# 16

# THE WARS FOR
# THE RHINE

# THE RING OF FIRE SERIES

*1632* by Eric Flint

*1633* by Eric Flint with David Weber

*1634: The Baltic War* by Eric Flint with David Weber

*1634: The Galileo Affair* by Eric Flint with Andrew Dennis

*1634: The Bavarian Crisis* by Eric Flint with Virginia DeMarce

*1634: The Ram Rebellion* by Eric Flint with Virginia DeMarce et al.

*1635: The Cannon Law* by Eric Flint with Andrew Dennis

*1635: The Dreeson Incident* by Eric Flint with Virginia DeMarce

*1635: The Eastern Front* by Eric Flint

*1635: The Papal Stakes* by Eric Flint with Charles E. Gannon

*1636: The Saxon Uprising* by Eric Flint

*1636: The Kremlin Games* by Eric Flint with
Gorg Huff & Paula Goodlett

*1636: The Devil's Opera* by Eric Flint with David Carrico

*1636: Commander Cantrell in the West Indies* by Eric Flint with
Charles E. Gannon

*1636: The Viennese Waltz* by Eric Flint with
Gorg Huff & Paula Goodlett

*1636: The Cardinal Virtues* by Eric Flint with Walter Hunt

*1636: The Ottoman Onslaught* by Eric Flint  (forthcoming)

*1635: The Tangled Web* by Virginia DeMarce

*1635: The Wars for the Rhine* by Anette Pedersen

*1636: Seas of Fortune* by Iver P. Cooper

*1636: The Chronicles of Dr. Gribbleflotz* by
Kerryn Offord & Rick Boatright

*Time Spike* by Eric Flint with Marilyn Kosmatka

*Grantville Gazette volumes I-V*, ed. by Eric Flint
*Grantville Gazette VI-VII*, ed. by Eric Flint & Paula Goodlett

*Ring of Fire I-IV*, ed. by Eric Flint

For a complete list of Baen books and to purchase all of these
titles in e-book format, please go to www.baen.com

# 1635

## THE WARS FOR THE RHINE

## ANETTE PEDERSEN

1635: The Wars for the Rhine

Copyright © 2016 Anette Pedersen

A Baen Books Original

Baen Publishing Enterprises
P.O. Box 1403
Riverdale, NY 10471
www.baen.com

ISBN: 978-1-4767-8222-5

Cover art by Tom Kidd
Maps by Michael Knopp

First printing, December 2016

Distributed by Simon & Schuster
1230 Avenue of the Americas
New York, NY 10020

10  9  8  7  6  5  4  3  2  1

Pages by Joy Freeman (www.pagesbyjoy.com)
Printed in the United States of America

# Contents

Maps     vii

*1635: The Wars for the Rhine*     1

Afterword     293

Cast of Characters     295

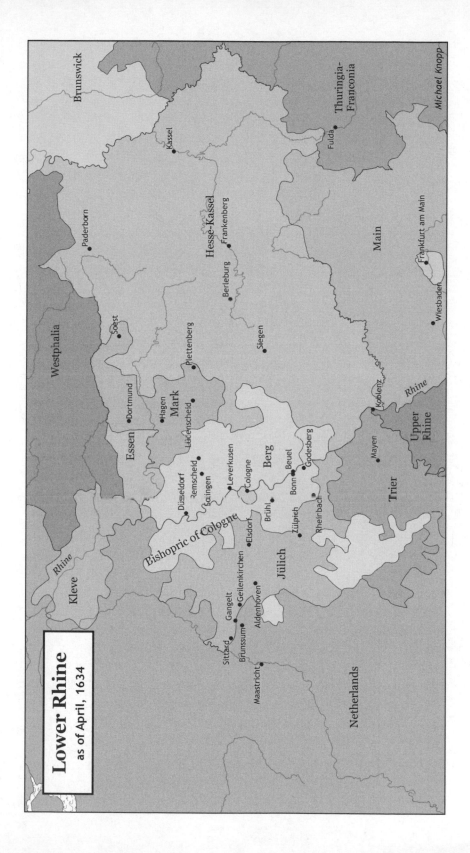

**Lower Rhine**
as of April, 1634

Michael Knopp

Brunswick

Thuringia-Franconia

Kassel

Fulda

Paderborn

Hesse-Kassel

Frankenberg

Berleburg

Main

Frankfurt am Main

Wiesbaden

Westphalia

Soest

Plettenberg

Siegen

Rhine

Koblenz

Dortmund

Hagen **Mark**

Lüdenscheid

**Essen**

Upper Rhine

Mayen

Remscheid

Leverkusen

**Berg**

Godesberg

Beuel

Düsseldorf

Solingen

Cologne

Bonn

Brühl

Zülpich

Rheirbach

**Trier**

**Bishopric of Cologne**

Elsdorf

**Kleve**

Rhine

Geilenkirchen

**Jülich**

Sittard

Gangelt

Aldenhöven

Brunssum

Maastricht

Netherlands

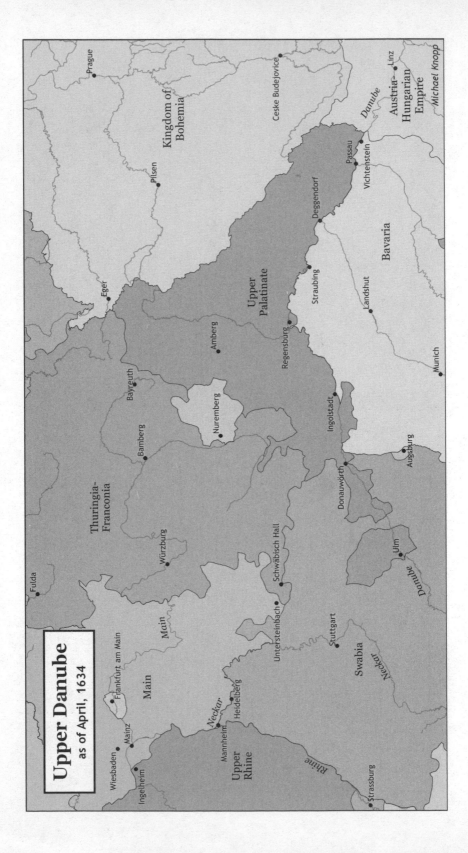

**Upper Danube**
as of April, 1634

Prague

Kingdom of Bohemia

Pilsen

Ceske Budejovice

Eger

Danube

Passau

Vichtenstein

Austria–Hungarian Empire

Linz

*Michael Knopp*

Deggendorf

Bavaria

Upper Palatinate

Straubing

Landshut

Amberg

Regensburg

Bayreuth

Nuremberg

Ingolstadt

Munich

Bamberg

Thuringia-Franconia

Donauwörth

Augsburg

Würzburg

Schwäbisch Hall

Fulda

Ulm

Danube

Untersteinbach

Stuttgart

Main

Swabia

Neckar

Main

Frankfurt am Main

Neckar

Heidelberg

Wiesbaden

Mainz

Mannheim

Upper Rhine

Rhine

Ingelheim

Strassburg

# Prologue

**Cologne**
**Spring 1634**

"Agreed."

"*D'accord.*"

"Agreed."

Two of the three men at the table stood up, bowed, and left, while the third refilled his glass with wine and took it to the east-facing window. There were no lights visible on the ground. The moon was still up, turning the Rhine River into a glittering band of silver, but in the horizon the first pale traces of the false dawn were beginning to show.

Archbishop Ferdinand of Cologne sipped slowly of the wine, and looked towards the section of the Rhine once known as Bishop's Alley. The Protestant conquest had not stopped until Mainz had fallen, and now only the archbishopric of Cologne remained. But that would change. The Rhine formed the link between central Europe and the western oceans, but Cologne sat as the gate, and Cologne was still his. Tonight he had irre-vocably joined in on a desperate and dangerous gamble, but he would win. Not just what had been lost, but all of the middle Rhine, proving to the entire world his might as a statesman of the Church. At whatever cost.

# Chapter 1

*Düsseldorf, the Castle*
*May 1634*

"Katharina Charlotte, you cannot desert your God-given husband!"

"I'm not going to, Elisabeth," Charlotte replied, without turning from the window to look at her sister. "I'm simply considering making a short journey up the Rhine to Cologne to ask our mother's old friend, Archbishop Ferdinand, to help me pray for the safety of my husband and his heir. That I also don't trust Marshal Turenne, and think that he is making my husband attack Essen for some secret French purpose is entirely beside the point, and probably just one of those funny ideas pregnant women sometimes get."

"You keep looking for excuses to leave your home and husband, Charlotte, but he was quite within his rights to beat you. It is your duty to obey him in all things, and you told me yourself that you had talked back to him."

Charlotte shrugged. Three years ago at the barely nubile age of sixteen her father had married her off to his old first cousin, Duke Wolfgang of Jülich-Berg. As the third of six daughters she had looked forward to having a household of her own, and all things considered it hadn't been a bad marriage until the previous autumn, when Ferdinand Phillip, the son she had so proudly—and painfully—borne, had died, and her husband had berated her for

3

her weakness in bearing such a fragile wimp. Her answer: that bearing children before she was fully grown was not her idea, had cost her a front tooth, the most unpleasant night she had ever spent, and daily beatings until she showed pregnant again. A plea to her father for protection had resulted only in a lecture on obedience, but now her father was dead, and her husband was taking his heir and his army to try to conquer the rich industrial area of Essen just north of his own land.

Charlotte felt no grief for the death of her father, and certainly didn't expect to feel any if her husband got himself killed. All scraps of daughterly—never mind wifely—duty and affection had long since been worn away, but if Philipp, her stepson, died she would be carrying the heir to not only some of the Neuburg lands on the Danube, but also the lands of Jülich and Berg here on the Rhine. If that happened, then the guardianship of a living son would be a windfall wanted by every German prince, and that of a living daughter only slightly less so. And if the child died—thus leaving Wolfgang without an heir—then the codicil to her marriage contract that her father had somehow talked Wolfgang into signing meant that Charlotte herself became the trophy. She would be hunted like a twelve-point stag unless she was safely within the protection of someone she could trust. Preferably that would be her young brother, Friedrich. He had been in Italy on his Grand Tour when their father had suddenly died, but he should be coming home by now. Archbishop Ferdinand of Cologne was another possibility, but if she could not reach Friedrich, it might actually be safer just to hide herself somewhere in the City of Cologne. Especially if Wolfgang didn't do her the favor of getting himself killed. The archbishop would certainly just send her back to Wolfgang, but darling Friedrich was now count palatine of Zweibrücken and the new head of her family, and he had quarreled bitterly with their father, when he had agreed to the marriage in return for that mine near Saarbrucken.

Wolfgang of course expected to return in triumph with the gold of Essen at his disposal and all the lands once belonging to his mother's family firmly within his grasp. This, he believed, would enable him to strike west and start taking the Protestant holdings within the USE. In Charlotte's opinion that made as much sense as the mad fantasies of Wolfgang's maternal uncle, Phillip the Insane, whose lack of an heir cost them the lands in the first place.

The campaign had been proposed by the French marshal Turenne, who had first gotten both the archbishop's and Wolfgang's permission to move French troops a few at a time across their lands to gather in Düsseldorf before striking northward. Turenne had paid well for the privilege, and then talked Wolfgang into joining the undertaking of some complex maneuvers that would supposedly take the army of Essen completely by surprise. Charlotte didn't know enough about warfare to judge whether the plan stood a chance of success, but her question about what the French would actually be gaining in return for their money and men had only resulted in yet another black eye.

As the sound of shouting reached her, Charlotte moved her eyes from the harbor to the street below her window. Cavalrymen wearing her husband's colors were forcing what was obviously the last speed out of lathered horses. Charlotte opened the casement and leaned out.

"They are dead! They are all dead! The French betrayed us, and the army of Essen is right on our heels!"

"Elisabeth." Charlotte turned from the window. "Send Harbel to see that the boat is ready, and Maria to attend me in my bedchamber. Then go pack your most valuable possessions, but only what you can carry yourself. We are leaving as soon as I am ready."

### Vienna, The Palace

"I assure you, the child is mine." Melchior von Hatzfeldt, count and general of the Holy Roman Empire, looked with frustration at the man he expected to soon become his liege-lord and emperor.

"I do not doubt you," Archduke Ferdinand of Austria said with a slight bow of his head, "but it was born less than ten months after old Mansfeld's death and allowing you to claim it would create a nasty heritage squabble. And I do want their goodwill. I'm sorry, my dear General, but it is in the best interest of the Holy Roman Empire that you allow your child to be reared as the heir to a quite sizable fortune, and an apparently ever growing influence within the Catholic world. And talking about the Catholic world: I have a task for you."

Melchior swallowed his protests and rubbed his eyes before nodding. "As you wish."

"I want you to pay a visit to your family in Cologne, look around the area and report to me when you return. My sister's marriage to Duke Maximilian should ensure our alliance with Bavaria, but Cologne is an important link to our Spanish cousin in the Netherlands." Archduke Ferdinand rose from his chair in the sun, and went to pick up a stack of papers on a nearby table. "The furlough, permits, etc. should all be in order. Didn't you mention that your brother was marrying into the von Worms-Dalberg family this summer?"

Melchior nodded again, not quite trusting his voice.

"Well, that should serve as a reason for your presence in any casual conversation." Archduke Ferdinand looked directly at Melchior and sighed. "I truly am sorry, Melchior, both for you losing the one woman to break down that chaste reserve of yours, and for denying you the right to claim your child. But the child is more likely to be spoiled by doting aunts than mistreated, and the cost would simply be too high."

"I understand."

Melchior bowed himself out in the correct manner and went slowly down the stairs to the entrance hall, absently nodding to colleagues and acquaintances. His mother had always predicted than when Melchior would finally fall in love, he'd fall hard, and sweet Maria with her big dark eyes and lively manner had completely stolen his heart. He had always been a firm believer in the sanctity of marriage and total fidelity, but even the fact that she had been a newly married woman when they first met had not been enough to completely kill his interest. Maria had clearly been unhappy in her marriage, as well as too young and impulsive to hide her dislike of her husband, but Melchior had very carefully kept their relations completely platonic for almost two years, playing the role of a friend and occasional escort whenever his duties took him to Vienna. Only when her husband had died, and Melchior had found her alone—except for her Nubian slave—when paying a condolence visit after the funeral, had he lost his head and his hold on his emotions. Maria had refused to publish their relationship with a betrothal before her mourning year was over, even when she proved pregnant with a child that she assured him could only be his. Instead she had promised that as soon as the child was born, she would come back to Vienna, and marry him before the summer was over.

But she had never recovered from the birth, and when he had gone to the Mansfeld estate to attend her funeral, Melchior had been denied all access to the baby. And now his last frail hope of having the crown interfere on his behalf was gone as well.

"Sir?"

Melchior look blankly at Lieutenant Simon Pettenburg, the courier who had come with him to Vienna, then pulled himself together. "We're leaving for Linz this afternoon. I need to talk with General Piccolomini first. Go pack our belongings, and I'll meet you at the inn."

## Magdeburg, House of Hessen

Amalie Elisabeth of Hanau-Münzenberg, wife to Wilhelm V, landgrave of Hesse-Kassel, was widely acknowledged as one of the most astute players on the new political scene. So it was no wonder to anyone that she was having morning tea with the equally astute Abbess Dorothea of Quedlinburg and Princess Eleonore von Anhalt-Dessau, whose husband, Wilhelm Wettin, many people expected would become the next prime minister of the USE.

That Amalie chose to hostess the small gathering in the only finished room of what was to become the new House of Hessen, rather than in her apartment in the government building, might seem a bit odd. But then all official areas were getting so overcrowded that there were no possibility for privacy. Besides, the noise of the carpenters putting up the wall panels in the next room served nicely to disguise anything being said over the tea cups.

Both Dorothea and Eleonore were quite aware that Amalie had an extra agenda, so once the official business of inviting young female relatives to visit and benefit from the abbess's political lessons was done with, the abbess asked with a smile in her eyes. "And if no one has anything else to talk about, I believe that we are finished?"

"Very funny, Abbess Dorothea." Amalie filled the cups again. "Have you ever known me not to want to run down the political situation as well?"

"No, but sometimes you so want to be devious that it takes you forever to get to what you really want to talk about. And

I've had more than enough recently of rehashing the situation with that tiresome King Christian of Denmark and the situation in the Baltic." The abbess grinned and suddenly looked several decades younger than her actual years. "But if you've got the wind of something new brewing? That is of course a different matter."

Amalie smiled and tapped a fingernail on the teacup, making the fragile porcelain chime. "Cologne."

"Wha—" Eleonore coughed and swallowed her tea. "Amalie, do you have an army of small gnomes listening at keyholes all over town?"

"No."

"Then what do you know about Archbishop Ferdinand?"

"That the captain of his personal guard has traveled to hire some of Wallenstein's former mercenary colonels, and that the archbishop's personal torturer, Felix Gruyard, has been seen entering Duke Wolfgang von Neuburg's castle in Düsseldorf late at night. Nothing conclusive." Amalie leaned back in her chair, easing her stomach, which was just beginning to swell in her tenth pregnancy. "Some members of the Bavarian ducal family have a tendency towards obsessions. Often religious, but not always. Archbishop Ferdinand has been obsessed with becoming a cardinal since the death of his brother Cardinal Philip. But since Ferdinand never had his brother's intellectual and spiritual qualities, the only way he can achieve his ambition is by gathering power. The Protestant conquest of most of Bishop's Alley along the Rhine has severely reduced his power, and with the USE looking to stabilize and consolidate their hold, it should be only a matter of time before he tries something desperate."

"And you are waiting like a cat outside a mouse hole for him to stick out his nose?" Eleonore frowned at her friend.

"Fairly much so," answered Amalie, quite unruffled. "My husband is going south to rattle his saber at the archbishop in the Wildenburg-Schönstein area. The branches of the Hatzfeldt family have long been divided between those looking towards Hessen and those owing alliance to Cologne or Mainz, but we hope to persuade that entire area to join the new Hesse-Kassel province."

"The newly elected prince-bishop of Würzburg, who went into exile when the Protestant army conquered that town, was a Hatzfeldt," Eleonore mused. "Would it help if he had his diocese back?"

"Could be. Prince-Bishop Franz von Hatzfeldt is the younger brother of General Melchior von Hatzfeldt, whose second-in-command is his cousin, Wolf, who is one of the Wildenburg Hatzfeldts." Amalie smiled. "My father knew old Sebastian, the father of Franz and Melchior, quite well, and I met the boys several times as a girl. Sebastian had five sons, but was the guardian of several more, and usually had the three Wildenburger boys in tow as well. He was a very caring man, who loved children. He was very bookish too, and whenever he visited Hanau, he'd sit in the evening and tell stories."

Amalie shook her head. "I'd be hard pressed to put a name to any of the boys I remember, except for Melchior, whom I saw in uniform just before my marriage."

"I've heard that he is quite handsome." The abbess held out her cup for a fresh cup of tea. "Have you been carrying a torch, my dear?"

"Of course not," Amalie answered, refilling their cups. "Melchior wasn't ennobled at the time and a Catholic as well. It was just a girlish fancy." She shrugged. "I'm quite satisfied with Wilhelm. We want the same and work well together."

"Hm. I realize that you cannot permit small enclaves in the new province that are under control of someone else, especially not Archbishop Ferdinand. But why not try for a deal?" the abbess asked.

Amalie sighed. "I expect you have both studied the American books just as closely as I have. Do you remember what they said about Hessen?"

"Actually, not very much," said the abbess, frowning, while Eleonore looked thoughtful.

"Exactly. A minor industrial area with Kassel as the only town with slightly more than local importance." Amalie's eyes suddenly glittered in anger and determination. "*That* is not acceptable."

"The proposed province of Hesse-Kassel is quite a lot larger than Hessen was in the American world," said Eleonore mildly, "and your husband is going to be its representative in the House of Lords."

"Larger, yes." Amalie looked cross. "But mountainous and rural except for the northwestern part of Mark, and Gustavus Adolphus might end up selling that to De Geer in Essen."

"I see," said Eleonore. "So, are you planning to expand all

the way to the Rhine? The Rhine trade is valuable and likely to grow even more so."

"Yes." Amalie shrugged. "We would have preferred Essen, but Gustavus Adolphus apparently prefers De Geer to my husband, and expansion in that direction would be too costly, at least while De Geer is in power."

"Any indications that De Geer is falling? I've got quite a lot of investments in Essen." The abbess put down her cup.

"No. But the favors of princes are fickle—and that goes double for kings and triple for emperors. Wilhelm was once Gustavus' most favored ally, now he is apparently to be reduced to just another provincial governor. Sooner or later De Geer's star is bound to drop as well."

"How about the Düsseldorf area?" Eleonore asked, "It was as important as Essen to the Americans. And while Duke Wolfgang's second wife, Katharina Charlotte, is Gustavus' cousin by marriage, Wolfgang has made himself so unpopular with absolutely everyone within the last few years that I cannot imagine much opposition to taking him down. Especially since Wolfgang's heir is by his Bavarian first wife."

"Hesse mentioned the possibility in passing to Chancellor Oxenstierna after Brandenburg's betrayal, and the answer was a clear refusal. Princess Katharina of Sweden is Gustavus' favorite sister, and she is very fond of her niece and namesake. Unless Wolfgang does something very stupid, taking Berg from him is not an option. That Archbishop Ferdinand has sent his pet-torturer to talk to Wolfgang in secret seems promising, but I need more details. What do you know, Eleonore?"

"You're going to owe me for this, Amalie." Eleonore gazed sternly at her friend. "This information only arrived last night, and even the government hasn't yet been told."

"I see." Amalie smiled. "From Moses Abrabanel, then. Well, I don't want to go try to squeeze it out of him, so: debt accepted with the abbess as witness, for one political favor of your choice."

"Archbishop Ferdinand has hired four regiments of cavalry with money received from Richelieu. It seems to be related to those French military movements south of Trier that have been worrying the government lately."

"And their target?" Amalie leaned forward.

"Unknown. But if some kind of a deal has been struck between

Richelieu and Archbishop Ferdinand, then there is nothing capable of stopping a French army from striking north and taking Jülich from a base within the diocese."

"How about Banér?" the abbess interrupted.

"He cannot move that far west unless it's in response to an attack. The situation to the east and south is simply too unstable." Amalie shook her head and tapped her fingernail on her teacup again.

"And with an alliance with Don Fernando in the Low Countries they would be able to take Rheinland Pfalz at their leisure and make everything west of the Rhine Catholic." The abbess sighed. "Most of the USE regiments are already occupied far to the east and north. Any information about timing?"

"No. But Don Francisco Nasi put another interpretation on the news last night." Eleonore leaned back, her stomach every bit as round as Amalie's. "That Felix Gruyard has been visiting Wolfgang may suggest that there is an alliance there as well. And *that* puts the combined forces in position to attack Essen."

"Yes. Or Hesse-Kassel." Amalie suddenly looked very alert, and put down her cup hard enough to chip the saucer.

"No offense intended, my dear," the abbess smiled, "but Essen is actually the more valuable area."

"Yes." Amalie leaned back again and smiled at the abbess. "But not even Oxenstierna could blame us for defending our land against a Catholic conspiracy."

### Bonn, Archbishop's Palace

"Ah! Please come in, Father Johannes. Did you have a pleasant journey here from Grantville?" Prince-Bishop Franz von Hatzfeldt of Würzburg rose from his desk, and greeted the tall ascetic looking priest with a smile that didn't quite reach his eyes.

"Yes, thank you. The roads have dried out nicely, and I even had the opportunity to ride the new railroad for a short stretch. A most comfortable way of traveling once you get used to the speed." Father Johannes gave a quick look around the room, while sitting down on the chair his new patron indicated. Dark oak panels, dark oak furniture, dark and slightly shabby velvet upholstery, all in all a quite depressive room for a man in exile.

Father Johannes had met Bishop Franz while doing some paintings in Bamberg several years ago. At the time Franz von Hatzfeldt had been a diplomat in the service of the prince-bishop Johan Georg of Bamberg, and a full member of the Church administration in both Bamberg and Würzburg. Father Johannes remembered him as a calm and likeable man with a keen eye for beauty. Now, however, the man fiddling with his pen on the other side of the desk seemed filled with a kind of restless worry that made Father Johannes wonder if Francisco Nasi was right, and there was more going on in Cologne than a group of exiled clerics wanting their bishoprics back. Franz von Hatzfeldt had proved himself an excellent diplomat in negotiations with Tilly, and had slowly gained more and more influence until he was elected bishop of Würzburg just a few months before the Protestant conquest of that diocese. Surely the loss of land and power should not mean that much of a setback to a competent diplomat with proven skills and contacts that would make anyone with ambitions want to hire him?

"I have the pardon signed by Archbishop Ferdinand for your behavior against your superiors after the sack of Magdeburg. As I believe my secretary Otto Tweimal explained to you: the pardon will officially be a part of your payment for your work on my family's property in Cologne. The property is several old houses—all of which are worn and drab—so officially I'm hiring you to paint murals for the ladies, and advise on the restoration and decorations. I know of old that your taste is unerring." Bishop Franz took a deep breath and forced another smile. "Unofficially I want you to tell me all that you can about the Americans and how they are likely to affect the political situation. You are not to mention the unofficial part of your duties to anyone without my permission. I'll be coming to Cologne from time to time, to see my family and to follow your progress with the house."

"Are you considering approaching somebody in Magdeburg about a wish to return to your bishopric?" Johannes asked. "I have no interest in politics, but I have heard mentions of people of importance in the new administrations. Even met a few during my stay in Grantville."

Bishop Franz sat for a while without answering. "I make no secret of my wish to return to Würzburg, but there are various ways in which that can be accomplished. Some naturally more attractive to me than others." He rose from his chair. "I'll ride with you to Cologne, and introduce you to Sister Maximiliane. She is Archbishop Ferdinand's cousin, originally Countess Maria Maximiliane von Wartenberg, and she is to take up residence in my house along with most of the women in my family. Your luggage can follow in a wagon. Otto Tweimal mentioned that you were involved in developing a European porcelain industry. Perhaps you would tell me more about this. Würzburg and Bamberg are traditionally winemaking areas, but it might be an idea to diversify a little."

# Chapter 2

*Cologne, Hatzfeldt House*
*May 1634*

Hiding behind the curtains in a noble lady's bedroom while she was undressing! Father Johannes bit his lip to keep back a totally inappropriate giggle. During his stay in Grantville he had read a few of the so called "Romances" the Americans had brought with them, and this was straight out of one of them. There were differences: he was not a young nobleman in trouble, but a middle-age priest and painter in trouble. And the lady in question was not a beautiful and willful young virgin, but a very competent spinster his own age. A very handsome spinster in Father Johannes' opinion, but there really wasn't that much similarity between the adorable Annabella of *Love Conquers All* and Sister Maximiliane, former Countess von Wartenberg.

Sister Maximiliane had come from Bavaria to Bonn the previous winter to nurse her cousin, Archbishop Ferdinand of Cologne, during an illness, and she had accepted an offer to stay and take charge of the Hatzfeldt household in Cologne, as the four Hatzfeldt brothers' feud with their stepmother, Margaretha von Backenfoerde, had left them with no one presently capable of the task. The house was an old and worn complex of buildings acquired from the Nassau family by the brothers' father, Imperial Knight Sebastian von Hatzfeldt, and left in his will to his third son, Franz. It was a shabby residence for such a prominent family, but after Crottorf, the main castle of the Hatzfeldt family, had been invaded by the Swedes in 1631, causing the death of old Sebastian, it had been decided to shelter as many family members as possible behind the defenses of Cologne. Bishop Franz had for that—and other—reasons contacted Father Johannes in Grantville the previous autumn, and hired him to transform the old Nassauer Hof into something worthy of the name Hatzfeldt House.

At the moment only Sister Maximiliane and a few servants had arrived in Cologne, and all in all it should have been the best time for Father Johannes to do a bit of snooping around. Not that he wasn't free to enter any room during the daytime, but what possible reason could he give for taking down a picture in Sister Maximiliane's bedroom, and searching both front and back through a lens? Only—time had slipped away from him, and Sister Maximiliane had come back from Evening Mass before he'd had the time to get out. Now all he could do was to wait for the maid to leave and Sister Maximiliane to go to sleep.

"I wish thee would come forth." Sister Maximiliane's voice was sharp and firm.

But the maid had just left! She could not have seen him. He had not left open a hole to peek through. Or moved.

"It is thee behind the curtain I'm talking to. If I shall have to leave my bed to come pull thee forth, I shall be most annoyed."

Father Johannes moved the curtain slightly to the side and saw Sister Maximiliane sitting in the bed staring straight at him.

"Well?"

"It's only me, Sister Maximiliane." Father Johannes took a few steps forward and bowed. "I most humbly apologize for intruding on your privacy, but assure you that I intend you neither harm nor disrespect."

"Hmpf! Father Johannes." Sister Maximiliane frowned. "I'm not in the habit of holding evening levees, but come sit on the bed and give me an explanation."

Father Johannes sat as he was told. "I just wanted to study the painting on the wall. 'The Heavenly Madonna.' I believe it's by Paul Moreau. Do you know him?"

"You put it back upside down."

"Oh!" Father Johannes half-rose to turn the picture.

15

"Never mind that. Just what are you up to with that young whipper-snapper Franz von Hatzfeldt?"

"Milady?"

"Father Johannes, Franz might be the prince-bishop of Würzburg these days, but I have known him all his life. He's only seven years younger than I, a friend of my brother, Franz Wilhelm, and our families have known each other since before the Deluge. He's up to something." She shrugged. "So is just about everybody else these days, but in my estimate Franz would just about sell his soul to get his diocese back from the Protestant occupation. With the Americans being the blank shields in this cabal, and Franz hiring a painter straight from their town—not to mention giving you free-hands and an open purse—I would have to be dumb as a door not to suspect something. And no one has *ever* called me stupid, Father Johannes."

"N-no, milady. Quite the opposite. S-surely." Father Johannes swallowed and tried to gather what was left of his wits. Sister Maximiliane was unsettling enough when being the formal grand lady, but once she dropped her formality, she was absolutely terrifying. He could either try to play dumb or confess everything, and hope for her kindness. And he really wasn't that much of an actor. And Sister Maximiliane was better known for her competence than her kindness. "My commission from the p-prince-bishop is quite genuine; a written contract filed with the authorities here in Cologne, money for my payment as well as expenses deposed with the bankers. It's a very generous agreement, but then I am well known within clerical circles. A-as a painter, I mean."

"Certainly. I cannot say I approve of all the uses you have made of your gifts, but I do not deny they are great. So, what is not in the files?"

Father Johannes swallowed nervously. "Everybody wants to know about the Americans, milady. My patron just wants me to tell him about them. W-when he comes here to visit his family."

"Father Johannes, no one is that ingenuous past the age of twenty. You are making me angry."

This wasn't working. "Sister Maximiliane, I'll be putting my life in your hands." Father Johannes dropped his cringe and looked Sister Maximiliane straight in the eyes.

"It is already there, Father Johannes." Then Sister Maximiliane's stern face eased in to a little smile, "but if it's any consolation to you, I consider you far too talented a painter to waste."

"Your cousin, Archbishop Ferdinand, felt the same way about my friend Paul Moreau. So after he faked the evidence for Paul's trial, your cousin ordered his torturer to spare Paul's hands and arms and concentrate on the lower part of his body. I do not find your words much of a consolation." There was absolutely no answering smile on Father Johannes' face.

Sister Maximiliane gaped, then pulled herself together. "Are you absolutely sure of this? My cousin is politically ruthless, that goes with being part of the ducal family of Bavaria, but this!" Sister Maximiliane took a deep breath. "To spare the hands of a talented painter would be a kindness. If the man was guilty, the evidence genuine..."

"Not a chance. Paul's mother was a friend of my mother, and we have often studied and criticized each other's paintings. Four or five years ago Paul was accused of painting votive pictures for the Black Mass. Three years ago I was in Bonn just before going to Magdeburg to paint the propaganda broadsheets for that campaign. By accident I saw those evil pictures attributed to Paul. And he never painted those. I recognized the work of Alain van Beekx, a painter from Holland. Van Beekx is known to work for Felix Gruyard, your cousin's torturer and executioner."

"I've met Gruyard." Sister Maximiliane looked up at the Madonna painting. "You saw the protocol as well? No chance Gruyard acted on his own? Faked the evidence without my cousin's knowledge?"

"The record for Gruyard's expenses included a very large fee to van Beekx, and your cousin signed personally for full payment. Paul later managed to escape somehow and disappear." Father Johannes looked up at the picture, too. "I didn't do or say anything at the time. Closed my eyes and told myself I could do nothing. None is so blind as he who will not see." He looked back at Sister Maximiliane. "My stay with the Americans taught me that there is so much—even in the mortal world—that I'll never understand. That all a man can do is to put his faith in God, and try to do what is right. I want to find my friend and help him if I can. Bishop Franz might be planning to double-cross your cousin. Or they may be up to something together. I don't particularly care. The Madonna on your wall is painted by

Paul, the greenish blue of the sky is a shade Paul was developing when I last met him, and the motive is Catholic. It is recent, but it is not something a Calvinist like Paul would ever willingly have painted."

"It was a gift from my cousin." Sister Maximiliane sighed. "Ferdinand was very ill last winter. With stomach pain and vomiting blood. Gruyard tried to convince him it was poison. My life in München had soured on me, so I came to nurse my cousin, and a diet of very bland food solved the problem. I had admired the picture and he gave it to me as thanks, but..." Sister Maximiliane stopped and frowned at Father Johannes. "The picture was hanging in my cousin's bedroom in Bonn—so that he could see it from the bed. At night when the pain was especially bad, he told me to take it down and remove it from the room. Shouted at me when I wanted to wait for the morning. I took it down myself, and when he was well, he told me to keep it. I fear your story is true, Father Johannes." She looked up at the painting again. "You need not fear I'll tell anyone of this, but please let me think now. We'll talk tomorrow."

The next morning Sister Maximiliane came into Father Johannes' major workroom with the painting of the Heavenly Madonna in her hands. The room would eventually become the biggest parlor in the house, but on this bright spring morning it was filled with craftsmen and work-tables loaded with paint and fabrics.

"Good Morning, Father Johannes. Could you find the time to examine this picture for me? I wonder if the wood is beginning to crack. Just store it until you can find the time."

"Good Morning, Sister Maximiliane, I promise mine shall be the only hands to touch it." Father Johannes bowed and took the picture.

"Thank you. Just take your time. I think I'll find something else for my bedroom, as I find I no longer like it as much." Sister Maximiliane nodded her thanks; she looked tired, but no emotions showed in her stern face. "Bishop Franz is expected to arrive from Bonn any day now. I would like to examine his rooms."

"Certainly, Sister Maximiliane, the bishop's bedroom and study were finished as the very first rooms. Only the new carpets have not yet arrived."

In the study Sister Maximiliane sat down behind the carved oak table and looked at Father Johannes. "When Franz arrives I'll find out if he knows anything about what happened to Paul Moreau. I'll also write to Cousin Ferdinand in Bonn for any information he has about the painting and the painter. I'll pretend I worry about the wood it's painted on being faulty. There's no reason for him not to help me. But just what did the interrogation protocol tell about your friend? Any indication he was hurt enough to die?"

"No, and I found some private correspondence as well. I didn't realize it at the time, but Gruyard must have kept—probably stolen—letters. Letters with potential for blackmail." Father Johannes moved restlessly around the room. "Paul survived for at least four months after the interrogation. Archbishop Ferdinand had ordered him moved to Bavaria. Paul was to travel up the Rhine and then over land with a troop of mercenaries going to Würzburg. From there Bishop Franz would arrange the rest of the transportation. But the troop of mercenaries was scattered by a Protestant attack near Aschaffenburg, and when they reached Würzburg their leader, Captain Eltz, claimed that Paul was nowhere to be found after the attack. Paul might have managed to escape, but Eltz is a distant cousin of the Hatzfeldts, and used to serve in the army under Bishop Franz's brother, General Melchior von Hatzfeldt. Eltz had been hired by Bishop Franz to strengthen the defenses at Würzburg against the approaching Swedes. I don't think your cousin—or Gruyard—knows where Paul is, but I think Bishop Franz might know something."

"Franz's archives are here in Cologne. Both his personal files and what he managed to save from Würzburg. They are stored in the muniment room together with the archives from Fulda."

"Huh! I've seen the sealed crates, but why are Fulda's archives here?"

"The Fulda monks, who brought the archives—and the abbey's treasure—with them when they fled here from the Swedes, find that they cannot agree on what to do with them. Prince-Abbot Schweinsberg of Fulda has made a deal with the Americans, and while my cousin might not have the power to excommunicate Schweinsberg, he is not obliged to help him either. Cousin Ferdinand has always disliked Schweinsberg; it's an old quarrel, so . . ." Sister Maximiliane shrugged and smiled wryly at Father Johannes. "The monks have kept the treasure among themselves, but most of them are noble-born and probably think archives are for clerks. Franz's sister, Lucie, has just become a widow and is coming here to stay. Like me, she is very good at administration, and I think I'll suggest that she and I sort all those Würzburg and Fulda crates this summer. We are very good friends and while she would not betray her brother's trust, she'd certainly be willing to help me by noting anything in connection with your friend Paul."

"Lady, I'll be forever in your debt."

"I want my Madonna back on my wall, Father Johannes, but I find I cannot enjoy it now. Perhaps I'll be able to do so again, when your friend has been found."

"If not, I swear I'll paint you another, Sister Maximiliane, to the very best of my abilities."

"Thank you. I might want to accept that. And please call me Maxie."


A very talented painter, as well as a Jesuit priest, Father Johannes Grünwald had come to Grantville while fleeing from the Inquisition after the atrocities at Magdeburg had made him rebel against his superior's "Holy War" campaign. He had settled down among the Americans as a teacher and painter, while waiting to see what his Church would do about one of their most important propaganda painters thus running off—and while making some adjustments in his own faith and beliefs.

His faith and trust in his God had been the first to heal, and the quiet stability of Father Mazzare had shown him that it was perfectly possible for a Catholic priest to be both a human with mundane interests and joys, and yet still be deeply religious and virtuous. However, in one area Father Johannes had not been able to take Father Mazzare for a role-model: Father Johannes' abilities as a painter made him an important tool—and weapon—for the princes striving for power—both inside and outside the Church. Of course, as a Jesuit priest, obedience to his superior should have been of primary importance to him, and he should just be doing what they told him to, but Magdeburg had taught him never, ever to place his talent under the control of anybody else.

The Americans too wanted to use him, and as Father Johannes walked through the early morning streets of Cologne on his way to Claude Beauville's Emporium of Fine Arts, he enjoyed the peace away from the constant hustle and bustle of the Hatzfeldt

House, and thought about his talks with Don Francisco Nasi the previous autumn. The young head of the Abrabanel family's financial network in Germany had also become the unofficial head of the Americans' information network, and after Father Johannes had accepted Franz von Hatzfeldt's offer of employment, Father Johannes had also agreed to pass along information about the situation in Cologne to Don Francisco. Not due to pressure or in return for money, but because Father Johannes shared Don Francisco's belief in the benefits of the American influence.

Father Johannes stopped and looked at the new Mocha House; during his two years in Grantville, he had grown used to the American habit of drinking coffee in the morning, but this was still too early for the coffee shop to be open, and it was still the only one of its kind in Cologne.

The Americans had brought so many changes in so few years; from a new budding empire to the habit of drinking coffee. Still—fads and empires had always come and gone, what lasted was the ideas that grew from and in people's minds—and the American had brought an unbelievable treasure of those. Father Johannes smiled a little bitterly as he continued his walk; officially Bishop Franz von Hatzfeldt had hired him to oversee the restoration of Hatzfeldt House, unofficially the bishop had wanted Father Johannes to tell him about the American ideas in return for a pardon for Father Johannes' rebellion at Magdeburg, but privately Father Johannes was certain that the bishop's ultimate goal was to get his diocese back, and never mind the cost. That Father Johannes had a private line to negotiations with the USE might eventually be of more value to the bishop than anything else. And in the meantime Father Johannes had no qualms at all about keeping Don Francisco informed about Archbishop Ferdinand's intrigues. Ruthlessness was expected of a man of power, but the uses the archbishop had made of his personal torturer, Felix Gruyard, had gone way beyond what was acceptable.

Claude Beauville's office was fully lit when Father Johannes arrived. The Beauvilles had once been an important family in Toulouse in Southern France, but the collapse in the woad dye trade had brought the family to near ruin. Monsieur Claude had since done quite well for himself by trading in all kinds of dyes as well as paints, paper and fine textiles, and his new emporium occupied an entire house in the center of Cologne. Father Johannes had bought a lot from him during his years with the Catholic army, and now, since Father Johannes had started working on Hatzfeldt House, he had gone to the emporium at least once a week to use the Beauville family's many contacts to acquire the materials he needed—and even to order a few of the exciting new colors from the Americans. The business didn't usually open this early, but the night before a note had arrived at Hatzfeldt House: the American cargo had arrived under the aegis of Herr Moses Abrabanel, and if the honored Father Johannes would come as early after dawn as convenient, he would be given first choice among the many fine marvels.

So Father Johannes had risen before dawn, and as he stood admiring the new smooth glass in the windows shining in the first rays of the morning sun, he considered exactly what to say to Moses Abrabanel. The general situation was well known: most of the dioceses in the Rhine Valley—also called Bishop's Alley—had been conquered by the Swedes in 1631, and most of the exiled bishops were now in Bonn planning heaven-knows-what with Archbishop Ferdinand. Prince-Abbot Schweinsberg of Fulda had defected—made a deal with the USE—and was back in Fulda, but with little of his former power and riches. And Archbishop Ferdinand's fury at the defection made it totally clear that Schweinsberg had burned all his bridges behind him.

During his meals with his sister Lucie, Maxie and Father Johannes, Bishop Franz had talked freely about his fellow refugees and about his host in Bonn. The bishop of Trier had quarreled with Archbishop Ferdinand and left, so the most important clerics remaining were Archbishop Anselm of Mainz and Maxie's brother, Bishop Franz Wilhelm of Minden. According to Bishop Franz, his old friend Franz Wilhelm seemed to be patiently waiting for something, but Archbishop Anselm was visibly chafing under the patronizing charity of Archbishop Ferdinand. None of this was really secret, and could readily be picked up among the gossip at the Mocha House, but at least Father Johannes could send confirmations of those rumors back to Don Francisco. And perhaps Archbishop Anselm of Mainz was ready for an approach from the USE.

In the end, though, it really all depended on the most powerful cleric in the area: what was Archbishop Ferdinand of Cologne going to do? A treaty between him and the USE could mean peace along almost the entire western front of the USE, greatly strengthening the chances for at least an armistice with the Spanish occupation in Holland, hinder the French in stirring up trouble, and generally add greatly to the USE's security. For the archbishop it would be a chance to save what he could before he was negotiating with a knife on his throat. Or at least with a USE army coming down the Rhine from Frankfurt.

On the other hand the archbishop was a member of the strongly Catholic and ambitious ducal family of Bavaria, so was he instead planning to reconquer the lost dioceses? The French agents had been sniffing around all spring, and according to Bishop Franz the newly arrived dragoons at Bonn had been paid for with French money. Officially the dragoons were a warning to Wolfgang von Neuburg, Duke of Jülich-Berg, never the safest of neighbors, but considering Duke Maximilian of Bavaria's upcoming marriage to a Habsburg princess, the Holy Roman Empire might also get behind an attempt to push the USE away from the Rhine—with Richelieu stirring up troubles on the sideline.

No one expected Father Johannes to actually spy to discover military plans—not least because the archbishop lived in Bonn and Father Johannes was in Cologne—but Bishop Franz had come from Bonn to watch the progress Father Johannes was making on the house. And incidentally to deliver to Father Johannes the promised full pardon for his "momentary loss of reason" at Magdeburg. In return Father Johannes had answered as many questions about the Americans as the bishop had cared to ask.

Father Johannes sat down on the horse-plinth outside the entrance to the emporium's office to consider a point: what Bishop Franz had really been interested in was, what kind of people had gained power—and how—in the Americans' home world. In fact the only here-and-now political or military subject the bishop had asked about had been Fulda and the American team there. Why no questions about Würzburg, the bishop's own diocese? The Americans were there too.

One other question Father Johannes had not been able to answer was just what Bishop Franz was planning to do? The bishop had the backing of his wealthy and powerful family, so in Father Johannes' estimate Bishop Franz wasn't likely to settle for anything less than a major part of his former power and riches. He certainly wasn't likely to accept a powerless return like Prince-Abbot Schweinsberg's. And if Bishop Franz wanted better terms, he'd have to have something to offer the USE in return. A peaceful deal for the entire Cologne area might involve something for Würzburg—and Bamberg too given the bishop's strong connections to that diocese as well—but Bishop Franz had not asked who to approach for an official peace conference. Which fairly much left him either double-crossing the archbishop to gain favor with the USE, or riding the archbishop's coat-tails on a military campaign and hope to win back his diocese that way. The ladies, Lucie and Maria, had asked far more directly about Bishop Franz's plans than Father Johannes ever could, but received only evasions.

Claude Beauville personally opened the door beside the window. "Ah! *Bon Matin*, Father Johannes. Monsieur Abrabanel is here and would like a few words with you in private about the materials available."

The muniment room in the basement of Hatzfeldt House was packed with crates and leather-wrapped bundles. Not much light entered from the windows high on the walls, but several bright lamps turned the big table in the center of the room into a suitable place for paperwork. Thick pillows and a sheepskin were heaped in a big armchair to support the crippled hip and back of Lucie von Hatzfeldt. The young widow had gladly accepted Maxie's suggestion about sorting and listing the many papers in the crates and now spent several hours each day in the silent, whitewashed room—usually with one of her husband's children sitting by her feet to run errands.

Lucie had been the last of the nine children of Sebastian von Hatzfeldt's first marriage, and had been born only a few weeks before her mother's death. Four years later her father had acquired a papal dispensation to marry his cousin, Maria von Hatzfeldt-Wildenburg, a widow with a son and two daughters from her first marriage, and Sebastian's second wife had simply added all Sebastian's children and wards to her household and raised them absolutely equally with her own children.

Sebastian's third marriage—to Margaretha von Backenfoerde, widow of the wealthy Franz Wilhelm von Hatzfeldt-Merten—had been much less fortunate for his children, and despite Lucie's handicap, all her four brothers had flatly refused to place Margaretha in control of the new Hatzfeldt House. That Backenfoerde Woman had her widow's seat at Zeppenfeld, and that was all she was getting from this branch of the family! Margaretha was a great favorite of Archbishop Ferdinand, who had arranged her marriage to Sebastian, so Franz had been less vocal than his brothers in his denunciations of his stepmother. His asking Sister Maximiliane, who was nursing her cousin in Bonn, to come to Cologne and take command of the household had been an almost Solomonic solution that pleased everybody—except of course Margaretha.

Normally it would have been Lucie, as her father's only adult daughter, who had taken command over her unmarried brother's household, but she had suffered a carriage accident after her wedding to a fellow officer and friend of her brother, Melchior, and had never healed beyond the ability to limp slowly and carefully with the aid of a cane. As she healed, she had patiently handled the papers and finances of her husband's estates in Jülich, while overseeing the upbringing of his increasing brood of illegitimate children. Melchior—her favorite brother—had at first violently protested this arrangement and even challenged his friend to a duel, but Lucie had told her family that she didn't mind the arrangement: she liked children, but apparently the damage to her back and hip made it impossible for her to carry a child to term. Less than a year ago her husband had been killed in Bohemia, and she had now left her estates in the hands of Johann Adrian von Hatzfeldt-Werther, her distant cousin and her father's former ward, and moved to Cologne with all her husband's five surviving children.

Father Johannes liked her. She seemed a bit dull next to the impressive Maxie, but Lucie's ready sense of humor and genuine kindness had brought back much of the joy and mischief Father Johannes had lost during his years with the Catholic army. It might be a bit hard on his dignity that she sometimes seemed to regard him as just another of the children she was caring for—she was after all more than ten years his junior—but all in all it was nice to be teased a little again. And she did take his worries about Paul Moreau completely seriously, and told him every little bit in the papers referring to painters.

"Lady Lucie? Your stepmother Margaretha has arrived with her daughter Dame Anna and her niece Lady Sophia von Backenfoerde." Father Johannes came into the muniment room to aid Lucie in rising from her chair. Normally the child on page duty would have done that, but a Spring Fair was held today, and all the children had been allowed to go there with Thomas, the old head groom.

"Thank you, Father Johannes." Lucie lifted a cat from her lap, stretched slowly and looked down on the papers on the table. "This is slow work. Everything was just gathered helter-skelter in Fulda as well as Würzburg, and mixing the two lots in this room haven't helped. We have only just managed get the origin of the last bundles identified, and some of the papers my brother has asked for don't seem to be here. I'm sorting the Würzburg papers first, but there is nothing so far about your friend."

"Is Captain Eltz mentioned?"

"My brother hiring cousin Bobo and his men to defend Würzburg is all I've found so far. Bobo was killed there by the Swedish attack, you know."

"Yes." Father Johannes walked slowly beside Lucie along the basement corridor, pushing away the cat trying to twine around the lady's legs. "Did you know him well?"

"Not really. A rowdy, young boy. He was very eager to become a soldier, never really wanted anything else. The war didn't seem to bother him the way it does my brothers, Melchior and Hermann. They are good fighters, competent officers, but dislike the violence and gore of the battles." Lucie climbed the stair, one step at the time. "Bobo on the other hand once told a story about the rats on a battlefield. He found it funny." Lucie shuddered. "Talking about rats: have you seen Otto Tweimal lately?"

"In Bonn, on my way here this winter. I think he was just leaving for Bavaria. Why?" Father Johannes stopped on the narrow stairs and smiled down on Lucie; she really was a nice woman.

"Tweimal does Franz's dirty work the way Felix Gruyard does Archbishop Ferdinand's. Having Franz mention Tweimal and Gruyard in the same letter makes me smell rats. Dirty little rats scuttling around behind the panels." Lucie whacked her cane against the wall before hoisting herself up the next step. "Some kind of pamphlets against the Americans and Hesse. Drawings were mentioned, but nothing about your friend. By the way, has Sobby had her baby yet?"

"Sobby?"

"Lady Sophia. She's Margaretha's niece, and expecting her first baby within the next month. The two of them are staying at the old Wolfer Hof. Sobby doesn't just cry over spilled milk, she turns it into a major passion-play. Complete with fireworks in the end. My maid told me there was a fire at Wolfer Hof last night, but if Sobby is going to stay here—not to mention Margaretha—I think I'll have my future meals in the muniment room. Care to join me?"

"With the greatest delight, Lady Lucie."

# Chapter 3

*Düsseldorf, The Castle*
*June 1634*

"Sister Maximiliane to see you, milady."

Charlotte looked up from the letter she was writing to glance around the room to see if everything was in order. Two weeks ago she and Elisabeth had been about to board the boats arranged to take them up the Rhine to Cologne, when a dispatch had arrived from Wolfgang to the captain of the garrison left behind. As it turned out the cavalry that came running back to Düsseldorf with the news about the French betrayal had been only partly right: Turenne and his men had gone off on their own as soon as they had crossed the river Ruhr, but her husband was very much alive, and locked in a battle with the army of Essen. Faced with this news, Charlotte had decided to stay in Düsseldorf, and wait for the arrival of her brother, rather than to try hiding from Wolfgang in Cologne. Unfortunately Friedrich had been delayed by spring flooding in the Alps washing away the roads, but according to his latest letter he had now arrived in Metz and would come north as soon as possible.

In the meantime Wolfgang's plans to catch the army of Essen in a vise and crush it to a quick victory had been changed into a long drawn-out battle and attacks against the fortifications surrounding Essen. He had sent for the heavy cannons from

Düsseldorf—as well as all available troops from Jülich and the cavalry the archbishop had promised him—but the news coming from the front was so contradictory that the entire town—not to mention all the servants at the castle—were in a constant state of uproar. As a result Charlotte was constantly called upon to deal with some new crisis, and whenever she sat down to think and make plans, somebody would interrupt. Elisabeth, who was supposed to help her run the castle as well as keep her company, was actually worse than useless in dealing with a crisis; her mind had never been agile, and the life as a postulant, who never had to think outside the rules, suited her perfectly.

"Thank you, Frau van der Berg, that'll be all." Charlotte nodded to her castellaine, and turned her attention to her visitor. Sister Maximiliane, former Countess von Wartenberg and a cousin to Archbishop Ferdinand of Cologne, had come from Bavaria to nurse her cousin through a serious stomach disorder the previous winter. She was well known as a strong fighter for women's right to enter total sequestration and concentrate fully on the glory of God, but to everybody's surprise she had accepted taking charge of the Hatzfeldt household in Cologne instead of returning to München. Speculations as to why had been running rather wild all spring, and ranged from a love affair with Prince-Bishop Franz von Hatzfeldt to financial problems in München making it impossible for her to return. Elisabeth had been partial to the first theory on the basis of the many mistresses kept by the males in the Bavarian ducal family, but Charlotte knew the kind of money it took to enter total isolation, and found it far more likely that the strong-willed Maxie had bitten off more than she could chew and simply wanted to raise some money before going home.

Well, as the hostess it was Charlotte's task to direct the conversation, so perhaps she could direct it in that direction—and if nothing else then at least an afternoon spent with the apparently intelligent and capable older woman would serve to distract Charlotte from all the problems otherwise running her ragged.

"My sister Elisabeth is unfortunately bed-bound with a stomach disorder today, but she has so much wanted to hear your opinion about the religious opportunities for women in Cologne. My own time is presently very much taken by the practical tasks of running this castle, but if you would be as kind as to give me your impression of the most needful undertakings, I'm sure my sister would be delighted to join you in whatever you feel would do the most good."

"I am no longer actively involved with religious matters." Maxie smiled a little bitterly and sipped delicately on the sweet, fine wine Charlotte was serving in costly Venetian glasses.

"Oh." That was unexpected.

"My male relatives had promised me their support, but played me false." Maxie looked directly at Charlotte and grinned without real mirth. "I'll not deny that it hurt to give up the plans for which I had fought so hard, and I still believe that women should have the same opportunities as men, but personally I find that there is a certain liberty in no longer needing so many people's goodwill. I rather believe I'll enjoy speaking my mind for a while."

Charlotte found a wry answering smile tucking her own lips. "Yes, that would be wonderful."

"I rather heard—between his words—from my archbishop cousin, that you have had some problems in that direction." Maxie's words were almost, but not quite a question.

"Yes." Charlotte looked down into her wine to hide her thoughts. Not only would Maxie be a valuable ally if Charlotte went to Cologne, but Maxie's openness about her own life made Charlotte want to trust her with her own problems. Still, Maxie was known to her only by reputation, so it might be wise to feel her way a little. "Do you think the Americans in Thüringen have been sent by the Devil?"

"No," Maxie's eyebrows had lifted in surprise, "but unless that was an abrupt change of subject, I'm most interested in the connection."

"Wolfgang was three times my age when we married, but not at all a bad husband—or a bad man. He was quite tolerant of what I wanted, fair in his judgments, and both concerned and capable in running his lands. He often went to Essen, being interested in what De Geer there was doing, and usually came home with new ideas and plans. Then, a little more than two years ago, an American had been there to tell about all the new things they claimed were possible, and when Wolfgang returned he was very quiet and didn't want to talk about it. In fact he forbade anyone to even mention the Americans. Then he started losing his temper over quite insignificant matters. Would fly into a rage if something had been moved, or his son voiced a different opinion from his own. Previously Wolfgang had been proud when Philipp had made a clever argument, but now it made him furious. And it wasn't just with Philipp and me. It was the servants, in courts, everywhere, as if he had been bewitched into a totally different person. And it only got worse." Charlotte shook her head and looked up at Maxie with a weak attempt at a smile. "You are very well known for your nursing skills, do you think he could be ill?"

"Not from any disease I have ever encountered," Maxie looked thoughtful, "but the mind is a strange place, and I might have heard about something. Has he been very opposed to anything new?"

"Yes, anything new, anything changed."

"Well, first of all, I'm not personally familiar with any Americans, but Father Johannes, a person whose judgment seems quite sound, has lived with them since shortly after they arrived. He claims that they are quite ordinary people, special only in being most excellent craftsmen, but morally neither better nor worse, neither stronger nor weaker than what you'll find in any German town. However, one of the crafts they excel in is that of medicine, and their studies of the human body have included that of the mind. One of the books Father Johannes read and found especially interesting described things that are not actually diseases, but rather too strong or twisted reactions to things happening in a person's life. I recognized the description of shellshock in a patient I once had, who previously survived a heavy cannonade during a siege, and what has happened to your husband could be something similar called future shock. As far as I have understood, it's what happens when your mind cannot adjust to all the changes in your life, and try to escape into unthinking rages, drink, or apathy."

"I don't understand."

"Well, truly neither do I," said Maxie smiling warmly, "but Father Johannes assured me that things like the flying machines are quite real, and I suspect that a flight in one of those could drive me more than a little out of my mind. Perhaps your husband experienced something like that, something his mind could not understand or accept, but which Essen embraced, and he therefore would soon find on his northern border. Your husband's recent behavior certainly seems to indicate that he finds Essen a danger to him."

"Yes," Charlotte said, absentmindedly refilling the glasses, "and Turenne played him like a viola. Will you be staying long in Düsseldorf?"

## Magdeburg, House of Hessen

*My Dearest Uncle,*
  *I write in the hope of finding you and your family in your usual good health, and in the hope that your beloved wife...*

Amalie lifted the pen from the paper. No. Better not mention her last skirmish with Ehrengard at all. Uncle Albrecht would have had all the details from his wife anyway—in fact he would probably have had them morning, noon and night ever since last Christmas—and she *had* to find a way to make the family stand together if they were to retain any kind of prominence. So...

  *...will permit your lovely daughters to visit me here in Magdeburg, and take advantage of the abbess of Quedlinburg's advanced lessons in the new political system. As you know, the abbess was a member of the Chamber of Princes and one of the people who worked on the new constitution, but Princess Eleonore von Anhalt-Dessau, whose husband, Wilhelm Wettin, everyone expected to become the next prime minister of the USE, and I, have prevailed upon the abbess to offer lessons to those of her former students, who might find themselves in a position where such knowledge would be to their advantage.*

There. Implying that Albrecht's daughters were expected to make marriages of political importance ought to tickle his vanity. Though from the little Amalie could remember, they were all rather insipid and really difficult to keep apart. But the fences had to be mended, and this invitation—written in her own hand— could only be taken as an extended olive branch. So, now all that was left to write was the usual polite regards and inquiries, and then she could go see what Eleonore had heard about the situation in Denmark.

## Cologne, Hatzfeldt House

The four Hatzfeldt brothers had arrived together in Cologne after meeting in Bonn, and the entire family was now gathering in preparation for the youngest brother, Hermann's, marriage to the heiress Lady Maria Katharina Kaemmerer von Worms-Dalberg on the first Sunday in June.

The fire at Wolfer Hof had not done much damage, but Lady Sophia—with her cousin, Dame Anna, in attendance—had moved to Hatzfeldt House, so she could have her baby away from the fearful fire. They were still in residence along with the nine Wildenburg and Fleckenbuehl cousins, who had been able to come. And even with the twelve Weisweiler and Werther cousins having their own lodgings, and the eight Merten and Schoenstein cousins staying with Margaretha in Wolfer Hof, the Hatzfeldt House was now bursting at the seams, and Father Johannes' work came to a complete hold.

The orphaned Lady Maria Katharina, called Trinket by the Hatzfeldts for her love of finery, would come to Cologne later together with Archbishop Ferdinand, and stay with him in his palace until the wedding. Fortunately the big feast following the church ceremonial would also be held in the archbishop's palace. That Trinket's Worm ancestors descended from King Clodomir I of Cologne was almost certainly just a myth, but the archbishop nonetheless used it as an excuse for a big celebration in Cologne. And to get the council's permission for him to enter the town to perform the ceremony. Cologne was staunchly Catholic, but also a free trading town with many special privileges, and since the citizens of Cologne had successfully rebelled against their clerical overlord in 1288, the following archbishops could enter the town only with the council's permission. In Father Johannes' opinion, the wedding celebration was a quite clever move, since having the town's backing and support would most likely be crucial to any plans the archbishop made. And—of course—everybody loves a wedding.

Lucie had stuck to her plan to take all meals—except formal dinners—in the muniment room for as long as Lady Sophia was in residence, and Father Johannes usually kept her company in both places. The formal dinners really weren't that bad. Sure,

Lady Sophia's overblown histrionics got a bit tiresome with repetition, but usually the dinner was in the honor of this or that cousin's arrival in Cologne, and even if it wasn't enlivened by one of the lively feuds the Hatzfeldts entertained themselves with, at least Father Johannes gained major orders for porcelain from the Magdeburg Meissen factory he was part owner of. The ovens were presently being built in Magdeburg, and hadn't gone into production yet, but his few test samples fired in Grantville had convinced everybody that he could deliver.

Maxie obviously enjoyed herself hugely by needling Margaretha whenever That Backenfoerde Woman had to be invited. And usually Maxie had the enthusiastic help of the Wildenburg, Weisweiler and Werther cousins, while the dignified Fleckenbuehls tried to calm things down and the Merten and Schoenstein cousins sniggered up their sleeves at their unpopular matriarch's problems with keeping her sharp tongue under control when faced with the archbishop's favorite cousin. All in all, dinner parties from hell—except that everybody seemed to regard it as business as usual, so Father Johannes relaxed and let himself be entertained by the antics.

During the daytime Maxie came to the muniment room whenever she could find the time, and she and Lucie soon included Father Johannes in their old and firm friendship, talking about everything between Heaven and Earth, while sorting and listing the huge piles of paper. Father Johannes sometimes helped the sorting, but usually worked on lists for the restorations, sketches for the new buildings, or—lately—plans for a library—such as shown in the latest number of *Simplicissimus Magazine* and fast becoming extremely fashionable—to house the family's collection of books.

Lucie's four brothers also came to visit the muniment room from time to time. Quiet, calm-looking Heinrich Friedrich, the oldest of the Hatzfeldt brothers, was the least frequent visitor. Old Sebastian had spent most of his life serving the archbishops of Mainz in one capacity or the other, and he had bought his oldest son an expensive position as a domherr at St. Alban in Mainz. Here Heinrich had remained during and after the Swedish conquest of the town, and he now spent most of his visit in Cologne with the exiled Archbishop Anselm of Mainz.

All the Hatzfeldt brothers had studied theology for a while in their youth, but only Franz, the sturdy and dark third brother, had taken the priestly vows and made a career within the Church, first as a diplomat in the service of the prince-bishop of Bamberg, later as a prince-bishop himself in Würzburg. Normally this would have made him the most powerful—and the wealthiest—of the brothers, but with his exile following the Swedish conquest, his prospects were now most uncertain. Especially since his main heritage from his father, the Castle Crottorf, was also behind the present USE borders.

Hermann, the spindly and narrow-shouldered youngest brother, was a colonel—but well known to be much more of an administrator than a warrior—and always ended up serving as quartermaster of whatever army he was serving in. With none of his three elder brothers showing any signs of marrying, Hermann was now withdrawing from warfare and concentrating on handling the family's estates and possessions, a life Father Johannes felt certain would suit him just fine. Not to mention that he'd probably get much better results negotiating with the USE for the conquered parts of his family's lands near Mainz than he would trying to fight for them.

Melchior, the ruddy and most handsome second brother, had planned to become a Knight of Saint John on Malta, but broke off his studies after several years in Fulda, Würzburg and France to become a soldier. As such he had made a very fast career to general under Wallenstein, and had since gathered a sizable fortune during his campaigns. Before going to Cologne, Father Johannes had searched the library in Grantville for information about the Hatzfeldts, and in the Americans' world Melchior had—in 1635— become an imperial count, field-marshal and imperial councillor as a reward for remaining loyal to the emperor during Wallenstein's intrigues. Now Melchior was an imperial count a year early, but just that, none of the other titles. And rather than fighting against Wallenstein's rebellion in Bohemia—or against one of the Protestant armies elsewhere—he had been given furlough to visit his family. He had, of course, left behind his regiments in Linz. Nevertheless, while he wasn't as famous as Tilly and Wallenstein, he was still the highest ranking and most respected Catholic war-leader now in the West. Sending him to lead an attempt to push back the USE occupation along the Rhine would make sense, but was that the plan? A messenger from Don Francisco had come to Cologne a few days after Melchior's arrival: Duke Wilhelm of Hesse-Kassel was most alarmed by General Melchior von Hatzfeldt's presence so near his border, and any sign of military mobilization would be viewed as intended aggression. Any information from Father Johannes would be appreciated!

The Fleckenbuehl cousins—with estates in Hesse and a long history of service to the ruling family there—repeatedly tried to corner Melchior for a private discussion, so after a few days Melchior took to spending all his afternoons with the ladies and Father Johannes in the muniment room. And to his great mortification Father Johannes found himself jealous of the other man's easy relationship with *his* ladies. It was of course an unworthy feeling. Illogical. Ridiculous. And altogether to be ignored. And beside Melchior's presence in the muniment room might provide some insights in what dastardly deeds were going on in Bonn. That Father Johannes liked—really liked—the two ladies didn't mean their male relatives weren't both ambitious and ruthless. Father Johannes really should spend as much time as possible with the ladies. Eh! With Melchior. He owed it to... To his American friends. And the chance for a better world that they represented. And as a priest he should certainly try to prevent a renewal of the fighting in this part of Germany. Eh! As a Catholic priest he should prevent a Catholic archbishop from using this Catholic imperial general to re-take areas presently occupied by the Protestant? Argh! What a bloody mess. Father Johannes stopped to rest his head against the door before entering the muniment room.

Inside, the two ladies and Melchior were laughing at two cats sitting on each end of the table and alternately hissing at each other and ignoring each other with contempt. "Come in, Father Johannes," said Lucie, smiling up at Father Johannes. "Two new toms have been added to the household and they are being absolutely ridiculous."

"Yes," said Maxie leaning back in her chair and smiling wryly at Father Johannes, "and their names are Melchior and Father Johannes."

Melchior stopped laughing and stared at Maxie, while Father Johannes sank down on a chair and kept his eyes on the cats. The silence stretched for a while, then Melchior started chuckling. "I didn't think we were being that obvious, Father Johannes."

Father Johannes sighed and looked at the other man; when he dropped the harsh authority of an officer and his smile reached his eyes, Melchior really looked like a male version of Lucie. Kindness and humor at least somewhat included. "If my behavior has been offensive or in any way improper, I most humbly apologize," said Father Johannes with a bow towards the other man.

"Don't be silly, Father Johannes." Once again Lucie made Father Johannes feel like a school boy. "Compared to most of the clerics I know, you are an absolute pattern-card of moral rectitude and proper behavior. But you and my dear brother have so much in common that it's silly so formal you both have been. Why don't you start by telling Melchior about the Americans' notion of democracy? Papa studied for years in Strasbourg, and was most interested in philosophy. Melchior has inherited this interest."

## Hessian camp outside the town of Frankenberg

Wilhelm of Hesse-Kassel had been commanding troops since he was a teenager, including several years of learning everything he could from Gustavus Adolphus, and now every bit of experience he had told him that this campaign was getting too complex. His wife Amalie took the greatest delight in political intrigues, and the more complex the better. But while he had the greatest respect for her brain and knowledge, she didn't really understand military realities in the field.

He had perfectly agreed with her that the new province of Hesse-Kassel needed a major center for industry and trading, preferably on the Rhine. With Gustavus Adolphus blocking both Essen and Düsseldorf, the only possibility left was Cologne. So, he'd made plans for a feint towards Wildenburg and Schönstein followed by a quick raid across the mountains southwest of Hessen to take first Bonn and then Cologne before the summer was over. That Archbishop Ferdinand had been hiring some of Wallenstein's old colonels was not a problem, especially since the names mentioned were definitely second-rate. It made a somewhat plausible excuse for those excessively nervous types in the government who insisted that armies should only be used for defense. The French had been sniffing around the area all spring, but Richelieu liked to have a finger in all pies, and the French troops south of Trier had not been reported moving north, so that was fairly much business as usual too.

That General Melchior von Hatzfeldt had suddenly shown up in Bonn a few weeks ago was slightly more worrying, but since he came without his regiments, it was probably just some kind of scouting mission for the HRE. But now! Hesse sighed and looked down on the telegram in his hand. A special courier from Amalie had arrived only a week ago with a letter saying that Wolfgang of Jülich-Berg was in league with the archbishop and Richelieu in planning an attack on Hesse-Kassel, and that the plans should be changed to head due west for Mark and Düsseldorf. Today she had sent a telegram using the radio between Magdeburg and Kassel to get the message to him faster, if less secretly, saying that the Catholic Alliance had already attacked Essen, and that he should head northwest towards Paderborn and Dortmund to hit them from the rear!

Both changes made sense on the basis of the information, but what Amalie really didn't understand was that you could not keep changing where your army was going and still expect it to get anywhere. Doing so undermined the men's confidence in the leaders, and backtracking on roads already churned by a passing army meant that the cannons and supply wagons were almost guaranteed to get stuck. He could recall the cavalry and send them north to Paderborn, or he could let them take the mountain paths to the road past Plettenberg, but the cannons and the infantry were already strung out along the southern route, and there was no way he could turn them north before Siegen.

In the meantime he needed to leave the army and go see old Ludwig of Sayn-Wittgenstein. That stubborn old fool was almost on his deathbed, but still determined to make troubles. His heir, Johannes, was a sensible young man, who had almost immediately seen the benefits in having his small mountain realm incorporated in the USE province of Hesse-Kassel. But the old man had flat out refused to even discuss it, declaring in the most pompous phrases that he would see every mountain stream run red with the blood of both his own people and any invaders before he gave up the land built on the bones of his ancestors.

The army Wittgenstein could field wasn't even a single regiment, so it was of course possible to simply ignore the old man and press ahead. But since the old man's daughter-in-law was the sister to Hesse's sister-in-law, it might be better to try diplomacy once more. Hesse's brother Herman really doted on his new bride, and if Hesse—even by accident—made Juliane's sister a widow, there really would be trouble when he returned to Magdeburg.

# Chapter 4

*Düsseldorf, The Castle*
*June 24, 1634*

"My lady? Pardon me for disturbing your vigil."

Charlotte turned her head at the voice of General Merode, and rose stiffly from the pad where she had been kneeling. She had gone along with her sister's suggestion that they would keep the old custom of holding a vigil, praying in the chapel on Saint John's Night, hoping that the quiet of the night would enable her to put her options in order and make some plans for the future.

"My lady?" Merode reached out to touch her sleeve. "Are you unwell?"

Charlotte shrugged and tried to smile. She felt dizzy and lightheaded. Holding a vigil while short of sleep and more than seven months pregnant had probably not been very wise. "You bring news, General Merode?" The man looked as worn-out as she felt, but she couldn't read the emotions in his weathered face.

"Yes, my lady. And I'm afraid it's very bad news." The general bowed. "Your husband and his son were both killed yesterday afternoon, and the troops suffered heavy casualties. The army of Essen may be expected to reach Düsseldorf either today or tomorrow, and I think you had better flee. The battles have been unusually bloody, and unless the Essen command is able to reestablish discipline very quickly, things could get badly out of hand. I've got only a few hundred men, but I believe our best option is to head for Jülich."

"Thank you, General." Charlotte pulled herself together and ignored the agitated babbling of her sister and the other people around her. "But I would like for you to try organizing some kind of defensive lines stopping Essen from taking more of Berg than the area here around Düsseldorf. The sack of the town should buy you some time, and heaven knows the mountains form their own defenses. I shall travel up the Rhine to Cologne. Archbishop Ferdinand is an old friend of my mother. Stop wailing, Elisabeth, and go pack."

## Cologne, Hatzfeldt House

On the evening of Hermann's wedding Father Johannes sat sketching lamps for the new library on a piece of scrap paper when Maxie and Lucie came into the muniment room. He had received an invitation to join the celebrating in the palace, but though the invitation had come from Melchior, and had no other motive than their fast growing friendship, Father Johannes had not wanted to catch the attention of the archbishop—nor of Felix Gruyard.

"Back so early, ladies?" Father Johannes rose with a slight bow and helped Lucie to her chair.

"We used Lucie's leg as an excuse, and borrowed Peter von Hardenrat's carriage," said Maxie with a frown. "Neither of us liked it there. No one talked about anything but that mess with Essen and Wolfgang of Jülich-Berg except Cousin Ferdinand, who would not talk to me about anything except the food—which he didn't touch. And everyone who came with him from Bonn drank too much and their smiles never reached their eyes. I wish my brother had come with the archbishop, but Franz Wilhelm remained in Bonn. And immediately after the banquet Ferdinand and some of his friends pulled Melchior aside and withdrew from the hall; such rudeness towards the mayors and the city councilors worries me. Ferdinand is the son of a duke, he cannot just sit waiting for his land and power to be eroded; it's totally against his nature and upbringing. But if Melchior is more important than the support of the Council of Cologne... Damned." Maxie's striding up and down the floor came to an abrupt end when her thin embroidered slipper connected hard with a crate.

"Do sit down, Maxie." Lucie tilted her head a bit and looked at her friend. "Melchior will tell us something when he comes back. Like you, I favor negotiations, but I cannot blame Archbishop Ferdinand and Franz for wanting to negotiate from a position of power. We've all heard how Schweinsberg's doing in Fulda after simply going back to his diocese. Franz would hate to be so powerless. He might do it if he thought the people of Würzburg were being badly mistreated, but Father Johannes has made it clear that this is unlikely."

"Actually, your brother has shown far more interest in the conditions in Fulda than in Würzburg," said Father Johannes.

"Fulda? Why Fulda? I think my toe is broken." Maxie winced as she eased off her shoe and moved her foot. "Help me get my stocking off, Father Johannes. I want to take a look." Maxie leaned back on the big table and pulled up her skirts to show her pink embroidered stocking tied with a matching garter above her knee.

"Maximiliane!"

"Oh bother, Lucie. I cannot bend down in this boned stomacher, and you are in pain already. Besides, if Father Johannes hasn't untied a lady's garter before, then it's high time he did."

Knowing his face would be beet-red, Father Johannes knelt down in front of Maxie, and was trying to figure out which ribbon to pull when the door to the room opened.

Melchior walked slowly from the archbishop's palace back to Hatzfeldt House. There was something seriously wrong. Archbishop Ferdinand was up to something that he wasn't willing to talk openly about—and he was involving Franz in the intrigue. That would not necessarily have been a problem if Melchior had any confidence in the archbishop's ability to succeed, but every bit of military experience Melchior had gathered during almost twenty years as a mercenary officer told him not to rely on Archbishop Ferdinand as a leader.

Melchior nodded to the servant by the entrance, and went down the steps to the muniment room where the candles still burned along that passage. He opened the door and stopped in surprise at the sight of Maxie with her skirt drawn up to show her legs leaning against the table with Father Johannes beetroot-red in the face kneeling before her—and with Lucie broadly grinning in her chair.

"Oh my God!" After a surprised stop, Melchior collapsed in a chair and bent over with laughter.

Father Johannes totally by chance pulled the right end and eased off the stocking by touching only the heel and toes. Then he returned to his chair scowling at the still-laughing Melchior— and carefully avoiding the eyes of either lady.

"Will you stop laughing, Melchior? It's not that funny. And that toe will certainly be blue and black in the morning." Maxie frowned at her toes before dropping her skirts and sitting down. "I said stop it!"

Melchior dried his eyes, but kept smiling. "I really needed that, dear Maxie. It was such an antidote to the poison I've inhaled tonight."

"Glad to be of service," Father Johannes half snarled, "but could you possibly explain what is going on with the archbishop; because the rest of us haven't got a clue."

Melchior leaned back in his chair and looked far more somberly at Father Johannes. "No offense intended, Father Johannes, but though you are a Catholic priest—a Jesuit of all things—I need to ask if your primary loyalty is to the Catholic Church or to the Americans."

"The Americans *are* Catholics." Father Johannes shrugged. "At least some of them. They have sent a delegation to the pope to clarify their status within the Church, and I refuse to consider it a problem until and unless it becomes one. Also, I've never given any kind of oath to the Americans; they never asked for one or even mentioned the idea. What I give to them I give freely, without pressure or obligation, based only on my own judgement. As for the Church?" Father Johannes sighed. "I broke my vow of obedience towards my superiors at Magdeburg, and I'm totally certain I never did anything more right. Your brother arranged a pardon for this from Archbishop Ferdinand, but no one has asked me to renew my broken oath. And I'd much prefer no one did. I serve God to the best of my abilities, but there are things I'd never again do for the Church: making propaganda for a 'holy' war is one; attempting to stop the American ideas from spreading is another. I really do believe they'll do more good than harm."

Melchior nodded. "My own oath of loyalty is, of course,

to the emperor I serve, and the most important part of 'Holy Roman Empire' is first, last and always: Empire. I was sent here partly to evaluate the military situation in the West, partly for an irrelevant personal reason, and I'm far from certain that the archbishop's plans are in the emperor's best interest. Maxie, are you quite certain your cousin is of a sound mind?"

"Ambitions are encouraged in the ducal family, especially for the boys." Maxie looked down on her hands, fingers twisting her shining rings. "The only subject where I have known Ferdinand to be lost to reason concerns his older brother Philipp. There was only a year between them, and they were as close as twins, played together, studied together in Ingolstadt, and went to Rome together when Philipp became a bishop at the age of sixteen. Philipp was a cardinal when he was killed by a fall from a horse only six years later. That was more than thirty years ago, but Ferdinand still wants to become a cardinal like Philipp. He really has neither Philipp's brilliant flair for theology nor his genuine interest in spiritual matters and charity. So for thirty years Ferdinand has slowly been building a power base." She looked up at Melchior and Father Johannes. "You should understand, that for Ferdinand it is not the land, the people, the wealth or the fame, it is influence in clerical circles that has his main interest. This is illogical as he doesn't really want to be a cardinal for any purpose; it's just a goal. But watching that power base erode, seeing that dream fade, feeling he failed his dead brother...Despite his long experience and political acumen, he could be making decisions based on other than logic."

"Sorry, Maxie, but I do not think logic or reason has any part in his decisions anymore." Melchior started twining his goatee between his fingers, a sure sign he was thinking hard. "Father Johannes, how would you estimate the chances of winning against the USE here in the West—providing the Americans remain in alliance with the Swedes?"

Father Johannes sat up, suddenly very alert. Was there a danger to that alliance? "Winning by military means? None, unless the Catholic countries suddenly started working together and didn't count the cost. The present engagement could barely stop the Swedes and their German allies, and the addition of the Americans has made the Protestant army much more efficient. The Americans are very good at fighting, but their real value is their handling of resources, which they call the Sinews of War. Oh, winning a few battles against them would be entirely possible, perhaps even regaining a major part of Bishop's Alley while they were occupied elsewhere. But sooner or later, they'd turn this way to push back. And then they'd just keep pushing until they reached the sea. Something like the entire French and Spanish armies might get them to accept a border not drawn by American conquests, but I wouldn't count on it. The concept of accepting defeat gracefully appears to be incomprehensible to them."

"As for winning by negotiations?" Father Johannes shrugged, "I don't think that's possible at all. Not because of the terms and deals that might be made, but because the American 'land' will always be defined by ideas rather than borders; and those ideas are going to spread. Those Committees of Correspondence we discussed the other day are just a small part; no matter the result of a negotiation, people will sooner or later hear those ideas and chose for themselves among them." Father Johannes gave a grin. "Of course people don't always choose wisely, so I also want the Church around to guide them. But guide, not dominate."

"Hm!" Melchior kept pulling his beard. "The archbishop wants me to lead an army—nothing surprising in that—but those regiments he has been hiring don't stand a chance of success even as far up the Rhine and Main as Frankfurt. My own regiments are quartered at Linz under the temporary command of my cousin Wolf, ready to strike northwards if Wallenstein makes a move. Since it's highly unlikely that Wallenstein would do anything so stupid, Archbishop Ferdinand wants to borrow me and my men from the emperor. If that cannot be done, he plans to use his own dragoons as a kind of decoy, to draw attention while he strikes in some other fashion. Wouldn't give me the details, but hinted at discrediting the Americans in some way. One of the Bamberg clerics was very drunk and started giggling about a renegade Jesuit, spying and corrupting for the Americans: nurtured like a snake at the bosom of the Church. The way Franz cut him off made me wonder if you might not better keep your saddlebags packed, Father Johannes. You could also come with me back to Linz."

"I'm getting really annoyed with Ferdinand," said Maxie, tapping her fingernails against the table, "and *that* he can just forget about!"

"But Maxie," Melchior's broad grin was an open challenge, "since you are a nun, an archbishop is surely in a position to give you orders."

"Nun, my bare arse!" Maxie suddenly slammed her hand against the table. "I've spent fifteen years trying to make it possible for nuns to enter seclusion for the contemplation of God same as it is for monks, and I've gotten nowhere! Nuns are supposed to work for their support. Teaching young girls and tending the sick. Not even studying medicine. Oh, no. Just cheap nursing. When Ferdinand sent for me last year I was this close," she held up two fingers barely an inch apart, "to renouncing my vows, and telling my ducal relatives to go to hell. I'm sick and tired of trying to placate everybody to get their support. Playing by the rules while every male relative I've got is flouting any that don't suit them."

"Well, I don't blame you, dearest Maxie," Melchior was openly laughing now, "and if you find yourself in need of gainful employment, I could certainly use an officer with your talent for organization."

"No, thanks. Trousers don't become me, and I've got enough people owing me debts and favors to set myself up for any life I fancy. And now I want to get rid of this pearl-encrusted armor I'm wearing. Good night. Lucie, do you want to come?"

## Magdeburg, Government Palace
## June 26, 1634

"Welcome back to Magdeburg, Chancellor Oxenstierna." Amalie smiled up at the spare face of the Swedish chancellor, while maneuvering in the crush of people attending the party celebrating the Congress of Copenhagen to place herself directly before him. "Did the journey go well?"

"Yes, thank you, my lady." The chancellor seemed to decide that escape was impossible, and that trying to direct the conversation was his best option. "And how is the organization of the new Hesse-Kassel province coming along? Are you having any trouble with getting the last commitments?"

"None whatsoever, Chancellor." Amalie fixed the smile on her face. The chancellor was very good at keeping informed, even when traveling around the Baltic Sea. Some members of the Nassau family were indeed still making trouble. Oh, they'd agree in the end, but not until they had squeezed every bit of advantage out of the situation. She continued. "I assume that the whole of Berg is to be included in Hesse-Kassel, now that both Duke Wolfgang and his heir are dead."

"I'm quite certain that the emperor does not wish to make a final decision on that question until after Princess Katharina's young cousin, Katharina Charlotte, has given birth to the child she is carrying." The chancellor smiled back at Amalie. "So, you've got the final holdouts among the Nassau family to agree to the proposed structure for the province? Impressive."

"Has a guardianship been settled for the unborn child?" Amalie headed into battle. "We have written Gustavus Adolphus offering our house for this. Katharina Charlotte is little more than a child herself, but with Hesse-Kassel as overlord we would have—"

"You overstep yourself, my lady." All traces of a social smile had now disappeared from the chancellor's face. "The child has plenty of relatives on its mother's side, and any guardianship for the child and the land will be settled within the Vasa and Zweibrücken families. Also, according to a codicil to the marriage contract, the late Duke Wolfgang settled the entire Jülich-Berg on Katharina Charlotte as her dower and heritage, if the duke died without heirs of his body. So, whether the child lives or dies, Jülich and Berg are not necessarily included in your province. Now, if you'll excuse me, I'll go have a few words with Duchess Hedwig. Christian August, her oldest son, would be next in line for Jülich-Berg if it had not been for that peculiar marriage contract."

"I think I'll go with you, Chancellor. I haven't yet had the opportunity to inquire after Christian August's health. As you know, he had trouble recovering from the pox that killed his father and brothers. Quite a crush here tonight, don't you think?" Amalie took the chancellor's arm and thought quickly. Oxenstierna's care for the interest of the Swedish royal family was well known, but he would never have spoken for Gustavus Adolphus like that unless he really was certain that this was the emperor's decision. Had she just made a major mistake? It was too late to stop the letter.

"Quite so, my lady. And talking about crushes, there seems to be quite a lot of soldiers gathering west of the proposed borders of

Hesse-Kassel, so I've sent a message for your husband to remind him not to engage in any combat with the army of Essen presently occupying Düsseldorf. The emperor does not want a battle with Essen."

"Oh, and does Gustavus Adolphus intend to donate to his good friend De Geer the entire lot of land once belonging to Johann the Insane—or just those areas the Americans tell us potentially form the most important industrial area of Europe?" Amalie very nearly lost control of her temper to see the chancellor silently laughing at her. With Wolfgang gone—and Brandenburg turned traitor—Jülich, Berg, Cleve, Mark and all the smaller areas should be up for grabs. And to be blocked by the emperor, who owed Hesse so much for all those years of faithful support! Making Hesse-Kassel the center of a USE province was *not* enough, when it included nothing but rural backwaters.

"Good evening, Amalie, Good evening, Chancellor. You look a bit out of temper, my dear." Hedwig of Holstein-Gottorp leaned forward to brush a kiss on Amalie's cheek, and just looking into the kind eyes of her old friend made Amalie calm down. Hedwig was a very nice woman, even if they might now be rivals. It should be possible to reach some kind of accommodation with her.

"Good evening, Hedwig. I was just discussing the Jülich-Berg problem with the chancellor." Amalie smiled. "I think he was needling me a bit. But, where do you stand my dear? Is Christian August well enough to handle that mess Wolfgang left behind?"

"A twelve-year-old, sickly boy?" Hedwig smiled wryly. "No, thank you. I may not have your interest in politics, Amalie, but I'm not a complete idiot. As soon as we got the information about the demise of both Wolfgang and his heir, I sat down and wrote a statement leaving all claims on behalf of my son to the emperor's discretion."

"I see." Amalie looked up at the chancellor, whose eyes were still laughing in an otherwise completely somber face. "And do Wolfgang's two other siblings agree with Hedwig, Chancellor?"

"Since Hilpoltstein's wife, Sofie Agnes, is Hesse's first cousin, I'm sure you know that she has been unable to carry a child to term. And that the American doctors couldn't help. Anna Marie von Neuburg is still undecided, but little Elisabeth Sophia is her only living grandchild, so Saxe-Altenburg also plans to follow Hedwig's example. Apparently some of your peers believe in trusting the emperor to do what is best, for their class as well as for the USE. Ladies, if you'll excuse me."

This time Amalie let the chancellor escape and sat down silently beside Hedwig, slowly using her fan to cool her face, while automatically nodding and smiling to the people passing by. Damn! It simply hadn't occurred to her to seek the emperor's favor by leaving the decision to him. If Gustavus Adolphus was heading towards becoming one of those absolute monarchs that the American books had told about, then the old ways of playing for power simply had to be dumped. Mary Simpson had more than indicated that the time for independent military conquests was over, but this quickly and with no protests? Amalie looked at Hedwig sitting serenely next to her. Jülich and Berg had come to the Neuburg family from Wolfgang's mother, Anna, who was one of Johann the Insane's four sisters. With all her other children out of the way there were none who could contest Wolfgang's marriage contract on the basis of consanguinity, since the nearest male heir after the baby would be Katharina Charlotte's brother, Count Palatine Friedrich von Zweibrücken.

Hesse's artillery had been stalled for weeks crossing the mountains south of Ludenscheid, while the Hessian cavalry had wasted their time hunting French cavalry, which had not been attacking Essen, but rather coming rapidly first north and then south near Soest. With the army of Essen now firmly in control of Düsseldorf, this entire month of campaigning had been a total waste, and there didn't seem to be anything else to do but go back to taking Cologne. Amalie rose from her seat with a brief invitation to Hedwig for a visit the next day, and headed for the door. She had to get another telegram off to Hesse, but first her bladder demanded a visit to a water closet.

# Chapter 5

*Cologne, Hatzfeldt House*
*July 1634*

"You could move your regiments here by way of Trier!" Bishop Franz was almost shouting at Melchior, and obviously far from his usually calm self.

"No, dear Brother, I could not." Melchior went to put his hand on Franz's shoulder trying to calm him down, but Franz shook it off and went to stare out the window at the masons building the framework for the new stable wall.

"I've told you before," Melchior continued, "that unless I had permission from every ruler along the way—starting with Bavaria or Bohemia, both of which are equally unlikely at the moment—I would be fighting a new army every time I crossed a river or a mountain pass. Usually small armies, true, but even if I had a direct order from the Holy Roman Emperor, I would still try to talk my way out of it." Melchior took a walk to stand beside his brother and put an arm around the shorter man's shoulder. "I cannot do what you want, my dear Brother," Melchior smiled, "but then you never did have the slightest understanding of military matters. Why don't you tell me what's going on? You know I want to help you regain your winegrowing kingdom on the river Main, but why do you insist on trying to do so by fighting, when all that you have ever achieved has been gained through

49

negotiations? You are acting totally out of character, and none of us understand it."

Franz turned to his brother and opened his mouth—then shook his head and walked out the room, slamming the door behind him.

## Cologne, Beguine of Mercy

The market stalls were closing down, but a fair number of people were still standing around talking. Not, Charlotte noted, the usual gossiping housewives, who had gone late for the market looking for bargains at the end of the day, but men from all walks of life standing around with serious and slightly worried expressions talking in low voices that fell silent as Charlotte came near.

Well, Charlotte was worried too. Worried about the fate of the child frequently kicking in her womb; worried about the lives of General Merode and his men fighting the army of Essen as the Hessians moving in from the East; worried that her brother had once again been delayed; but most of all worried about the letters from Archbishop Ferdinand in Bonn getting more and more insistent that she should seek his protection and place herself and her unborn child under his authority. She had not intended to even let the archbishop know that she and Elisabeth had taken refuge in the Beguine of Mercy in Cologne, but her stupid sister had written to the man, when Charlotte didn't, and since then he had kept pestering her to come to Bonn. He had even gone so far as sending that disgusting lackey of his, Felix Gruyard, whom Maxie had told her was actually a torturer from Lorraine.

Maxie had come to visit her twice at the Beguine, and Charlotte was becoming more and more impressed with the sheer number of people Maxie knew, and the amount of information they brought her. Charlotte had rarely left the Beguine since her arrival, not just because her growing belly made it difficult for her to get around, but also because she didn't want anybody to recognize her. Hopefully Friedrich—or at least one of her uncles—would come soon in response to her letters. She felt vulnerable in the Beguine knowing that both De Geer of Essen and Wilhelm of Hesse-Kassel now had armies in Berg and certainly would have agents searching Cologne for her and her unborn child.

Today, however, Elisabeth's nagging and fretting had been driving her up the walls, and after the evening meal, Charlotte had covered her face with a veil, quietly slipped out, and headed for Hatzfeldt House to spend an hour with Maxie before the Beguine closed its doors at sunset. Unfortunately Maxie had left Cologne to visit her brother in Bonn, and was not expected back until late tonight, so instead Charlotte had walked slowly around the market until they started to close down.

Heading back towards the Beguine, Charlotte was startled to see the cadaverous shape of Felix Gruyard, the archbishop's messenger and torturer, talking with two men on the street across from the Beguine, and she made a quick turn to head for the side door, only to feel her thin leather shoe slip on the uneven cobbles. Curling her arms around her belly to protect her child as she fell, Charlotte felt a strong grip on her dress and shoulder pull her back upright again, and she looked up to see the man she had just passed smiling down at her.

"I do not see your maid, milady. May I be of any assistance to you?"

Charlotte made a quick glance over her shoulder to where Gruyard was still talking, then looked back at her rescuer, and nodded. She couldn't see much more of his face than a rather ragged red goatee beneath the broad-brimmed hat, but his language assured her that he was well educated, and his clothes were new and in a cut that allowed easy movements and reminded her of General Merode.

"Yes, please. I had left the Beguine for a brief visit to a friend, but I seem to have become more fatigued than I had realized. If you'd be so kind as to lend me your arm across these uneven cobbles?"

"Certainly." The man turned around and held out his arm, obviously intending to take her to the main door.

"To the side door, please. It is down that street. It would be much closer to my room." Going that way would also keep the man between her and Gruyard. She really didn't like that man.

The walk to the door was brief, and Charlotte didn't feel like talking, but it felt nice and calming just walking with the strong arm to lean on. The man beside her smelled faintly of lavender and horses. He was probably an officer of some kind, and she briefly considered asking for his name. No. That meant that she would have to give her own, and she wanted as few people as possible to realize where she was.

At the door she said a polite goodbye, and slipped unseen back to her room. The walk seemed to have calmed her mind as much as she had hoped a talk with Maxie to do, and it now seemed possible to write a few letters before going to sleep.

An hour or so later Charlotte was just pressing her seal into the warm wax on the final letter when the door to her room was opened without a knock.

"The archbishop bids you come to Bonn."

"What!" Charlotte looked up startled from the letter she had been writing. The Beguine would have closed its door for the night by now, and she had expected the person entering the room to be her sister, Elisabeth, but instead Felix Gruyard stood in front of her. She had thought him a most unpleasant person ever since he had first come to speak with her husband, but now just facing those cold, unwavering eyes for some reason frightened her out of her wits.

"I'm sorry, Master Gruyard. Did you come to bring me a letter?" Charlotte had barely managed to pull herself together when a scream from another part of the building made her jump up from the chair and turn toward the door leading to the inner courtyard.

"No. You will come with me." Gruyard grabbed her arm.

"But what is happening? My sister, Elisabeth? The other women?" There were now several voices screaming and shouting.

"That does not concern you." The flat voice showed no sign of human emotions, only a total concentration on his task. He pulled Charlotte out of the room, and past what looked like soldiers standing in the hall with drawn swords. Outside the main door a carriage drawn by four horses was standing with two more soldiers beside it, and Charlotte was bundled inside before she could formulate a protest. Gruyard entered after her, and the carriage went off with a speed quite unsuited to the cobbled streets it was traveling over.

### Cologne, Hatzfeldt House

"Good morning, Simon." Melchior took the reins his courier extended towards him and looked towards the sun not yet visible above the roofs. "It'll be hot today."

"Yes, sir. Do you want to cross the river and take the forest roads? I can go get the rest of the troop waiting by the eastern gate and we'll meet you by the ferry. We might have to wake up the ferryman though." Simon sounded much too fresh and eager for this time of the morning, and his boyish enthusiasm made Melchior feel old—especially now after a very late and rather emotional night.

"No, that'll be too slow. We'll stop at the Black Goat on the other side of Bonn for the warmest hours, and then try to get as close to Koblenz as possible before stopping for the night."

Melchior swung into the saddle just as Father Johannes came out the door still yawning and rubbing the last sleep from his eyes.

"I wish you a safe and pleasant journey, and success in your endeavor." Father Johannes gave a slight bow.

"Thank you." Melchior smiled down at the man he had so quickly come to consider one of his best friends. "And thanks also for your attempt at inserting a little sanity in the discussion last night, Father Johannes. I got a little heated after dinner. My brother, Franz, used to be a most rational and level-headed man, but now..."

"I find all four of you—and your sister as well—to be both competent and calm, but I do believe the prince-bishop is what the Americans call 'caught between the Devil and the deep blue sea,' and that must be a most unsettling place to be."

Melchior gave a grunt. The two years that Father Johannes had spent in Grantville teaching and reading as many of their myriad of books as possible had given the man a taste for using these odd, but very vivid expressions.

"After you had retired for the night, Maxie remembered yet another person whom you might contact in München, and went to write a letter of introduction. Did you find it this morning?"

"Yes, but I have a nasty suspicion that reason is not going to carry the day. If Maxie cannot talk Archbishop Ferdinand into changing his plans, it's unlikely that anything short of overwhelming force is going to. But on a totally different subject: I was wondering if you would be willing to do an errand for me, Father Johannes?"

"Certainly."

"Yesterday I escorted a quite pregnant young woman to the Beguine of Mercy. She didn't give her name, and the veil keeping the dust off her face made it impossible for me to see her clearly, but there cannot be that many pregnant women staying there. The servant bringing me my shaving water this morning mentioned a disturbance last night in that part of town, and I would like for someone to see if she is in any kind of distress."

"I'll make a detour on my own errands this morning." Father Johannes gave a little grin. "And should I try to discover if she might be a widow?"

"Never mind that, Father Johannes, and fare thee well."

As Melchior and Simon let their horses amble slowly over the cobbles, Melchior noticed Simon sneaking peeks at him, as if gauging his mood. Lieutenant Simon Pettenburg was a rather bright young man, and one of the most promising officers Melchior had trained, so he caught Simon's eyes and raised an enquiring eyebrow.

"It is said that in China the wish 'May You Live in Interesting Times' is considered a most powerful curse." Simon had obviously decided to ask his question in a roundabout way.

"I've heard that too."

"And you visiting old friends all around the area—that was at least partly to see if anything interesting was going on?"

"Yes. And unless you are a lot more stupid than I think you are, you must have realized that I was gathering a report on the military situation around Cologne for the emperor."

Simon nodded. "And the archbishop seems likely to make things very interesting indeed? And also for your brother, the prince-bishop of Würzburg, so you have to do something about it? Only your brother wants you to fight for him to get him Würzburg back, and that wouldn't be wise?"

Melchior nodded. Simon's boyish looks hid a sharp mind, and those big blue eyes saw more than most men twice his age could manage.

"There were men from the mercenaries Archbishop Ferdinand has stationed at Bonn visiting Cologne last night. Not just for a lark, but doing something with the archbishop's Lorrainian torturer, Gruyard. I don't know what." Simon finally volunteered the information he had been leading up to, just as they came into sight of the rest of the troop, so Melchior just said thank you. Whatever the archbishop was up to, the best Melchior could do was get those letters to Münich and Vienna, and hope someone there would and could rein in Archbishop Ferdinand.

# Chapter 6

*Cologne*
*July 1634*

Some weeks after midsummer Father Johannes was enjoying the clear summer morning on his way back from Beauville's store. The river was sparkling beneath the green curtains of the weeping willows, and the white and yellow larkspurs dotted the gray stone walls and piers. The war seemed so far away and such a long time ago.

Father Johannes sat down on a stone plinth and threw a pebble into the still water of the shallows to watch the rings spread. His work here in Cologne was nearly finished. The entire town area belonging to the Hatzfeldts had been cleared of unwanted structures, and the new stables and outbuildings were planned. Building those didn't need Father Johannes' skills, and all that remained to do in the main house was install the new furniture and textiles Trinket had ordered from France. It had been a disappointment that there had been nothing in the Würzburg papers about Paul—the ladies had moved on to the Fulda archives a week ago—but at least the fact that no one seemed know where Paul was also made it unlikely that he was still in the hands of the Inquisition.

He would miss the ladies and Melchior. Melchior had never gone into details about the personal part of his reasons for leaving

Vienna, but he had gathered what information he needed to make his report to the emperor about the military situation, and had left Cologne a few weeks ago.

Father Johannes really liked the calm and competent soldier, but unfortunately the inquiries on Melchior's behalf about the pregnant woman at the Beguine had been met with a firm brush-off. It had been obvious to Father Johannes that something had happened to frighten everybody badly, but no one would even admit to having seen a pregnant woman. At Lucie's suggestion, he'd set the Peters to spy on the Beguine, but they hadn't seen anyone fitting Melchior's description either. Maxie had offered to go herself, but she'd been so busy with the archbishop that Father Johannes had told her not to bother.

The evening before leaving, Melchior had a major quarrel with Franz, when Melchior once again flat-out refused to bring his regiments to Cologne, and use them on behalf of his brother—and Archbishop Ferdinand—to regain first Bishop's Alley and later as much of Franconia and other USE areas as possible. Afterwards Franz had managed to quarrel with nearly everybody, and by the time he went with the archbishop back to Bonn, he really wasn't on speaking terms with anybody in the family.

On the positive side, there wasn't much chance that the archbishop's plans still involved Father Johannes in any way. That Maxie had grown up as the oldest of sixteen siblings—and was definitely in the habit of making decisions—apparently more than compensated for her being ten years younger and nominally the archbishop's subordinate. Darling Maxie. Father Johannes threw in another pebble.

Maxie had used all her powers of persuasion to get Archbishop Ferdinand to back down from whatever it was he had planned, but had been unable to make her cousin listen. Instead she had written letters to their family in Bavaria, and as Melchior was going to Vienna by way of München, he had offered to personally deliver the one to Duke Maximilian. Hopefully the duke would see the folly of stirring up trouble in an area already so unsettled, and call the archbishop to order.

Instead they'd had a letter from Melchior yesterday, delivered to Lucie directly from the hands of one of the two lieutenants who had accompanied Melchior to Cologne. Apparently Bavaria was in complete chaos following the flight of Duke Maximilian's

Habsburger fiancée, and no one with enough authority was willing or able to come to Cologne. Melchior had met Duke Maximilian in Landshut, and more than indicated in his letter that the Bavarian elector was even more unbalanced than the archbishop. Melchior's letter had also confirmed the rumors that the third brother, Albrecht, was now fleeing from his brother with a price on his head. And that Duke Maximilian had almost certainly been involved in the death of Albrecht's wife and one or more of their children.

Melchior also wrote that he had changed his mind, and now hoped to be able to bring some of his men to Cologne. The main part of his army could remain in Linz under the command of his cousin and second in command Colonel Wolf von Wildenburg-Hatzfeldt, but in Vienna Melchior now intended to ask for permission to bring his dragoons westwards. He did not intend to place them at Archbishop Ferdinand's disposal, but wanted to take control of the Cologne area himself before it went completely up in flames, and could be had by anybody coming along to pick it up. The ties between Bavaria and the archdiocese of Cologne had always been strong, and with chaos in Bavaria, Cologne was fast becoming totally isolated. Duke Wolfgang of Jülich-Berg had not been regarded as a particularly safe neighbor lately, but the death of both him and his heir, followed by the disappearance of his pregnant wife, had left Jülich and Berg without much in the way of leadership, and Essen, Hessen, and the Low Countries were all showing interest in the situation. In Melchior's opinion, the main reason conquering armies were not already pouring in from all sides, was simply that they didn't want to risk ending up fighting each other. What a mess! And Melchior's brother was caught right in the middle unless Franz could be persuaded to break with the archbishop.

Father Johannes had passed on a report of the latest news this morning, and it should reach Don Francisco within a week. Perhaps that clever young man could figure out the archbishop's plan. Of course doing something about it in time would be another problem. Father Johannes suspected that some kind of radio was available to Moses Abrabanel, but people still had to travel from place to place, and news had spread about a peasant rebellion around Würzburg, which might slow down travel on the Rhine if it spread.

Still, all Father Johannes could really do today was try to convince Trinket that Hermann, her rather ascetic new husband, would not be pleasantly surprised by her cleverness if he came back from buying a steam engine in Essen, and found that her newly furnished pink and gold parlor had been completely—and even more opulently—refitted in the new fashionable pale lilac. The combination of gold, pale lilac and Trinket really was enough to make a strong man cry.

Some ducks were swimming closer to see if the disturbance of their waters was something eatable, and Father Johannes rose to continue back to Hatzfeldt House.

✧    ✧    ✧

When Father Johannes entered the hall, one of Lucie's children sat waiting for him on the stairs. According to Maxie, Lucie's husband had been a cheerful man with very dark skin and hair due to some Moorish blood on his mother's side, while his long-time mistress had been a very temperamental red-haired Scot with absolutely no interest in her children. This had resulted in a series of copper-curled, cheerful and independent children as alike as peas in a pod. Lucie could tell them apart, but everybody else had taken to following Father Johannes' lead and simply addressed them all—boys and girls—as Peter. Lucie had been a bit doubt-ful about this, and Father Johannes' explanation—that they were obviously all Wild Boys at heart—had not been accepted until Father Johannes had started telling American stories about Peter Pan and the Wild Boys in the muniment room. As those stories spread via the children on page-duty, even Lucie had given in to the pressure and started calling them Peter.

"Father Johannes," said the fairly-big-but-probably-not-oldest Peter, "Lady Lucie requests your company in the muniment room." The formal words and bow were somewhat spoiled by a big grin and an attempt to pull Father Johannes along by his hand.

In the muniment room Lucie sat looking like a cat in a cream pot. "Come take a look at this, Father Johannes," she said while pushing a ledger across the table towards him. "Entry four and five, plus the upper half on the next page."

Father Johannes sat down and looked. "The Church of Saint Severi. A stone grinder, oil and minerals."

"Isn't that exactly the kind of grinder you mentioned using to grind your paints, Father Johannes? And I'm sure these are minerals that you have mentioned buying from Beauville."

"Oh yes, these are for paints, probably for Al Fresco murals. Where is Saint Severi and what's said about wages for the painter?"

"That's just it, Father Johannes," Lucie's smile got even brighter, "there are no wages. About four years ago Saint Severi started buying paint for decorating, but no payment for using what was bought, and no mention of by whom. I haven't yet found the yearly reports from the church to the abbey, just the accounts. It could be an old monk or somebody just doing it for free, but it had continued for two years when the monks fled from the Protestant army, so the painter must have been good. And look at the date of the first entry; it's six weeks after your friend disappeared near Aschaffenburg. And Saint Severi is in Fulda; some seventy miles north from Aschaffenburg."

"Fulda! Again! That town has come back like a bad coin all spring."

"Perhaps somebody was trying to tell you something, Father Johannes." Lucie was now laughing out loud. "Do go there and see what you can find." Lucie turned somber. "Peter, go tell Maxie and Cook that I want lunch in the blue room today, on a trestle table in the sun."

"Yes, lady, but Sobby is going to protest sitting in sunshine."

"Lady Sophia to you, young man! And she can eat in the Grand Salon as usual if she wants to, but find her and ask."

When the door closed behind the child, Lucie reached across the table to caress Father Johannes' cheek. "I'll miss you, Father Johannes. More than I had planned to. Will you be coming back?"

Father Johannes turned his head to kiss her hand and sat holding it, absently rubbing an ink spot. "I had planned to settle in Magdeburg once I'd found out what happened to Paul. You know I'm a major shareholder in the porcelain factory being built there. It's well under way, and I want to work with the production too. There's no reason I should not come to sell our products in Cologne from time to time, unless of course the situation here gets really bad. And in that case you and the Peters should certainly come to me instead. Have you thought about moving to the USE? Your family has plenty of land on both sides of the border, and you'll probably be safer there. I know your brothers, Heinrich and Hermann, talked with your Fleckenbuehl cousins about the Crottorf branch's estates in the occupied areas. It would be easier for you to keep them if more of you lived in the USE. Heinrich does his best, but he is needed by his church in Mainz, and could use your help."

"I've thought, yes, and discussed it with Maxie. And Heinrich, Melchior and Hermann. Melchior is in favor of coming to an agreement with the USE, both for the family and for what remains of Catholic western Germany. This is largely due to you, but also because Bavaria is the last full-strength Catholic area in Germany, and Bavaria has been paralyzed since the duchess died. France, Spain or even the Habsburgs might someday overcome the USE, but we cannot wait for that to happen. Everybody here needs some stability to get on with their lives." She sighed. "Hermann too is in favor of negotiating with the USE. He's the most pragmatic of my brothers, and he has been studying those laws, etc. you got for him, as well as talking to Heinrich. The way the Americans do things is not what Hermann would prefer, but he claims he can work with them. And land behind an enemy border is no use at all. Heinrich doesn't think we have any realistic alternative. But Franz... Franz is the problem. I think it would kill him if the rest of the family just disregarded his loss and accepted the USE's authority."

"He is an adult, Lucie. If he chooses to throw in his lot with the archbishop..." Father Johannes shrugged. "Hope for their failure or hope for their success, but in any case be there for him when it's over. Family is important no matter what happens." Father Johannes smiled and kissed her hand again. "But how about Maxie?"

Lucie removed her hand, leaned back and smiled. "Maxie needs things to do, challenges, battles to fight, people to manage. She is so bitter about her failures in München and the lack of support from her family, she doesn't want to go back. And considering the temper she is in combined with what we hear about Duke Maximilian, I seriously think she'll get killed if she does. The American way of doing things would suit Maxie just perfectly. She would so love to battle this bureaucracy you have told us about. Maria knows just as much about law as Hermann, and while she isn't as good at splitting hairs and debating sub-clauses, she is very, very good at kicking arse until she gets things her way. Magdeburg or Cologne? She'll be the same anywhere." Lucie tipped her head a little and grinned. "With a little address you could probably talk her into going with you."

"Lucie..." Father Johannes stopped. "Lady Lucie, I am most grateful for your information about Paul's possible whereabouts.

If you'll excuse me." Father Johannes' exit was followed by a gentle chuckle behind him.

The installation of a stained glass window in Trinket's private parlor, "to complete the illusion of a Rose Garden," had been Father Johannes' last work on the Hatzfeldt House. It had nearly also been That Last Straw Which Broke the Donkey's Back. Perhaps he should try talking with Martin about a series of articles about taste for the *Simplicissimus Magazine*. Still, everything was now in order: all work done, accounts settled, bags packed, and the miniature paintings he had made for Maxie and Lucie were finished. Lucie had cried when he gave her the chain with five medallions, each with a portrait of a Peter, and Father Johannes had ended up promising—on his faith—to write at least every fortnight, and come back to her as soon as possible.

Maxie had gone to the archbishop's palace to bully one of her many contacts—a secretary—for news about the trouble around Fulda. The trouble appeared to concern either land for railroads or the structuring of the new province proposed, but just who was protesting what—and why—wasn't clear, so Father Johannes sat waiting for her in what had been his work room for more than the past six months. It had been a good time: Trinket aside, the work had been artistically satisfying, and economically sound, and the cut he'd get from the porcelain-shares and wares he had sold would ensure that he'd never lack money again. And while he didn't think his reports to Don Francisco had changed the world, he was finally doing what he felt was right. But the best of all had been the ladies and Melchior. Lucie's suggestion that Maxie might be more interested in Father Johannes than was strictly proper had taken him by surprise. Since his late teens sexual urges had just been something that was there; they popped up when he met an attractive woman; that was acceptable, and just ignored. That he found Maxie—and Lucie—very attractive had just added a bit of spice to how very much he liked them, but that either—or possibly even both—might be attracted to him!

Marriage was impossible for Father Johannes unless he was either excommunicated or secularized by papal edict, and an illicit affair with either lady just felt too odd. Sure, lots of priests had more or less formal arrangements with women, some—for all practical purpose—a marriage and a family. But while Father

Johannes had always felt such to be his fellow priests' private affairs—and not really that much of a sin—it simply was not an arrangement he could imagine. Not with Lucie, and certainly not with Maxie.

The other way around where a man became the cicisbeo—or lapdog—to a powerful woman as it was the fashion in Italy? He had seen a few such affairs during his work as a painter, and had no problem imagining that for Maxie, but...

When Maxie came into the room Father Johannes jumped to his feet and felt blushes color him from neck to hair.

"There was no news about a rebellion, Father Johannes, and Frau Vollsig's son, she's my brother's friend's landlady's neighbor, came from Fulda less than a week ago. Traveling is probably as safe now as it ever is."

"Thank you, Maxie, you have been most kind to me." Father Johannes bowed and held out a small, oval, framed picture, no bigger than the palm of his hand. "If you would show me the honor of accepting this with all my gratitude."

"A Heavenly Madonna!"

"Yes. You did whatever you could for Paul, and I really think you should hang his picture on your wall again, but if you do not want to, then perhaps this may please you in its place."

"It is beautiful, Father Johannes, and I'll gladly hang it by my bed when I'm not wearing it." Maxie smiled and placed the picture carefully on a table, before putting her arms around Father Johannes' neck and rising to her toes to kiss him.

Father Johannes cooperated to the best of his abilities and it was a while before she broke off the kiss and rested her head on his shoulders. "I finally find a man I want, and he is not just the wrong rank, which I had expected, but a priest as well. This must be the final proof that God is a man."

"Maxie!"

"Yes, yes, I know. It still stinks."

"Perhaps we could convince ourselves this is a platonic love."

Maxie kissed his throat and gave him a squeeze. "I don't think so. Don't you want me, my dear Johannes?" She looked up at him and smiled.

"Of course I do. Darling Maxie. There's nothing I want more than having you manage me for the rest of my life—except, that is, for having Lucie and the Peters around too. But Maxie," Father

Johannes placed his hands around Maxie's face and gave her a quick kiss, "We cannot marry. And reducing you to a priest's concubine is something I refuse to even suggest."

Maxie grinned, "My dear, I'm perfectly capable of making any suggestions I want on my own, and what vows I keep or break is a matter between me and God. At my age a child is unlikely, and I have no estates to tie me to a liege lord. What fortune I can lay my hands on is my own, and while my family would not approve of us living together, they also haven't approved of a lot of other things I've done over the years. Duke Maximilian would once have tried to interfere, but at the moment he has so many problems of his own that he doesn't even keep Ferdinand in line. And Albrecht—even before Mechthilde's death—would not have done anything. Especially if we are living in Magdeburg."

"Do you want that?"

"I think so. It sounds like a place where something is happening. But first things first: you go to Fulda and see if you can find your friend, while Lucie, Melchior and I see what we can do about Ferdinand and Franz. And don't forget to kiss me properly before you go."

# Chapter 7

*Bonn, the Archbishop's Palace*
*July 1634*

Another spasm of pain wracked Charlotte's body, but she barely flinched. The baby could come or not, live or not, kill her or not, she didn't really have the strength to care.

In Cologne she had felt vulnerable and uncertain, but at least she had been in contact with her family, had received reports from General Merode in Berg, sent orders to the caretakers in Jülich and Berg, and generally tried to pick up the reins of the mess her husband's death had left behind. She might have longed for her family to come help her, but she had not been considering Archbishop Ferdinand a very serious problem, after all: while he wasn't a relative, he had been her son's godfather, and she knew her mother considered the archbishop a friend of the family. But then he had sent Felix Gruyard into her life, and an uncertain situation went straight into the hell of cold, unwavering eyes showing no sign of human emotions, only a total concentration on his task and his duty.

After arriving at Bonn in the middle of the night she had been kept isolated for almost two days, and when she had finally met the archbishop, the slightly indulgent old man she remembered from the baptism had seemed a totally different person. She had of course asked for an explanation for what happened at the

Beguine, and why she had been dragged to Bonn in the middle of the night, but he had brushed her off with a few words about the political situation being tense, and that she would be safer in Bonn. She was now to concentrate on giving birth to a healthy child, while he would take care of everything else.

Charlotte had not liked that, and she had liked it even less when he started pressing her for a letter giving him full power to act in her name. She had not received a single letter during her weeks here in Bonn, and while she kept writing her own letters and giving them to Sister Ursula to send, she became more and more certain they never left the archbishop's palace. She—with her baby-heir-to-be—was in fact the archbishop's prisoner.

At the end of her first week in Bonn Charlotte made the mistake of telling Sister Ursula how much Gruyard upset her. The same evening, when she once again refused to write to the archbishop's dictate, Archbishop Ferdinand claimed her mind was obviously unsettled, and she should enter seclusion with that Loyal Servant of the Lord, Felix Gruyard, as her only contact with the world.

As the weeks dragged by, Gruyard now started haunting her nights and days as well as her nightmares. He would enter her small whitewashed cell whenever she had fallen into a fitful doze, wake her and say it was time to pray. Or worse: not wake her, just stand there looking at her when she woke in a cold sweat of fear. And, as the last week of her pregnancy went by, she could feel her hold on reality slip more and more with her lack of sleep, until—when the labor had started in the early hours of the morning—she barely seemed to notice. It was just another nightmare, and she couldn't put two thoughts together and even consider what to do.

Sister Ursula had come that morning after the water had broken. Presumably Gruyard had brought her, though Charlotte couldn't remember having seen him—or her—enter. The grim older woman was now sitting on a stool, murmuring soothing words and prayers, but not doing any of the things the midwife had done at the birth of baby Ferdinand. Presumably she was loyal to the archbishop, and that was all that mattered. Perhaps that was the way it should be. Perhaps she would soon go away too.

It was dark again now outside the small deep-set window, and Sister Ursula had been frowning for a while when she went to the door and said: "I think we need to send for the midwife, the contractions are getting weaker." She stepped back and Gruyard entered the room, going to the narrow cot where Charlotte lay with open, unseeing eyes, barely breathing. He reached out and shook her shoulder. "Katharina Charlotte, it is time to wake." At his words Charlotte screamed and tried to scramble away from his touch, but only managed to fall to the floor before fainting from the pain.

When she came to herself two strange women were moving around the small room with linen and hot water, and Sister Ursula was sitting by the cot holding a steaming mug. She lifted the mug towards Charlotte and said with an attempt to smile that looked almost painful: "Drink this. Frau Eigenhaus and her sister have come. They will make your baby come out."

"Never mind that." The largest and most determined looking of the two women took the mug and pushed Sister Ursula aside with a swing of her hips. "You just drink this and relax." She lifted up Charlotte and helped her hold the mug with the warm, honeyed drink. "I am Frau Benedicte Eigenhaus, and this is my sister Irmgard, who is the best midwife in Bonn. We have both been bringing children into this world since long before you were born, so you just leave everything to us."

"Y-you'll keep him out?"

"What my dear?"

"G-Gruyard."

"Gruyard!" The two sisters looked at each other, then turned their heads to look at Sister Ursula, whose pale, hollow cheeks suddenly showed two bright red spots. "And pray tell, Sister Ursula, just what does the archbishop's torturer have to do with this nice, young mother-to-be?"

Sister Ursula straightened her back and took a deep breath. "The archbishop has delegated the responsibility for this woman to Master Gruyard. She is not of sound mind." The nun's eyes started waving under the stern gaze of the midwife and her sister. "It is probably just temporary fancies, brought about by the pregnancy and the loss of her husband."

"I see." Irmgard exchanged a look with her sister. "A common occurrence, those not-sound-fancies in a pregnant woman, and usually very convenient to somebody."

A muted scream from Charlotte interrupted. "Benedicte, you lift her up again and support her; that potion she just drank should ensure that the baby will be coming fast."

## Linz, Austria, The Scribe

"Melchior! You're back." Wolf von Wildenburg-Hatzfeldt jumped up from his chair and enfolded Melchior in an obviously heartfelt embrace. That his cousin was to be found in a tavern rather than in the garrison with his men wasn't really a surprise to Melchior—and neither was the fact that Wolf paid absolutely no attention to Melchior's frown—but this was an unusually warm welcome. Unless of course Wolf was a lot more drunk than Melchior would expect for this time of day.

"Just passing through on my way to Vienna. But what kind of trouble are you in to make you that glad to see me?"

"None, my dear Cousin." Wolf returned to his chair and waved at the barmaid for more beer. "I'm just bored out of my skull with garrison duty, and hoped you had a new campaign for us. I could use a little action."

"Hmpf! Well, I admit that you are quite singularly bad at garrison duty." Melchior removed his hat and sword and sat down across from Wolf. "But in this case I must ask you not to go stir up any action on your own. I rather strongly expect that we'll soon have all the action even you could want."

"Where, when, and with whom?"

"All over the place, any time, and with everyone." Melchior accepted the beer and waited for the barmaid to move away before continuing. "Archbishop Ferdinand of Cologne has hired Irish Butler and some of the others of Wallenstein's discards, and is up to some kind of cabal that's bound to bring the Protestant army down on him even if Hesse stays in Berg. And the Habsburgs—Vienna as well as Spain and the Netherlands—are not going to like seeing Cologne as part of the USE. Duke Maximilian of Bavaria, whom I hoped would be willing to call his brother to order, has no interest in anything beyond his own personal concerns, which seems to center on hunting down his missing fiancée—and just about everybody else. Banér is rattling his saber north of the Danube, and your guess is as good as mine as to whether we'll end up fighting him or Bavaria. Wallenstein in Bohemia and Bernard in Swabia don't appear to be making any moves we'll need to respond to at the moment, but I'm not prepared to wager any sizable sum on that continuing. Not to mention Gustavus Adolphus, who made peace with Denmark last month, and is probably getting just as bored as you by now."

"I think Gustavus Adolphus is actually planning to do something about Saxony at the moment."

"Good riddance to bad rubbish."

"The Saxony court is amusing but expensive. I've always rather liked it."

"Not to my taste. But Wolf, I need to make my report in Vienna as soon as possible. There's not much chance of the emperor—or rather Archduke Ferdinand—doing something directly to stop the archbishop, but they still need to know as soon as possible. Young Simon is picking out my court gear, and we'll be leaving as soon as he meets me here with fresh horses. I don't expect us to go directly into battle any time soon, but talk with Colonel Dehn about having all scouts as well as minor training maneuvers circulating in the direction of the Bavarian border."

"Will do. Maid! Pack up some travel food!"


## Magdeburg, House of Hessen

Amalie carefully leaned forward and look down to the street without touching the draped lace curtains, not just because lace was still expensive despite the new machines making it, but she also didn't want her guests to realize that she was looking them over before they entered the house. There was only uncle Albrecht, two young girls and a maid descending from the fine new carriage, so Albrecht had been clever enough to leave Ehrengard at home. Amalie smiled a little. While she had been looking forward to a few skirmishes with her aunt-in-law, this showed that Albrecht was prepared to make peace and cooperate—at a price of course and probably a stiff price, but it would be fun haggling with him. Besides, with five daughters and only one yet wed, it was quite likely that he would settle for bridegrooms instead of money or political favors.

The two girls would be his two youngest, Elisabeth, called

Litsa, and Maria Juliana, who as far as Amalie knew usually answered to Ria. Due to her feuding with their father, Amalie had never spent much time with her younger cousins, but the girl dropping her gloves as she descended from the carriage was probably Litsa, who had seemed rather coltish and shy when Amalie had last been to their home in Schwarzenfels, while the one smiling up at her father and shaking her head to make her curls dance, was pretty little Ria. According to Abbess Dorothea, Litsa was actually rather intelligent, but Amalie preferred to make up her own mind about that; intelligent had different meanings to different people, and someone merely bookish would be of no interest to Amalie.

As her guests entered the main door, Amalie went to sit down on the high-back chair in the middle of the room arranging her skirts to show off the embroidery. She'd better use her pregnancy as an excuse to remain sitting while receiving them. The waddle of a walk she was reduced to was not impressive.

## Ludenscheid
## July 1634

"There's another message for you, sir."

Wilhelm of Hesse-Kassel looked up at young Lieutenant von Rutgert serving as his secretary, and bit back a curse. This campaign was hexed! Not by witches, but by that damned American radio. Sure it was nice being able to get information from one end of the country to the other, much, much faster than any horse could run, but it also made everybody and his uncle think they could direct an ongoing military campaign from wherever they were sitting. Hesse did not approve of vulgar language, but right now he fully understood the American concept of Rear Echelon Motherfuckers. Hesse broke the seal and read quickly.

"Rutgert! Send for von Uslar. I want to talk to him as soon as possible."

"Yes, sir."

As the young man left the room, Hesse went to look again at the large map covering the trestle table. Half his artillery and infantry had gone north to Hagen, before a direct order from Gustavus Adolphus had made it clear that no excuse about hunting French troops would get an attack on Essen overlooked. The other half was presently stalled in a three-way death-lock in Remscheid with the troops from Essen occupying Düsseldorf, and what remained of the Jülich-Berg army holding Solingen and Remscheid. He wasn't allowed to have any of those troops actually engage those they were facing, but he had stalled any movement, while hoping to get his hands on Duke Wolfgang's widow and prospective heir. That would have given him a good claim on at least those areas of Mark and Berg he was now holding, and probably Düsseldorf as well. Unfortunately she was now reported to be for certain within the archbishop's palace in Bonn, where none of his agents had been able to get to her.

Which brought him back to his original plan for taking Bonn and Cologne. Which he would probably already have done if it hadn't been for those radio messages sending him helter-skelter all over these damned mountains. Not to mention leaving him with his cannons more than fifty miles of bad mountain roads away from where he needed them. At least Amalie had managed to get a commitment to have some of the USE field cannons sent by boat down the rivers from Frankfurt, so he could afford to leave the artillery at Hagen where it was, but withdraw the infantry regiments south to Remscheid. Then negotiate with De Geer for access up the Rhine for both the men and artillery from Remscheid. Hesse sighed and went back to plotting.

# Chapter 8

*Fulda*
*August 1634*

The horse Melchior had chosen for Father Johannes in Cologne had plodded on steadily up along the Rhine and Main rivers, across the new bridge at Frankfurt and then north along the Fulda river to Fulda town. The countryside had so far been peaceful but active with the harvest under way, but the closer Father Johannes got to Fulda, the more people seemed to be looking back over their shoulders. The guards at the border stations had given him no problems—though he had had to be careful which of his two sets of letters he let them see—and those guards willing to chat had known of no fighting.

Rumors had come down from Fulda: vague talks about expected rebellions once the harvest was over, but nothing had seemed alarming until the night before. Father Johannes had stopped for the night at the Inn of the Red Bear and sat talking to a southbound postman named Martin Wackernagel, who claimed to have seen troops moving in the area between Fulda and Kassel. Father Johannes would have liked to know more, but the entrance of Felix Gruyard surrounded by three soldiers had made him withdraw from the common room before Gruyard saw him. Gruyard had last been heard of in connection with the disappearance of Duke Wolfgang of Jülich-Berg's

71

young widow, and finding him now near Fulda was not a good omen.

Fulda looked like a disturbed anthill in its broad, fertile valley when Father Johannes approached. As expected, the overcast sky made a few farmers hurry around getting the last grain into the barns, but aside from that, all kinds of people seemed to be moving around, not fleeing, not looking frightened and not all carrying weapons. The guard at the gate politely stopped Father Johannes and asked the usual questions: identity, origin, destination and business in town. He also wanted to know if Father Johannes had noticed any people—perhaps soldiers—transporting one or more prisoners. Father Johannes mentioned Gruyard and the three soldiers, and upon hearing that a henchman of the archbishop of Cologne had been in the area until the night before, an officer was called and Father Johannes had to repeat the entire story plus as much as he knew about Gruyard.

It was thus late in the evening before Father Johannes made his way to the Church of St. Severi. The small gray church had been built two centuries ago by the important Wool-Weavers Guild on a small rise between the council hall and the cathedral, and the new, tall, surrounding half-timber houses seemed to hover protectingly around it. The evening service had just ended, and the congregation dispersed along with the priest with softly murmured goodnights. Father Johannes approached the sexton snuffing out the lights by the door. "Blessed evening, Goodman, I was wondering if you would be so kind as to help me. My name is Father Johannes Grünwald and I'm a painter. I've been told your church has been richly decorated within the last few years, and I would very much like to come see the church properly in daylight tomorrow. For now, could you tell me the whereabouts of the painter? I would enjoy talking to a colleague."

"The painter is here in the church, but he keeps to himself, and I doubt he wants company."

"Perhaps, you'd be kind enough to ask him. Say Father Johannes Grünwald wishes to see him." Father Johannes placed a few copper coins on the wooden bench beneath the window, and went to put a few more in the collection box by the door into the nave. The sexton swiped the coins from the bench and disappeared, only to come back followed by a small, thin man in rag-shoes and a worn tunic.

"Paul! So it is you." Father Johannes went to embrace his friend, but was stopped by the lack of reaction in the other man's face.

Paul blinked his eyes a few times, "Yes, I'm Paul." He seemed to pull himself together. "Please, come in. We can talk in the sacristy."

In the sacristy a half-open closet showed a collection of stoles, albs and other priestly garments, while an oak table with neatly lined-up painting paraphernalia, and a pallet and a slop-bucket made it clear that Paul both lived and worked out of the small room.

Paul waved Father Johannes toward a stool by the table, then kicked off his shoes made of braided rags before sitting down on the pallet and pressing his back against the wall; the skin on his feet and legs was scarred and twisted, and several toes were missing.

"Paul..." Father Johannes stopped and hesitated.

"Please sit down, Father Johannes, you lean so." Paul pulled his feet up under his tunic and looked away.

Father Johannes sat down, pulling a bottle from inside his doublet. "I'm staying at the Inn of the Wise Virgin; they had bottles of the plum-wine you used to like. I wasn't sure you were the painter at St. Severi, but I brought along a bottle. Just in case. Do you need anything?"

Paul shook his head and, rattled by his friend's silence, Father Johannes went on, "Three years ago I saw the Black Mass pictures by van Bcekx that you were accused of painting. And read the interrogation protocol and what else the archives contained. I should have come looking for you in Aschaffenburg, but I didn't. I'm sorry. I should have."

Paul remained silent.

"I was on my way to Magdeburg. To paint propaganda for that campaign. You know I'm very good at closing my eyes to those things I don't wish to see, but Magdeburg was too much. I rebelled and had to flee. Ended up with the Americans in Grantville. Last winter I accepted a commission from Prince-Bishop Franz von Hatzfeldt of Würzburg and went to Cologne to try to see if I could find you. I know I should have searched when I first knew that you had been in trouble. I'm sorry. Paul? Is there anything I can do?"

Paul turned his head back to look at Father Johannes. "No. And it would have made no difference if you had come earlier. By the time Magdeburg burned I had been here for more than a year. And this is where I want to be. Right here. Some of my Aunt Louise's Baril relatives are here, working for the American administration—and the parish supplies me with food and paint in return for me decorating the church. I want nothing but to stay here and paint."

Paul looked down on his hands, rubbing them against each other before continuing. "I've gone to see the American people twice. It was the right thing to do. Felix Gruyard has been doing his dirty work here. I wanted to stop him, but I don't want to go outside. I want to stay here. This is sanctuary." Paul looked up again at Father Johannes, his eyes wide open, "Isn't it funny? A torturer working for a prince of the Catholic Church hurt me until something inside me broke, and I did what he wanted me to do. Yet once a shot made my horse panic, and I had the chance to escape, it was in that same Church I felt safe. I don't want to go anywhere."

Father Johannes rose and went to kneel before Paul, touching first his shoulder then his cheek. "Dear Paul, this will change. After Magdeburg I fled to my childhood home, hiding in a cabin like a wounded animal in its den. Encountering Evil in your fellow man taints you, destroys your innocence, and you will never again be able to delude yourself that such Evil isn't real. But as pain and evil are real, so are joy and love. The Bible tells us not to put our Faith in princes, nor in the sons of man; I agree on the first but not on the second. We are all sons of man: princes and beggars, soldiers and painters, even Our Lord Jesus Christ came to us as son of man."

Father Johannes stopped and swallowed before continuing. "Paul, I'll come to see your paintings tomorrow, and we can talk again. I'll stay in town for a while. I'm going to see the American people about the archives from the abbey. If you don't want to come with me when I leave, I'll arrange to leave you some money with them, as well as addresses for people who will know where I've gone. If you ever want—or are forced—to leave, you can use the money to go to your family or come to me. I'll most likely be in Magdeburg working with porcelain." Father Johannes rose and smiled, "And by the way: your Heavenly Madonna is beautiful, and it no longer belongs to the archbishop, but to a most lovely lady called Maxie."

# Chapter 9

"Charlotte, I have had enough of your willfulness and lack of gratitude." Archbishop Ferdinand pushed open the door to Charlotte's room with a bang, causing her nursing son, Philipp, to let go of her nipple and scream. The archbishop paid no attention to the baby, just frowned and motioned for Sister Ursula to leave. He calmed his face and smiled, but his hand's jerky movements showed that he was extremely upset. "You are nothing but a silly girl and in no way capable of handling the affairs of your son and his estates. You will now write letters naming me the sole guardian of my new little godson and entrusting all his affairs—and yours—to me. You will also make it quite clear to your family that it is entirely to your wish that the two of you are staying here as my guests."

"No!" Charlotte rose with the screaming baby in her arms. "My son's guardians will be my brother and my family. You cannot keep us here forever. You and your two jailers have kept me from all information about what is going on outside this room, but I know my family. My aunt, Princess Katharina of Sweden, will have written to her emperor brother, and my mother will have the entire Simmern family alerted. They haven't heard from me for more than a month, and even those who don't care for

75

me personally will know the importance of my baby. You risk having not just the Swedes coming at you from the north and east, but also the entire Pfalz rising against you in the south. And judging from the last news I heard before you locked me up, your ducal brother in Bavaria has far too many problems on his own to come to your aid."

"You are entirely right, my dear," the archbishop kept smiling, "and that is just half of my problems. Which is why my faithful Gruyard will have the care of your baby until I get those letters." He snatched the swaddled baby, and had the door locked behind him before Charlotte could reach him.

Sister Ursula had stepped back from the door so quickly she fell, and rose stammering an apology, but the archbishop just thrust the screaming baby at her and said: "Get a wet-nurse."

Charlotte sat staring at her bloody hands in the fading evening light when Sister Ursula opened the door and entered with a covered tray and a burning candle. "You miserable monster! Where is my son?" Charlotte grabbed the empty cradle and aimed it for the nun's head, but it slipped in her hands, which were weak and torn from battering against the door all day. She stood panting and glaring while Sister Ursula calmly set the tray on the table and placed the cradle right way up in the middle of the floor. Then from the tray she took a sealed clay pot with long piece of thin rope sticking out from the top, and placed this in the cradle.

"Katharina Charlotte," said Sister Ursula, looking straight into Charlotte's eyes. "I have loved and served Archbishop Ferdinand all my life. I was even his mistress briefly in my youth. But he has now gone too far. The end may justify the means—but not all means. And Ferdinand has gone beyond all that is reasonable. He is no longer the person he once was." She sighed. "Gruyard has left for Fulda and your baby is waiting for you at the home of Irmgard Eigenhaus. There is a man outside waiting to take you there. I'll go tell the archbishop you were gone when I came with your dinner, and create a mystery with this." She held the burning candle to the end of the rope, which caught fire and started a sputtering burn. Then she grabbed Charlotte's arm and pulled her out of the room, leaving the door open behind them.

✦   ✦   ✦

The late Master Eigenhaus, councillor of Bonn and master of the Merchant's Guild, had sired four daughters on his wife and four more on his mistress. This was not in itself an unusual situation for a prominent man, but insisting that both women with all the children live together in his house had been regarded as rather eccentric. Not to mention that he dowered all the girls equally. Still, he was wealthy, well liked and well connected, and contributed freely to both church and civic projects, so nobody made that much of an issue of the arrangement.

The girls had been brought up to consider themselves a family, and to aim at making that family wealthy and powerful. As females they were barred from sitting in Bonn's ruling council, but six of the eight girls had married prominent guild members, and they were now a major force in town.

Irmgard, the oldest of the illegitimate daughters, had never married, but instead used her dower to buy the shop from the town's apothecary and officially set herself up as a midwife. She first paid the old apothecary to remain the official head of the business, but everybody knew that his shaking hands made it impossible for him to make even the simplest tisane. After he died, Irmgard simply kept on running the business.

After Sister Ursula had delivered Charlotte to a big, limping man, he had hidden her in his waist-high, fish-smelling basket, and actually carried her on his back to the back door of the apothecary shop. Irmgard had been waiting with the baby in her arms, and even before the archbishop had calmed his household after the explosion in Charlotte's room, Charlotte and the baby had been fast asleep in the attic above the shop.

The next morning Irmgard set about changing Charlotte's appearance by bleaching her hair with chamomile and darkening her pale skin with walnut water. So by the time the archbishop had accepted that the baby had unexplainably disappeared from his new cradle at the wet-nurse's room, the pale and delicate brunette, Countess Palatine Katharina Charlotte von Zweibrücken, had become the buxom, fair-haired and sunburned Lotti, widow of a soldier from Trier. And by the time he had picked up the trail of the young mother traveling into Berg in Charlotte's clothes, Lotti was just another of the many refugees the Eigenhaus family took in and briefly employed before finding them a position through their many friends and connections.

The matriarch of the Eigenhaus family was the oldest legitimate daughter, Benedicte, who ran the family trading affairs as well as the household. Every major concern of the town from polluted wells and garbage removal to new wall-cannons and the women's militias went by way of Frau Eigenhaus. Her devoted husband had inherited a series of wineries, and—while no bad merchant himself—was more than satisfied to concentrate on winemaking and leave the general trade to his wife.

Frau Benedicte's household was big and busy with all the matriarch's activities, so no one found it the least bit unusual when Charlotte—as Lotti—was hired to embroider the gowns for the wedding of Frau Benedicte's youngest daughter. Charlotte—along with baby Philipp—was given a room in the attic and a place at the servant's end of the family table, and—to protect the expensive fabrics—Frau Benedicte had arranged for Charlotte to do her work in the main parlor. Charlotte had no problems with the delicate needlework, and she could keep her baby beside her while she worked, but the parlor was also where Frau Benedicte spent most of her day, and just thinking about all Frau Benedicte's projects made Charlotte feel exhausted.

Still, the abundance of writing material gave Charlotte the opportunity to write new letters to her family, and in the few quiet moments when the two of them were alone, Frau Benedicte talked to Charlotte about the previous visitors and conversations, asking what she had understood and clarifying this and that. Eventually—as Charlotte slowly recovered and started showing an interest in what was going on around her—the older woman also began asking Charlotte for information and opinions. Charlotte might feel woefully ignorant about business matters on more than a household scale, but as a member of the nobility she knew her peers—and their politics and follies—inside out. And as the weeks passed, and the archbishop kept chasing rumors of Charlotte up and down the Rhine, a genuine friendship evolved between the two very different women. Charlotte started making tentative plans for taking control of her son's heritage once her brother finally managed to disentangle himself from the upsets caused by the crisis in Bavaria.

## Linz, Austria, The Scribe
## August 1634

"I am quite certain I told you not to stir up trouble, so what were you doing getting into a duel with a Bavarian nobleman?" Melchior tossed his hat on the table and sat down on the chair by Wolf's bed.

"Well, you also told me to keep an eye on Bavaria. So it's really all your own fault." Wolf leaned back against the pillows stacked high behind him. Despite all the trouble his cousin cost him whenever they were in garrison, Melchior was actually pleased to notice that Wolf looked fit and healthy—aside from a slight pallor and a bandaged shoulder.

"But what were you doing in Regensburg? Aside from the obvious, that is," Melchior added when Wolf started to smirk. "I did hear about you and the nobleman's wife."

"The day after you left for Vienna, I had a letter from the lady in question. The dear Duke Maximilian appears to be throwing his weight around pretty badly. I just went to see for myself how bad things were."

"And visit the lady."

"Of course." Wolf opened his eyes wide and tried to look innocent—something he wasn't very good at. "After all she was the one who had made contact with me."

"But you are healing now with no sign of a fever?" Melchior decided to drop the topic. Wolf had been in and out of trouble since they were children, and he wasn't really likely to change now.

"Yes." Wolf also stopped playacting. "And how did your errand go?"

"I'm going back to Cologne. But you're staying here," Melchior quickly added when Wolf sat up fast and then grabbed at his bandaged shoulder.

"If you think you'll leave me behind just because that fat ninny managed to prick my shoulder, you can just think again." Wolf had narrowed his eyes and looked ready to jump Melchior for a wrestling match.

"Calm down, Cos. I cannot take the regiments with me. It's not that Archduke Ferdinand refuses permission," Melchior held up a hand to forestall Wolf's protests, "it's the situation with Bavaria being too tense. There is no way the duke would not consider it an attack on top of the insult given by his runaway fiancée. I'll be taking just Simon and Sergeant Mittelfeld, plus this bunch of papers." Melchior tapped to his breast bulging slightly from the document purse he was carrying.

"Money?" Wolf looked interested.

"That too. But mainly writs giving me not only ambassadorial status but also plenipotentiary powers in negotiating on behalf of the HRE in all matters concerning the middle Rhine area. Now, I want you to take over as commander while I'm away. I know I usually put old Dehn in that position when we're in garrison, but the entire situation is so uncertain, and while Dehn's a good solid commander, his mind just isn't very flexible."

"I hope you don't intend to give that as a reason," Wolf remarked dryly.

"Of course not, I'll tell him it was high time you grew up. I'm sure he'll agree to that." Melchior grinned a little; Dehn's dignity had been the target for Wolf's pranks more than once, and while the old man had borne them with good humor, he had definitely disapproved of Wolf's behavior. "But on a totally different matter: is your shoulder good enough for you to write? I'll be around for a day or two, and your family would expect letters from you when they see me."

"Better send Allenberg to me. I can write, and I'd like you to take a letter at least to my sister in Bonn, but Anna complains about my handwriting even at my best."


## Ludenscheid, Hessian headquarters

"Please come in, Von Uslar." The stairs to the tower room Landgrave Wilhelm of Hesse-Kassel had chosen for this meeting had obviously been hard on his cavalry leader's wounded leg, so Hesse waved him towards a chair, while going himself to check that no one was lurking on the stairs.

"I apologize for making you climb all those stairs with your bad leg, but I intend to ask you to attack a fortified town without artillery support," Hesse closed the door and returned to his desk, "so I'm sure you'll agree that secrecy is of the uttermost importance."

"As long as it isn't Kronach," von Uslar replied in his usual laconic voice.

"No, it's Bonn. Your brother is coming westward with fresh troops, and I want you to head east and meet him at Berleburg, as if it was an ordinary exchange of troops. Together you'll then go up the Eder valley, cross to Sieg at the headwater, and then down that valley to Siegen. From there you must reach Beuel as fast as possible, take the town and the ferry, and cross the Rhine to gain at least a foothold on the other side. Landgravine Amalie has arranged for new cannons to come down the rivers from Frankfurt, but by the time they arrive, I want the country-side and as much of Bonn as possible to be under our control."

"The archbishop's palace in Bonn is said to contain quite a lot of gold and jewels." Von Uslar now looked vaguely interested.

"Yes, and I'll need that to cover the cost of the new guns, and other expenses."

"And the infantry?"

Hesse sighed. "Eventually I'll reach an agreement with De Geer for access to the Rhine, and we'll meet you at Cologne. Cologne is of course our real goal, but I cannot sail the new artillery past the cannons on the river wall at Bonn."

"Not to mention the gold from the palace."

"Yes, that too."

# Chapter 10

Charlotte looked down at the gun in her hands. She had of course seen such before, even held her brother's first set of pistols and tried to admire them, but guns had always seemed like something that had no place in her personal life, something other people had and knew how to use.

"Rest the butt of the gun on the ground, and lean the gun against the crook of your arm, while you measure out the powder from your horn." When Frau Eigenhaus had first mentioned the possibility of Charlotte joining the Women's Militias, Charlotte had protested that she didn't want the risk of anybody recognizing her—and didn't have any interest in guns anyway.

"Pour the powder into the barrel of the gun." Frau Eigenhaus' assurance, that nobody would recognize her with the way she looked now, or even consider that she might still be in Bonn and stand on the wall with the rest of the Eigenhaus' adult female servants, had not persuaded Charlotte at all.

"Next take a lead ball from the purse, and wrap it in one of the small squares of greased cloth before sliding it into the barrel of the gun." The story of the American woman shooting Wallenstein was one Charlotte had heard before, though it had not occurred to her to take it as proof that with training a woman was in no way inferior to a man as a fighter.

"Now place another piece of greased cloth in the barrel, and very carefully use the stopper to press the ball and the powder together in the bottom of the barrel." Only when Frau Eigenhaus had given a very stern talk about the duty of a woman in protecting her family and children, had Charlotte seriously considered the suggestion.

"Go to your post and take your stance." Her darling little Bobo, so tiny and helpless. As Charlotte lifted the gun to her shoulder, faces started flickering before her eyes. Her father, husband, the archbishop, all swirling around while their voices babbled in her ears, shouting at her, yelling orders. Suddenly Felix Gruyard swam into focus. Charlotte fired the gun, and sinking to her knees, started to cry.

## Mainz, Church of St. Alban

The building housing the office of Domherr Heinrich Friedrich von Hatzfeldt was neither new nor luxurious, but to Melchior the warm and slightly shabby surroundings looked like an extension of his calm and patient older brother.

"Welcome, dear Brother." Heinrich laid down the papers he was reading and rose smiling from the bench to greet his brother. "Come sit in the shade with me, Melchior. As you can see, I've moved my office to the courtyard to take advantage of any breeze from the river. Judging from the heat and humidity, we should have thunder any day now." He looked to the western sky. "But probably not today. Do you come alone?"

Melchior felt himself relax and smile. He really ought to find a way to spend more time with his family. It wasn't that he regretted his youthful decision to abandon his plans of becoming a Knight of Saint John, and instead become a mercenary soldier, but it seemed that the rank and fortune that path had gained him had come only at the cost of quiet happiness and contentment. He had hoped to settle down with Maria and start a family of his own, but now... "My sergeant took a spill from his horse and landed badly, but the American remedies available in Frankfurt should keep him from losing his leg. I left Simon, my courier, with him, and told them to contact you in case of trouble. I hope that is all right with you?" Melchior sat down on the bench beside his brother and leaned back wearily. It had been a hard journey with long days in the saddle and camping wherever they could at night.

"Of course. But did Wolf and the rest of your men stay behind in Austria?"

Melchior looked more closely at his normally unflappable brother and noticed the furrow in Heinrich's brow. "Yes, it's not possible to take them across Bavaria at the moment, but what has happened here, Heinrich?"

"While you were gone, Archbishop Ferdinand made his move— or rather several moves—but the one that has upset everybody here was sending his torturer, Felix Gruyard, along with several of the mercenaries to Fulda, where they kidnapped Abbot Schweinsberg and tortured him to death."

"What? Why ever would he do that?"

"I have no idea. Archbishop Anselm suspects it was just a minor part of a bigger scheme, but doesn't know for sure. I suppose it could just be Archbishop Ferdinand settling his old scores with Schweinsberg."

"If so, then he's even more deranged than his brother."

"Yes. Now Anselm might not have been all that friendly with Abbot Schweinsberg either—I suspect fighting his way to prince-abbot of Fulda from such an obscure background made the man a lot of enemies—but there was an eyewitness to him being tortured to death by Felix Gruyard. Not a very prominent person, but one with no reason to lie. Schweinsberg's body has now been retrieved and given a proper burial, but everybody is upset and worries about Ferdinand's next move. Having your regiments here would be really nice. Is there no way you can send for them, or at least for somebody who might be willing and able to do something now?"

"I cannot think of anything. Bavaria has been in complete chaos since the duke's fiancée ran off last month, and since she was a Habsburg archduchess, the relations between Bavaria and Vienna are really tense right now. Maxie gave me letters for almost anybody who might have been willing or able to come to Cologne, and she especially put her hopes on Maximilian and Ferdinand's younger brother, Albrecht. But at the moment Albrecht is fleeing from his brother with a price on his head, and there's little doubt that Duke Maximilian was involved in the death of Albrecht's wife and one or more of their children. Might not have ordered it, but he was involved."

"I cannot believe this." Heinrich stared blindly into the golden sunshine dancing in the fallen leaves across the courtyard. "You didn't by any chance encounter four riders on your way?"

"One of them riding a pale horse? No, not that I noticed." Melchior leaned his head back against the rough stone wall, and closed his eyes. "I've never believed in omens and portents, but whether the coming of the Americans heralded a change or caused it doesn't really matter. According to Father Johannes they themselves believe that they have come from the future, only their arrival will have changed the past, so that they are now from a future that will never be. A paradox and as such better left alone by practical men like you and me. After all, if the apocalypse is coming there's very little we can do about it except carry on with our tasks." Melchior sighed. "And at the moment my task is trying to keep things stable and preferably Catholic in the middle Rhine area. If I had my regiments, I could just have taken control, but as it is I'll probably need to negoti-ate. Archduke Ferdinand gave me plenipotentiary powers, and if everything else fails, and the archbishop looks about to send everything up in flames, I might be able to make some kind of deal with Don Fernando in the Netherlands. Essen and Hesse seems nicely locked in a stalemate in Berg, but that's not going to last forever, and once the deadlock breaks, you can bet that fine new cassock of yours that all that might keep Essen, Hessen, and the Netherlands from trying for Cologne as well will be if they don't want to risk ending up fighting each other."

"And our darling brother is likely to get caught up in the middle unless Franz can be persuaded to break with the arch-bishop. You will try talking to him again?"

"Of course. I'll leave for Koblenz tomorrow, and continue on to Bonn the next day. I've got a letter from Wolf for his sister, and plan to look up Franz as well. But enough about that." Melchior sat up straight and looked at his brother. "How are your trading schemes coming along?"

## Magdeburg, House of Hessen
## August 31, 1634

"Please come in, Abbess Dorothea." Amalie put down her pen on the letter she was writing, and rose to greet her visitor. "Eleonore is not coming today; the heat is bothering her a bit."

"I know. I just brought her a potion against stomach upsets. An American recipe that is not going to harm the baby. And how is your pregnancy coming along, my dear?"

"Healthy as a hog as usual. But I am aware that some of the old remedies contained abortifacients." Amalie gave a slight smile. "And I faithfully promise to use only Quedlinburg American Herbal Remedies if I develop any problems. How is the production coming along?"

"Very well, actually." The abbess sat down at the elegant table by the window overlooking the Square. "We had the still-rooms already, and the students have been most interested in both learning the new recipes and earning a bit of money by producing enough for sales. That American herbal book might have been very expensive, but it was one of the best investments I've ever made. I'm hoping to persuade Eleonore's youngest sister, Eva, to go to Quedlinburg after her stay here in Magdeburg. We need someone to develop new recipes for problems the Americans could solve in other ways, and Eva has shown a real understanding of what each herb actually contains and can do."

"And with her pox-scars she's unlikely to find a husband." Amalie shrugged and poured a glass of raspberry cordial for her guest. "Becoming an herbalist would be a sensible choice. I was just penning a note telling Eva and Anchen that my young cousins, Litsa and Maria, are expected any day." Amalie took a sip of the cold mint tisane she habitually drank instead of wine when she was pregnant. "Once they are here you can start your advanced lessons in the new political system. How is the final work with the new constitution coming along?"

"Slowly." The abbess sighed. "Every time I think we have a consensus in the committee, somebody raises a new question. I still hope to get it ratified within the next months, but the election must be postponed until next year."

"Come spring?"

"Or late winter."

"Hm. I'd hoped it would be done faster. There are far too many areas of unrest, and we need a firm government to keep everybody in line." At Amalie's words the abbess started laughing so hard she had to clutch her side.

"Really, Dorothea. That wasn't a joke." Amalie looked affronted.

"Everybody in line but you and Hesse, I presume?" The abbess was still chuckling.

"Oh, that."

"Yes, that. How is your campaign going, my dear? That is of rather more importance than a kidnapping in Fulda or yet another peasant uprising."

Amalie shrugged. "The entire summer has pretty much been wasted. Von Uslar and the Hessian cavalry have dealt with any troubles in all of Berg except the area around Solingen and Remscheid, but De Geers wants too much for permitting the infantry access to the Rhine. Hesse could strike at Bonn and Cologne tomorrow, but without infantry and artillery to back up the initial strike, it would be a chancy undertaking." She frowned. "It looked like such a golden opportunity what with Archbishop Ferdinand's attention seemingly so firmly fixed on his old quarrel with Abbot Schweinsberg in Fulda, but this campaign has turned into a highly depressing affair. Unless you can come up with a really good idea, I'd much rather talk about something else. Did you know that Hermann and Sofie Juliane are moving into House of Hessen?"

# Chapter 11

*Bonn, Eigenhaus House*
*September 1, 1634*

All traces of Charlotte's calm routine had disappeared on the day of the wedding. From before dawn she, like everybody else in the household, had been up and around making preparations for the feast to be served after the wedding ceremony. Charlotte had been given all the lists of ordered goods, and now stood by the gate to the kitchen yard in charge of getting everything distributed to the right parts of the house. On the street outside the tall, half-timbered house, chopped pine bark had been spread to dampen the noise of wagons rolling over the rough cobbles, and in the calm morning air the smell of the pine mixed pleasantly with that of freshly baked cinnamon cakes and wood-smoke from the cooking fires.

Old man Steinfeld, the porter, had gone to the tubs of live eels and carps, and—after grumbling good morning to Charlotte—started cleaning the fish. On the sturdy bench beneath the kitchen window two of the maids borrowed from Frau Benedicte's sisters sat, yawning and gossiping while plucking the feathers of two big geese. The younger of the two cats keeping the house free from mice and rats twined around their feet, meowing and batting at escaped feathers, while the older cat had climbed on top of the handcart beside the gate and crouched there, staring at the live eels and the basin with fish guts.

"Silly bugger!" As the old cat disappeared under the cart with a bit of fish, and the old porter shook his fist after it, Charlotte felt her face crack into the first smile for a long, long time. "Arrh, leave it be, Steinfeld. We'll all have plenty to do today. There's no sense in wasting any energy on a bit of fish gut."

Hilda Mundi, the cook, had been running back and forth between the kitchen and the washing house half the night. The big fireplace built into the wall of the main kitchen had been filled with roasting meats, so the two big iron cauldrons used for boiling the sealed pots of rabbit-stew, the soup hens, and the nets containing whole stuffed cabbage heads had had to be moved to the washing house. It would have been easier with one cook in each building. When Charlotte had passed through the kitchen on her way to the yard, Heidi, the cook borrowed from Frau Clara, had been boiling spiced meatballs for the saffron soup, and Madelaine, Frau Elisabeth's French cook, had been swearing in French at her helpers in the bakery. Frau Benedicte's feast might be small compared to the entertaining Charlotte's parents had done in Zweibrücken, and she had herself arranged bigger in both Jülich and Düsseldorf. But those feasts had been held in castles with all the space and servants one could want, and she had never before realized how much timing and planning it took to make something like this in a more ordinary household. Bigger obviously didn't always mean more complicated.

Frau Mundi stretched her arms above her head and twisted her back. "Breakfast is set out at the end of the big table, Lotti. It's all cold, and you'll just have to snatch it when you can. I've added one of the big spiced fruitcakes that didn't rise properly. And once the fish are clean, Steinfeld, do sprinkle them with a bit of salt and place them in the wine cellar. I'm not ready for them yet and the master has given permission for the use of his cellar. Which reminds me. Lotti, as soon as the bottles of sack arrive, you are to send for the master; they are to go straight to the hall, not into the cellar. And Lotti, Frau Benedicte told me that you have never done much cooking since your husband was an officer, but surely you can peel apples?"

"Yes, Mutti." Charlotte smiled at the friendly gray-haired woman, and made a notation on the paper with one of the crayon sticks one could now buy from the Americans. Such notations might not last the way good ink did, but it was so much easier to handle. "And a sugar baker showed me how to decorate cakes when I was a girl. It's not that I've never learned anything about cooking, it's just that I haven't done anything but give orders since my marriage. The camp followers did the actual cooking."

"Excellent." The cook smiled back and shook her head. "Stina was supposed to do the garnishing and decorating, but Frau Benedicte has kept her in the dining room to arrange the settings there. There has been a problem with the best linen not bleaching properly in the cloudy weather we have had lately, and this has upset the planned pattern of the dishes. Steinfeld, you direct any deliveries to Lotti in the pantry; she'll tell them where to go from there."

As Charlotte and Frau Mundi passed Ilse, the young kitchen girl who was cleaning carrots and onions in narrow scullery between the yard and the kitchen, a pile of big loaves of bread cooling on the table started slipping into the water basins. Ilse, trying to grab them, cut her finger and started crying. This might have been partly from peeling the onions, but a few drops of blood did fall, so the cook shouted at Steinfeld to come finish the onions. She then told Ilse to wash and wrap her hand in a clean cloth before going to Frau Benedicte's warehouse at the riverfront for more of the sago imported from Malaya. She allowed Charlotte to snap up a piece of bread to eat, while explaining that the lowest layer in the sago casket in the larder had turned out to be damp and moldy. It was needed for a cold ginger soup in the third course. Did Charlotte know how to make parsley roses for such a soup?

In the pantry, where Charlotte was to work, the dishes were to receive the final touch before leaving the kitchen area. The major soup, fish and meat dishes for the first course would then go straight to the table in the dining room on the first floor, to be placed in a carefully calculated symmetrical pattern, while the cheese, fruits and sweet dishes for the third course would be arranged as impressively as possible on the special banquet table. The lighter meats, pies and vegetables for the second course had to be stored somewhere while waiting for their turn, and as there was no room in the kitchen, the two male servants were lifting the doors from their hinges and placing them on top of the beds to serve as extra storage space.

On the long narrow table in the pantry, Charlotte was decorating a roast sirloin of beef with swirls of candied lemon peel and honey-glazed onions when she heard Ilse screaming hysterically in the kitchen. As she entered she saw Frau Mundi throw a ladle of cold water in the girl's face and tell to pull herself together.

"Ah, Mutti, it is soldiers on the pier!" The girl was gasping and her eyes looked fit to roll from her head. "A-and it's on fire. A-and they are shooting. We are all going to be k-killed."

"Lotti, go get Frau Benedicte." Frau Mundi pulled the shaking girl down on her lap and wiped the water off her face. "Take a deep breath, Ilse. Now, what was on fire?"

In the dining room, Frau Benedicte was setting out the blue and white delftware plates, while Stina straightened the candles in the big silver epergne at the center of the table. Despite the obvious haste of the two women's movements, there was a marked contrast between the bustle of the kitchen and the silence of the elegantly paneled and plaster-decorated room. Both the lamplight and the pale morning light entering through the beveled windows glittered in the glass and polished silver on the white damask cloth. For a moment Charlotte felt her thoughts swirl again in the dizzy confusion from her time in the archbishop's palace, and she stood staring mindlessly at the pattern of glitter and shadows.

"Good morning, Lotti, is there a problem belowstairs?" Frau Benedicte's words jerked Charlotte out of her daze.

"No, Frau Benedicte, it's outside. There appears to be fighting and fire at the warehouse. Ilse saw it and awaits you in the kitchen."

# Chapter 12

*Rhine Valley, southern side, between Koblenz and Bonn*
*September 1, 1634*

It was pitch-black and pouring rain by the time Melchior reached the Inn of the Black Goat just outside Godesberg. He had planned to spend the night in Bonn before continuing to Cologne in the morning, but the clouds had gathered on the long desolate stretch of cliffs between Uberwinter and Godesberg, and the resulting darkness had forced him to slow down. By now everybody would be asleep, but Andrew the Scot, the innkeeper, had made enough money out of the four Hatzfeldt brothers over the years that he would not mind Melchior stabling his horse and dossing down in the hay himself. No chance of the mountain bacon and the hot whiskey posset that were the Goat's specialties, but—as any old campaigner—Melchior kept a bit of food in his saddlebags. That would have to do for tonight.

"Wen d'you tink di cannens gonna get hir?" The singing Swedish accent of the question made Melchior freeze just before turning into the cobbled stable yard.

"No idea. Faster than if we'd tried to lug them over those damned mountains."

"Those wiren't mountains." The Swedish voice chuckled. "Just little hills with a few little hillsides. Berg is so much easier to move in than Sweden. River valleys everywhere. Up the Eder and

92

down the Sieg. And once you're all the way up, it's easy downhill all the way. Just as with a woman."

Letting the laughter cover any noise he and the horse made on the wet gravel, Melchior backed away and turned the horse. Eder and Sieg? Those rivers led northeast to Kassel, the capital of Hesse-Kassel. Landgrave Wilhelm of Hesse-Kassel had been moving his armies around in the mountains of Berg all summer, obviously trying to grab as much as he could, while the problems left by Duke Wolfgang's death were still unsolved. But when Melchior had left for Vienna, the man had been safely stuck at Remscheid up near Düsseldorf. So what would soldiers coming from Kassel be doing this far south and on this side of the Rhine? And were they Hessians or the main USE army?

As far as Melchior knew, those regiments of the main USE army not in the east at Ingolstadt were far north near the Baltic. Of course a single Swede didn't mean that it was the USE army— Melchior knew quite well that he had a few Swedes in his own regiments—and it could just be that Hesse had hired a few extra regiments to break the deadlock at Remscheid by attacking the Jülich-Berg army from the south. On the other hand Archbishop Ferdinand of Cologne *had* been trying to stir up something in Fulda, which was inside the area occupied by the USE. Twenty years of campaigning made it perfectly clear to Melchior that he needed more information before proceeding with his journey.

Andrew the Scot had acquired the Black Goat by marrying the daughter of the old owner, Nicholaus, and old Nic had now retired to a one-room stone cottage a bit down the road from the inn. A major reason for the Goat's popularity had always been the cheap-for-the-quality of their spirits, and the old man's contacts with smugglers—and heaven knows what else—had always ensured that he knew everybody and everything that went on along the Rhine. Old Nic would not take kindly to being woken, but if an army came to Bonn, it was almost certain that Cologne was their ultimate target, and with Melchior's family living there, he'd brave the old reprobate to get that information right now.

As Melchior approached the cottage he saw squat old Nic taking a leak from the doorway. He didn't seem overly surprised to have Melchior pop out of the rain, just told him to take the horse to the empty woodshed and throw the blanket there over it.

Inside the cottage the toothless old man kept the lamps out, but stirred the coals in the fireplace, making his shadow dance weirdly on the rough wall. "Sit down, boy. On y'way t'Bonn or from't?"

"I'm on my way to Bonn, Nic, but just what has happened?" Melchior folded his long legs to sit on the low stool beside the fireplace.

"Hessian cavalry. Surprise attack at dawn this morning. Came down Sieg and went through them archbishop's mercenaries at Beuel like a knife through hot butter. Got some men across t'Rhine on t'ferry and took that old toll-tower." Nic spat into the fire. "Them ropes on this side's cut, and t'ferry sunk. They'll come across sooner or later, never-you-fear, but it's not that easy without t'ropes to guide."

The four mercenary regiments Archbishop Ferdinand had hired as part of his plans were led by the Irish colonel Butler and three of his friends. Although their equipment had looked good, Melchior had no confidence in their ability to fight as a unit. He knew all four men from Wallenstein's army where they had been his peers and colleagues; neither of the four was incompetent, but they also had no sense of responsibility towards their men. Even Melchior's usually very easygoing cousin, Wolf, loathed their carelessness with the lives of their own men. Melchior had always tried to make his men as good a fighting unit as possible, not just to win but also to survive and become even better and more efficient fighters in the next battle. Butler and those like him believed that they could always hire new men to fill out the ranks, and make the princes pay for their hire. That veterans fought better than novices was of much less importance, especially since those who didn't survive the battle couldn't claim a share in the loot.

Aside from the two thousand or so cavalry, the archbishop had only his personal guard, but in Melchior's estimate that should be enough to stop anything the Hessians could ferry across the Rhine—providing of course that the troops were properly led and nobody lost their head and panicked. However, if the Hessians managed to gain a beachhead, and hold it for long enough to land cannons, then the situation would be entirely different.

The "normal" method of conquering a fortified town was to send cavalry to stop all traffic in and out, while the artillery slowly moved into position to shoot holes in the walls. Then infantry would attack through the holes to open the gates for the cavalry, and finally there would be fighting in the streets until the town surrendered. If the walls were very thick or the town's population big compared to the attacking army, a prolonged siege might weaken the town by starvation.

When the archbishop—and Franz—had tried to talk Melchior into leading an attempt to take back Mainz, Würzburg and the other conquered bishoprics, he had repeatedly pointed out that those towns were defended by garrisons behind solid fortifications and walls, and that the archbishop had no artillery worth mentioning. Without artillery the gates would have to be opened by tricks or treason, and while the archbishop expected the populations to rise against the occupying USE garrisons, Melchior was firmly convinced that the prelate was deceiving himself. From what Father Johannes had told him about the Americans and their ways, some of the leaders of the occupied towns might prefer the return of the ruling bishops, but the main population would probably be quite satisfied with the new rules and freedoms.

Still, with some luck—and especially if the archbishop had succeeded in talking Melchior into leading his forces—it might have been possible to regain Koblenz and Wiesbaden, and perhaps even Mainz. But the next town up the rivers was Frankfurt am Main, filled with Protestant troops and supplies, ideally posed for a quick trip down the Rhine to kick the archbishop's regiments all the way to the Dutch border. Not a good plan. There could be situations where it made sense to conquer a town that you could hold only briefly, but as far as Melchior could see, nothing would be gained here to make it worth the cost.

The archbishop had claimed to have some kind of secret plan involving Fulda to break up the USE and presumably make them need their troops elsewhere. But he wouldn't give Melchior the details, and Melchior frankly didn't trust the old man to know what he was doing. In fact, if it had not been for Melchior's younger brother, Franz, prince-bishop of Würzburg— who hoped the archbishop's plan would eventually regain him his lost bishopric—Melchior would just have washed his hands of the entire mess. Then, when the USE came in response to the archbishop's troublemaking, the Hatzfeldt family could have concentrated on negotiating a deal with the occupying forces. The

Schönstein Hatzfeldts with their long history of serving Hessen as administrators would have helped. Sometimes, with no way to win the battle, you just had to save as much as you could.

Heinrich and Hermann, the oldest and the youngest of the four brothers, completely agreed with Melchior. Heinrich, a canon at St. Alban in Mainz, had stayed during and after the Protestant conquest, while all his superiors fled to Cologne. As a result he had spent two years dealing and negotiating on behalf of his church, first with the army, then with the American NUS administration. He had told the family that the Americans followed different rules, but once you knew those, it was entirely possible to function and even prosper.

Hermann had recently sold his commission as a colonel to concentrate on handling the family estates on both sides of the border, and very badly wanted to join the new industries starting in Essen and around Magdeburg, so he wanted firm treaties all around.

But Franz, Melchior's third brother, would not accept the logic of this. He had only been bishop of Würzburg for little more than a year when he had fled from the Protestant army sweeping down from the north. Franz had made so many plans for his bishopric: new schools, agricultural improvements, helping all those Catholic refugees from the north resettle and build new lives. Now, it was breaking his heart to be reduced to a powerless refugee, forced to depend on either the support of his family or the charity of the archbishop.

In Melchior's opinion, Franz needed to make a deal with the USE, so he could go back to Würzburg and start working. True, a bishop under American rule had little earthly power compared to a ruler of a bishopric, but the people would be there to care for and help. And Franz had spent eight years as a diplomat in the service of the two previous prince-bishops of Bamberg. Surely he could negotiate something better for himself than Abbot Schweinsberg had in Fulda. But first of all Franz had to stop chasing the archbishop's rainbows and settle for what was possible.

When all else failed, Melchior had gone to München hoping to persuade Duke Maximilian to put an end to Archbishop Ferdinand's wild schemes. Unfortunately Bavaria had been in total chaos after the disappearance of the duke's fiancée, Archduchess Maria Anna, and in Melchior's opinion the duke had been even more unbalanced than the archbishop. Melchior had done what he could, but nobody had seemed to both care about the danger to Cologne, and have the power to call the archbishop to order.

In the end Melchior had given up in Bavaria, and instead tried to get permission from the emperor in Vienna to take his own regiments west to Cologne and take command of the area. The old Emperor Ferdinand had been too ill to make any decisions, but his heir, Archduke Ferdinand, had told Melchior to return to Cologne and try to hold things together until reinforcements could arrive. A bit vague, but then everything was quite unsettled at the moment, and the archduke had supplied Melchior with some unusually potent papers and writs.

Old Nic had been heating a pot of water while Melchior sat musing, and now silently gave him a mug of hot brandy. "All four of the archbishop's regiments were billeted within or around the walls of Bonn when I left," said Melchior frowning. "Do you know how many were moved across the Rhine to the Beuel and how big the Hessian army is?"

"Some moved to Beuel and some to that camp outside t'west gate. Them colonels had left; no discipline and rioting in town." The old man harked and spat again. "Old Pegleg from Beuel came across today. He'd seen the attack. Looked like them Hessians have about half real cavalry and half them mounted infantry. Don't know how many. Everybody in Bonn who can's fled west t'Cologne or t'Aachen. There's a few Hessians this side already. Prob'ly scouts crossing before the attack. One group's at t'Goat."

"I know. Are your family well?"

"Yeah, nobby wanna fight armed soldiers, but there's only a handful. They can stop travelers if they want to, but they make much trouble and me girls gonna bash their balls. Big fine girls."

Melchior, remembering a surprisingly intimate encounter with one of the old man's granddaughters some years ago, didn't really doubt that. "Have you heard anything about my brother, Franz, or the archbishop?"

"Nope. Somebody just mentioned them mercenary colonels not being around, and wondered where you'd gone."

# Chapter 13

*Outside Bonn*
*September 2, 1634*

In the early morning foggy drizzle Melchior had no chance of getting a good view of the situation from the road following the top of the river bank. The old toll-tower, where the town wall reached the Rhine, rose squat and solid out of the mist. Hesse's attempt to take Bonn with a surprise attack not supported by artillery had been a daring maneuver—quite in the style of Landgrave Wilhelm's mentor, Gustavus Adolphus—and one with a fair chance of succeeding even now after the first rush had been stopped. Presumably the town's cannons had now been moved along the walls to cover the occupied tower, but reducing it to rubble would be impossible without damaging the wall too.

Melchior stopped to consider his options. No one seemed to be around outside the walls at the moment, but using the gate by the toll-tower would expose him to fire from above, so he turned the horse inland towards the next gate. It was sure to be occupied with defenders ready to fire along the walls to keep more Hessians from reaching the toll-tower gate, but if he came slowly and openly they were unlikely to fire on sight.

"Ho, the gate!" Melchior called as soon as he could see the second tower.

"Yeah, who goes?"

"General Melchior von Hatzfeldt returning from Vienna. My cousin-in-law, Commander Wickradt, can vouch for me. But hurry, please, I'm feeling a bit exposed."

In the whitewashed guards-room at the base of the gate tower, Melchior was offered a breakfast of hot beer, rye bread and cheese by the distant relative of his sister Lucie's late husband. Commander Wickradt had been a siege specialist in the Dutch army before returning to his hometown to take command of Bonn's defenses. Bonn had always played second fiddle to Cologne, but when the archbishops of Cologne near the end of the thirteenth century had been thrown out of Cologne and forbidden to enter except to fulfill their clerical duties, they had settled in Bonn. Here they had built the walls and fortifications, and generally given the small provincial backwater town some importance. Where Cologne was an important free city in its own right, and ruled entirely by its council, Bonn belonged to and depended on the archbishops—and the town's council usually did what they were told.

The archbishops had always maintained their own guards. Sometimes just the Palace Guard and an escort for their travels, sometimes an actual private army, but always something separate from the town's defenses and taking their orders directly from the archbishop. During the last few years, as the war had come closer and closer, Commander Wickradt had taken personal control of the town's militias and started training as many of the town's citizens as he could. The archbishop—and his guards—had sneered at that: bumpkins waving around cutlery, pretending to be soldiers. But when the archbishop's mercenary regiments had tried to bully their surroundings, it had been the men trained by Wickradt who had stepped in and beaten up the worst offenders, proving that being lofty cavalry was no protection against cudgels in a dark alley.

In the flickering torchlight on this particular morning Commander Wickradt looked every one of his sixty-some years, and despite keeping the mood light while Melchior was eating with humorous tales about "his" people's ability to defend themselves against their rough mercenary "guests," the old man was obviously deeply worried.

"My thanks for your hospitality, Wickradt," said Melchior,

refusing the offer for another serving, "but I think we better move on to more serious matter. Or are you waiting for someone?"

"The mayor, Herr Oberstadt, should be along shortly, but there's no reason to wait with the military information. A few people have crossed the river in fishing boats and one of them, Karl Mittelfeld, is an old friend of mine. He used to be a musketeer until an infected wound gave him a limp. From what he and the other fishermen told me, the Hessians have brought four or five regiments of cavalry and at least a few companies of mounted infantry with muskets, say two or three thousand in all. It could be more, but people don't tend to underestimate the size of an attacking force. No sign of their artillery."

"The cannons are coming later." Melchior looked blankly at the wall trying to recall what information he had on the Hessian army. "A few years ago, Hesse could field ten to twelve thousand soldiers including around three thousand cavalry. So it's not the entire Hessian army—at least not yet or at least not around Beuel—but it could be most or all of his cavalry."

"Cavalry are not my specialty, Herr General, but if Hesse had been hiring heavily I would have heard. And I haven't." Wickradt kept his eyes at the younger man. The Hatzfeldts were one of the most prominent families in the area, and while Melchior wasn't as famous a general as Wallenstein or Tilly, he was by far the most reputable military leader presently west of Bavaria. "Any ideas about the bigger picture? Should we expect the Swedes too?"

"I am almost completely certain that the main armies of the USE are fully occupied northeast and southeast of here." Melchior dipped a finger in his beer and started drawing a map of wet lines on the table. "Ingolstadt has fallen, and the USE border with Bavaria now follows the Danube. I passed close enough to be certain that General Horn has not moved in this direction. Nor have any major units left Frankfurt to travel down the Rhine. Gustavus Adolphus must still need most of his army in the northeast, but might have been able to spare a few units or even some American specialists. When I left Cologne, Hesse was stuck around Remscheid with the Bergian forces between him and Cologne, and the army of Essen between him and the Rhine. Are there any reports from that area?"

"No. As of the day before yesterday there were no movements along the Rhine, and no reports of attacks on the Bergian fortifications. With De Geer and Essen firmly in possession of Düsseldorf, I suppose it would make sense for Hesse to try expanding westward and take Cologne. And I'm quite aware that he could easily have moved his cavalry. But he cannot hope to take Cologne or even Bonn without artillery to break the walls. And where would that be coming from?"

"My guess would be down the Rhine from Frankfurt." Melchior continued drawing wet lines on the table. "There really are three routes Hesse could take. The first is up the Fulda River from Kassel, and down the Rhine from Frankfurt, thus hitting Bonn on the way to Cologne. Number two is west through Berg or Mark to the Rhine and going upstream to hit Cologne first. And the third is up the Eder valley and down the Sieg to take Bonn. Which we know he used for at least some of the cavalry now on this side of the river. Option number one makes sense for any cannons he might have left behind when moving into Berg. That would be much easier than dragging them across the mountains. Option number two would need a deal with De Geer, but when I left for Vienna the rumors in Cologne were quite insistent that Archbishop Ferdinand played a role in that mess with Duke Wolfgang and the French raid this spring, so such an alliance is far from unlikely. That reminds me: has Wolfgang's widow been found?"

"It is known that Felix Gruyard brought her to the archbishop's palace here in Bonn, and that she gave birth to a living son, but no one has seen either her or the baby since the birth. The archbishop's people searched for her into Berg, but found nothing. I have my own ideas about what happened, and think she is safe and with friends."

"Hm, poor girl. I took a cousin of hers prisoner at Augsburg a couple of years ago—nice young man and an excellent card player. The Zweibrücken family is heavily intermarried with the royal family of Sweden, and I suppose she could be part of the reason Hesse is here. Somebody in Vienna mentioned him trying to become the baby's guardian." Melchior frowned. "Do you think you could find her if necessary?"

"Probably, but you might have to swear to her your personal protection from the archbishop as well as from Hesse. Your cousin, Dame Anna is here in Bonn. She is a friend of Irmgard Eigenhaus, the midwife. Paying a visit to the dames might be a good place to start."

"I see. I've got a letter to Anna from her brother, Wolf, who is now my second-in-command. I had planned to visit her anyway. And Archduke Ferdinand told me to do what I could to keep Jülich-Berg as well as the Archdiocese of Cologne under Catholic control." Melchior frowned and re-drew the drying lines on the table. "But back to the military situation: Hesse used the Eder-Sieg route for his cavalry, but their presence here might be mainly to ensure that the cannons can get down safely from Frankfurt to Cologne. Bonn isn't that important in the overall picture. I haven't seen any signs of infantry coming from Frankfurt, but they could be following the cavalry on the Eder-Sieg route or coming via Essen. Do you know who is actually leading the Hessian cavalry?"

"It's said to be Wilhelm of Hesse in person, but that's not verified. Could be one of his generals, probably von Uslar." Wickradt frowned at the wet lines on the table. "You don't think Hesse is just trying to remove Archbishop Ferdinand before the archbishop does whatever he hired those mercenaries for? We had mail from Cologne yesterday, and they are not expecting an attack. You cannot move infantry around in complete secrecy."

"Stopping the archbishop is probably a part of it. And if Hesse isn't bringing his infantry, he might settle for that and a tribute. But taking Cologne is his most likely goal. What do you have to oppose him with here in Bonn?"

"If you are right about the cannons coming from Frankfurt, then our cannons on the river-walls could sink any boat trying to pass in the daytime. Sailing the Rhine at night is extremely dangerous, but can be done with a local pilot." Wickradt smiled. "I'm fairly certain Karl and his friends don't live entirely on what they catch fishing."

Melchior shook his head. "Sailing the Rhine past Bonn at night is something much too chancy to base your artillery movement on."

"Well, you're the expert on field-maneuvers. Outside the town the situation is that the archbishop's regiment at Beuel is completely gone, and with them the lieutenant colonel given the overall interim command while the four colonels were up-river doing something with Felix Gruyard."

Melchior interrupted. "The archbishop's torturer went with Irish Butler and the others? And the overall commander was across the river in Beuel?"

"Yes and yes. And while I'm glad not to have that Lorrainian creep Gruyard around polluting the wells, things might have gone better if those mercenary colonels had stayed."

"Possibly, but go on."

"When the Hessians took Beuel, they went straight to the ferry and continued the attack across the Rhine. They failed to take more than the old toll-tower, but there's an arsenal in there, and a frontal assault would in my opinion not just be costly, I think it would fail completely. Those walls and gates are strong. Reducing the tower to rubble with the wall-cannons might turn out to be necessary, but it would seriously weaken the wall, leaving a hole in the defenses. And if we can just stall things for a few weeks, we'll starve them out." Wickradt sighed. "The archbishop's other three regiments were supposed to patrol the river brink, to prevent more Hessians from crossing. But last night, when the rain started, the Hessians managed to get several barge-loads of musketeers across the Rhine before anybody noticed—or at least before anybody reported it. When the news reached the mercenary camp, two lieutenant colonels couldn't be found, one was so drunk he was incoherent, and the rest started quarreling. Eventually just one squadron went, only to return in panic, shouting that the Hessian cavalry were across and right on their heels."

"Any idea if that was true?" asked Melchior.

"None. The only Hessians I have seen are in the tower. But the panic spread. The mercenaries struck their camp during the night, and most moved west. Judging from what was left behind, it was not entirely an orderly maneuver. Also around midnight the archbishop packed his guards and left town. He is taking direct command of his mercenary regiments from a field headquarters until Butler and the others return. With your brother as his interim general-in-charge."

"What! Is Hermann here?"

"Oh no, your brother Franz, the prince-bishop of Würzburg."

"Franz? Impossible. He has only the bits of military training our father insisted on. He cannot lead an army."

"Be as it might. The label 'General von Hatzfeldt' commands quite a lot of respect."

"Oh, God, poor Franz. The archbishop must be totally out of his mind."

"In my opinion the archbishop still hopes to put you in charge, Herr General." The entrance of the portly mayor had gone unnoticed by Melchior. "Of course, I rather hope to do the same. Only for my town rather than for the mercenaries. I'm not qualified to judge the archbishop's sanity of mind, but I am definitely sure I do not want my town sacked and burned. Nor do I want its people starved to death by a siege."

The mayor sat down carefully on the low stool and continued talking. "The Hessians appear to have come without cannons, so the archbishop claims the city is safe. But even if they don't get siege weapons built or brought, they could still starve us out. We have stores for some months, but not for all winter."

"The cannons are coming, probably down from Frankfurt," said Melchior absently. "I overheard a scout last night at the Inn of the Black Goat. And I don't think Hesse is willing to wait for Bonn if he has his sights set on Cologne. What's the military situation inside the town, Wickradt?"

"My guard is up to three hundred men, including reserves and artillerists, all well trained and equipped. The council agreed to the expenses when Mainz fell to the Protestants. The militias all have guns, and know how to use them. The old militia also follows orders fairly well," Commander Wickradt stopped and grinned. "But the new part has some problems. They are women."

"I beg your pardon?"

"Yes. They heard the story of the American woman shooting Wallenstein at the Alte Veste. Do you remember Frau Benedicte Eigenhaus? She trounced your stepmother, Margaretha, over that affair with the Neumarkt property in Cologne. About a year ago Frau Benedicte headed a delegation to insist that the strongest women in town should also be taught to shoot. I wouldn't want to do anything complicated with the Little Dears, but to put them on a wall and tell them to fire at an enemy on the outside should be safe enough. They have even set up a rather efficient shooting method. Somebody told someone about the musketeer's system of 'one man fires while one man loads' in alternating rows, so the Little Dears have paired off and one sits down and loads both guns while the other stands up and fires them. Once the shooter gets a sore shoulder, they'll change. They can actually manage a quite respectable rate of fire that way. If I had enough guns I would have dragged in some of the weaker women just as extra loaders."

"That explain some remarks I overheard from the Palace Guard just before I left for Vienna." Melchior kept making drawings on the table with a wet finger, of what he remembered of the wall and fortifications around Bonn. "But how many guns do you have? And what about cannons?"

"The gun situation is good: almost one thousand new, good quality muskets. There are also a few hundred older—but working—guns in the arsenals, and some militia men prefer their own. The wall-cannons are the old ones, except for the river-wall." Wickradt frowned. "The old ones will keep battering rams from the gates, and might take out a badly placed enemy artillery bastion, but they are far too slow in adjustment to stand any chance of hitting mounted or marching men."

"What about balls and pikes?"

"Lots of balls and gunpowder for everything, but only my guards have much in the way of swords. The militia's men have cudgels, pikes and staffs according to preference. The Little Dears?" Wickradt shrugged, "I haven't tried to do anything. They might in fact be better off not looking too warlike if it comes to fighting in the streets."

"So for all practical purpose: getting in without cannons would be very costly for the Hessians, and Landgrave Wilhelm is not one to spend his men unnecessarily. But once their cannons get here, only the archbishop's cavalry can keep them from pounding this tower, while they get in through the toll-tower gate. How much have you done with barricades in the streets?"

"Nothing so far, but wagons are ready to be rolled into the area in front of the toll-tower. The slope towards the river should make them roll in place without exposing my men to fire from above. But I still want to retake that bloody toll-tower." Wickradt banged his mug into the table. "Once the Hessians get inside the walls it'll be a bloodbath. For us and for them. No matter how much we slow them. And to depend on the archbishop and those mercenary to keep the cannons away? Forget it. They'll fuck up even if they try."

"I would very much prefer not to rely on that cavalry myself," said the mayor, "and the rest of the council agrees. We were rather hoping you would be willing to help us avoid that necessity, Herr General."

"In what way, Mayor Oberstadt? Commander Wickradt has

far more expertise in town defenses than I have, and I do not carry an army in my pocket. My own regiments are still in Linz, and getting them here could not be done in less than two months. I may decide to do what the archbishop wanted, and go take command of his regiments. But they are not well trained and the Hessians appear to outnumber them. Sooner or later the Hessians will still come to your gates."

"We realize that, Herr General, and the council and guilds have spent the entire night debating what we should do. We were still in session when the news of your arrival came to the Town Hall, and a quick agreement was reached to place the matter fully in your hands."

"What?"

"Yes, Herr General, according to our best lawyers, the archbishop has abandoned the town in the face of an enemy, and withdrawn his soldiers and protection. He gave no orders about what we are to do before he left. And so the council—and citizens and guards—are not breaking any oaths or committing treason by choosing you to do whatever you can for us. As long as a single enemy soldier is within the area controlled by the Council of Bonn, you are empowered to use all our resources and make any negotiations you want. The papers are being written at the Hall." The mayor folded his hands over his velvet-clad stomach and smiled at Melchior, while Wickradt broke in to a slightly hysteric laughter.

Melchior closed his mouth. This was not expected! He wanted to find Franz and get him away from the archbishop. Melchior could then take charge of those damned mercenary regiments, and gather as many more fighters as possible to harass the Hessians until Wolf could bring his regiments to the west. But Bonn? Bonn had been where they went for fun and fairs all his childhood. If he was right about Hesse trying to conquer this entire stretch of the Rhine, Bonn didn't stand a chance. And if they chose to trust him like that, he couldn't just turn his back and leave. Damned!

A guard came to wave Wickradt out, and Melchior scowled at the smiling mayor. "And what if I choose to negotiate a surrender? Or to have Bonn join the USE?"

The mayor stopped smiling. "We trust you to make the best of a very bad situation, Herr General. On our own we face either a conquest or a surrender without negotiations. You are the one person here that Hesse is sure to take seriously. Everybody else would just get the terms dictated, but if you stand for Bonn, you'd be listened to. By Hesse and by the USE." He sighed. "We do not like this, Herr General, but last night—after the archbishop left with his soldiers but before we knew you had returned—the council and guilds majority were in favor of applying for membership of the USE. Either as a free town or as part of a province. The Committee of Correspondence is not very vocal in Bonn, but they are here and claim to be able to make the necessary contacts in Mainz. They'll wait for your orders before leaving; just tell us what you want."

"Very well." Melchior took a deep breath and nodded. "I accept the task. I'll write letters for the USE and for my brothers. Please have two couriers ready aside from the person from the CoC. I'll see Commander Wickradt about the rest."

"Certainly, Herr General, and thank you." The mayor rose and bowed deeply. "Just . . . There might be one small limit to your power here in Bonn. Please don't call the Women's Militia 'The Little Dears' within the hearing of any female; the consequences would be entirely beyond the council's control."

"Ah, General von Hatzfeldt." Commander Wickradt was standing just beyond the ironbound tower gate with the sun reflecting from his helmet and breastplate. "There is some news about the mercenary colonels."

"Excellent. Please walk with me, Commander, I'm staying for a while and would like to see the toll-tower for myself." Melchior breathed deeply of the fresh air and looked up at the still hazy sun. The rain clouds from last night were gone and the mist had just been the usual morning mist hanging over the river. Both good and bad. It would make the couriers more visible, but also give earlier warning if the Hessians started moving in on the town.

"So you accepted the council's offer?" said Wickradt in a much lower voice, as they walked between the half-timbered houses toward the river, their boots making small splashes in the rain puddles.

"Yes, and I'll be sending off letters as soon as we have spoken. Please leave the western gate open until the couriers have left, but keep men standing by to close immediately if any large parties approach." Melchior looked around at the wet cobbles sparkling in the sun. He had been a professional soldier for almost twenty years, and had been on the winning as well as losing sides of several sieges. But Bonn was so much a part of his childhood that the thought of blood running over these cobblestones made him feel sick.

"That is already done, General, and they'll also close the gate if mists gather again to obscure the view of the approach. This time of year that's entirely possible." Wickradt had to stretch his shorter legs to keep up with Melchior. "The news I just had was that Butler, MacDonald and Deveroux rode in through the western gate this morning, and left again less than an hour later going west. Felix Gruyard was with them. No sign of Geraldin. Also, the scouts I sent out earlier have returned to tell that the Hessians are crossing near Vesseling, and the road via Bruhl to Cologne is still open."

"All good, but if Geraldin turns up I'd like to see him." Melchior stopped before turning into the open area before the toll-tower gate. "How much do they fire from the toll-tower?"

"Not much. I went to the gate yesterday under truce to ask for their surrender. They refused, but we reached an agreement. Neither side sets fires until the town is actually attacked, and they can empty their slop-bucket safely over the outside wall in return for not deliberately targeting civilians. They are native Hessians, well disciplined, and prepared to just hold on until the rest of their force get here. I refused them food and extra water, but offered to let any wounded into care in the town. They replied that none of them were hit in the balls and none were catamites, so they preferred to stay away from Felix Gruyard and the archbishop's dungeons. I had to admit that I could not guarantee their safety."

"Very well." Melchior removed his hat and briefly scanned the tower by leaning round the corner. "No frontal attack on that, and reducing it to rubble only if negotiations fail. Let your wagons roll in to block as much of the gate as possible, and barricade all the streets just out of range. Where else might they attack? I remember the north wall missing some towers."

"If they can breach the north wall on the middle, they cannot be reached with cannons while entering town. But I've concentrated as many cannons there as I dared, so getting close would cost any attackers dearly. The west walls are good, and I'm sure we can beat anything they send at the river walls."

"Good. Letters next, and I'll need a place to sleep."

"Let us walk to the Town Hall." Wickradt looked sideways at Melchior as they crossed the gutter to walk on the big flat stones set along the middle of the road. "Is there any chance of getting your own regiments here?"

"Not in time." Melchior looked at the older man walking beside him and decided to be a bit more forthcoming. "I had some both personal and political problems in Vienna last winter, and was given furlough this summer to visit my family and make an evaluation of the military situation in western Germany for the emperor. I went back to report when it became obvious that Archbishop Ferdinand was about to stir things up along this part of the Rhine, but Bavaria is in chaos and the Habsburgs are waiting for the old emperor to die, so no one was willing to interfere."

"How about the emperor's heir, Archduke Ferdinand? Couldn't he do something?"

"Could, yes, but there's a long way from Austria to Cologne, and at the moment Duke Maximilian of Bavaria is likely to believe that any military movement in this direction is an attack on him. He is already seeing an enemy conspiracy every time somebody sneezes." Melchior smiled wryly. "At the moment I'm under oath to the old emperor as an imperial count, but only on retainer as a general, while some of my men are hired by me and others by the Holy Roman Empire. I tried to get permission to bring my personal regiments to the west, but in the end I had to accept waiting for the new emperor to take command. My plans must then depend on his plans. If Hesse is still around when the old emperor dies, Wolf, my second-in-command and cousin, should be able to bring my men here. They'll probably have to move either through Bavaria or along its southern border. Once they get here, we can try to hold as much of this part of the Rhine as possible." Melchior stopped and lifted his hat in greeting to a vaguely familiar old woman dropping into a curtsy as he passed.

"And if Hesse has conquered Cologne and Bonn? Could your men take them back?" Wickradt looked grim.

"Not on our own. At least not unless we can get the population to rise against Hesse." Melchior answered. "On the other

hand, if Hesse succeeds before Wolf can get here it would leave
the Holy Roman Empire fenced in behind Bavaria and entirely
dependent on Italy and France. So even if the new emperor
would prefer to keep his troops in the East, he might still find
it necessary to send them."

"Even with Bavaria unstable?" Wickradt lifted an eyebrow.

"It would not be an easy choice." Melchior frowned. "When
I left Vienna I didn't expect to do more here than placate whoever the archbishop had managed to upset, and keep things calm
until reinforcements could arrive. Still, Archduke Ferdinand gave
me quite a lot of power to counter whatever the archbishop
was up to, including plenipotentiary powers to negotiate on the
emperor's behalf in matters concerning the interests of the HRE
west of Bavaria. Hesse's attack across the Rhine came as a complete surprise to me. It makes sense for him to expand his new
province into Berg, but any attempt on Cologne I would have
expected to come from the south, and Rheinland-Pfalz is simply
too divided to do that right now." Melchior smiled and bowed to
another woman curtsying to him before continuing. "I suppose I
could take the archbishop's mercenary regiments and try to stop
him by military means—certainly most of my colleagues would
do so—but there isn't much chance I'd be able to succeed. And
from the emperor's point of view a Cologne with a negotiated
membership of the USE is very much preferable to a Cologne
conquered by Hesse."

"So you'll try negotiations." Wickradt nodded to himself.
"Sensible thing to do. With Hesse or above his head?"

"Above, if I can manage it. Gustavus Adolphus must have
permitted—or at least accepted—Hesse's plans." Melchior stopped
and looked at Wickradt. "If you are right about the Jülich-Berg
heir being here in Bonn that might enable me to stop Gustavus
Adolphus from openly backing Hesse. The baby's aunt is Gustavus Adolphus' sister Katharina, and he is said to be most fond
of her. And the second most powerful man in the USE is Mike
Stearns, an American. My brother Heinrich has been dealing with
the Americans in Mainz for the past two years, and my friend,
Father Johannes, has lived among them for longer. They have told
me that the Americans know the value of a willing ally—or at
least semi-willing one—over a conquered area."

Wickradt scowled. "So all we have to do is keep Hesse at bay until we get the negotiations opened? Well, we'll do our best. May I spread the news about you taking charge of the town? There have been a few reports of looters already, and I expect your name would squelch that again."

"Sure, but do put up a gibbet and don't expect me to walk on water too." Melchior slapped his hat against his leather trousers and started composing letters while he walked.

# Chapter 14

*Field Headquarters of the archbishop of Cologne
September 2, 1634*

*To Franz von Hatzfeldt, Bishop of Würzburg
From Melchior von Hatzfeldt, Count and General of the
     Holy Roman Empire*

*Dear Franz,
     I have accepted taking charge of Bonn, and I shall
begin negotiations with Hesse on the town's behalf as soon
as contact is made. Kindly inform the archbishop that you,
my brother, are the only person I shall acknowledge as
speaking on behalf of the archdiocese in those negotiations.*

*Loving regards from your brother,
Melchior*

Archbishop Ferdinand of Cologne crumpled the letter in his
hands and hissed. "Has Franz seen this?"

"No, Your Honor. I thought a message from Bonn would be
so important that Your Honor should see it immediately." Otto
Tweimal cringed and smiled, and wondered once again if it was
time to find another employer. Being secretary to the newly
appointed prince-bishop of Würzburg had offered all kinds of

opportunities for power and grafts, and the exile at the arch-bishop's palace in Bonn also the hope of an even better position there. But now? A failing power was not worth cultivating, and military life was far from his taste.

"Your Honor," Felix Gruyard had been reading over the archbishop's shoulder, "with three of your colonels back, Bishop Franz von Hatzfeldt isn't really needed here. I suggest he is sent off to Cologne after reinforcements, with, of course, an escort."

"No, he is going to Mainz after that turncoat Anselm von Wambold. Pick the escort from my personal guard, they leave within the hour." The archbishop banged his fist against the table in anger, and rose from his chair.

"Your Honor, it might be better not to tempt von Hatzfeldt into joining..."

"Pick an escort that'll see to it he doesn't. Herr Tweimal, place yourself at Gruyard's immediate disposal. Franz von Hatzfeldt no longer needs your service."

*Cologne, Hatzfeldt House*
*September 2, 1634*
*To Colonel Hermann von Hatzfeldt, Hatzfeldt House, Town*
*    of Cologne*
*From Melchior von Hatzfeldt, Count and General of the*
*    Holy Roman Empire*

*Dear Hermann,*
*    I accomplished nothing in München and little in Vienna, and returned to Bonn on top of an attack from Hesse. Archbishop Ferdinand has left Bonn, along with Franz and the mercenary cavalry. I have accepted taking charge of the town, but there is nothing I can do to stop Bonn from falling once the Hessian artillery gets here, and I shall begin negotiations as soon as contact is made, both with Hesse and the USE.*
*    The information as I write is: major contingent of Hessian cavalry came down Sieg and took Beuel. They are as I write crossing the Rhine near Vesseling. Only minor number of infantry (mounted) with them. Artillery expected to arrive soon, probably from Frankfurt, but may also come from Essen and thus reach Cologne first.*

*Please spread the news among our contacts and warn the council of Cologne. If you can get a mandate from them, and contact the USE before Hesse encircles Cologne, we might be able to pull something off for the entire area, including the family estates and perhaps even Würzburg.*

*Your loving brother,*
*Melchior*

"Oh dear," Lucie von Hatzfeldt looked across the table at her youngest brother, "I hoped the refugees exaggerated, and it was just a minor force aimed at stopping the archbishop's wild schemes. But if Melchior doesn't think so ... Do you think the Hessians could conquer Cologne?"

Hermann shrugged. "Their entire army could close off the town, and given enough artillery they could breach the walls. It would either take a very long siege or be extremely costly in men, but it could be done." He shrugged again and rose from his chair. "I'll pick up young Count Palatine Friedrich von Zweibrücken and go see the council; they'll be in session all night. Please find the letters Father Johannes wrote from Fulda, and make notes of the Americans he mentioned in Mainz and Frankfurt."

*Beuel, Hessian Field Headquarters*
*Archdiocese of Cologne*
*September 2, 1634*

*To whom it may concern, Hessian Field Headquarters,*
  *Archdiocese of Cologne*
*From Melchior von Hatzfeldt, Count and General of the*
  *Holy Roman Empire*

*On behalf of the Town of Bonn I, Melchior von Hatzfeldt, Count and General of the Holy Roman Empire, have opened negotiations with the United States of Europe concerning said Town's inclusion among said States. In view of this I hope for an end to hostilities, but also inform that I have accepted taking charge of the Town of Bonn, and shall defend it to the uttermost of my abilities.*

*By my hand and under my seal,*
*Melchior von Hatzfeldt*

Landgrave Wilhelm of Hesse carefully refolded the parchment. This wasn't good. That the initial attack across the Rhine had failed to take and hold the river-walls of Bonn was not a problem; it would have made things simpler, but no one counted on unsupported cavalry taking a fortified town.

Having General von Hatzfeldt as an opponent was bad, but at least he wasn't leading his regiments, and von Uslar could surely beat those mercenaries the archbishop had hired. Having Bonn—or any other part of the Archdiocese of Cologne—independently join the USE was on the other hand totally unacceptable.

Having the entire area between Hessen and Cologne more or less up for grabs after the removal of both Georg William of Brandenburg and Wolfgang of Jülich-Berg was surely a God-given opportunity, but it would all be worth next to nothing unless he could get the rich trading center of Cologne too. If the Hessian army could take Cologne, the emperor would surely give him Berg and Mark. It had been necessary to promise De Geer parts of Mark as well as several other concessions in order to get the Hessian infantry access to the Rhine, but Gustavus Adolphus would consider it a small price to pay for removing the last fully Catholic enclave in the west. If, however, the Archdiocese of Cologne—or parts of it—joined the USE on its own, Hesse stood to lose quite a lot of face and favor. He had long been one of the emperor's favorites, and considering his long and loyal service it was unlikely he would get into serious trouble for anything less than treason. Still, when Amalie had attempted to get the guardianship of the Jülich-Berg heir, Axel Oxenstierna's reaction had made it perfectly obvious Hessen had seriously overstepped their privileges and that any further presumptions would be slapped down.

So, a second misstep could remove him from his status as one of the emperor's most trusted German allies, which meant that it *had* to be a victory. Bringing in a new area by negotiation would not do now. It was too late to stop von Hatzfeldt's messengers, but he would have at least a month before orders could arrive from Magdeburg.

"Rutgert, send a troop to find out what's keeping the cannons and where. Also, I want the artillery bastions around Bonn built first."

"Bonn?" The lieutenant serving as secretary looked up from the American style writing-board, and looked puzzled.

"Yes, Bonn. Move all the building teams there, and have Colonel Brenner plan for all the cannons from Frankfurt to be placed around Bonn first; I want the town in rubble within a fortnight."

*Mainz*
*September 12, 1634*

*To whom it may concern in USE administration*
*From Melchior von Hatzfeldt, Count, General and Agent*
*    Plenipotentiary of the Holy Roman Empire*

*With the power granted me by the Council and People of*
*Bonn I, Melchior von Hatzfeldt, hereby apply, on behalf of*
*the Town of Bonn, for the opening of negotiations concern-*
*ing said Town's inclusion in the United States of Europe.*

*By my hand and under my name and seal,*
*Melchior von Hatzfeldt*

Bennett Norris looked up at the big, rough-looking man standing in front of his desk. "Herr Karl Mittelfeld, the CoC in Mainz vouches for you as a committee member in good standing from Bonn."

The big man nodded and shifted his weight, making Bennett remember his limp, and gesture him towards the chair. "Do you know the content of this letter?" Bennett continued.

"It's from General von Hatzfeldt, who's been given command of Bonn to deal with an attack from the Hessian army, Herr Norris. Bonn is asking to join the USE. The general's brother, Colonel Hermann von Hatzfeldt, is here with a similar letter from Cologne, but your soldiers didn't want to let him through to you. The general said to me to say to you that your mother-in-law, Andrea Hill in Fulda, has told his friend, Father Johannes the painter, that the Americans want people to join them instead of being conquered. The councils of Bonn and Cologne want to do so, but the Hessians must be stopped while a deal is made."

"I see. And I shall act upon this. Thank you for bringing me this letter. Will you remain in Mainz?"

"I'm taking another letter to the general's brother, Heinrich von Hatzfeldt, at the Church of St. Alban. He will find a place for me to stay until you can give me a letter to bring back to Bonn."

"Fine." Bennett smiled a little. "I usually see Domherr Heinrich von Hatzfeldt several times a week anyway; at least we will now have a new subject to debate."

When the big man had limped out the door Bennett Norris sat a while staring at the letter without seeing it. A lifetime of small town administration combined with civic duties on school and church boards had not prepared him for this. The year he had spent as the Grantville liaison to the Council of Jena, while Marian, his wife, had trained the nurses at the hospital, had taught him to work with the German version of bureaucracy, but being an inspector of the upcoming elections was as much as he had volunteered for. Not this. Heading the NUS administration in Mainz was supposed to have been a brief stay while the permanent staff recovered from a bad bout of food poisoning, but those who had not died were still bedridden.

Bennett put his head in his hands and groaned. He really, really, really did not want to make decisions about wars.

# Chapter 15

*Bonn, the river wall*
*September 21, 1634*

Charlotte shifted the musket below her cloak, and wiped away the raindrop under her nose with the back of her hand. Despite the situation she smiled a little; whoever would have thought this?

Once she had recovered from her breakdown on her first training session, she had actually become quite good at shooting, but had still felt that for a woman to shoot a gun was somehow indecent. But standing by her baby's cradle on the morning of the Hessian attack, watching him make small suckling movements in his sleep, Charlotte had completely changed her mind. She had spent a good deal of time helping to make the infirmary ready for the siege, but otherwise she had taken to spending every moment she could on practicing with whatever group of militias was on the walls, even talking the instructors into letting her train with the men, and finally taking regular watches. And it felt good! For once in her life she had the feeling of actually being able to defend herself against an enemy wanting to hurt her and her son. For once she wasn't completely helpless and able to only rely on the goodwill of others.

It was probably just an illusion. The Hessian army had completely surrounded Bonn, preventing anyone except those able to travel the Rhine at night from entering or leaving the town, and the militias took turns spelling the town guard manning those sections of the walls—such as the river wall—not likely to be targeted for a direct attack. Still, Charlotte felt safer than at any time since her marriage, and not a single nightmare about Gruyard had plagued her since she had first picked up a gun and taken her place on the walls.

"*Alles in Ordnung?*" Charlotte turned her head at the question and looked at the officer coming along the wall. The hood covered most of his face, but judging from the rain-dripping reddish goatee it was General Melchior von Hatzfeldt, who had been given the command of the town.

"Yes, Herr General. Nothing has been seen moving on the river all morning."

"Your accent sounds southern. Have you been in Bonn for long?" Melchior von Hatzfeldt put his foot up on the cannon wheel beside Charlotte and rested his arms on his knee.

"Just a few months."

"And already you are willing to fight for this town?"

"I have a baby son here, Herr General, and I am most certainly willing to fight. Fighting is good." Charlotte patted the gun she was leaning against her leg to keep it out of the rain.

"I see." Charlotte could hear the amusement in the man's voice and frowned at him as he continued. "After having spent more than half my life as a soldier, I'd rather say fighting is sometimes necessary. I'd also say that it should not be necessary for a young mother to risk her life standing behind a gun on a parapet." A bit of steel crept into the general's voice. "I will not order you to leave the militias, but I cannot approve of this new American fashion for female soldiers."

"No." Charlotte looked across the gray rain-dotted river towards Berg, which—God willing—her son would someday rule. "I refuse to hide behind my own skirts. Fighting might get your body killed, but not being allowed to fight may destroy your mind and soul. And as for female soldiers?" She turned her head, and smiled bitterly at the handsome man beside her. "With all respect, Herr General, get used to it. A gun is more effective than a frying pan, and the Americans have proved that with training women can fight just as well as men."

"Hmhf!" General von Hatzfeldt pushed back his hat, and smiled back at her. "Certainly, some of the most competent people

I know are women." He hesitated a moment. "You seem quite passionate about this. Were you caught in a battle yourself?"

"Sort of. Just not one where guns were the main weapons. I think I'll prefer guns."

"You think so? I find myself hating them more and more."

"But . . . But you're a general! A famous one!" Charlotte nearly dropped her gun.

General von Hatzfeldt shrugged and looked across the river. "A general might do less actual combat himself, but it's still the same. The blood and the gore. Seeing men's brains splattered all over from a bullet hitting their head. I suppose that's why I so much dislike seeing a woman holding a gun. I'd like to believe there exists something clean and perfumed, and untouched by the gore."

"Untouched!" Charlotte spun on her heel to face the man beside her. "Untouched! A pawn. Moved by anybody's will but her own. Bended, broken, used in other people's schemes and deals." She stopped with a gasp, frightened by her sudden loss of control, and feeling the hot tears mingling with the cold rain on her face.

"I see." The general reached out to touch Charlotte's chin with a finger, his wet leather glove only smearing the moisture. "I'm sorry for your pain, my lady, but while a gun might seem to me an odd bandage for your wounds, I do wish you ease from it." He smiled sadly, bowed and left to continue along the wall, while Charlotte spent the rest of her watch staring across the river and into the past.

# Chapter 16

*Magdeburg, House of Hessen*
*September 30, 1634*

### Magdeburg News, 30 September 1634

*Newly Arrived in Our City is a Delegation from the Free City of Cologne. As the Honored Reader Might Know, Rumors of Military Movements and Civil Unrest along the Middle Rhine have Reached Us following the Death of Duke Wolfgang von Neuburg to Jülich-Berg and His Heir. The Leader of the Cologne Delegation is the Late Duke Wolfgang's Cousin and Brother-in-Law, Count Palatine Friedrich von Zweibrücken, who has newly succeeded His Late Father Johann II, as Head of the Neuburg Family. Also in the Delegation is found Princess Maria Maximiliane of Bavaria, Councillor...*

Elisabeth von Schwarzenfels frowned at the newspaper she was reading, and put it aside. There was something important about this, and she wanted to discuss it with Abbess Dorothea of Quedlinburg when she arrived. Elisabeth looked around the so-called little drawing room and smiled a little. Cousin Amalie—in no way slowed down by her tenth pregnancy—had barely moved into her brand new house when Elisabeth and Maria arrived, but of course the rooms needed for entertainment and political gatherings had been finished even before the final flooring had been put down in the servants' quarters. The house was situated between the Governmental Palace and the new House of Wettin built by her equally pregnant friend, Eleonore. Eleonore had moved to Magdeburg with her two youngest sisters, Johanna and Eva, when her husband, Wilhelm Wettin, had decided to abdicate as duke of Saxe-Weimar and run for prime minister in the first general democratic election in the USE. Wettin spent most of his time at the palace, but Eleonore enjoyed entertaining in her own house, and when Elisabeth and Maria arrived, the four young girls had quickly formed the core of the abbess's political school and took turns hosting the afternoon gatherings in either of the two houses.

Today the gathering was to be in the House of Hessen, and Maria had already moved to stand under the chandelier in the middle of the room so she could greet the visitors with as much light shining on her blond hair as possible. Elisabeth smiled wryly at her sister; Maria was the youngest and prettiest of the five Schwarzenfels daughters, and no one—least of all her one year older sister—believed she had come to Magdeburg to learn about politics. Not that Maria was stupid; she was just spoiled rotten and not really interested in anything except her own desires. If there was something Maria wanted, she could in fact be extremely clever about getting it. And at seventeen what she wanted was a richer and more powerful husband than their oldest sister's.

At the sound of voices from the entrance hall Elisabeth rose from her seat by the window and went to stand beside her sister.

"For Heaven's sake, Litsa, go wash your hands," Maria hissed as they went forward to greet the abbess.

Elisabeth looked at her dirty fingers, and smiled at the abbess. "If ink from books doesn't smudge the reader, why does a newspaper?"

"I truly don't know my dear, but give me a kiss instead." The abbess offered her cheek to Elisabeth, who kissed the soft skin and enjoyed the familiar fragrance of oranges and spices that always seemed to surround the abbess.

"You always get dirty, Litsa, but at least that dull dress of yours doesn't show the stains." Maria cast a superior look at her sister and smoothed the sleeves of her own new pale blue velvet gown.

"Nonsense, Maria, Litsa's gown is according to the latest fashion in the *Simplicissimus Magazine*, while all that lace you are wearing makes you look rather old hat." Johanna, who had entered the room at the abbess's heels, came quickly to the defense of her friend, while Elisabeth just shrugged. She knew how easily she could get dirty or torn, even while sitting quietly on a chair, and had chosen the plain brown wool just so the wear and tear wouldn't show easily.

Johanna had been Elisabeth's best friend while they were both staying at the abbess's school in Quedlinburg, and now that they were living next door to each other, they had soon fallen in to their old habit of doing everything together. Not that they were all that much alike, Elisabeth thought as she went to get a damp towel from the tea table. Sure, their circumstances were very much alike; same past as second youngest daughters of families of almost the same class, same present as a younger relative of one of Magdeburg's most important political hostesses, and same rather limited future of either marriage or the Church. But where Elisabeth liked to just sit quietly and think things over, the lively Johanna enjoyed the hustle and bustle of the Magdeburg social-political life to the fullest.

Another difference was that where Elisabeth's cousin Amalie had played an active role in furthering Hesse's political goals from the day of their marriage, Johanna's sister, Eleonore, preferred to support her husband only as a hostess, and by cultivating her very large number of friends and social connections. The two houses of Wettin and Hessen formed the hub around which the social-political life in Magdeburg turned, but where Amalie's gatherings and conversations were first, last and always centered on politics, Eleonore liked to fill her house with guests likely to be amusing, original and knowledgeable about art and culture. This meant that Johanna met by far the most entertaining people, but Elisabeth had by far the best idea about what was actually going on behind the official political scene. And that was what made her worry about that newspaper!

"Mother Dorothea, do you know who is actually writing the newspapers?" Elisabeth asked while passing the cups of Chinese tea around to the seated ladies.

"Really, Litsa, sometimes you sound as if you have spent your entire life in rural seclusion in Schwarzenfels." Johanna frowned at her friend sitting in the light from the beveled window. "You must have noticed those men with pens and papers in their hands, hanging around Hans Richter Square, asking questions of the people leaving the palace. They are writing down the news."

Elisabeth shook her head and smiled at her old friend. Johanna's quickness rarely gave her the time to look for any deeper meaning, until somebody—usually Elisabeth—made her realize she was missing something. Also, Johanna's habit of answering questions not directed to her had always irritated the abbess, who now gave a firm rebuke while setting down her cup. "Mind your manners, my dear Anchen. You are correct, but as always a little too hasty. Litsa asked the question to me, and presumably for a reason. Please, elaborate your question, dear Litsa."

"In Quedlinburg," Elisabeth spoke carefully, wanting to put her thoughts very precisely into words, "you very strongly emphasized the importance of understanding politics. And aside from shoving family unity behind the new province of Hesse-Kassel, the reason our parents agreed to let Maria and me come here to stay with Cousin Amalie this winter was your argument: that the coming of the Americans had changed politics so much that we needed new lessons to understand what was now going on. But last night Tante Anna Marie talked with Cousin Amalie about how the Committee of Correspondence was using newspapers to spread propaganda pretending to be factual news. And this paper I read just before you arrived called Friedrich von Zweibrücken the 'head of the Neuburg family' and Sister Maximiliane of the Wartenbergs a Bavarian Princess."

At her words various giggles and laughter erupted at the table, and even the abbess had to smile; the tante was the abbess's harridan of a stepmother, Anna Marie von Neuburg. And since the Neuburg family had originally split off from the Zweibrückens, that statement was tantamount to calling the Neuburg family extinct. To make matters worse, the death of Anna Marie's brother, the late and otherwise unlamented Duke Wolfgang of Jülich-Berg, actually had brought their family to the brink of extinction, and the old lady was well known to be like a bear with a sore tooth on the subject. The abbess took a moment to gain control of her visible amusement before answering. "Well, everybody knows that dear Maxie does not hold her Bavarian ducal relatives in the highest of esteem at the moment, but young Zweibrücken might in fact end up with considerably more influence than he has at the moment. Though not—I expect—within the Neuburg family. But you were saying, Litsa?"

"That that's the point." Elisabeth became eager. "Everybody does not know. If those men on the Square are the ones writing the news, and they do not know who people are, then the news will end up false even if they want to write them true. And people read the news. Not just those people who do know what is going on, but all people. Does that not mean that newspapers are now a part of politics?"

"Litsa, who cares?" Maria looked up from buffing her nails on her gown and shrugged. "Those who need to know will know. I'm much more interested in this Friedrich von Zweibrücken. Is he in line for Berg? It would be so nice to marry somebody with land near our dear sister Katharina in Birstein."

"No, Ria, Litsa is right." Johanna scowled at the younger girl. "The very point of this election is that everybody is voting, so correct information is important. And you need extra lessons in geography: Berg is not near Birstein."

"Well, it's west from home!"

"So are the Americas!"

"Children!" At the word from the abbess the two girls subsided and sat down again. "Elisabeth and Johanna are right about the importance of correct public information. It used to be a minor matter, but with more and more power moving from the old families to the common people it is a problem—and becoming more so. Litsa, do come with me when I go visit Maxie tomorrow. She did arrive with young Zweibrücken yesterday, and she is staying with one of her cousins. I had a long letter from her less than a month ago and she mentioned that a friend of hers was connected to the *Simplicissimus Magazine*; she can help you find more information about the Origin of News."

"Anchen, you too should meet Maxie. Maria..." The abbess stopped, sighed and continued in a very patient voice, "the last duke of Jülich-Berg-Kleve died insane and childless, and his lands were divided between his four sisters with the major portions going to the two oldest. The heir to the eldest sister—and thus the lands of Jülich and Berg—is the rumored new-born baby of the late Duke Wolfgang of Neuburg and his second wife, young Zweibrücken's sister Katharine Charlotte. Charlotte and her baby are presently guests—or prisoners—of Maxie's uncle, Archbishop Ferdinand of Cologne. The Republic of Essen is laying claim on part of Berg by right of conquest after Duke Wolfgang's attack on them in June, but Jülich and the rest of Berg legally belong to the baby. If the baby dies, the usual heirs would have been Wolfgang's two brothers, but Johann von Hilpoltstein's children keep dying within a year, and August von Sulzback's widow, Countess Hedwig of Holstein-Gottorp, has made it quite clear that she wants nothing to do with this inheritance mess. Hedwig is a very sensible woman, and claiming those torn and disputed lands on behalf of a twelve-year-old sickly boy would only lead to trouble."

Maria's dimpled cheeks had gone very red during the abbess's careful explanation; as well they should, in Elisabeth's opinion. That entire problematic heritage had been the center of any number of conflicts and intrigues for all their lives, and while not everyone needed the political acumen of the abbess—or Cousin Amalie—neither could Ria afford to be that ignorant. Still, she was very young for her age, and—to draw the abbess's attention from her sister—Elisabeth asked: "But how about Tante Anna Marie? Could she not make a claim?"

The abbess frowned at the thought of her stepmother, and answered in a softer voice. "Tante Anna Marie could indeed make a claim on behalf of my half-brother, Johann Philipp von Saxe-Altenburg. But little Elisabeth Sophia is his only child—in fact after the Muensterberg-Oels family was recently killed in Bohemia she is Anna Marie's only grandchild—so they might choose to stay out of it too."

"But not wanting land?" Johanna interrupted, now frowning and obviously getting interested in the problem. "Countess Hedwig has been to talk with Eleonore and Wettin about this, and since her son is so young and still weak after the pox that killed his father and siblings, I can see the point in preferring to gain the emperor's favor by leaving the matter in his hands. But Hilpoltstein might still get a living heir, and surely Tante Anna Marie would want those lands even if she was the last Neuburg alive—and on her death-bed as well. The inheritance cannot be totally worthless."

"Yes, Anchen," said the abbess seriously, "it's not worthless. Northern Jülich is a fertile area, and Berg's location by the Rhine makes it important, but both areas are largely Catholic, they are far from secure USE borders, and they are so drained of everything by Wolfgang's mismanagement these last few years that you would need to spend a fortune securing and holding them. Also, the changing political structure—with the constitution replacing so many of the old ways—makes the title to more land of much less importance than making what you already have productive and well administered." The abbess hesitated a moment. "This subject is extremely sensitive right now. While the emperor was just the king of Sweden, he needed not concern himself overly much about how his allies managed their land. But now those areas have become his direct power base, and lands in the hands of supporters who cannot manage what they have are going to be almost as dangerous as lands in the hands of opponents. And so—as Hedwig has already realized—admitting your limits, and leaving the fate of an area in the hands of the emperor is a very sure way to gain you favor with him." The abbess smiled at Johanna and Eva. "Your brother-in-law, Wettin, is a prime example of the value of political favor over title to land. And while my stepmother might not have realized this, I'm quite certain my half-brother has."

"Do you think Zweibrücken is here on behalf of his sister and nephew, Mother Dorothea?" asked Elisabeth. "Or on his own behalf? I think I remember that he too is heir to Johann the Insane."

"He is, dear Litsa." The abbess nodded approvingly at Elisabeth. "Young Zweibrücken is heir to the third sister, and the heirs to the second sister are the Brandenburg family." The abbess turned grim. "And after the recent unpleasantness—I trust you have all heard of that—they are not in a position to lay claim on Berg or anything else.

"I do not know young Zweibrücken's plans," the abbess continued, "and there is said to be a rather odd recent codicil to Charlotte's marriage contract, but if Charlotte's baby dies, her brother could put forth a claim on behalf of the Zweibrücken family, not only to Neuburg's areas of Jülich and Berg, but also to Brandenburg's areas from the second sister. Hilpoltstein, Hedwig, Tante Anna Marie, and my half-brother could all challenge that claim, but with no young, strong male to build up the land and secure the border, their claims might annoy the emperor. Also, young Zweibrücken's uncle is married to the emperor's oldest sister

Princess Katharina of Sweden and their son is second in line for the imperial throne after Princess Kristina. In the American world he became the king of Sweden after she abdicated."

The abbess frowned and shook her head. "Never mind that. Young Zweibrücken is far from a nobody, but whether or not he can gain the emperor's support for whatever he wants, will depend entirely upon what kind of man he proves himself to be. He is only eighteen, a year older than you, Maria, but a message last week from the Americans in Mainz told us that he comes as head of a delegation from Cologne. That town has now broken completely with Archbishop Ferdinand and is seeking membership of the USE. They are probably only applying to stop Hesse from besieging the town, but still: if Zweibrücken brings Cologne into the USE," the abbess spread her hands and smiled, "with his combination of legal claims, royal connection and political benefits, he could end up with Berg and perhaps other parts of those disputed areas."

"Especially since his own lands are on the French border." Eva sat with her back to the window. Like Maria she was the youngest of her family, but rather than being vain and slightly spoiled, Eva was quiet and bookish, and never said very much. When asked, she joked that she never had the chance to speak because Johanna always said it first, but in Elisabeth's opinion the main reason was that an attack of pox had left Eva's face scarred. As a result, she was usually reticent, at least in public.

"Ah, I did wonder if any of you would think that far ahead," the abbess's eyes twinkled with approval. Elisabeth knew that the abbess considered Eva one of her most intelligent students and had tried to talk the brainy young hermit into a life as a nun. Eva, however, would not even consider it, claiming that she had no vocation. Still, what other possibilities were there for an intelligent noble woman with no marriage prospects? Elisabeth didn't have a vocation either, but surely a life like the abbess's would be better than that mess of a life their sister Katharina was living in Birstein. "Yes, France is a problem that must be watched most carefully," the abbess continued, "and Zweibrücken as an ally—or even a part of USE—would be a major benefit. Just permission for a garrison to keep an eye on Trier would probably be worth making young Zweibrücken his nephew's guardian. But enough about politics for now; would anybody care for a game of cards?"

# Chapter 17

*Bonn, Eigenhaus House*
*October 1, 1634,*

"It looks as if he has gotten used to the smell of gun oil."

Charlotte looked up from her nursing son and smiled at Frau Benedicte sitting at her table. "Yes, he just wrinkled his nose for a few days if I didn't wash between taking off my kyras and feeding him, but now he doesn't seem to notice. I suppose you can get used to just about anything."

"And how about you, my dear? This is a life quite different from the one you were brought up to live."

"Yes," Charlotte looked down at her nursing son, "but not necessarily one that's worse. I was very young when I married, and not just in years. I had been taught to cope with running a household, and warned against getting too attached to a baby before it had survived those first dangerous years. That I could not keep my distance to my first little baby, and don't think I'll ever be able to just leave a child to my servants, is another matter, but Wolfgang's deterioration..." Charlotte sighed and leaned back against the hard back of the chair. "I still don't understand what happened. Wolfgang was a good man once."

"You call it deterioration. Could it be nothing more than old age? He was more than three times your age."

"It didn't seem like old age to me. One of my mother's old

129

friends became more and more odd and forgetful as she grew old, but Wolfgang..." Charlotte sat up and looked at the older woman. "When Maxie—that's Archbishop Ferdinand's cousin—visited me in Düsseldorf, she told me about some American theories about too many changes and the kind of pressure they could put on people's minds. I suppose that could be what happened to Wolfgang. In a way I suppose that was what Felix Gruyard did to me: putting so much pressure on my mind that I went irrational and could not think straight. It was in a different way from Wolfgang, but perhaps it really was the same."

"Could be, my dear. Women trying to take care of too many children—and especially if one is a baby cutting a tooth and preventing her from sleeping—can certainly do things they would never have done in their right mind."

"Do you think it's wrong for me to like guns? Or perhaps a sign of mental disorder?" Charlotte leaned back again and thought about her conversation with General von Hatzfeldt.

"No, I think being able to defend yourself and your baby is very necessary for you if you are to regain your peace of mind. Seeking safety from a protector either in the shape of your brother or a new husband might be the more ordinary solution for a young girl, but you are turning out to be an unusually strong and capable young woman. One might always need the support of God, but there is nothing whatsoever wrong with wanting to be able to do for yourself rather than rely on other people."

"I suppose not. And I'm not totally opposed to a new marriage, I just..." Charlotte suddenly sat up in anger, causing her baby to let go of her breast and protest. "And I also suppose that was why the archbishop set Gruyard on me—to make me feel so helpless that I would be willing to seek his protection. I want to kill Gruyard—and the archbishop too—and Turning the Other Cheek Be Damned." Charlotte kept her voice soft and gently rocked the baby.

"Lotti, my dear, I think you've gotten into bad company in my militias."

Charlotte looked at the smiling older woman over the baby dropping off to sleep, and felt her face split into a broad grin. "Yes, and isn't it nice?"

## Bonn, the Guardhouse

"You have mail," said Commander Wickradt entering the guard-house.

"Another diatribe from the archbishop?" Melchior looked up from the papers he was reading.

"No, it's actually a letter from your sister."

"What?"

"Yes, young Jakob Eigenhaus, Frau Benedicte's youngest son, brought it to me a few moments ago, along with the information he has gathered from their contacts along the river." Wickradt removed his helmet and sat down. "The cannons you have been expecting from Frankfurt landed at Godesberg this morning. They are on their way here, and even with the soggy ground they should arrive at the Hessian bastions the day after tomorrow. The Hessian cavalry have moved their main camp from Vessel-ing to Bruhl, and the road to Cologne is now completely closed. The archbishop's cavalry tried to gather for an attack while the Hessians were moving, but barely got started before they were scattered. There are now small mounted skirmishes all over the areas between Bonn and Cologne. The main Hessian army has come upriver from Düsseldorf—also as you expected. They have set up a camp at Leverkusen, and have encircled Cologne. It sounds as if they have brought along some artillery too, so the cannons from Frankfurt might have been extras borrowed from the Swedes. The new cannons can hit a lot harder and reach a lot farther than the walls were built to cope with, so the Coun-cil of Cologne expects the casualties to get really bad once the cannons start. They are trying to negotiate, but the first attempts didn't turn out well."

"Hesse is almost certainly seriously annoyed about the attempt to join the USE by treaty, instead of letting him make a conquest."

"Most royally pissed according to the scuttlebutt." Wickradt leaned back and tried to stretch his back despite his armor. "One bit of good news is that the Hessians are finding it extremely difficult to blockade a river as wide as the Rhine against those willing to sail at night; so Jakob and his friends expect to be able to get information in and out for quite a while yet. Oh, and both Landgrave Wilhelm and General von Uslar are around."

"Please give Jakob Eigenhaus my thanks, and offer rewards for information." Melchior cut off the seal from the thick letter, and started reading. "Karl Mittelfeld should have been here at least a week ago, so I'll give ten thalers to those helping the CoC contacts back inside the walls. Hmm! Lucie writes that the Council of Cologne managed to get two delegations for the USE out of Cologne before the Hessians closed them in; the official one going north directly for Magdeburg by way of Hannover with Count Palatine Friedrich von Zweibrücken in nominal charge, the other trying for Mainz with my brother, Hermann, as leader. It is a bit early to expect anything to have come back from Magdeburg, but Hermann might have joined up with Karl."

"Your brother is a good choice for a negotiator, but Zweibrücken? A Kleve? Should I know him?" Wickradt poured himself a glass of beer, and stretched his legs. The looting had stopped after the first two hangings, and the town was as calm as anyone could expect. Still, the old man obviously worried too much to rest, and had been patroling the walls and streets almost round the clock. Melchior guessed Wickradt would calm down once the attack actually started, but for now he kept searching for more preparations to make.

"Personally, no. Friedrich is a very young man, only eighteen, and according to Lucie eager to become a hero by saving the rich town of Cologne and bringing it into the United States. What is actually important about him is that his mother is a Simmern, and that his father's brother is the husband of Princess Katharina of Sweden. This makes him a relative of both Hesse's wife, Amalie, and of Gustavus Adolphus, not to mention Saxony, Bavaria and just about everybody else of importance."

"I see. And he'll be traveling through land he might claim through his grandmother. Especially if he can make a name for himself, and with Bavaria and Brandenburg out of the picture. What was he doing in Cologne?"

"Looking for his sister, Charlotte, who is the missing widow of Jülich-Berg. He started by contacting Maxie, that's Sister Maximiliane von Wartenberg, who is staying at Hatzfeldt House. I expect she and Hermann put the notion of representing Cologne into his head." Melchior kept reading. "And Maxie has gone along to Magdeburg too. And listen, this is very interesting: 'Our dear brother, Franz, along with Maxie's brother, Bishop Franz Wilhelm of Minden, and Archbishop Anselm von Wambold of Mainz, are all said to have left Archbishop Ferdinand, and returned to their dioceses. I'm not sure how or why, but Archbishop Ferdinand is supposed to have killed Abbot Schweinsberg of Fulda. And Melchior, whatever is behind those rumors of the archbishop having Franz impersonating you? I've practically had to sit on Maxie to keep her from hunting down her archbishopally cousin to demand an explanation.' The rest is just family news."

"Sounds like the rats are deserting the sinking ship—no offense to your brother—but I think we can just about ignore the archbishop from now on." Wickradt rubbed his eyes and looked up at the map on the wall. "Mainz may be reached in a week even without a horse, but Magdeburg cannot be reached in less than two weeks no matter how fast you ride. I'm not sure we can hold off Hesse for that long."

"No, but Father Johannes told me the Americans in Mainz have ways of sending news around very, very fast, and even if Bonn surrenders, it'll take Hesse two more days getting his cannons past Bonn to Cologne. So, let us think about stalling."

# Chapter 18

*Magdeburg*
*October 1, 1634*

"Mother Dorothea, did you know uncle Hesse intended to attack Cologne? Is he acting on the emperor's behalf?" Elisabeth turned her head to look at the abbess and managed to step with both feet into a big puddle of dirty water. The paving was fairly good on the streets around the palace but the drainage couldn't quite handle the recent heavy rain.

"No, I didn't know. And officially the campaign is entirely Hesse's own idea, and no one knew his plans. Unofficially?" The abbess waved at the two following footmen to carry her and the two girls across the puddle, and continued on the other side. "Unofficially, somebody might have known or guessed why the Hessian army went west this summer. It is only natural for Hesse and Amalie to be concerned about the future prominence of their new province. Those maps from the Americans' future show Kassel as the only major town in a not very important area. At the moment Hesse's prominence depends on political favors, but to ensure that the prominence continues they need a future important industrial area or trading center. And Cologne is the only target that is not guaranteed to land them in more trouble than they can handle. Cologne is not a natural expansion of Hessen, but—as a von Hanau—Amalie understands the importance of the Rhine. And that the importance of Cologne will only increase when American ships increase the ocean trade."

"Huh! I mean: why that? Cologne doesn't produce that much, and it is not on a coast." Now it was Johanna's turn to get her feet wet. "We really should have borrowed the carriage."

"It's only three streets, my dear, and we have all been sitting around too much. The Americans are the healthiest people I have ever seen, and all their medical books emphasize the importance of movement and fresh air." The abbess stopped and sniffed. "Fresher outside towns, of course, but at least the cold keeps the malodor down. And as for your question: small ocean ships may travel up the Rhine as far inland as Cologne, but from there they must reload to boats, barges or wagons. And Cologne gets its share of every load. Here's Maximilienne's house now."

Much to the annoyance of his brother Wilhelm the Holy, Duke of Bavaria, the late Archbishop Ernst of Cologne had fathered a number of illegitimate children, and legitimized four of them. Maximilienne, his second daughter with his long-time mistress Magdalena Possinger, had married the second son of one of her father's French advisers, but left him after one too many quarrels with her Spanish mother-in-law. It wasn't that Maximilienne objected to praying for her father's salvation, but he had been a grown man who presumably knew what he did. She felt no obligation to spend all her days and half her nights on her knees in the small dank chapel on the family estate. So after an especially acrimonious evening she had packed up her belongings, dowry and children, and left. She took along two highly gifted silversmith brothers from her husband's estate, and went to Aachen to set up a workshop soon famous for its delicate silver filigree objects. An energetic woman in her late thirties, she had gone first to Grantville to see what new methods the Americans had to teach, and then on to Magdeburg to create jewelry for the nobs in what looked to become the capital of the new leading area in Europe.

Maximilienne had bought a new well-built house in the business district nearest the palace and paid the owner—a cloth merchant—more than market-price to vacate the prime location. Now the shop filled the entire ground floor of the front house, and she lived with her two daughters and youngest son in the spacious rooms above.

Not as opulent as the houses of Wettin and Hessen—Elisabeth looked around while two maids gathered the short, fur-trimmed cloaks from the visitors—but with everything in good taste and quality. Neither Mistress Maximilienne nor Maxie were apparently the kind to sit idly waiting for visitors, but by the time the abbess and the two girls were seated in the inglenook to warm their feet at the fire, their hostess and her cousin arrived from other parts of the house, and conversation took off at full speed immediately.

Once the initial chatter of introductions, inquiries regarding family and friends, and exchange of news and rumors from the war was over, the abbess turned to her old friend, near contemporary and sometimes colleague, and asked, "Dear Maxie, you wrote to me—several times—about Father Johannes the painter, and mentioned a connection to the *Simplicissimus Magazine*. Litsa here is interested in the who's and how's of writing news; can you help her?"

"Father Johannes is here in Magdeburg." Maxie smirked. "He is heavily involved with the new porcelain manufacturing, but I expect he is also sending news to his nephew, who is the publisher of the magazine."

"Maxie!" the abbess interrupted, frowning. "I know that smirk of yours. Didn't you decide to devote yourself to enabling women to enter seclusion and spend their lives in prayer and contemplation? When we last met three years ago you even planned to enter seclusion yourself."

"I did and I did." Maxie's smile turned bitter and her eyes briefly showed her fury. "That my relatives were reluctant to lose my skills as a nurse and hospital leader, and therefore never gave me much support was one thing, but that they sent me to nurse cousin Ferdinand in Cologne and then used my absence to sabotage the support I'd found elsewhere was too much. I'm never going back to München! It'll be years—no, probably decades!—before my temper has cooled enough to let me enter any kind of contemplation."

"And in the meantime you're planning to scandalize your family as much as possible? You know, dear Maxie, converting to Lutheranism would probably be more effective—not to mention dignified—than following in the footsteps of your male prelate relatives."

"I didn't know either of them ever lived in sin with a Jesuit priest, dear Dotty." Maxie went back to grinning broadly at the abbess, who gave an irritated wave in answer. "But that's not really what and why I'm doing it." Her smile faded a little. "We both know my temper and that my fury is a mortal sin. But when I'm with Father Johannes I'm not angry. I'm just happy, and my family's betrayal doesn't really seem so important."

"Hmpf! I realize you have grown most fond of this priestly painter, and heaven knows I'm not opposed to clerical marriages, but you are both Catholics and your habit of forming the most unsuitable alliances has been an embarrassment to your friends—never mind your family—for far too long. It's becoming undignified. It really is time you settled down and stopped upsetting everybody."

"But I *am* planning to settle down." Maxie kept smiling. "My archbishop cousin paid me quite handsomely for my nursing, and I'm planning to buy a house and settle down right here with Father Johannes, Lucie von Hatzfeldt and Lucie's late husband's bastard children. Father Johannes is quite serious about his faith, and probably isn't going to abandon it to marry either of us." She shrugged. "But he isn't totally opposed to getting seduced, and everybody needs something to confess. I'm not likely to get a bastard at my age, and even if I do that wouldn't be so bad." She accepted an enameled tankard of warm spiced wine from the maid and raised it in a smiling salute to her hostess before drinking.

"Maxie!" The abbess shook her head before drinking, and Elisabeth pretended to cough to keep from laughing at Maxie's audacity. The abbess couldn't even protest or continue this line of conversation without being rude toward their hostess. Besides, the abbess had told the two girls that her dear friend had never seemed quite happy running that cloister in Münich, and she certainly seemed happy now.

Maxie now turned her infectious smile on Elisabeth. "I'll introduce you to Father Johannes, so he can tell you more, but I do know that monthly magazines like *Simplicissimus* buy both news and written articles from a large number of people. A weekly or biweekly newspaper is different. I'm not sure exactly how, except that they employ people to seek out and write down enough news to fill every number of the newspaper."

"Thank you, Sister Maximiliane." Elisabeth smiled and nodded. "And so: to a newspaper it's probably more important to find enough interesting news for an issue than it is to make certain that the person writing it knows what he is talking about."

"Exactly. I suppose you have seen the recent edition of *Magdeburg News*?" Maxie laughed. "I would actually gladly forgive them their mistake about me, if I could only have seen Anna Marie's face when she read the part about darling young Zweibrücken being the head of her family."

"Maxie! Not Zweibrücken too. He could be your son." The abbess spilled wine on her embroidered dress front and started rubbing it with a handkerchief, while a nod from her hostess sent the maid standing by the door hurrying to assist.

"Of course not, Dotty. He is just a darling boy: handsome, earnest, wanting to be a hero and save the world. He was in Verona on his Grand Tour when his father suddenly died, and when he hurried home, it was to hear the news of his sister's capture by my mad cousin the archbishop."

"H-how tragic." Johanna had always been the lively one, both in her family and at school, but Maxie seemed to leave her almost stunned with delighted awe.

"Well, he absolutely despised his father for marrying Charlotte off to old Duke Wolfgang, and rushing to his sister's aid gave the young Sir Knight all the excuse for adventure a young man could want."

"I saw the brief message the Americans sent from Mainz"—the abbess accepted a damp cloth brought by a second maid—"saying that Cologne and Bonn have broken with your cousin and want to join the USE, but are under attack from Hesse. Amalie confirmed the attack, and said that it was to free Charlotte and her baby, and to establish a safe western border for the USE. She also claimed that Cologne's petition for membership was just a plot to gain time for the archbishop's Bavarian relatives to come to his aid. Prime Minister Stearns and his supporters wanted to stop Hesse immediately, and the House of Lords was split down the middle until the emperor finally cut the knot and ordered Hesse to stop, but not withdraw his troops until the matter was settled. Hesse doesn't have a radio with him, so the order probably hasn't reached him yet, but should do so soon. No one is certain if Hesse attacked with or without the emperor's knowledge, and is in or out of the emperor's favor. Certainly, Hesse stepped on a lot of toes this summer, when he tried to become both guardian and heir to Charlotte's child, but that *was* a possible solution to the problem at the time—and Hesse is one of the emperor's oldest supporters. So, start at the beginning, Maxie, and tell me what you know."

Maxie smiled. "As far as I know, the emperor, or at least somebody high in the government, knew Hesse wanted to take his regiments towards Berg and Cologne this spring, but not the details. After running around all summer chasing shadows, Hesse sent his cavalry down the Sieg Valley last month to try to take Bonn. That's where Charlotte and her baby were rumored to be. But he had to move his infantry and artillery by way of Düsseldorf, getting De Geer's permission in return for promising undisputed annexation of Western Mark and Kleve."

"What!" The abbess nearly spilled her second serving of wine too. "Are you asking me to believe that Hesse and Amalie agreed to make a deal that involved promising the emperor's land to somebody else?"

"Lucie von Hatzfeldt's youngest brother Hermann has a lot of contacts in Essen, and that's what he discovered just before he left for Mainz, and we went here to Magdeburg." Maxie shrugged. "Hesse and De Geer are both in good favor with the emperor, and if they can bring him Jülich, Berg and Cologne, he might well let them keep those lands, and add Mark and Kleve too. And while Essen's present claim on Kleve might be based on a rather suspect 'public vote' . . ."

She shrugged again. "Actually it isn't—or wasn't—such a bad plan. Only, when Hesse arrived at Bonn, Charlotte and her son had disappeared, and the two councils of Cologne and Bonn decided they'd rather join USE than get conquered. Before the sieges enclosed the towns, they managed to send out two delegations. Hermann von Hatzfeldt was in charge of the one heading for Mainz, and from what you tell he obviously managed to reach the Americans there. Zweibrücken had arrived in Cologne just before Hesse surrounded the town, and once he received word from some discreet friends that his sister and nephew were safe and sound beyond the archbishop's reach, the darling boy accepted leading the delegation here. He is to spend today with Axel Oxenstierna, but meet with the House of Lords tomorrow."

"But how about Charlotte and her baby? Where are they?" Johanna looked excited, and Elisabeth suspected her friend found this almost as good as those American novels. Zweibrücken had to be the hero, but then his sister could not be the heroine. Still, this was good.

"I've been told that they are still in Bonn, but my archbishop cousin believes them to have escaped into Berg, and wasted an awful lot of time and money searching for them before the siege. Lucie's older brother, General Melchior von Hatzfeldt, has taken command of Bonn's defenses, so they are as safe as anyone can be in that area. Hesse, I'm sure, doesn't know where they are." Maxie smiled. "But who's in town right now? Zweibrücken is to be introduced to the emperor tonight, and I'm invited to the soiree at the palace and need to plan my strategy. I assume you'll be willing to support Zweibrücken as his nephew's guardian, Dorothea, but what else is on your agenda, and who can we bully, bribe and blackmail for support?"

# Chapter 19

*Linz, Austria, The Scribe*
*October 1, 1634*

"My, my, look what the cat just dragged in." The lean dark-haired man threw the cards he was holding down on the scarred table and picked up his goblet. "Hansi, my dear, stop fondling Dannwitz's purse and find Lieutenant Peckerbun a mug of hot beer."

The other card players half-turned in their seats and looked at the mud-splashed young officer standing in the doorway. Despite the table littered with cards, dirty plates, bottles and smoking pipes, the room had suddenly taken on a decidedly businesslike air.

Lieutenant Simon Pettenburg gave a silent sigh, and handed the dispatch to his—hopefully temporary—commanding officer. Colonel Wolf von Wildenburger-Hatzfeldt was a good combat officer, but off the battlefield, the Wolf tended to spend his time drinking, gambling, wenching, and setting up elaborate jokes of a kind he really should be too old to find funny. Having his own name repeatedly changed in some ribald way hadn't really bothered Simon once he realized that the Wolf was always extremely correct and polite towards people he didn't like, but Simon's slight build and boyish face already made it difficult to get the respect due an officer, and the nicknames didn't help.

"Where's the general?" Captain von Dannwitz reached behind the Wolf to pull a stool around for Simon.

"In Bonn." Simon sat down and accepted the mug from the barmaid, while trying to ignore the breasts she pressed against his neck when leaning over to remove the empty jugs in the middle of the table. "Landgrave Wilhelm of Hesse-Kassel is besieging the town, but the general managed to get out letters before the town was closed off. This came through his brother in Mainz." Simon nodded towards the dispatch, which the Wolf was slitting open.

"And just where were you and Sergeant Mittelfeld?" Like the other men around the table Colonel Lorentz had known General Melchior von Hatzfeldt since serving with him in Wallenstein's campaigns several years ago, and hadn't liked their old friend and commander-in-chief going off with only the sergeant to guard his back and Simon to carry his messages.

"The sergeant took a tumble when his horse slipped. His thigh landed on a wooden spike and the wound festered. We got him to Frankfurt and the general paid for the new American medicine so the leg didn't rot, but the general ordered me to stay with the sergeant, and only continue when we both could travel."

Simon drank of the warm, spicy beer, and felt his body starting to thaw. It had been a cold two weeks' journey across Bavaria with soaking rain and temperatures close to freezing. He hadn't quite been able to avoid the fighting along the Danube, and considering the general chaos, he'd kept his armor on even at night. As a result the padded tunic he wore under everything else had never really dried, and he'd never really been warm.

"What's the situation in Bavaria?" The Wolf looked up from the dispatch with no sign of his previous lazy amusement.

"Bad, sir." Simon lifted his mug and looked at the barkeeper to signify that he wanted another serving. "The Protestant armies under Banér have taken Ingolstadt and are said to be in control of everything north of the Danube."

"Never mind Banér." Wolf leaned forward and fixed his full attention on Simon. "I want to know if Bavaria is passable or would we have to fight our way across it?"

"Perhaps you better tell us what's in the dispatch from the general, Wolf." Old Colonel Dehn met the Wolf's angry stare with calm. Dehn had been the officer usually given the overall command when the general had to leave the regiments, and while he had made it clear that he didn't mind the younger man being put in charge this time, everybody also knew that the Wolf would need his support for anything involving all the regiments.

"Are you challenging my authority, Dehn?" Wolf leaned back in his seat and picked up his goblet with his narrowed eyes still fixed on Dehn.

"Hmpf! Pretty words from somebody who usually thinks authority is a town up by the Baltic Sea." Dehn looked totally undisturbed by what Simon knew could easily lead to a duel. "What I'm saying is that you're excellent at scouting missions, not bad at tactics, but your big-scale strategies stink. So if you plan to take some of my men along on one of your harebrained escapades without a direct order from either the emperor or the general, I'll box your ears, m'boy."

The Wolf looked somewhat surprised at the words from the usually taciturn Dehn, then he threw back his head and roared with laughter with the other officers joining him only a moment later.

"Very well, old man. You win this one." Wolf smiled and reached across the table to hand Dehn the dispatch.

"Hm." Dehn quickly scanned the two handwritten pages. "So the general is cornered, has nothing with which to fight his way out, and will try stalling and negotiating. And the date?" He turned back to the first page. "Almost five weeks since he wrote it. When did you get this, Lieutenant?"

"The dispatch was almost two weeks from Bonn to Frankfurt, probably because it was brought to Mainz by the sergeant's cousin who had to row up the Rhine while playing hide and seek with the Hessians. After that I was more than a week in reaching Bavaria, as the shortest road is almost destroyed by the heavy rains, and finally another week across Bavaria from Regensburg." Simon looked around the table. He was the most experienced of the couriers in the six regiments under contract to General Melchior von Hatzfeldt, and while he didn't have the long-standing relationship with his superior officers that would permit dropping all formality, he also didn't want the general to lack the backup he needed because Simon wouldn't open his mouth for fear of overstepping his rank. "There'd be problems getting even a single regiment along the northern roads in time to be of any help for the general, but taking the Bavarian route might take even longer despite the better roads. It's bad there. Everybody is looking over their shoulders and putting up defenses, but it isn't Banér they are worried about."

"A peasant uprising?" Dehn frowned at Simon.

"No. The Ram was mentioned, but only in whispers." Simon swallowed and tried to gather his thoughts to explain what had bothered him. "Colonel Lorentz, you once told about the Inquisition gaining force in your home town, how everybody feared to gather or talk, and were watching their neighbors. It was more like that. My papers were checked several times during a single day rather than just when I wanted to enter a walled town for the night. It was also difficult to buy travel food even in inns, as if everybody were hoarding their stores. No one was really willing to talk to me, and what I managed to overhear indicated that strangers of any kind simply weren't welcome." Simon took a deep breath. "And that the people they were most worried about were those working for Duke Maximilian. The opinion seems to be that he's gone insane."

"Well, those rumors made it here as well." The Wolf looked up into the smoke curling about the blackened beams beneath the roof. "Before starting back towards Cologne in August Melchior told me that he couldn't take the regiments with him across Bavaria without a direct order from the emperor, and even then Maximilian might decide to take it as an attack. The old emperor was dying in Vienna, but Archduke Ferdinand gave my cousin plenipotentiary powers in making any deal and taking any action that would keep the middle Rhine in Catholic hands."

"Was that the exact wording?" Dannwitz pushed away his goblet, and waved away the maid.

"I didn't read it, but that was how Melchior phrased it."

"Hm. And no new orders from Vienna since the funeral." Dehn started rubbing his goblet with a fingertip, a sure sign that he was thinking and didn't like his own thoughts.

"Exactly." The Wolf started to grin. "And asking for new orders would add at least another couple of weeks. Any dispatches going on to Vienna, Lieutenant?"

"No, sir. Just the letter for you. Unless somebody else has traveled faster than me, Vienna is unaware of Hesse's attacking Bonn and Cologne. When the general left us in Frankfurt, he was only concerned with the problems created by Archbishop

Ferdinand of Cologne, and Hesse seemed fully occupied with conquering Berg."

"Legally the general would have the power to bring at least his two personal regiments to Cologne." Dannwitz, who had studied law before becoming a soldier, was now reading the dispatch. "And this part about stalling until reinforcements can arrive in a dispatch sent to Wolf could be taken as an order for him to get those reinforcements to the general as quickly as possible."

"I'm pretty certain the general expects Wolf to take this letter to Vienna to speed up the permission to bring the all or most of the regiments to Cologne." Dehn frowned at the Wolf. "Anything else would be quite contrary to the Melchior's way of operating."

"I completely agree." The Wolf looked at Dehn, still grinning. "But my cousin did put me in charge, and that's not the way I operate. And before you get your dander up, old man, remember that my cousin has known me all my life, and he did not write a direct order for me to do this or that."

"So," Wolf looked around the table, "we're leaving tomorrow morning with three regiments. Dehn, you take over as commander here. I'll lead Melchior's old regiment. Lorentz, you leave behind the newest recruits and those companies who failed to follow orders in Pisek. There'll be absolutely no room in this for laggards or those who put their comfort above getting things done. Dannwitz, your regiment is the smallest at the moment, so see if you can pad it a bit. Dehn might be willing to lend you some of his fastest riders, but Schierstedt and Mettecoven are not around to give permission. See what you can do, it need not be three full regiments, but I want the absolute best. We'll take no wagons, and only those noncombatants who can ride at least as well as the soldiers. Food and tents must be packed onto the spare horses. I don't intend for us to do any fighting until we reach the general, but I want us to reach the Rhine in little more than the time it took Pettenburg to get here. Pettenburg," Wolf stopped and looked at Simon as if measuring the inside of his skull, "I want you to take charge of our reconnaissance, and that'll be not just the couriers and scouts, but also our best saboteurs, spies, thieves and forgers. Talk with Allenberg about the permits and papers."

Simon swallowed and mumbled something he didn't know for sure was a "yes, sir" or an oath.

## South bank of the Danube between Vichtenstein and Passau, two days later

"And just how are you enjoying your first command?"

At the sound of Wolf's voice Simon looked up at the grinning man and wondered how much trouble he would get from giving the answer that first came to his mind. No, he was much too angry to give an honest answer, so instead he jumped to his feet, gave his most elegant bow and stood straight shouting: "Sir! Yes, sir! Everything as you ordered, sir!"

Wolf's jaw literally dropped for a moment, then he laughed out loud and clapped Simon on the shoulder. "As bad as that, boy?"

The two men looked down the hill at the camp being organized on the meadow around the rickety barn. The general's dispatch had given an estimate of the Hessian cavalry as two or three thousand, and Wolf had brought fewer than fifteen hundred, but there was just no way to get all the regiments to Bonn in time, and no one expected Wolf to try meeting the Hessians in open battle anyway. The men on the meadow represented the absolute maximum strike force the regiments could field in the least number of bodies. They were all veterans proven and trusted by their officers, all expert riders on well-trained horses, and all equipped with the best weapons to be had in the HRE. All—that is—except for half of Simon's little group of six persons now gathering around a campfire slightly removed from the rest.

Pettenburg's Specialists—as they were called in the files—had been handpicked by Wolf, and only Marsch, Lenz and Niederthal were to do the work General von Hatzfeldt would normally have assigned them to. They were—like Simon—couriers and scouts supposed to ride very fast horses behind and through enemy lines carrying messages and gathering information about troop movements. Occasionally that also meant fighting—and usually against rather bad odds—so they were also better than average with both saber and pistols. Of course slender, red-haired Marsch, who was the son of a very well-to-do locksmith, could also open any lock except the American ones, burly, swarthy Lenz, whose father owned a mine, was very good at setting off small precise explosions, and nondescript Niederthal, who never spoke of his background, had a padded crate filled with bottles and packets of

American chemicals. Still, they were all three fine fighting men, and Simon would have been proud of being made their leader.

Ferretlike Schaden, on the other hand, usually worked at curing the sick horses in Lorentz's regiment, and while he was really good at using any kind of knife, he was also well known for being unable to hit a barn with a musket at ten paces, and likely to do more damage to himself than his opponent with a sword. What he could do better than anyone else, was to sneak close to an enemy camp and silently remove any guards or other inconvenient persons. Not a skill often called for in the normal order of things, but being able to get that close to the enemy camps also meant getting really detailed information about their number, equipment and fighting morale.

Allenberg was a relative newcomer to the regiments, and normally the head quartermaster of Melchior von Hatzfeldt's old regiment. He had joined shortly before the last campaign, and had made no secret of his lack of fighting ability and experience, but he was—in addition to being able to squeeze all kinds of information out of papers and ledgers for the general—also quietly known to be able to produce a most amazing range of papers and permissions. The general presumably didn't know about Allenberg's little *nebengeschäft*, but the Wolf had absolutely no objection to getting over a difficult ground as lightly as possible, and Simon's talk with Allenberg had resulted in the finest set of forged papers Simon had ever seen. Simon rather liked the calm and solid looking forger, but Allenberg didn't socialize much, and usually went back to quarters after buying his round at any tavern.

Allenberg's assistant, "Rosy" Ross, on the other hand was usually the life and soul of any party. He was a fair and rather fragile looking Scot, who had all kind of outrageous stories about his background, but in Simon's opinion the one about running away from his strict parson father to become an actor sounded the most likely. Whether he had ever been the foremost player of female roles at the royal theater in London was a different matter, but he could in fact get away with impersonating a woman long enough to gather all kinds of information in a market, and had an almost uncanny ability to gain friends quickly in any tavern. What he could do in a fight no one had ever seen, but judging from the minimal training the general insisted on, it really wouldn't be much.

"The road north from Passau is no easier than the one you rode from Nürnberg to Regensburg." Wolf turned to look westward, squinting his eyes against the setting sun. "That leaves us with Deggendorf, Ingolstadt, Donauwörth, or Ulm. I want you to enter Passau tomorrow, while the rest of us cross the Inn, and see what information you can gather."

"Very well, sir. I'll take Niederthal and Rosy with me. We'll leave Rosy on his own, and go inquire about permission to set up a recruitment table at the Christmas Fair." Simon stated calmly.

"Recruiting at Christmas is rare." Wolf remarked "What'll be the excuse for not waiting until the hiring fair in spring?"

"Unsettled times. Farmers seeing the harvest cannot last until spring." Simon shrugged. "I'll think of something."

"While looking young, earnest and just a little naïve." Wolf laughed and slapped the younger man on the shoulder. "Carry on, boy, carry on."

# Chapter 20

"The last of the Hessian cannons are being moved into position, Frau Benedicte." Charlotte leaned her gun against the wooden panels in the hall, and removed her helmet. "All the rain has softened the ground, which is slowing them down, but the Town Guard I spoke to expected they would be ready to start bombarding us from all sides the day after tomorrow."

"I know, my dear. Commander Wickradt came by earlier today. But go remove your kyras, and spend a moment greeting your son. Then come join me and Irmgard. We need to make plans."

When Charlotte entered Frau Benedicte's private parlor, she found the two sisters looking at maps spread all over the biggest table.

"Good evening, my dear." Irmgard came smiling forward to hug Charlotte. "I took a look at your baby earlier. A very healthy boy."

"Yes, very." Charlotte smiled and hugged the friendly midwife back. "I wish I could have nursed him for longer, but my milk dried out after a few weeks. Fortunately Frau Siemens has milk to spare, as her little girl doesn't seem to need very much, so she can give him a little extra while I'm on the walls. But I went by the infirmary on my way back." Charlotte sat down in the chair, where she used to sit repairing the Eigenhaus linen, leaned back her head and sighed. "I never went to the hospital in Düsseldorf, where the wounded from Wolfgang's campaign were taken. They sometimes sent a request for this or that—mainly food and linen or money for medicine—but I just passed those on to my chatelaine. I never realized how bad it would be. How children would also be wounded, when cannons were firing at a town. I suppose you both know that the Mittelfeld household was among the first hit? That Karl's wife was killed immediately, and that two of their children died this afternoon?" She looked at the two older women, who nodded silently to her questions.

"Yes. There's only the oldest daughter and the baby left, and Karl isn't back from Mainz yet," said Irmgard. "That'll be some homecoming for my old friend."

"Knowing how busy you both are with the infirmary, I presume you didn't ask me to come here to discuss my little Bobo?"

"Well, only indirectly," said Frau Benedicte. "It looks as if neither von Hatzfeldt's regiments nor any orders from Gustavus Adolphus are going to be here in time to stop Hesse from attacking. We might be able to prevent him from taking the town before help arrives, but those walls weren't built with modern cannons in mind, so it's going to cost a lot of lives." Frau Benedicte looked straight at Charlotte. "You might be able to prevent that."

"How? Giving myself and my baby into his hands would keep only the two of us safe—or relatively so—but Hesse would still want Bonn. Or are you considering trying to trade us for a promise?"

"Not quite." Frau Benedicte answered seriously. "Hesse definitely wants both Bonn and Cologne, but not—we believe—at the cost of severely angering Gustavus Adolphus. And that is what would happen if Hesse killed or seriously endangered the favorite niece of Gustavus Adolphus' favorite sister. Don't you agree?"

"Yes. Probably. And I know I owe you for your help and protection." Charlotte rose from her chair and started wandering back and forth across the floor.

"My dear," said Irmgard. "We know that publishing your whereabouts would place the two of you in a vulnerable position, but if Hesse knew you were on the walls, and also that Gustavus Adolphus knew that Hesse knew, this might buy us the time we need. Once the siege is lifted, I promise you we'll do anything in our power to get you and your baby safely back to your family. We'll not agree to any deal involving turning you over to Hesse."

Charlotte stopped her pacing and nodded. "I've been thinking too. A bad fight. A long siege. Such increases the risk of a massacre. Everybody knows that after Magdeburg. No leader, no matter how strict, can be certain to keep his men under discipline during a sack. I've been trying to come up with a way to use my presence to protect the town, without placing myself and little Bobo in more danger than absolutely necessary. So, what do you both know about General von Hatzfeldt? I mean, as a person. His military life must be well known to everyone in this town by now."

"We haven't seen that much of him for the last twenty years," said Frau Benedicte with a frown. "But before that he was a very nice boy and young man. Studious like all of old Sebastian's children, and very idealistic. I cannot imagine what made him abandon his plans to enter the Order of Saint John, and instead take up a life as a mercenary. I know he has done very well for himself financially, and Commander Wickradt has told us that in addition to being ennobled, von Hatzfeldt has also been given plenipotentiary powers from Vienna to act on behalf of the HRE with regard to the entire Cologne area."

"What General von Hatzfeldt was like twenty years ago doesn't help," said Charlotte curtly. "Wolfgang wasn't a bad husband until the external pressure and threats mounted to more than he could take."

The two older women looked at each other, then at Charlotte. "Husband?" asked Frau Benedicte. "Are you considering marrying Melchior von Hatzfeldt?"

"Yes," said Charlotte harshly. "And not just for the siege. Sooner or later I'll have to let people know where I am. My brother, Friedrich, will do his best to protect me and little Bobo, but Friedrich is still very young, and the rest of the family—including both Gustavus Adolphus and Aunt Katharina—are going to want me to remarry. And to their benefit, not necessarily to mine. The only way I can see for me to retain some control of both Bobo and my own life is if I am already married when they find me. I want a husband powerful enough to protect me and Bobo, but of a rank too low for him to aspire to Bobo's heritage. A birth lower than mine would also make it difficult for him to get away with treating me the way Wolfgang did, but a commoner is not a possibility. That would make my relatives demand the marriage be annulled. General and Imperial Count Melchior von Hatzfeldt seems to fit my requirements fairly well."

"Benedicte told me you had met him on the walls," said Irmgard. "How do you feel about him?"

"That doesn't matter." Charlotte stopped pacing and sat down, wrapping her arms around her body. "I don't know." She frowned. "He seemed intelligent. And kind. And didn't seem to mind me talking back to him."

"No," said Frau Benedicte firmly. "I'm sure he knows how to keep his soldiers in line, but none of old Sebastian's children would ever try to suppress another person's mind. The entire family is rather extreme in that regard." She smiled at Charlotte. "It would not have done for you as a first marriage, but as a widow with lands of her own, there would certainly be benefits for you in such a marriage. I suppose the solution had not occurred to me because his ennoblement is so new; I'm simply not used to thinking about Melchior von Hatzfeldt as an imperial count."

"Yes, yes, Dicte. We can all see the practical benefits, but there is more to life than that, and Charlotte doesn't need a second bad marriage." Irmgard was still frowning. "Charlotte, if you disregard all the practical considerations, would you still at least consider marrying him?"

"I don't know." Charlotte sat silent for a while, still huddled and looking down on the floor. "He's quite handsome." She looked up. "I wanted to talk with him again after that first conversation, but while he has come by on all my watches, Commander Wickradt has always been with him. We've only been able to exchange the most commonplace remarks. Asking my name, and how Bobo was doing. Things like that." She smiled a little. "Few of the other women in the militias are still on wall duty, and he definitely wanted me to stay away too. But he didn't order me away, and he could have."

"I see." Now Irmgard was smiling too. "Sounds like the two of you have at least some natural interest in each other."

"So you both think it would be a good idea?" Charlotte looked at the two sisters.

"For Bonn? Yes. For you?" Frau Benedicte gave a wry smile.

"If you are asking whether you'll be happy, then that's impossible to know. But you are no fool, Lotti, and heaven knows you no longer trust easily. If you think beyond the present difficulties, and imagine taking control of Wolfgang's legacy, then would you rather do so on your own, or would you prefer to have Melchior von Hatzfeldt at your side?"

Charlotte sat for a while, then she slowly unfolded from her cramped position, and smiled at the two sisters with a twinkle in her eyes. "Do you think you could come up with a gown that would look good as a background for my gun?"

# Chapter 21

*Bonn, Eigenhaus House*
*October 6, 1634*

Melchior took his hat off, slapped it against his leg and put it back on while looking at the stout half-timbered house. "Is there anything in Bonn that the Eigenhaus family is not involved in?"

Wickradt chuckled. "Probably not. But having just one place to go when needing something does have its benefits."

"Are you sure this is where the Jülich-Berg heir and his mother are staying? If we don't find some way to get Hesse to stop the cannons, I'll have to surrender, or the town will be nothing but rubble in a few weeks. Those new cannons are devastating, and Hesse shows far less regard for casualties than I'd expected."

"No, but I'm sure this is where we should start if we want to find them." Wickradt knocked on the door.

"Good evening, Lotti." Melchior smiled at the young woman from the militias. Without her helmet he could see that her blond hair had dark roots, as if she was lightening her hair with chamomile or chemicals in the manner of certain Viennese court ladies. Few hausfraus would permit such behavior in their servant, but Lotti's language showed that despite her sunburned skin, her birth and upbringing had to be far above the servant class. That she had given her name only as Lotti and made no mention of a family name was a bit odd, but with all the shady deals and

154

betrayals following in the wake of the war, many previously honorable names were now a matter of shame. The mystery of Lotti's name was probably nothing more than a young woman's disapproval of her family's actions. Her passionate outburst about being a pawn in other people's games at their first meeting had certainly indicated something of that nature.

Melchior shook his head at his own thoughts as they were guided through the house. He really liked the passionate young woman, and admired her determination to fight for herself and her child. Most of the other women had been withdrawn from the walls once Hesse had encircled the town, and his snipers proved that the walls were well within the range of his new American rifles.

Lotti showed them into a pleasant room with five chairs arranged in front of a fireplace. Two of the chairs were occupied by their hostess, Frau Benedicte, and her sister, Irmgard, whom Melchior vaguely recognized as the woman in charge of the hospital set up in one of the Stift's buildings. Turning from greeting their hostess and finding Lotti sitting in the fifth chair made Melchior raise his eyebrows.

"Please sit down, General von Hatzfeldt." Lotti looked both tense and amused. "And you too, Commander Wickradt. I have something to say of importance to the defense of Bonn."

Melchior gave a brief bow, and sat down in the chair beside her.

"Actually it's more in the nature of a proposal," Lotti continued. "Will you marry me, General?"

"My dear young woman..." Melchior tried to think fast. She couldn't be the missing Jülich-Berg widow. No one got that sunburned that fast. Was one of Hesse's sisters missing? The two youngest would be about the right age. "I am of course deeply honored and flattered that such a lovely young woman would consider me as husband, and I am quite aware that your birth must be at least equal to my own, but since you have mentioned the defense of Bonn, I am afraid I must ask you for an explanation before I can give the question its due consideration."

Lotti gave a brief laugh at Melchior's eloquence. "It sounds as if you've been spending more time at court and less on the battlefield than rumor has it. I am Katharina Charlotte von Zweibrücken, the widow of Wolfgang of Jülich-Berg. Hesse has been turning over most of the stones in Berg, searching for me and my son."

"I see. And were you perhaps in the habit of going for long rides in the sun?"

"No. Why?" The young woman now looked confused.

"Charlotte's skin has been stained with a walnut concoction, General," Frau Benedicte interrupted with a smile. "She really is whom she claims to be."

"Ah." Melchior had heard about ways to lighten the skin with lemon juice and milk, but of course no one he knew would have wanted to make their skin appear darker. "Please pardon my suspicion, my lady." Melchior hesitated. "Given our previous conversations about pawns, I cannot imagine you being willing to seek the protection of Hesse. But would you be willing to pretend doing so? At the moment we are rather desperately looking for a way to stall Hesse's attack, but he knows both Bonn and Cologne have applied for membership of the USE, so only something that he really wants would make him hesitate."

"No." Charlotte shook her head, and her eyes looked even harder than when Melchior had first met her on the wall. "I'm sorry, General, but I must think beyond the present danger both for myself and for my son. If you are willing to offer me your protection as my husband, I have a letter ready announcing both the marriage and that I'll be defending Bonn as a fighter on the walls in case of an attack. Frau Benedicte assures me that she can get copies of the letter to Gustavus Adolphus as well as to my family. That he would knowingly have killed his emperor's niece should be enough to prevent Hesse from attacking Bonn. At least if you make certain Hesse knows that Gustavus Adolphus knows."

"You'll literally be gambling your life on that assumption."

"Yes." Charlotte took a deep breath, "but I'll take death from something I can at least shoot back at, before surrendering myself into a powerless position."

"So: Death before Surrender, but: It's Better to Marry Than to Burn." Melchior's sense of humor suddenly bubbled to the surface. His feelings for the young widow weren't anywhere nearly as strong as for his lost Maria, but getting a wife of breeding, courage and spirit in addition to the best solution to the siege he could hope for here and now was an excellent deal by anybody's standard. "You are placing a lot of trust in a man you barely know, my lady," he continued seriously. "I am quite willing to protect you to the best of my abilities without asking for your hand in return."

"No." Charlotte looked Melchior straight in the eyes. "As an unmarried woman I am far too tempting for my family—as well as for Hesse—to use in their political maneuverings, and I cannot fight them on my own. Frau Benedicte has assured me that considering your upbringing it is highly unlikely that you'll ever try to control my thinking—or even speaking. Anything else I can live with."

"Certainly." Melchior said. "My late mother was a woman of a most original and independent mind, and I would never..." He stopped and shook his head. "That is not important right now. If you are sure this is what you want, then I am yours to command."

# Chapter 22

*Magdeburg, House of Hessen*
*October 7, 1634*

"Will you be at the palace all day again today, Cousin Amalie?" said Elisabeth, while spreading honey onto a fine wheat bun. She wanted to talk with her cousin, and so had left the bedroom she shared with her sister early to have breakfast with Amalie and the males of the household before they left.

Amalie leaned back in her chair and tapped her tankard of hot beer with a fingernail. "Probably. The Cologne delegation has been introduced to the emperor, and is to be heard by the House of Lords this morning. Did you spend the afternoon with the abbess yesterday?"

"Yes, and the day before we went to visit Sister Maximiliane von Wartenberg. She was very interesting." Elisabeth smiled at her cousin. "Do you know why the Hilpoltstein heirs keep dying?"

"Taking an interest in politics, my dear?" Amalie raised an eyebrow. "Maxie might well be the most intelligent living member of the Bavarian ducal family, but her passions occasionally led her to follow her heart too much and her head too little. As, for Hilpoltstein: Sofie Agnes went to see the American doctors and they told her that her blood does not mix well with Hilpoltstein's. Something called rhesus. It will only get worse, with each pregnancy producing a baby weaker than the previous one, and as she can no longer carry to term, she had better stop before

158

she kills herself. I'm told the problem is with Hilpoltstein, and that she would probably have no problem with a child sired by somebody else, so Hilpoltstein has not asked for a divorce. Yet."

"One of the American books I've read talked about rhesus as a problem in the English royal family; it is something different in the blood in some families—or part of families." Elisabeth's eyes became distant as she slowly continued. "The Zweibrücken and the Veldenz branches have no shortage of strong children, but the descendants of Philipp von Neuburg and Anna of Jülich-Kleve-Berg are close to dying out. Countess Hedwig's children seem to have been the only numerous group, but that might have been due to the care she lavished on them. The way the pox killed half and has left the rest weak for years ... Tante Anna Marie had four living children, but none of them have produced more than one."

"Hmm. Interesting." Amalie smiled at her young cousin. "I hadn't put that together myself. How about you, Hermann?" She turned her head toward her brother-in-law.

"The American doctors have made it quite clear that they cannot predict which marriages would be fertile and which would not." Hermann of Hesse-Rotenburg had obviously grown more than a little careful about what he told his relatives since becoming the USE secretary of state. Not that they were not loyal to the emperor and the USE, but they also had private agendas and in the traditional maneuverings of the old families he now had to be completely neutral. "I'm having a meeting with Oxenstierna before the session in the House of Lords. Good Day to you all."

The speed with which the young man left made Elisabeth suspected he slightly regretted moving from the palace to his half-brother's house a few months ago, when he married Sofie Juliane of Waldeck. The wedding between the two childhood sweethearts had been planned for the previous winter, but when it was put off due to the expected election, the building of their house had also been put on hold. This had not pleased the passionate and independent Soffy, so an officially premature baby was now expected to arrive any day, and the couple had temporarily moved into the House of Hessen.

"I think you are making him nervous, Sister." Philipp Moritz von Hanau looked after the hastily departing young man.

"Hesse isn't trying to rival or undermine the power of the emperor, but if USE is to remain stable and grow, this mess left by

Johann the Insane needs to be dealt with once and for all. Hesse is loyal and able, and our bloodline is strong and healthy—whereas the entire Neuburg family seems to degenerate more and more."

"But as Elisabeth pointed out, the branches of Zweibrücken and Veldenz seem healthy enough." Albrecht zu Schwarzenfels smiled fondly at his daughter. Elisabeth smiled back. She knew her father took great pride in his five daughters and sole surviving son, but usually it was the pretty Maria who was his favorite. Still, after fighting his niece and her side of the family for decades over this and that property he had gained a great respect for Amalie's mind, and if Elisabeth could prove her own abilities, she might be able to get his support for something more interesting to do than another marriage into the Isenburg family.

"Zweibrücken is young and unproven, Uncle Albrecht, and the present Veldenz is an infant. Despite their Vasa mothers and grandmothers, the emperor might prefer those difficult lands in the hand of someone of proven loyalty and ability." Amalie shrugged. "The House of Lords will listen, debate and present the emperor with a recommendation—which he may follow or ignore."

"Didn't he indicate what recommendation he wanted last night?" Elisabeth asked.

"Young lady..." Amalie broke off her scold and joined the general laughter around the table. "Well, you have certainly woken up and started paying attention to the world around you. But no, unless you count spending the evening flirting with Maxie as an indication, the emperor appears to be waiting." She frowned. "Oxenstierna on the other hand seems to have taken a strong liking to Zweibrücken. Probably not surprising since the chancellor has always been close to Zweibrücken's aunt, Princess Katharina, and even tried to place Princess Kristina in her care."

"So even if Oxenstierna does not want Cologne to remain a free town, he might well favor Katharina's family regarding the Jülich-Berg heritage question." Elisabeth's eyes went distant again. "Especially over De Geer in Essen."

"Uncle Albrecht, I don't know what ever you have been teaching your daughter at Schwarzenfels," Philipp rose from his chair, "but having her in the same house as Amalie is making me nervous. Let us leave for the safer rooms in the palace, where all that threatens is a bit of backstabbing, character assassination and revolution."

# Chapter 23

*Regensburg*
*October 8, 1634*

"They have arrested the Wolf." Simon startled at the low voice, but managed to keep from turning around. He had sent Schaden into Regensburg in the guise of a horse-leech looking for a job, while Rosy and Simon went pretending to be two very young officers on their way from Passau to Landshut. In either case it made perfect sense for them to ask about Duke Maximilian's troop movements, and Rosy and Simon had been doing very well in a party given by a wounded officer in the inn, where they had taken a room. Simon had pretended to be a lot more drunk than he actually was, but to keep the pretense from getting real he still had to go outside and stick a finger down his throat from time to time to rid himself of most of the wine and brandy he had consumed.

"Schaden?"

"Yeah. The Wolf went to visit his mistress, and her husband found them and had him arrested as a spy. He's been locked up in the old wall-tower."

"Not in the jail?"

"No. The husband is a town councilor, and is trying to talk the captain of the guard into just cutting the Wolf's head off and sending it to the duke in Landshut."

"That would be highly irregular." Simon shook his head trying to clear the brandy fumes so he could think.

"Be as it might. The councilor is rich and the captain is building a new house."

"Damned! In that case the risk is too great to wait for help from the camp." Simon stood for a moment and listened to the roar of laughter following one of Rosy's stories. "Is the councilor the same man that the Wolf dueled with in August?"

"I have no idea." Schaden sounded irritated. "If you decide to do something and it involves me, you can find me in the tack-room behind the Moor."

"Wait!" Schaden's words distracted Simon for a moment. "Don't you care about the Wolf?"

"I like horses. I'm not too fond of men—or women."

"I see. But you go tell the camp, while Rosy and I go take a look at the tower. Get Rosy from the taproom. Say..." Simon hesitated.

"That his little friend has finished vomiting, fallen down and gone to sleep. Rosy can take it from there."

Rosy and Simon came staggering along the street following the wall, singing a raunchy song in English. At least Simon assumed that it was raunchy, but since he didn't speak more than a few words in English, all he could do was to repeat what Rosy had just sung about half a beat later. There were no guards outside the door to the tower, but a light was shining behind a window, and an extremely loud and angry female voice could be heard. Simon stopped their stagger just outside the door by simply sitting down on the dirty street, and claiming that he wanted to listen to the lady singing instead of Rosy sounding like a tortured cat in some foreign tongue. They had barely spent a few minutes with Rosy trying to wrestle Simon back up on his feet, when the door slammed open, and a tall, curvaceous and very angry lady came out shouting curses and running right into Rosy.

"Are you the Wolf's mistress?" Rosy whispered.

"What? Yes, but..."

"Scream and shout for help to get us inside," Rosy whispered, while Simon, admiring his fast thinking, threw his arms around the lady's legs and started singing the dirtiest song he knew.

"Pretty lady, pretty, pretty lady. We're two lost little sheep looking for a friendly shepherdess. Wanna find a little hay to play in with me?" Rosy's voice was now raised high enough to be heard above Simon's singing, until they were both drowned out by the lady screaming like a banshee, while starting to beat Rosy on the head.

The two rather portly men who came to the lady's rescue and dragged all three of them up the stairs to the lighted room would have been child's play for Simon and Rosy to handle in a fight, but the big scarred man leaning against the barred door was an entirely different matter.

Simon staggered to the chair nearest the big guard and kept his attention apparently fully on the scene enacted by Rosy and the tall lady, whose named appeared to be Madeleine. In reality, however, Simon was watching the distorted reflection of the guard in the window glass, and trying to come up with an idea before somebody ran out of steam. With the brandy still fuzzing his brain, Simon didn't think he could come up with anything clever, but when Madeleine changed track and went from berating Rosy to attacking the officer for arresting a fine upstanding young officer just because he had succumbed to a woman's weakness, instead of making the streets safe for decent women, Simon noticed the big guard licking his lips, and had an idea. It depended rather heavily on Madeleine playing along, but then the Wolf had always had a strong preference for intelligent women.

"My lady, you are so right. A pretty young woman really shouldn't limit herself to an old and worn-out husband, but would be much better off taking a strong, young soldier to her bed." Simon stood up and clumsily tried to put his arms around Madeleine, while whispering, "Push me at the guard," under the sound of her husband's shouting.

The push she gave him was strong enough to create a most convincing stumble ending up with Simon clinging to the big guard's kyras with one hand and the helmet with the other. As Simon heard the sound of wood breaking behind him, he kneed the guard in the groin, pulled off the helmet, and used the guard's own cudgel to knock him down and out.

When he turned, the fight behind him was already over with both Madeleine's husband and the officer groaning on the floor. Madeleine grabbed the keys from the officer's desk and hurried over to open the door behind the big guard, while Rosy quickly and expertly started binding and gagging the men with their own belts and cravats. Simon grabbed their confiscated swords and knives and went to help Madeleine support the rather battered Wolf out from his prison.

"Sir, we need to leave before Schaden brings the rest of your men. Are you able to ride?"

"Yes, but getting out of the gate at this time of night might be a problem."

"I'll take care of that." Madeleine let go of Wolf. "Drag the men into the cell, and go get your horses. I'll meet you at the southern gate in about half an hour."

"Madeleine, my dear. How can I ever repay you?"

"I'll think of something. I'm coming with you."

"But..."

"Forget it. My family might keep that old fool from locking me in a cloister, but one more evening with my mother-in-law and I'll murder that old bitch and go to prison anyway. I'm coming with you!"

# Chapter 24

*Magdeburg, House of Hessen*
*October 10, 1634*

"Very nice girls." Duchess Hedwig nodded towards Amalie's two young nieces greeting the visitors beneath the chandelier in the middle of the big drawing room. Normally Amalie would have been standing beside them, but because of the feud she had been having with their father, she had no idea how well they coped with difficult social situations, and had therefore used the fact that she was expected to drop her baby any day now to let Litsa and Maria welcome the guests on their own. The mix of the girls' old school-friends—some of whom had made high-status marriages—and Amalie's politically important hostesses took both tact and poise to manage.

"Yes, very." Amalie smiled and nodded to Dowager Duchess Anna Marie von Neuburg, who gave back a rather frosty smile. Maria, the younger of the two girls, had always been lively and charming, but had never shown much interest in anything but dresses and fripperies. The best that could be done with her would probably be a marriage to seal a political alliance.

"Looks like the old lady still hasn't forgiven you for trying to become her nephew's guardian," said Hedwig, having noticed the byplay.

"No. She doubtlessly feels that she and her son would be the natural guardians for Wolfgang's heir." Amalie gave a small shrug. "But Gustavus Adolphus favors his own sister and the baby's Zweibrücken relatives."

If young Friedrich von Zweibrücken succeeded in getting a share in the Jülich-Berg heritage either for himself or his sister, it might be worth making a connection by marrying him to Maria. Amalie made a mental note to the point.

"Has Hesse found out anything about Wolfgang's widow and the baby?"

"Not much. The birth of a boy to Katharina Charlotte von Zweibrücken has been recorded in Bonn, signed and verified. But no one appears to have seen either the child or his mother, and judging from the way Archbishop Ferdinand has been searching all over for her lately, I'd say she didn't stay there willingly. If in fact she ever was there at all."

Elisabeth, on the other hand, was showing signs of developing some really capable political acumen. Amalie remembered the young Litsa as being rather shy in social situations, but so far she seemed to be handling her hostess duties just fine and with an obvious interest in the people she was meeting that was rather charming. Her observations the other morning had also been quite interesting, and if those promises came through, then the choice of a husband for her had to be much more carefully made.

"Oh?" Hedwig raised an eyebrow.

"I first thought the archbishop somehow knew that Charlotte had died." Amalie turned her full attention back to Hedwig. "Charlotte has had several miscarriages, and another one could have killed her. Since only the archbishop's people were supposed to have been present at the birth, he could then have picked any newborn boy and claimed that it was Wolfgang's heir. But that doesn't fit with his behavior." Amalie kept her face smiling, but let a little of her anger and frustration come out in her voice. "I simply haven't got enough information."

"Do you intend to join your husband once you've given birth?" Hedwig unfolded her fan and started moving it slowly.

"No." Amalie unfolded her own fan. The excessive use of candles showed off the gild and mirrors in the most lavish fashion, but it also made the temperature rise fairly quickly. That the campaign to take Cologne was going so badly upset her more than such setbacks usually did. "I rather expect that Hesse is already in control of both Cologne and Bonn, and I plan to stay here to see that we keep them."

# Chapter 25

*Bonn, Eigenhaus House*
*October 11, 1634*

"Good morning, Charlotte." Frau Benedicte greeted Charlotte with a smile, but looked a bit surprised to see her in the old, rough dress from her disguise as Lotti. "I believe your husband has gone to his meeting with Hesse."

"Good morning, Frau Benedicte. And yes, we had a lovely breakfast in the privacy of the big room you have given us." Charlotte walked to the chair by the window where she used to do the fine needlework and repairs for the Eigenhaus households. "General... My husband sends his apology for not taking leave of you in person, but I'm afraid we lost track of the time, so he had to leave in a hurry." Charlotte felt the color rise in her cheeks and bent down to put little Phillip in the American-style playpen. Old man Steinfeld had built it for her after a drawing in *Simplicissimus* in return for the gout remedy she had cooked for him after what she remembered of her aunt's recipe. The playpen had been quite a topic of interest for the female visitors to Frau Benedicte's parlor.

"Good." Charlotte could hear the smile in Frau Benedicte's voice. "And not to pry—but you *did* first meet your new husband while part of my household, however irregular the circumstances— so how was your wedding night?"

Charlotte looked up from fussing over Phillip, and couldn't help answering the older woman's grin with one of her own. "Surprisingly fun, actually." She sat down and took up the stomacher with the ripped embroidery she had begun mending.

"There's no need for you to keep working, my dear."

"Perhaps not, but I'm afraid I've lost the skill of idling gracefully, and I cannot imagine my new husband having any use for an idle wife anyway." Charlotte found her needles and the yarn she wanted from the basket beneath the chair. "Once we know how the situation with Hesse turns out, we'll need to sit down and make plans. But Frau Benedicte..."

Charlotte hesitated. She didn't really feel comfortable discussing her private life with anyone, but the older woman was the best source she had for information about her new husband, and he really wasn't quite what she had imagined. "Was my husband very humorous as a child? I mean... Despite his kindness he really seemed quite stern and somber. Only he isn't. And I was wondering if there had been some kind of big grief to change him, or if it was his life as a soldier?"

"Nobody gets through life without a certain amount of grief, and despite his fighting skills—and the fortune he has earned—I never quite understood why someone as idealistic as Melchior would choose to become a mercenary."

Frau Benedicte shrugged. "I know of nothing specific to have changed him." She leaned back in her chair. "All Sebastian von Hatzfeldt's children enjoyed having fun. Sure, they also had deep interests in religion and philosophy, but things like music, art and beauty also played very large parts in their life. Sebastian didn't have the means to anything like a court-life, but he had close ties to the archbishop of Mainz and wherever he traveled on the archbishop's behalf, he nearly always took along a gaggle of kids. Not just his own children and wards, but also any youngster he had just taken into his household. His third wife Margaretha definitely didn't approve, which reminds me: you better watch out for her when the two of you meet. Your rank might save you from any open actions, but she's a greedy, selfish back-biter, and you absolutely cannot trust her." Frau Benedicte grinned. "And no, I don't like her."

"What about the rest of the family. Are they close?"

"I think so. Melchior's cousin, Dame Anna, lives here in

Bonn, and since she is a close friend of Irmgard, I also see her from time to time. Her brother, Wolf, is Melchior's second-in-command, and like nearly all the Wildenburger-Hatzfeldts he is quite wild and something of a rascal. You'll probably like Anna, though, and also Melchior's siblings. Now, let's see what I remember. Heinrich, the oldest, who was a very musical boy, is now a canon in Mainz. He has recently become involved in some very interesting trading ventures—all Sebastian's children have a strong sense of the practical—and I think it might be worth it for you to discuss them with him. You'll need money to repair the war damage to your lands."

Charlotte nodded.

"Then came Melchior, and then Franz. Franz I remember as a quite ambitions little boy, very kind to those younger than himself, but also always trying to compete with the older boys. He was very fond of color and beauty, and always spending his pocket-money on pretty trinkets rather than sweets at the fairs."

"Was Melchior fond of sweets?"

"Yes, and honeyed figs were his favorite, but you better not serve those for him. He got stung in the mouth by a wasp while eating one at a Michael's Mass fair. He had a very bad time of it, and I don't remember seeing him eating one after that. Why are you smiling like that, my dear?"

Charlotte looked down but couldn't keep her mouth from smiling. "Melchior had somehow found a small box of candied fruits and chestnuts from France that he gave to me last night. We shared the entire box. Eh...Do you have any idea where I could find another?"

"Certainly, and I can get one for you before tonight. But back to the Hatzfeldts. Hermann is the youngest brother still alive, but I seem to remember a fifth brother who died quite young. I don't remember his name, but I think he died in an accident. Hermann followed Melchior into the armies, but his talents were not for strategy and fighting, but rather for organizing and negotiations, so he always ended up as a quartermaster, or otherwise in charge of supply. He married a young heiress of the Dalberg family this summer—I don't remember her name but everybody calls her Trinket, and she is supposed to be more than usually fond of finery and opulence. Hermann is supposed to take charge of the family's investments and estates, and is already getting a good name as a competent man when it comes to business." Frau Benedicte hesitated. "He could be of a lot of help to you, but I know many of his major deals and investments involve Essen, so you might prefer not to."

"I didn't particularly like De Geer the few times I met him, and I would much prefer Essen to withdraw from Düsseldorf, but Wolfgang's attack on them was to the best of my knowledge without provocation." Charlotte shrugged. "I certainly don't intend to let any deals with Essen get in the way of a cordial relationship with my husband's family." She stopped and looked towards the window. "It's odd, really, but Melchior already feels so much more like my husband than Wolfgang ever did. I *do* want him with me, whether I go back to Jülich or not. Do you think I ought to go to the wall?"

"No, my dear. Not until we are certain that Hesse is informed that you'll be there. And not to the hospital either; you need to be where a message from Melchior is sure to find you."

"Melchior said that they were hiding the entire town beneath my skirts."

"Did he seem to mind?"

"No, he said..." Charlotte stopped and grinned. "Never mind, but it didn't seem to hurt his dignity a bit."

"I see. Well, the Hatzfeldt brothers also have a little sister, Lucie. She suffered a carriage accident some time after her marriage to one of Melchior's colleagues, and now walks with a cane. I believe she has spent most of the past decade or so bringing up her husband's illegitimate children, and has brought them with her to Cologne. Her mother died of a fever a few weeks after Lucie's birth, and I remember her brothers—and especially Melchior—being very protective of their little sister. I know of nothing to her demerit, and making her your friend could be a good idea if you want to keep a connection to your husband's family."

"I do. But doesn't Lucie have any children of her own? The accident must have been many years ago."

"No. Irmgard once mentioned in passing that Lucie had been pregnant at the accident, and some inner organs had been removed. That is a very dangerous operation. And I believe that the person involved later got into quite a lot of trouble with the Church in Cologne. Not burned, but..."

"I see. There was an old midwife in Jülich, but Wolfgang sent her away, and insisted I should be attended only by an Italian doctor. I wish I'd had Irmgard."

"The boundaries between midwife, wise woman, and witch sometimes get a little blurred in men's minds."

"Didn't Lucie's husband mind that she couldn't give him an heir? Wolfgang would have been furious."

"I don't know, my dear. I don't really know the family that well. Aside from Irmgard's friendship with Dame Anna, the only reason I know more than common gossip is the dealings my own father had with two of your first husband's Amtmen: Johann Wilhelm of the Weisweiler-Hatzfeldt line and Hermann of the Schönstein-Hatzfeldt line. They both died before you came north, but you might have at least heard of their heirs. Melchior's stepmother is actually one of them from her first marriage, and she has managed to completely tyrannize her children and stash them away, so that she can rule everything. Fortunately for you most of the estates in Jülich went to old Sebastian's ward, Johan Adrian von Werther-Hatzfeldt, and to Johann Wilhelm von Weisweiler-Hatzfeldt, whose widow Adolpha von Cortenbach now runs them for her minor sons."

"I think I've met Adolpha, and I'm sure Wolfgang had a quarrel of some kind with a young man named Johan Adrian von Hatzfeldt, who was a major landowner. Do you know his relationship to Melchior?"

"Their last common ancestor must be at least three generations back, but they grew up like brothers, so I'm pretty sure you can count on Adrian's support."

Charlotte leaned back in the chair, and smiled at her hostess. "Melchior said my bridal gift would have to wait, but it seems he has already given me a network of useful connections. You know this marriage really may have some quite unexpected side-benefits."

### Bonn, the west wall

Climbing down a rope-ladder was not an elegant undertaking under any circumstances, and that the rain was pouring down again didn't make it easier. Still, this was the time agreed upon for a face-to-face meeting under truce between Melchior and Landgrave Wilhelm of Hesse-Kassel. Melchior had postponed the meeting for as long as he could, using two of the wounded Hessians in the toll-tower as messengers, but two days ago Hesse had started the cannonade for real, and as he targeted not just the walls but also the town behind them, the death-toll was rapidly increasing.

In the tent on top of the river cliff Hesse remained seated, and no chair was offered to Melchior. "Bonn will surrender now, or I will reduce it to rubble. Go get the gates open, there is no way you can win." The landgrave looked irritated and in Melchior's opinion also a lot more worried than he wanted anyone to see.

"No. A tribute is acceptable. In fact, you are welcome to the entire content of the archbishop's palace. I don't like the man either. But the gates of Bonn remain closed as long as you have any significant force near the town, and you cannot afford the time it'll take you to take the town by force." Melchior smiled. "Now stop trying to bully me, offer me a chair, and let us talk. I do think we can reach an agreement."

Hesse gazed for a while into Melchior's eyes, sighed and waved at one of his men to bring in a chair. "General von Hatzfeldt, if you are expecting anything from that little wet-behind-the-ears Friedrich von Zweibrücken, forget it. No one in Magdeburg will be willing to listen to a boy."

Melchior shrugged. "I don't know how high in the USE your campaign here is known and supported, but it is in the best interest of the USE to have Cologne join willingly. Also, as an American, Prime Minister Stearns will be especially in favor of that solution. And by now he already knows the situation, and will be discussing it with Gustavus Adolphus. If you want to get anything from Cologne, even some trade agreements or a tribute, you cannot afford to spend any time and force here at Bonn."

"There is no way even the fastest courier could have reached Magdeburg, much less brought back an answer before I closed the roads."

"No, but you are forgetting the American way of getting news moving fast by radio. I had a reply from Mainz this morning. The requests from both Bonn and Cologne for inclusion in the USE are known and being discussed in Magdeburg. I do not know if your emperor has already sent orders for you to stop your campaign, but I am quite certain he will do so once he gets the latest news even now traveling for Mainz."

Melchior smiled again. "You may congratulate me, Landgrave Wilhelm. Yesterday, your emperor's young relative, Countess Palatine Charlotte von Zweibrücken, widow of Jülich-Berg, became my wife, and she will insist on fighting beside me on the walls of Bonn in the American fashion." Melchior hesitated and frowned a little. "I do not quite approve of this, but she insisted that it should be a part of our marriage agreement. And Gustavus Adolphus will also know that you were told of this today."

Hesse gave no answer, so Melchior continued, "Now. The archbishop took his strongbox with him, and whoever takes charge of the town's administration is going to need the archives, but the palace contains..."

# Chapter 26

*Bavaria, south of Ingolstadt*
*October 15, 1634*

"So, what do you think of our latest recruit?" Rosy was barely visible in the moonlight as he passed the bread and bottles he was carrying on to Simon and Lenz, and squatted down beneath the big fir sheltering most of Pettenburg's specialists.

"I think the Wolf might have bitten off more than he can chew, but she sure looks good in trousers." Lenz popped the seal on the bottle, and looked towards the colonel's part of the camp from where a very loud and definitely female voice could be heard despite the order for a silent as well as dark camp. Madeleine had proven an excellent rider, but she definitely didn't like being denied a hot bath at the end of a day's hard riding. The previous evenings Wolf—or rather Simon—had managed to find farmhouses, where his "Mylady" could have her bath, and Madeleine had actually been extremely good at keeping track of his excuses for why she wasn't at the local manor house or at least in the finest inn. Tonight, however, they were passing very close to where the Bavarian army led by Duke Maximilian was gathered across from Ingolstadt, and to escape a confrontation Wolf had ordered the regiments to continue well past sunset and only make a brief cold camp to rest the horses before continuing. Simon totally approved, and none of the men did more than

174

grumble, but Madeleine made her displeasure very loudly heard, and Simon had sought refuge with his men instead of staying with the other officers.

"Where's Allenberg?" Simon took a swallow of the wine to wash down the rough bread before passing the bottle on to Schaden.

"He came back from the stream when I passed, but didn't want to join us. He's probably going to doss down on his own somewhere near the colonels—he usually did that on the Pisek campaign." Rosy was cutting slices of the sausage he had brought and passing them around.

"Thenk he's looken' for promotion or just a lil' extra business w' his papers?" Simon had never managed to identify Niederthal's odd twangy accent, but in a mercenary army you just didn't inquire into people's background unless they started volunteering information, and Niederthal had said less about his than anybody else.

"I think he's one of those nuuks." Schaden's broad Swabian accent could be difficult to understand, but this time it was his words that nearly made Simon choke on the wine he had been about to swallow.

"Please don't waste the wine, honored leader. It's the last of the good bottles from Passau." Rosy leaned over to slap Simon on the back. "Why do you think that, Schaden?"

"Ever seen his pecker?"

"No, but he could just be shy. Or perhaps have a small one." Rosy's even white teeth flashed in a grin.

"He also never gets a beard-shadow, even when everybody else looks shaggy." Lenz said. "There lived an Italian castrate singer in our street, when I was a child. My uncle was his barber and wig-maker, and he told me that he never had to shave the castrate."

"That's not enough reason to say something like that about a man." Simon had regained his breath, and decided to insert a little reason into the discussion before it really went wild. "My own beard is so sparse that I've given up growing a mustachio, and Rosy can pass for a woman all day, if he shaves closely in the morning."

"Well, Lenz can vouch for me being male." Rosy's grin flashed again. "We got into a pissing contest after Pisek. But what about you, oh honored leader? You are almost as standoff-ish as Allenberg."

"Very funny." Simon emptied the bottle and chucked it at Rosy, who caught it neatly before it could hit his head. "And for that insult you can help Schaden ready the horses in the morning. Now let's get tucked in for a few hours. We'll leave well before dawn."

## Cologne, Hatzfeldt House
## October 15, 1634

"Lady Lucie, Lady Lucie! There's a new letter!" The copper-curled youngster came rushing into the kitchen waving a bundle of paper. Lucie von Hatzfeldt and the cook both looked up from their list of the food stored in the larders, and broke off their early morning debate about what could be done to make it last as long as the siege.

"Thank you, Peter. Who brought it?" Lucie reached for the letter as quickly as her crippled back allowed her.

"Jacob from Bonn. He had to wait almost a week to get through the siege. Do you think the general has beaten the Hessians?"

"That is probably being a bit too optimistic. If Uncle Georg returns from the town hall please bring him to me." She removed the seal and started reading.

> To Lady Lucie von Hatzfeldt, Hatzfeldt House, Town of
>     Cologne
> From Melchior von Hatzfeldt, Count and General of the
>     Holy Roman Empire
>
> Dear Lucie,
>     Please spread around the following information: both applications for membership of the USE have reached Magdeburg and are under consideration there. Hesse has been informed of this today. Hesse has agreed to stop the bombardment of Bonn, but the town is to remain closed until the agreed upon tribute is delivered, and as the tribute includes the town of Beuel as well as other areas, the paperwork can delay this for as long as he wants it to.
>     I expect him to move most of his cannons to Cologne and make an all-out effort to take the town or force the council to surrender within the next few days. The council can try offering a substantial tribute, or they can decide to

*batten down and accept the damage until Magdeburg can interfere, but make sure they realize that the damage will be heavy and delay will not be possible. Hesse knows he must take Cologne now—or face a probably very costly failure.*

*Finally some information of less immediate interest to Cologne: Yesterday, Charlotte von Zweibrücken did me the honor of becoming my wife. She and her baby son remained incognito in Bonn after escaping the archbishop, and I met her on the wall during the siege. Charlotte has joined the women's militias here in Bonn, and has fought most valiantly at my side on the walls.*

*What is to be mentioned only within the closest family is that Charlotte has had a very bad time—both as a wife and as a widow—and that I am deeply honored that she is willing to entrust me with the safety of her baby and her person. I might wish that she was less eager to gain the ability to ensure such safety herself, but considering what she has been through, I do understand. It is a part of our marriage settlement that Charlotte may continue her military training, as well as any other skills she wishes to develop. I want it made perfectly clear to every member of the family—our stepmother Margaretha included—that no matter what happens I expect Charlotte to have the full support of the entire Hatzfeldt family, and that anybody not offering her this support will receive my strongest displeasure.*

*Your loving brother,*
*Melchior*

When Lucie looked up from reading the letter, the cook in the chair on the opposite side of the table had been replaced by the cousin whom everybody called Uncle Georg. The elderly man had had a fine career as dean in Fulda, and had seemed the only calm, financially secure and fully respectable member of the unruly Wildenburger line until he'd suddenly and violently fallen in love with Helene von Bellinghausen, left the Church to marry her, and settled on her estate southeast of Cologne. After the death of his beloved Helene, Georg had secluded himself on the estate and refused to see anybody until the previous year, when Maxie had made a brief stop on her way to her cousin in

Bonn, and dragged Georg off to Cologne. Georg had not liked the strong Counter-Reformation at the University of Cologne, so instead Maxie had set him teaching his young cousin, Wilhelm Heinrich of the Weisweiler line, how to manage the many estates he was soon to take control over. In the process Georg—as nearly everybody else—had run afoul of Lucie's quarrelsome stepmother, Margaretha von Backenfoerde, and the old administrator's ability to block that lady had made him a firm favorite with Lucie and her brothers.

Lucie smiled wryly at the old man and reached across table to give him the letter. "I think Melchior has fallen in love. Oh, and Hesse knows that he might have less than a week to take Cologne, so that's the reason for the recent attacks."

# Chapter 27

*Bonn, Eigenhaus House*
*November 1, 1634*

Charlotte snuggled a bit closer to Melchior, who gave a little grunt and put his arms around her.

"Cold, m'dear? Would you like me to close the bed-curtains?"

"No, but thanks. The room isn't drafty, and you make a very nice warming pan without the hazard of fire."

"Well, we could try for a little fire." Charlotte could hear the smile in her husband's voice as his hands started to drift, and gave a little giggle in response. She rubbed her cold nose on his shoulder. Getting married to Melchior was starting to look like a very good idea—even if he didn't like her fighting and didn't like closed bed-curtains.

"Is your dislike of closed bed-curtains from your campaigns?"

"No. There's very rarely any opportunity to stop drafts while camping." Melchior stopped what he was doing to raise himself on one elbow and lean down to give Charlotte a kiss, his beard tickling her nose and making her sneeze. "I gained the dislike in Vienna. Despite what the American books tell about the plot against Wallenstein, assassinations are not actually common among military leaders, but I do have a few enemies with fewer morals and more capacity for violence than they should have. And so I prefer to be able to see what's in my room the moment I open my eyes. But they are quite unlikely to come to this part of the world." Melchior lay down again and pulled Charlotte close.

"Do you need to go back to Vienna, and do you think the emperor will let you go without protests?"

"I'll certainly not need to go until things are quiet in this part of the world, and even then—unless Wallenstein gets ambitious—there's probably nowhere else I could be of more use to the Empire than here. You'll need to understand, my dear," Melchior was obviously getting serious now, "that even if I resign as general, I'll still be an imperial count, and I do take my liege oath very seriously. I have no qualms at all about my marriage vows to you, but if you decide to join your lands to the USE there could be a problem. Much as I respect Gustavus Adolphus I cannot formally enter his service."

"I've been thinking about that—I mean alliances for the future. Essen appears to be able to maintain independence, but I'm not De Geer and neither Jülich nor Berg has the resources to produce such wealth or maintain such an army." Charlotte shrugged. "On the other hand I most definitely don't want my baby's heritage nibbled away bit by bit. An alliance with France is out of the question, and—given what I saw when helping Irmgard at the infirmary—I would find it most difficult to be even coldly polite to Hesse and those who supported him in the USE." Charlotte shook her head to remove the memory. "I'm not entirely opposed to considering an alliance with Essen despite their war with Wolfgang, but I'm quite certain that would make every member of the Neuburg family my sworn enemy—probably Bavaria too."

"That leaves you looking to the west."

"Yes. What do you know about Don Fernando on Jülich's western border? He is a Habsburg like your own emperor, but could he be trusted?"

"To keep an alliance? Yes. To not covet Jülich if you remain neutral? No. To go to war with the USE over Jülich? I don't think so. I don't know the details of their negotiations, but at the moment the Netherlands just don't have the resources to win an all-out war with the USE."

"You obviously know a lot about this part of the world, I thought you had spent very little time here, what with you fighting in Denmark and Bohemia?"

"Archduke Ferdinand sent me to make an evaluation of the

middle Rhine area this summer. Hesse took me completely by surprise by attacking Bonn, but I really should have expected it. According to Father Johannes the American books claim that Cologne is destined for prominence, but Kassel for obscurity. Hesse is bound to try changing that."

"By fair means or foul?"

"I don't know. I've not well acquainted with the man, but just in case: I'm watching my back—and yours." Melchior's hands started roaming again. "And—while I haven't the slightest intention of dictating your decisions regarding your lands—I firmly advise you to stay right here until Hesse has withdrawn."

"I could perhaps be persuaded to see the wisdom in that."

# Chapter 28

*Magdeburg, Wettin House*
*November 5, 1634*

"Dearest Litsa, have you been waiting long?" Johanna burst into the parlor with even more than her usual speed and nimbly skipped to avoid the low table filled with books and papers that Elisabeth had placed next to the writing desk.

"I've been here for a while, but not idly waiting. Maxie took me to meet Father Johannes and Madame Louisa Tapié this afternoon; she is the wife of Father Johannes' nephew, the publisher of *Simplicissimus*, and she is also co-editor." Elisabeth gave the brightest smile Johanna had ever seen on her face. "She hired me."

"What!"

"She hired me. I'm the permanent Magdeburg correspondent for the *Simplicissimus Magazine*. With special responsibility for the magazine's political and aristocratic articles."

"Litsa, are you out of your mind?" Johanna sank down in the nearest chair.

"No, this is what I want." Elisabeth's smile turned serene. "I never had either the slightest interest in marriage or a vocation, but this is my vocation: information politics. I went to the palace afterwards and spoke to Uncle Hermann. I convinced him I was both serious and knew what I was talking about. He expects to continue as the secretary of state after the election and has not been satisfied with the work of his public relations—that's the people supposed to make sure the newspapers write the correct information—and if I show I can do the work for *Simplicissimus*, he'll try to get me hired by the government. Information is going to be very important."

"That might convince your father to let you do it, but your mother is going to have hysterics." Johanna left the chair and started pacing the room. "It would be too dull a life for me, but if this is what you want I'll help you all I can; I just don't think your father is going to stand up to your mother." She brightened. "You'll have to run away to prove yourself. You can hide with Maxie and then flee with Friedrich and me to Cologne."

"No." Elisabeth turned grim. "My honored mother might protest, but I know too much about buried Isenburg skeletons for her to stop me." She tilted her head and scowled at her eager friend. "Friedrich, who? And whatever are you up to now? Have you been reading those American novels again?"

Johanna grinned and threw herself into the chair. "I've been so busy too, dearest Litsa. After Friedrich—Zweibrücken that is—had been heard—or rather interrogated—by the House of Lords he had nothing to do except wait for them to debate, so I went to keep him company. Maxie was right: he is such a darling boy. And he completely understood how dull it is always being surrounded by adults and never being allowed to do anything on your own. He has had the greatest adventures on his Grand Tour, and would have loved nothing more than to lead an army against Archbishop Ferdinand to free his sister. Only Maxie and Lucie von Hatzfeldt convinced him that Charlotte and her baby were safe, and that the best thing he could do was to stop Hesse and ensure Charlotte had a home to return to. His own lands—Zweibrücken, Bischweiler and Birlenbach—are in perfect order, and no one really needs him there, so what he really wants to do is help Charlotte and her baby get back to Jülich... and help his sister get that land back in shape. And he invited me to come help him." Johanna took a deep breath, lifted her head and did her best to look virtuous. "After all, I did concentrate my studies on medicine and nursing, and Charlotte might need someone to take care of her and the baby after their hardships; Eleonore and mother would both surely support me."

"Probably. But he invited you? Just as a result of a few hours' conversation?" Elisabeth looked skeptical.

"Well, I might have delicately hinted that I would like to come." Johanna grinned.

"I see. And was young Zweibrücken by any chance darling enough for you to delicately hint at the benefits of joining the USE, and forming an alliance with one of its prominent families?"

Johanna opened her eyes wide and placed her hand over her heart. "Why Litsa, I would never dream of doing anything so indelicate." She grinned again. "I plan to have Maxie do so instead, since he has quite a lot of respect for that lady."

Both girls were laughing hard when the door opened. "Good evening, Anchen and Litsa." The abbess was wearing an evening gown, and behind her in the hall Tante Anna Marie, Hedwig and Eleonore looked ready to leave for the evening party at the palace. "You seem in very good spirits."

"Oh, we are, but why is a story for tomorrow." Elisabeth smiled. "But please, has the emperor made a decision about Cologne and Jülich-Berg?"

"They are still debating, but it looks like the former archdiocese and the free town of Cologne will become a republic with Hermann von Hatzfeldt in charge of the first election; he was the only suggestion acceptable to both Catholics and Protestants. Charlotte and her brother along with the emperor's sister and her husband all become guardians of Wolfgang's heir, but the heritage itself is split. To keep the matter settled even if the baby dies, Jülich is settled directly on Charlotte, rather than on the baby, and if she dies without an heir the land reverts to the crown, not to the Neuburgs or the Zweibrücken family. If Jülich joins the USE, which is expected, she also gets the seat in the House of Lords. The occupied part of Berg is confirmed to Essen along with Kleve, while the rest of Berg is given to young Zweibrücken in return for his oath of loyalty. His lands may also join the USE along with the other areas in his family, thus bringing the entire—or almost entire—Rhineland and Pfalz into the USE."

"Then Hesse and Cousin Amalie get nothing?"

"Hesse gets Mark, but he is told to settle his deals with Essen on his own." The abbess frowned. "Ravensberg and the other minor areas are settled on Hedwig's children, Anna Marie and Hilpoltstein, but all with the same condition about reverting to the crown. The emperor wants it as part of the constitution that all the ruling families must choose a way to pass on titles and land: male first, male only, with or without including morganatic marriages, or however they want it, but if the line ends according to their choice, then the land reverts to the crown. This was agreed on."

"So the tighter a family tries to hold its land, the more likely that they will lose it to the crown. Beautiful." Elisabeth smiled at the pen in her hand.

"Well, it should cut down on the dynastic quarrels," Eleonore said, waddling to the doorway. "But do come, dear Dorothea. Tante Anna Marie and Hedwig are already in the carriage. And girls: there is to be a major celebration of the new treaty before the Cologne delegation leaves, and the invitation is for members of the House of Lords with their family, so you can come. Probably the day after tomorrow."

"Forget your writings for tonight, dear Litsa," Johanna's eyes glowed with the joy of battle and adventure, "and come help me lower the neckline of my rose damask dress."

# Chapter 29

*Donauwörth*
*November 10, 1634*

Donauwörth looked extremely impressive in the morning light, and on his way into the castle Simon marveled that the Swedish king had even contemplated attacking it—not to mention that he had actually conquered it. Fortunately the Wolf had no such intention, and would be taking the regiments across the bridge some miles up the Danube. The captain of the guard there had accepted their papers—supported by a small bribe—as genuine proof that they were troops having left the service of Bernard in Swabia, and now heading north for a new contract with Gustavus Adolphus in Mecklenburg.

Once across the Danube the regiments would, however, be traveling through the new USE, and until they reached the Wolf's old home-territory west of Mainz, they would have no old contacts for ready information. That the Wolf had actually expressed a dislike for traveling blind, and once again tasked Simon with finding out whatever he could about troop movements or other potential problems, had made the irreverent Rosy wonder about the domestic influence of the temperamental Madeleine. In Simon's opinion it was far more likely that the Wolf's worry about the fate of his cousin and general made him unwilling to run his usual risks.

"A pity we couldn't take along Madeleine." Rosy turned his head to look across the cart carrying him and Schaden. "She is absolutely wonderful at distracting guards."

"We'll manage." Simon grunted. Having Schaden claim a toothache and go to get one of his miserable brown stumps drawn by the garrison blacksmith was a good enough excuse for Rosy and Schaden to enter the castle, and give Rosy a chance to chat with whoever was around. In the meantime the plan was for Simon to seek an interview with General Munro, while Allenberg as Simon's batman went to negotiate with the garrison's quartermaster for some fancy bits and pieces for Simon's equipment. They were keeping to the story about heading for a contract in Mecklenburg, and while General Munro certainly wouldn't spend his time on a lowly lieutenant, there was no reason some lower-ranking officer wouldn't be willing to spend a morning hour giving a personable young officer the benefit of his experience, and some details about the area he would be traveling through—especially if Simon admitted not having had any breakfast and invited the officer to join him.

"So, after I fried that fucking little frog-eater I went to Gustav—that's Emperor Gustavus Adolphus to you, my young friend, only he wasn't an emperor yet in those days—and said..."

Well, Simon had certainly found a major willing to talk. The problem was that what the man wanted to talk about was limited to how he had won every major battle in Europe during the past ten years. He had said a bit about the political situation along the Rhine, so the morning hadn't been entirely wasted, but Simon was still more than happy to see Allenberg hurry towards him.

"Please come. Quick." Allenberg had already passed the table by the inn, where Simon was sitting, and hurried on down the street, as some kind of disturbance broke out up by the garrison's storehouses.

"Excuse me, Major." Something was obviously seriously wrong, so Simon threw some coins at the table and set off after Allenberg.

"What's wrong?" Simon caught up with Allenberg just as they turned the last corner towards the stable where they had left the cart and the horses.

"My past caught up with me." Allenberg said curtly, and

pulled Simon into a gateway as horses thundered down the street they had just left.

Allenberg took a deep breath and looked at Simon through slightly narrowed eyes. "It has nothing to do with the company or the general, so you could just play it cool, and pretend to know nothing. Rosy and Schaden should be with the horses by now. There's no reason for Tapic to connect the three of you with me. You get the horses and get out. I'll leave once Tapic has stopped watching the gate. Those horses would have been him going to the gate with extra guards, but he's the only one knowing me well enough to recognize me if I find something else to wear."

"I do know nothing—and want to change that. Both the major and the quartermaster saw the two of us together. And can you imagine what the Wolf—and the general—would say if I just left you behind?"

"The general, yes. The Wolf, no. But it would probably be inventive." Allenberg leaned back against the wall, and relaxed a little. "Do you remember the big scandal in Metz two years ago? The one where a mob broke into the prison and hanged the lawyer responsible for setting up the American pyramid game?"

"Sure."

"That lawyer was my father."

"Ah. And did you have anything to do with the scheme?"

"Colonel Tapic and his family lost ten thousand thalers altogether."

"I see. So your guilt would be irrelevant. Well." Simon looked at the smooth cheeks and solid figure of the forger. "We should be able to get away with Rosy's favorite ploy and get you out dressed up as a female."

"Simon." Allenberg gave a sigh. "I *am* a female. And Tapic knows this."

"Oh, shit."

"That was the most harebrained scheme I've ever been a part of." Rosy pulled off his drooping hat and threw it on the ground. "And I've damned well taken part in some beauties. Mind telling me, my fair-haired boy, just where you acquired that talent of yours for pulling tricks?" Rosy stuck his hands at his side and glared up at Simon.

Simon wondered if a quelling stare would be enough to make Rosy back down, but as usual his boyish face spoiled any attempt to look threatening. And instead he looked around at his most irregular irregulars. They had trusted him enough to follow him—not into the ordinary danger of a battle—but into a situation where Simon's ability to talk his way out of trouble was all that stood between them and getting hanged as spies. Perhaps he should let trust run both ways—at least a little.

"Learned it at my mother's knees." Simon dismounted and handed the reins of his horse to Schaden.

"Literally or figuratively?" Allenberg calmly looked over his—no her—shoulder at Simon, while continuing to unfasten the wine bag from her saddle.

"Literally." Simon took a drink from the bag Allenberg handed him before passing it on to Rosy, and started rummaging for food in his own saddlebags.

"Huh! I thought your old man was a very respectable silversmith in Hamburg?" Rosy took a drink without removing his gaze from Simon.

"He was."

"And your mother, I believe Dehn mentioned, was a very beautiful French noblewoman." Allenberg took the food from Simon, and squatted down to cut the dried meat against a flat rock.

"Very beautiful, very French, and certainly high class."

"Yes, but high class what?" Rosy relaxed and started laughing. "You know, it's really starting to look as if Schaden is the most respectable person among us."

# Chapter 30

*The road between Bonn and Mainz*
*December 15, 1634*

"Do you think we got away?" Prince-Bishop Franz von Hatzfeldt of Würzburg pulled the reins to stop his horse beside his friend.

"Yes. Few military troops are eager to chase down two armed men on fast horses, but with no visible luggage to loot. Let us stop and rest the horses." Bishop Franz Wilhelm von Wartenberg of Minden turned his horse into the shadows between the trees along the road. The rain had finally let up earlier that evening, tempting the two men into leaving their hiding place, but then the sky had cleared completely, and the light of the almost full moon had made it easy for the dragoon patrol to spot them.

"I cannot believe Archbishop Ferdinand would just let us get away. He must have people searching for us. Perhaps even that creepy Felix Gruyard. He could have gotten in front of us, while we laid low in Rheinbach." Franz fumbled with his reins, making his horse dance nervously even after the hard ride on the muddy road. "Even if the archbishop hates our guts, getting the support of our families is the only chance he has left."

"There is no chance." Franz Wilhelm's face looked grim in the moonlight streaming through the half-bare branches. "There never was. The archbishop's plan to drive a wedge between the Americans and the German princes, and then grab back the

190

conquered bishoprics along the Rhine in the confusion, could not work without the full support of Bavaria. And he didn't have that."

"Duke Maximilian of Bavaria would have joined his brother once the initial step of taking Fulda had succeeded. The initial plan wasn't that foolish. It was only when Hesse got involved that everything went to pieces." Franz got off his horse, and started walking it around to cool it down.

Franz Wilhelm shook his head, and got off his horse as well. "No, my friend, he would not. Even if Hesse had stayed at home. You haven't seen Duke Maximilian since his duchess died. He doesn't really care about anything but his grief, and what is worse is that he has shown more and more signs of focusing on a few specific ideas to the exclusion of all rational thought and reason."

"Idiosyncrasies and monomania." Franz sighed. "That's what Father Johannes told me the Americans call it. Only he was talking about Archbishop Ferdinand and his plans for the Americans in Fulda."

Franz Wilhelm nodded. "It's probably a family trait. Their father had the same tendencies. Perhaps the new American teachings are right, and to keep marrying back and forth in the same families is not such a good idea. I'm certainly very, very happy about my low-born—but very sensible—mother."

"Well, at least he cannot send the Irish colonels after us." Franz's mind kept returning to worrying about the powerful archbishop, whose aid he had sought three years ago when the Protestant armies had conquered his bishopric in Würzburg. "Even if you are wrong about them going to defect with all their men, Archbishop Ferdinand is going to need them to keep Hesse at bay." Franz cast a last glance over his shoulder and started walking his horse down the road into the next valley.

"I'm not wrong." Franz Wilhelm was the oldest son in the morganatic marriage of the archbishop's uncle, and his upbringing in the ducal family of Bavaria combined with his Jesuit and military schooling gave him a firm grasp of the overall strategic situation. Franz, on the other hand, was the son of a knight of only local importance, and had been a diplomat working for the bishops of Bamberg before being elected to Bishop of Würzburg, so while he knew just about every clerical person worth knowing in western Germany, his knowledge about military matters was close to nil.

Franz Wilhelm continued. "The Irish colonels haven't got an especially firm grip on their men, and cannot make them go on fighting a losing battle against Hesse. Especially with no loot and bad camps. And even if Irish and Co. manages to make them do so, they'll all stop the moment the archbishop's money runs out."

"I know how much he took from the treasury at Bonn," said Franz, "and that'll run out in another month or so, but he might also have managed to get something from the palace in Cologne before Hesse's siege closed off the town."

"In any case we should be safe from pursuit now." Franz Wilhelm looked up at the sky. "We are unlikely to reach the town of Mayen before morning, and the clouds are moving in. Do you know of any place where we can stop?"

"The old man in Rheinbach said that between all the skirmishing, and unregulated looting by the dragoons from both sides, fairly much all the farms and small villages have been abandoned. With the archbishop now being pressed west towards Aachen, people might be coming back, but the best we can do is probably to find a house or a stable, and just sleep rolled up in our cloaks. There never were that many inns on this side of the river, and we cannot depend on finding one before Koblenz." Franz hesitated. "I know I've asked you this before, but do you think we are doing the right thing?"

"My dear friend," said Franz Wilhelm, sighing as they both climbed back on their horses, "we're both competent men of proven abilities, and—if we didn't want to just retire to our personal estates—I'm sure either the Church or the soon-to-be new emperor could find something useful for us to do. But if we want our bishoprics back, we must negotiate and compromise for them. And the longer we stay away, the firmer any arrangements made in our absence are going to become."

"I'm not sure I could accept being as powerless as Schweinsberg in Fulda was," said Franz kicking his horse into a slow walk. "I have no problem with prince-prelates with the power of kings being a thing of the past, and I could probably get along with a Lutheran—if not a Calvinist—co-bishop. But there is just so much beyond the spiritual care that I had planned to do in Würzburg: schools, agricultural improvements, new villages for refugees to settle in and start new lives. I must have some resources for starting these plans. To go back to Würzburg with only the resources of my estate at Crottorf at my disposal would be unbearable."

"Yes, you have told me all about your plans for your precious 'Kingdom,' but do consider this, my friend: Archbishop Anselm of Mainz has managed to keep most of the old church estates in his area. Surely we two old diplomatic rats should do no worse." Franz Wilhelm's strong white teeth showed as he grinned at his friend.

"My brother, Heinrich, remained in Mainz during Anselm's exile and fought with all the lawyers and records at his disposal against any attempt to remove property from the Church." Franz's voice was still morose, but he held his head a little higher. "He lost a few battles with the new bureaucracy when something had a fuzzy provenance, and of course all the removable valuables were looted earlier, but Anselm could still go back to a fairly complete property. You left your people in Minden with the same resources, but I was newly elected in Würzburg, and the records are scattered all over the place."

"You are being too pessimistic, my friend. Probably lack of sleep. That always makes you cranky. You sent young Schönborn to deal with the new USE people in Bamberg, he got us the safe-conducts, and once you're back in Würzburg and things have quieted down, you can send for the records you brought to Cologne and start doing battle. Win or lose you'll still be better off fighting for your own kingdom than following my crazy uncle Ferdinand around. Let us pick up some speed."

# Chapter 31

*Bonn, Eigenhaus House*
*December 21, 1634*

To General Melchior von Hatzfeldt, Bonn
From Lucie von Hatzfeldt, Hatzfeldt House, Cologne

*Dearest Melchior,*
*First let me offer you a belated congratulation on your*
*marriage. I never met the Countess Palatine Charlotte while*
*she stayed in the Beguine of Mercy, but Uncle Georg assures*
*me that she is a very nice young woman, and nowhere near*
*as hen-witted as her older sister, Elisabeth, whom I had the*
*dubious pleasure of meeting in Nancy. Please assure your*
*wife of the family's full support, but try to overcome your*
*dislike of tale-bearing, and warn her against Margaretha.*
*Our stepmother considers the entire mess with Hesse and the*
*USE a personal affront directed at her. Fortunately there has*
*been a minor raid at Castle Schönstein by what turned out*
*to be some of the archbishop's mercenaries, so Margaretha*
*is presently occupied with her "grave disappointment in her*
*dear friend Archbishop Ferdinand of Cologne, son of Duke*
*Wilhelm of Bavaria, you know, such a pious man and a*
*dear friend of my father." As usual her complaints get rather*
*boring, but at least this subject is not disrupting the family.*

*I know you and Charlotte must have all sorts of things to take care of—with Bonn, her lands and your regiments—but I hope to see both of you here as soon as possible. Hatzfeldt House is still standing, and the deal with Hesse was finally signed today, so the siege is being raised and we can get new supplies. In my opinion just having the cannons stop is worth more than the Council agreed to pay, but now we must just pick up the pieces and try to get back in shape.*

*That very nice young courier of yours reached Hatzfeldt House yesterday with a letter from Wolf, and he has brought your three oldest regiments plus something he called—I think—the Cherry-Brushers and the Wild Oafs. Really, Wolf's handwriting is atrocious. Reading—to the best of my abilities—between the lines, it seems he lied his way through Bavaria, while breaking most of the Ten Commandments and generally having the time of his life. Melchior, are you quite sure you knew what you were doing when you made him your second-in-command? And thank God that Wolf made contact with Old Nic at Godesberg before he broke the armistice by hitting Hesse in the rear. Still, I suppose Wolf's presence contributed to Hesse finally signing the deal, and having a nice little army of your own should make establishing order in Jülich much easier. Wolf will contact you as soon as the siege on Bonn is lifted, but he sent the letter to Uncle Georg here in Hatzfeldt House, since the Hessian ring around Bonn was so much tighter than around Cologne. Just what did you do to make Hesse so mad at you? Wolf also inquired about the whereabouts of Archbishop Ferdinand's Irish mercenaries, but I could truthfully reply that I didn't know. Didn't you mention some kind of bad blood between Wolf and at least one of them? Still, not even Wolf can go harrying after the archbishop to settle an old score as long as he is leading your army. Probably. I hope.*

*Anyway, Hermann came back from Mainz—smuggled along the river by night and he has the most horrid tales about it—with a thick letter from Franz that I was to pass on to Father Johannes! For the family there was just a brief note saying that his traveling papers were now in order, and he would leave for Würzburg. And would I please send him copies of Hermann's correspondence with Steve*

*Salatto as soon as possible. That was all! No explanation, no nothing. And after all our worries about him. He was no more forthcoming to Hermann and Heinrich when they met in Mainz; just said that he had had enough of Archbishop Ferdinand, and was going back to Würzburg with Maxie's brother, Bishop Franz Wilhelm of Minden. Our darling brother is driving me crazy!*

*Our oldest brother, Heinrich, was offered the position as archdeacon of Mainz by Archbishop Anselm in gratitude for Heinrich's work to keep the land and possessions of the Church together during Anselm's exile, but Heinrich wants to get back to his music, so he plans to decline the offer. We'll see what happens.*

*Hermann, on the other hand, has made new contacts in Mainz, and goes north to Magdeburg, as soon as our affairs here are in order. Trinket is sulking, and complains that as his wife she should go to Magdeburg and meet the emperor too. Sigh!*

*Father Johannes found his missing painter friend, and is now in Magdeburg. I plan to join him and Maxie there sometimes next spring. Maxie is buying a House.*

*Your loving sister,*
*Lucie*

## Hessian Field Headquarters, Archdiocese of Cologne
## December 26, 1634

Hesse looked up from the two dispatches on the table before him. One was an old-fashioned parchment with Gustavus Adolphus' seal and signature, the other a stained and crumpled radio transcript signed and sealed in Mainz. Together they made him wonder if God had for some reason turned against him, and he was no longer among His chosen.

"Thank you, Lieutenant." He nodded at the mud-splashed courier wearing the emperor's colors. "Lieutenant von Rutger will show you a billet, and I'll have an answer ready for you in the morning."

Hesse went to the open window of the small manor house

he was using as his headquarters, and looked at the setting sun. The rain, which had slowed down every movement he had made since crossing the Rhine, had stopped for a while and the clouds parted to make way for a glorious sunset. When the orders he had expected after his talk with General von Hatzfeldt had failed to arrive, he had hoped it was a sign of the emperor's favor, and while it annoyed him that he had let Melchior von Hatzfeldt trick him, Bonn really wasn't that important in the grander scheme. Instead the emperor *had* sent him the expected order to stop, but the courier from Mainz had been killed on the road outside Koblenz, where the rain had created a mudslide. It had been a trading caravan from Mainz to Aachen led by Moses Abrabanel that had come across the corpse and retrieved the metal cylinder with its official order. The Jew had personally brought him the still sealed cylinder two days ago, and since Hesse had dutifully stopped the bombarding after having read the order, Gustavus Adolphus couldn't blame him for disobedience. But "couldn't blame" was not the same as favor.

Hesse had never truly doubted that he was among the saved, that both he and Amalie were chosen to enter Heaven and take their place at God's side. And for so long the prosperity that had followed them had seemed proof of that for all others to see. Hesse had thrown in his lot with the man who was now an emperor, he had a long list of military victories behind him, an exceptionally clever wife who shared his dreams and goals, several strong and healthy children. Lately, even his own quarrelsome family was bowing to his superiority and accepted him as their leader.

This summer's attempt to add Cologne to his new province had been the first major failure he had suffered since becoming a man. But why?

Hesse went back to his table and took the parchment from the emperor with him to the window. Messages? It was radio messages that had interfered with his original straightforward plan to take Cologne. Was that a sign that the Americans were his enemy and would block him unless he somehow destroyed them? But what about the rain? The messages had cost him three months of useless maneuvering during the summer, but he had known quite well that the plans had gotten too complex and could just have continued on his original course. The rains on the other hand had delayed him in everything he did since early September, and that rain could only have come from God. And what about the death of the courier from Mainz? And Wolfgang's missing heir to Jülich and Berg? Hesse sat on the window bench for a while, slowly rubbing his finger over the emperor's seal on the parchment. No, he wasn't meant to rule Cologne. It was not that he wasn't one of God's chosen, it was just that he for some reason shouldn't have Cologne. Everything that had gone against him this summer had just happened to block him from that specific goal.

Hesse looked down on the parchment. What he did have was Mark. He owed De Geer the tip west of Dortmund, but Dortmund itself had been fairly big in the Americans' world. There had been channels. Lots of channels. Exactly what had been transported and why Hesse couldn't remember, but Amalie would know, and there would be detailed maps in Magdeburg. Hesse gave a sigh, then stood up and squared his shoulders.

# Chapter 32

*Bamberg, Geyerswoerth Palace,*
*SoTF administration land office*
*December 30, 1634*

"Welcome back to Bamberg, Bennett. How was Mainz?" Janie Kacere looked up over the stacks of ledgers and paper on her desk to greet the grumpy looking man entering her office. "You deeply resented getting pulled away from your work with the election, but was it worth it?"

"I still think getting the election properly arranged is just about the most important thing to be done right now." Bennett Norris removed a stack of heavy books from a chair, but finding no place to put them, held them in his lap as he sat down. "But I must also admit that you and Steve Salatto were right: politics of all kinds are totally tangled together all along the Rhine and the Main. A single clog can strangle everything else, and if we want to grow—or even just hold things together—we simply must have some sort of control over the rivers." He sighed. "Those half-forgotten history lessons really should have made me realize that the Rhine is the Mississippi river of Europe—and the river Main pretty much the Ohio. But," he smiled, "the Mainz office is running smoothly again. And things are settling down around Cologne. But whatever is going on around here? I made a detour to Fulda, so I haven't been to Würzburg, and the inns are full of all kinds of rumors. Is there anything that could seriously impact on the election process?"

"A fanatic witch-burner, Father Arnoldi, is stirring up troubles in Würzburg in his bishop's absence—or possibly in preparation of his return. A safe-conduct was issued to Bishop Franz von Hatzfeldt, and he is expected to turn up sooner or later. Did you, by any chance meet him while you were in Mainz?"

"No, Bishop Franz was hanging out with Archbishop Ferdinand in Bonn and Cologne until they fled west when Hesse attacked," Bennett rested his arms on top of the books, "but I did meet two of his brothers. And liked them both. Extremely sensible men and definitely not the kind to favor any kind of fanatics. Very political though, on the local scale, and very far from stupid."

Janie looked around her office, which was absolutely overflowing with ledgers and bundles of papers. She much preferred an orderly workspace, but with so many tangled ownerships and so many records missing she needed access to everything she had from the area she was presently working in. "Just put the books on top of the stack to your left."

"I don't think they'll balance. You have all your bundles tied with the knots used for easy access, rather than the flatter ones used for stacking in storage. Heinrich von Hatzfeldt, Bishop Franz's older brother, showed me the difference along with a very clever little wooden thingy which I plan to have someone copy for me in very large numbers. Medieval Clerkery 101." Bennett sighed. "I had a lot of contact with Heinrich von Hatzfeldt in Mainz. He's a dean of some kind, and held things together for the Catholic Church in Mainz, while his superiors fled. He called Bishop Franz the diplomat of the family, and I gathered that they were worried about him. The entire family is quite famous for their religious tolerance. Of course that doesn't mean that Bishop Franz is not a fanatic—or in favor of witch-burnings."

"No. He was suspected of being behind the attack on the auditors last year. Nothing was proved, but the few entries about him and his family in the history books certainly indicates ambition." Janie rose to put more wood on the fire in the stove. The ceilings in the administrative buildings in Bamberg were beautifully decorated but very high by up-time standards, making the rooms difficult to heat. "The Ram movement has actually made things easier in purely political terms. Muddled and missing records still provide a lot of opportunity for shady deals and nepotism, but the people with wealth and power now have a lot less opportunity to grab more than they did even two years ago. And they don't like that. And Father Arnoldi appears to have become their focal point."

"So it's political slash financial rather than religious? That's not the way the rumors have it."

"We don't know. Father Arnoldi's rhetoric certainly aims at the most irrational medieval fears and superstitions, but the men around him are known for their worldly ambitions, and are no fools."

"Hm. Any idea how widespread a support he has, and what kind of resources?" Bennet wanted to stand up and pace, but that was totally impossible in the tightly packed room.

"You'll need to ask one of the military people about that, or Steve Salatto when you see him."

"Who is around right now?"

"I'm not really sure. We're still more or less closed down for Christmas. Vince has gone to bring both his wife and his daughter here. Barbara broke her leg rushing around as usual, and it has not set quite right. She'll probably always walk with a limp, but she plans to organize the women's branch of Hearts and Minds into something like a Women's Institute and teach women how to apply up-time knowledge to housekeeping. Terrie is to spend the winter here with her parents before going back to Grantville to take her exams in May." Janie smiled. "It'll be nice to have some more Grantville families here. And Vince has missed Barbara very much. The new railroad from Grantville is almost at Kronach, and is expected to reach Bamberg some time during next summer." She looked around her crowded office. "As for myself: I'm taking advantage of the relative peace and quiet during Christmas to sort some files. The post-Ram calm has given a lot of people more time and energy to devote to old—and new—disputes about estates, and I'm seriously short of reliable records for most Church properties. Or possible Church properties. And a fire in two of Würzburg's main guildhalls combined with a flooding here in Bamberg has not made things easier."

"I wouldn't say lacking records was your most obvious problem," said Bennett looking around, "but I know how it is. Is my office still mine?"

"Aside from a few nuns." Janie smiled. "That's some of the more positive news. One of the clerics Bishop Franz left behind—or who returned—is a very nice young man named Schönborn. He's only a canon at the Würzburg Cathedral, but another person mentioned in the history books. And getting raaave reviews! The German Solomon, no less." She grinned. "Really cute too. The nuns are his doing. Though not because he's cute." Janie stopped smiling and said seriously. "They are from Bavaria. Duke Maximilian took a dislike to something about their order, and they had to flee. They went to Würzburg first, but Father Arnoldi apparently considers learned women to be the work of the Devil, and tried to get them accused of witchcraft and burned. There've also been tales about learned and outspoken women getting harassed, and even disappearing. Did you hear those rumors?"

"Yes, but when I left, the situation was nowhere near lawless enough for that to happen. Has it changed?"

"We think it's just a part of Arnoldi's attempt to put The Fear Into The Congregation. None of the stories that we've followed have led to anything, but . . ." She rubbed her brow. "Two women, who had gone against some of Arnoldi's followers, disappeared while traveling. No one's sure exactly where, and their wagons and servants have not been found. They just never arrived at their destinations."

"Which were?"

"One was traveling north to Fulda with three servants. All four of them riding horses. That was in September. The other was driving her own small wagon from Bamberg along the road to Würzburg with a single maid for company. That was only about a month ago."

"That makes no sense. The road north to Fulda has some bad stretches, but between here and Würzburg there's just a few wooded hills between the fields."

"Yes, and of course that means the Devil took the Wicked Widow from Würzburg for her wicked ways—such as driving herself home from a visit to her sister here in Bamberg. And her maid with her for taking service with such an evil woman. And of course the fact that she's a widow is also suspect, since just how did her husband die? That he was shot, while defending his farm from the invading Protestant army, is unimportant. At least compared to the fact that she refused to sell—cheaply—a very fine vineyard to the Würzburg councilor who wanted it."

"We are supposed to be out of the Middle Ages, right?"

"Sometimes I wonder. But back to your nuns. Schönborn and..."

"Just a moment. My nuns?"

"Well sort of. Our nuns then." Janie's smile came back. "Father Arnoldi and his cronies in the Würzburg city council had them locked up and claimed that they were both witches and spies for Duke Maximilian. Schönborn together with some of Johnnie's Hearts and Minds people got them away from Würzburg, and suggested we hire them. They really are learned. Literate in German and Latin, used to doing accounts, and very good at making trade contract and other juridical documents. Two went to work as nurses, but the rest of them were added to our staff as clerks. They are really good. Two of them have been assigned to your office and have been keeping track of—and cross-checking—all the updates we're getting from the Amtmen about voters, etc." She rose from her chair. "Come let me introduce you to your own private office dragons."

### Mainz, Church of St. Alban

"Come in, come in." Domherr Heinrich von Hatzfeldt rose from his writing desk and went smiling to greet his visitors. "You both look like drowned mice, but I've hot water for a tisane. Please, close the door, Franz. The drafts along those corridors are murderous." To Franz, the shabby and rather overfilled office of his brother looked like a vision of Heaven after the cold and wet journey, and for the first time since he had realized just how far Archbishop Ferdinand was willing to go to regain his power base, Franz felt himself relax.

"My dearest Brother, corridors are always drafty. They really are nothing but horizontal ventilation canals."

"Are you hungry?" Heinrich looked from his brother to the rather wan looking Franz Wilhelm, who both shook their heads.

"We had breakfast this morning before we left Ingelheim." Franz Wilhelm's voice was weak and slow. "I've been suffering from the most annoying stomach fever for the past two weeks, so we've had to travel very slowly. And where is the closest necessaire?"

"Two doors to the left. It's behind the screen in the choir

room." Heinrich twisted around to take a bottle and three mugs from the cupboard behind his chair, and went to the small fireplace for hot water. "This is a honeyed mint and thyme cordial. It'll calm your stomach. Are you running a fever as well?"

"Not anymore. We stayed at an inn near Koblenz until that passed. Thank you." Franz Wilhelm accepted the hot drink. "But please give us what information you have on the political and military situation. We've been on the road for more than two weeks, and before that Archbishop Ferdinand did his best to keep us in isolation since intercepting Melchior's letter to Franz in September."

"Archbishop Ferdinand wanted to send me off with Felix Gruyard and some of his minions," Franz leaned back and let the warmth from the drink seep slowly into his bones, "but Franz Wilhelm stalled him with some of the fanciest diplomatic footwork I've ever seen. I still don't know how you managed, my dear friend, but I'll be forever grateful. I absolutely loathe Gruyard."

"I've known Uncle Ferdinand all my life, and my sister Maxie nursed him during his illness last winter. She told me..." Franz Wilhelm paused and looked into his mug. "Seems he has been doing things lately that go beyond what would normally be expected even from an ambitious man. Employing Felix Gruyard as a private torturer for a start. Against Abbot Schweinsberg of Fulda, but probably also in connection with a friend of Father Johannes, the painter." Franz Wilhelm emptied his mug and sank a little down in his seat. "I could use his uneasy mind to stall him."

"Yes." All traces of a smile now disappeared from Heinrich's face. "I wasn't at all on friendly terms with Abbot Schweinsberg of Fulda, but there was an eyewitness to him being tortured to death by Felix Gruyard. Not a very prominent person, but one with no reason to lie. Schweinsberg's body has now been retrieved and given a proper burial."

Franz felt sick, but Franz Wilhelm just nodded.

"I had a letter from our dear sister Lucie last week." Heinrich poured another round. "Do you know that Melchior is holding Bonn, and has married the widow of Jülich-Berg?" Both his guests nodded, and Heinrich continued. "Hesse has concentrated his attack on Cologne, probably hoping to take it before it joins the USE. The casualties are increasing, but when Lucie wrote the letter no member of the family had been wounded. Hermann has been bringing letters out of the besieged towns. He is in Frankfurt right now, but I expect him back any day. Elsewhere?" Heinrich leaned back in his chair and contemplated the smoke-stained ceiling. "De Geer seems to be consolidating his hold on the Düsseldorf area. Magdeburg and everybody else in the USE have elections on their minds, but there's also some saber-rattling in the direction of Saxony. Bavaria is falling more and more apart, and the old Habsburg emperor is said to be dead. I haven't seen the official confirmation on this, but I'm getting information through my connections to the Abrabanel family. Which reminds me." Heinrich twisted around to take a bottle and two small beakers from another cupboard. "This is a blackberry cordial. I remember you used to like that, Franz. At your health to both of you."

The two guests drank, and Heinrich filled the vessels again.

"There's lemon and ginger in this as well as berries and honey. Is it an old bottle?" Franz Wilhelm smacked his lips, checking the taste.

"No, it was decanted only about a month ago." Heinrich smiled and waited.

"If you can afford lemons and exotic spices, you cannot be doing that badly." Franz frowned at his brother.

"We don't." Heinrich's smile broadened into a grin, and he changed the tone of his voice as if preaching a sermon. "Things they are a-changing, my children. There have been a lot of problems caused by the erosion of the old order and power bases, but if you embrace the freedom of the new ideas, the possibilities are endless." He changed back to his normal voice and continued. "I've invited in the Jews."

"What!" Franz was genuinely startled. Their parents had imbued all their children with an unusual religious tolerance, but that was very far from the normal attitude of the Catholics in the area.

"Yes, I trust that you both know from Melchior that I've gone into business with the Abrabanel family."

"Yes, and someday I'd like you to tell me how you got Archbishop Anselm to accept that." Franz Wilhelm smiled slightly, but Franz had no idea how shocked his friend really was. On one hand Franz Wilhelm was a deeply pragmatic person, who had proven his ability to work together with the most unlikely persons, but on the other hand he had been raised in the deeply religious environment of the Bavarian ducal court.

"Yes." Heinrich leaned forward and smiled at his visitors. He obviously wasn't the least bit worried about the changes. "Frankfurt is getting a real boost from becoming so important from a military point of view, but the council there was fighting every attempt to stop discrimination—especially against heretics. On the other hand the civil leaders here in Mainz are fairly friendly towards our Jewish community at the moment, and it's becoming more and more obvious that the American influence in the USE will result in a political system with Equal Rights for Everyone; if not initially then at least as an end goal. The times when prince-prelates—or other rulers—could make their own laws and change them at will are over. There are going to be uniform laws, and they are going to be enforced. The translation of the American history book I've seen suggests that having a strong Jewish community tends to boost economic growth, so I made contact with Rabbi David Cohen. We share an interest in music, and while any kind of joint musical arrangement has not been possible, we usually meet at the more public concerts here in Mainz. He was the one who introduced me to Moses Abrabanel, and when Abrabanel last came to Mainz, he brought one of the newer drafts of the proposed constitution, and the three of us sat down and discussed what would be most important to the Jews and how we got the council to accept the changes." Heinrich stopped talking and sipped a little from his beaker.

"And what did they want?"

"It turned out that what were the two most important issues to the Jews were the permission to become citizens and the removal of the limit to the number of marriages within our Jewish community. Oh, they would of course also like permissions to own business properties and open shops, but getting that past the guilds would be impossible until they actually saw a law saying so. Getting the council to agree wasn't all that difficult, but selling the plan to Archbishop Anselm took some very fast talking. I'm not really sure he didn't agree mainly because he knew how much it would annoy Archbishop Ferdinand."

Franz Wilhelm and Franz both nodded. That sounded completely likely.

"But on a more positive note," Heinrich smiled again, "David Cohen became the first Jewish citizen of Mainz a few weeks ago, and several Jewish families have moved to Mainz from the Frankfurt Judengasse, and are renting properties from the archbishopric. We've set it up with fifty-year contracts and the rents tied to the price of bread. Good rents but not more than we could probably get Christians to pay. The real payback for the Church, however, is the trading opportunities. One of the properties we've rented out will be a series of warehouses for the Abrabanel trading network, and part of that rent is that the Church can get the goods at cost. In other words: the Church can use the rent money to buy a share in the Abrabanel cargoes."

"And does that pay better than the original rent money?" Franz leaned back. He'd need money from somewhere, if he was to succeed in his plans for his bishopric.

"Yes. Even with reserves to cover lost cargoes, it's a minimum of ten times."

"Jesus drove the traders from the temple. So, from a purely theological point of view, aren't you likely to get into trouble for inviting them back in?" Franz Wilhelm didn't seem very upset at the idea.

"First: the Church itself became a trader, the moment we owned more property than the temple itself. Second: that temple wasn't a church it was a synagogue." Heinrich shrugged, then leaned back and smiled. "When Anselm and almost everybody else fled from the Protestant army, I remained behind to protect the Church to the best of my abilities. I'm not at all certain that what I've been doing is right, and I'm sure it isn't the only solution, but most of all I'm totally convinced that things will not go back to the way they used to be if we just wait out 'the present unpleasantness,' to quote some of my colleagues. The conquered bishoprics here in the Bishop's Alley along the Rhine cannot regain their freedom and power by fighting the USE—with arms *or* with lawyers and diplomats. The USE and the changes the Americans brought are not going to just go away. We need to work within this new system with a constitution. We need to grab every advantage and opportunity it presents. Because if we don't, then we are going to be bypassed by those who are willing to change."

Heinrich continued more calmly. "If the choice was between

only spiritual or only secular power for the Church, I would personally vote for spiritual. I just think that we still have the opportunity for both. The Catholic message is important, and I want money to pay for missionaries to spread it, for schools to teach it to the children, for shelters where people can seek its protection." Heinrich sighed and smiled. "I also want the Catholic Church to be the place to touch God's glory on Earth. With beautiful music written to his glory, and richly decorated rooms in which to listen. But enough sermon from me. What are your plans?"

"We would like to stay here in Mainz until I've recovered completely, but if the winter remains mild—if wet—we'll continue and try to reach our bishoprics before Chandlemas," answered Franz Wilhelm.

Heinrich nodded, "You are both more than welcome. We have lost some clerics since the Protestant armies came west, so there are plenty of rooms for guests."

"Did Abrabanel tell you anything about Würzburg?" Franz's mind returned to his own affairs.

"Only very little. Jews are becoming less and less welcome in Würzburg. Since the Americans moved into Bamberg, many of the most close-minded bigots have moved out. They seem to be finding a gathering point at Würzburg. Around a Father Arnoldi."

Franz sighed. "Just what I did not want. Any letters from Schönborn?" Franz leaned back in the chair and looked up at the ceiling without really seeing it. Instead he saw the grape-covered fields around Würzburg with the Main River winding between the hills. His family and friends teased him about his "Kingdom," but becoming the bishop of those beautiful hills had been the fulfillment of all his ambitions more than three years ago, and for all that time he had dreamed of returning. It would probably have been more sensible to consider his bishopric lost, and accept some of the offers he'd received from France and from the Habsburgs, but his Kingdom of the Hills had always remained the only thing he really wanted.

"No, but all the rain this autumn has seriously disrupted the postal services." Heinrich smiled wryly. "The Abrabanel traders on the other hand seem to manage just fine. Did I mention that the copy of the latest version of the new constitution contained a clause stating that the Church won't remain tax-exempt?"

"What!" That pulled Franz's mind totally back to the here and now.

"Oh, yes. It's been proposed as part of the new constitution, and apparently several of the USE princes feel that unless they remain tax-exempt none of the churches should either."

"Please, Brother. I need another cordial. And would you please give some more details about your trading ventures? It sounds as if I'll be needing money even more than I thought."

# Chapter 33

*Bonn*
*January 20, 1635*

"That's the Old Boys, my old regiment. And Lorentz and Dannwitz. Or at least in part. They're not in any standard configuration. And no wagons or baggage train." At Melchior's musing voice, Charlotte looked up in surprise to see her husband squinting to identify the riders approaching Bonn in orderly files.

"Surely you cannot see anybody's face from this far?"

"The colors on the banners and the way the files are arranged are enough." Melchior put his arm around Charlotte's shoulder and gave a little squeeze. "All military leaders have preferences in how they deploy their men—both for combat and for marching. It's vital to know this about your opponent, but you must also know your own side. It's not possible for a general to order every little detail, but you still need to know where everybody is going to be and what they'll do. Take a look at the middle regiment. There're scouts out on both sides even when approaching a friendly town, and if you look beyond the easily spotted outriders, there're more that are only occasionally visible. That's Dannwitz's way of marching. Dehn never does that."

"Do you think Hesse left any of his men behind? Perhaps to look for a chance to attack once the gates open?"

"Not a chance, my dear. That simply isn't done. No one would ever trust him again."

"He attacked without warning, and treaties have been broken before."

"It'll not happen in this case. Please trust my judgment on this."

Charlotte looked up at Melchior smiling down on her. "I'm sorry. It seems I'm developing a nervous disposition." She looked away and took a couple of steps along the wall walk to free herself from Melchior's arm. Despite her growing fondness of her new husband, she still found it difficult to accept any kind of constraints when she was upset.

"Hardly surprising, my dear," Melchior folded his arms, leaned against the battlement and kept smiling. "You've had a very rough year."

"Are you always this forbearing?" A flashback to the previous winter, when the slightest opposition would be enough to trigger Wolfgang's fury, made Charlotte's question sharper than she had intended.

"Charlotte, I've been a soldier for twenty years, and surely seen every possible way a human can react to battle—and please do not belittle what has happened to you. It's been fully as harsh as any soldier's campaign, you went into it without any kind of training, and it was certainly something for which you never volunteered. If anything, I actually admire the way you keep your head in a crisis. And if you fall a little apart, once the crisis is over?" Melchior shrugged. "I have no real problem with that. You'll find your feet again, and calm down."

"But what if..." Charlotte stopped. Most of the militias and as many councilors as could find room were gathered on the walls to watch the arrival of her husband's regiments. They kept their distance to give their general and his wife a little privacy, but they were still close enough to hear anything she said if she spoke too loudly. She forced herself to calm down, and looked around to smile at Frau Benedicte, while taking the few steps back to Melchior.

"You're right." She smiled up at Melchior and leaned over a little to rub her shoulder against his. "I'll be calm, put my life in order, and be so much stronger from what I've learned."

"Excellent." Melchior put his arm back around her shoulder. "Good plan. You know, my friend Father Johannes told me that some of the guns owned by the Americans could be kept under your pillow while you slept. Perhaps you would like to buy one of those?"

"I am *not* the kind of woman who takes a gun to bed!"

"Eh! And what kind of woman is that?" Melchior looked a little confused, as if he wasn't quite sure that she was joking.

Pleased to have for once managed to tease her husband back, Charlotte gave a sniff. "Never mind that. You're a married man now."

Melchior looked questioningly towards the Eigenhaus family, who generally looked away and hid broad grins. Only young Jacob was looking puzzled, as if he longed to ask Charlotte for an explanation.

"What I still don't understand," said Charlotte changing the subject, "is why your regiments are coming here in the first place. We should be going to Cologne in a few days or weeks at most, and could easily have come to wherever they were camping. Is there some esoteric military reason why they come to you?"

"No. Normally, Wolf would just have sent me one of my couriers, probably young Simon, and perhaps a few other officers if anything special needed reporting or coordinating, but otherwise I would just have gone to the camp and taken back the command. Why Wolf didn't send anyone I don't know, but their reason for coming here is probably Cologne. After a siege and bombardment like the one Cologne just went through, the soldiers driving the attackers away are sometimes hailed as liberators, and sometimes not welcome at all. Wolf developed a very fine nose for such situations during our Danish campaign and following occupation under Wallenstein."

"Dame Anna had a packet of the new American drugs against infections and pain from a friend at the hospital in Cologne along with a letter telling that Wolf had not come to visit his family. In fact, the only one of your men anyone had seen was Simon."

"That would fit. Simon is so obviously a nice young boy that I often send him into the tense situations. But we'd better get down now, if we are to reach the City Hall in time for the official reception. And there's a woman riding next to Wolf, for which he better have a good explanation."

"So," said Wolf with a grin later that evening, "what does your wife say to you dressing up your squeeze in trousers, and calling her a soldier?" Melchior had taken Wolf along for his usual evening patrol around Bonn, well knowing that he was in for some teasing, but also wanting some private conversation to catch up on the state of the regiments.

"What on Earth are you talking about? Madeleine is your problem and I definitely intend to keep her that way."

"Pity. She seemed quite taken with you." Wolf's grin got even wider. "But it was in fact Allenberg I was talking about, you sly dog. A bit too solid for my tastes, but with a nice enough rack if you like them large."

"Very funny. You know quite well I had no idea Allenberg was female." Melchior stopped to pop open the door to the Dry Barrel, usually the rowdiest of the town's five ale houses, but a quick glance around was enough to reassure him that his men were on fairly friendly terms with the locals. "Any idea what made her put on the disguise?"

"Not in any details, but presumably her abilities as a forger were involved."

Melchior stopped and looked at his still grinning cousin. "Forger?"

"Oh, yes. An excellent one. We couldn't have gotten across Bavaria without her."

"I see." Melchior started walking again and dryly continued. "Anything else I should know about?"

"I put young Simon in charge of the couriers, and added Allenberg, Rosy, and Schaden for spice. Pettenburg's Irregulars."

"Poor boy."

"Oh no. He did extremely well. I think you've actually underestimated the boy's abilities to handle the more weird assignments."

"Are you talking spy?" Melchior frowned. The mindset that made a good spy rarely mixed with the makings of a good leader, and that was the goal he had intended for Simon. "Or just a weather vane ready to be somber and earnest with me, but a bit of a rascal for you?"

"Could be either or none." Wolf was completely serious now. "I know you're fond of the boy, and heaven knows he's both clever and capable. I wanted to see how he dealt with situations outside those straight and narrow ways that you've been sending him along. And your fair, young paragon completely exceeded my expectations. He has even more of a talent for shenanigans than I have."

"Hm!" Melchior started walking again. "Ripe for a bit of a lark?"

"Nope. Completely serious. Might have enjoyed the challenge, but..."

"I've seen no signs of a delight in intrigues," Melchior mused, "but a young officer with a quick eye for problems and a talent for obscure solutions could be more useful off the battlefield than on it." Melchior took off his hat and slapped the light dusting of snow off it against his leg before putting it back on. "I'll have a talk with Allenberg, and if she can convince me not to sack her on the spot, she goes with my wife and me. But I think our young Simon needs a few more challenges. I want to see how he handles that kind of assignment when they come from me rather than you. He'll go scout around Jülich with Rosy Ross posing as a servant and Schaden as a groom. Between the three of them they should be able to ferret out any major problems awaiting us there. The rest of us go slowly and with a stop at Cologne. Or is there some reason we should avoid that town?"

"None, if we are going in the train of the courageous defender of Bonn heading west to claim his wife's domain. But as an unattached army led by the Wild Wolf of Wildenburg?" Wolf shrugged. "Our darling little sister, Lucie, sent me a warning that everybody's nerves were extremely tense after all the cannonades and heavy casualties, so if I let any of my men into town, I'd better make sure they behave like meek little lambs. You keep good discipline in the regiments, dear Cousin, but we might be spending a fair amount of time in this part of the world now, so no need to risk fouling the nest."

"Amazing." Melchior shook his head and grinned briefly. "Common sense from the Wolf! I wonder if it's a sign of the second coming?"

"Could be." Wolf shrugged. "The arrival of the Americans is certainly the weirdest thing I've ever heard of. But talk about fouling the nest: Archbishop Ferdinand was last seen heading for Aachen with his men and I guess it'll be impossible to avoid some kind of contact with the man. Sweeping the area for small groups of deserters and other bandits must be coordinated with the councils of both Cologne and Bonn, but I'd like to go find the archbishop right away."

"No." All traces of a grin had left Melchior now. "I know

Wallenstein prevented you from settling your score with Irish Butler and his friends, but the situation here is still too unstable. You will make no moves in the direction of Aachen without my express permission. That is a direct order, and not even you will get away with breaking it."

"Hmpf!" Wolf set off at a quick pace with Melchior a few steps behind him and not trying to catch up. The mood of the town seemed good; even the rowdiest voices had a friendly undertone, and there were more laughter and songs than shouting. That could change quickly, but the cold evening with a few scattered bits of snow beginning to fall would not lend itself to the kind of major gathering in the squares where things could get really out of control.

"You rarely demand that kind of obedience from me these days, Cos." Wolf had stopped and turned to face Melchior. "Has your faith in my judgment eroded?"

"Not at all, old friend, you did an excellent job getting the regiments here, and at a most impressive speed." Melchior smiled and slapped his hand on Wolf's shoulder. "But you've always hated politics, and despite your words about not fouling the nest, I'm not really certain that you've considered all the implications of my mar-riage to Charlotte. Not only are we no longer mercenaries moving from place to place, we are also no longer just the local Hatzfeldt family, who serve the higher ranking nobility in various capacities. Charlotte is a ruler in her own right now. Her cousin is third in line for the Swedish throne and thus—at least theoretically—for emperor of the USE. I don't know what'll happen with Archbishop Ferdinand, but Charlotte must maintain a good standing with the Church as well as with the secular powers. And that includes what is left of Archbishop Ferdinand's family in Bavaria."

"And you must protect your wife. Yes, I get that. But now I intend to find some bottles and get drunk."

"You know, my dear Charlotte, this is the first time I've ever met your husband's officers. Not quite what I had expected of Melchior." Irmgard's suppressed laughter made her voice quiver in the dusky light inside the Eigenhaus' light town carriage.

"Sister! Don't tease Charlotte." Frau Benedicte's voice was reproving, but Charlotte could hear that her hostess too was trying not to laugh.

"If that Bavarian hussy had kept fingering my husband one

second more, I would have drowned her in that bowl of spiced wine!" Charlotte knew she was overreacting to what she would merely have considered a light flirtation, if any woman had paid that kind of attention to her first husband. In fact, the Danish countess who had come visiting from Holland had offered a far more direct invitation to Wolfgang without arousing more than a light irritation in Charlotte—and that mainly due to the woman's vulgar laughter and bad manners at the table.

"If so, then I made a mistake in interfering. That wine truly was awful." Dame Anna's beautiful voice masked her amusement better than the Eigenhaus sisters, but Charlotte could see the twinkle in her eyes despite the dim light.

"Well, joking aside, Anna," said Irmgard. "What was going on with those two women among the officers? That this Madeleine had somehow attached herself to your brother was obvious, but Melchior didn't protest when Wolf introduced the big girl in trousers as Melchior's quartermaster."

"A quartermaster isn't usually invited to that kind of social affairs, so my brother was obviously bent on teasing Melchior—as well as stirring things up with the councilors to keep the official party from getting too dull. The last bit works better in a place where all the officials haven't known him since childhood, and our cousin Melchior has obviously gotten used to Wolf's pranks as well."

"I didn't mind Allenberg. She seemed quite stoic and patient about people staring, and while only that nice young Simon Pettenburg seemed in any way protective of her, the other officers seemed..." Charlotte shrugged. "Accepting I guess. Certainly not leering or disapproving."

"Well, get the story from your husband tonight, and tell us in the morning," said Frau Benedicte, opening the door to the carriage. "Anna, I want you to promise me to let the carriage take you all the way to your doorstep. I know it's only a short walk, but the town *is* filled with soldiers."

"Thank you, Benedicte, but I want to stop by the infirmary on the way, and I might stay for a while."

"As you wish. Irmgard, do you plan to join her?"

"Yes, but we'll return the carriage and ask Karl Mittelfeld to walk us home. He has been sitting at his daughter's bedside since he came back. We need to get him up and walking around. Pay some attention to the world around him again."

# Chapter 34

**Bonn, Eigenhaus House**
**January 30, 1635**

"I do think it's a little harsh of Melchior sending your young man into the snow after so short a rest." Irmgard set down her goblet of wine and smiled at Allenberg.

"Young man?" Allenberg looked up from the papers Charlotte had given her to sort.

"Yes. That nice young Simon has seemed quite protective of you at the parties."

"Oh, that." Allenberg gave a slow smile. "I believe that has been a case of mutual protection. Simon tells me he sometime feels like a hunted fox at balls and other social functions. The young girls can be quite forward—and the older women even more direct."

"And Simon is of course such a helpless little ninny, that you were positively doing him a favor by protecting him." Irmgard was openly laughing now. "That is one very clever young man."

"Ah, I see." Allenberg's placid surface seemed a little ruffled. "I had not considered that he might have been exaggerating his problems. He is after all a most charming young man." She fiddled a little with some letters and said with a small smile towards Charlotte who was walking around the room with her baby fretting in her arms, "I do not know if the general has told you, but Simon and I share a background with problematic relatives. I suppose that might have formed a bond between us, but our relationship is not of a personal nature."

"Melchior has told me your—problems—were not your doing, and that your experiences and skills could be very useful to me as a secretary and perhaps later as manager of some of my properties." Charlotte lifted little Bobo up to rest on her shoulder. The baby's cold had blocked his nose, and the women were taking turns walking him around to soothe him and ease his breathing. "You have been a very competent quartermaster for my husband, and I definitely have no problem with women wielding authority on their own." She stopped and looked straight at Allenberg. "But I need to know what you want from your life."

"Want?" Allenberg picked up her pen and smoothed out the feather with her fingers. "To leave the past behind me, and start a new life." She smiled a little wryly. "And never, ever have a mob after me. I like money as much as the next person, but some risks just are not worth the possible gain." For the first time she now met Charlotte's eyes full on. "If you accept me into your service, milady, I'll protect your interests to the best of my ability. My skills are not those one would usually find in the secretary of a noblewoman, but no one will be able to cheat you, and since nobody else is likely to give me such a chance, your interests would also be mine."

"Sounds reasonable. I'll pay enough that you should be able to either assemble a good dower over a few years, or eventually retire, but if you need or want more money faster for some specific purpose, I want you to tell me instead of trying for something shady—or something just not in my best interest."

"Yes, milady." Allenberg was now grinning broadly. "The general has already said something similar—if a bit more forcefully expressed."

"I can imagine." Charlotte's tone was dry, but her grin as broad as Allenberg's. "How about you, Irmgard? I do not expect Frau Benedicte and Dame Anne to leave their lives here behind, but would you be willing to come with me to Jülich? Wolfgang drove away many of his most loyal people in his rages, and those who replaced them are of very mixed abilities and morals. I hope I can get Frau van der Berg to come to me from Düsseldorf and take charge of the more practical aspects of running my households, but I'll need some kind of a lady-in-waiting, and I will not invite my sister Elisabeth to fulfill that position."

"No, Charlotte. I'm sorry, but Karl Mittelfeld is barely keeping himself together, and whether or not his two last children live, I think he is going to need me." Irmgard gave a slight smile. "At least I hope so. I've always been quite fond of him."

"I'll come with you." Dame Anna's quiet voice made everybody look at her in surprise.

"But . . . You're a Stiftsdamen! Why?" Charlotte's startled voice had woken her son, who started crying again.

"I'm bored." Anna smiled. "I am a Wildenburger too. And the recent excitement has woken my old lust for adventure."

"Excitement! Anna, are you out of your mind? Have you forgotten what's filling the hospital? All the new graves in the graveyard?" Irmgard looked as if she wanted to hit her friend.

"Not at all, my dear. And I'm not planning to follow Allenberg's example and try to disguise myself as a man." Anna sighed. "But I've been moldering. Slowly crumbling into dust with nothing stirring me out of my rut. It's time for me to go somewhere else for a while, and if Charlotte doesn't want me in her household, I'll go nag Wolf and Melchior into taking me along."

"Oh, I want you. Definitely." Charlotte started to laugh, while patting her son on his back. "You know, between Anna and Allenberg, and with Melchior to handle the military matters, I expect it'll only be a matter of time before Jülich becomes the center of a thriving little empire."

# Chapter 35

## Magdeburg, House of Wettin

Eva put down her pen and straightened her back. Grape blight. The American books were quite clear about the menace, and the destruction it had caused when the tiny root-destroying pests had reached the European vineyards from America. And now they were here. Spreading out from Grantville, following the rivers. So far only along the Saale, where grapes were rarely the main crop, but eventually the aphids would reach and destroy those fields along the Rhine and Main, where entire valleys with towns and estates depended completely on wine. In the American world the solution had been to graft every single grape plant growing in the European vineyards onto a root hard enough to hamper the pests. The Americans had brought along some of those roots too, and a project of producing rootstock for grafting was going on around Freyburg. But it would take millions of roots just for Germany, not to mention that the pests must eventually reach Spain, France, Italy, and all the eastern countries. She was not going to find a solution to a problem of that scale in her beloved still-rooms or even in the bigger facilities in the school at Quedlinburg, but what if she came up with a plan? Magdeburg right here and now would be the best time and place to get backing for whatever she came up with.

"The dressmaker's here." Eva turned as her older sister entered and went straight to the padded box holding Eva's precious new microscope.

"Please ask them to measure you and the other first, Anchen. And don't touch that."

"They already did, and are having a small lunch with the housekeeper. You're the one everybody knows has no interest in dresses, so they saved you for last. And I'm not going to break it. Getting our brother to buy you a microscope, even if it isn't an American original, almost took divine intervention."

Eva turned back to her papers, and fiddled a bit with closing her inkwell and cleaning her pen. With Eleonore's husband hoping to become the prime minister of the USE there would be occasions that Eva would have to attend. Hiding in the still-rooms in order to study would not be acceptable. And unless she was dressed in proper style, she would shame the family. Pox might be considered an act of God, and thus beyond human control, but a scruffy dress on a woman from a wealthy and prominent family would be taken as an insult to your host and his guests.

As the two sisters left the airy still-room in the back of the house and went along the corridors towards the front, Anchen kept glancing towards her younger sister until Eva had enough. "What's on your mind?"

"Just thinking." Anchen shrugged.

"Be careful with that or you might sprain something."

"Don't be rude, little Sister." Anchen hesitated. "Friedrich and I are announcing our engagement."

"Congratulations."

"Thank you." Anchen hesitated again, which finally made Eva pay attention as her sister was normally extremely straightforward and rarely hesitated before doing anything.

"Would you like to come with us?" Anchen said.

"To Zweibrücken?"

"Yes. Cologne first, but we'll probably make one of Friedrick's estates our main residence." Anchen took a deep breath. "We would like you to become our chatelaine, and run our homes."

They both stopped in middle of the hall.

"Please don't be insulted." Anchen rushed on. "It is an honorable position, even if it is not something a daughter of our father would normally consider. It wouldn't be right for you to do so in a stranger's household, but doing so to aid your sister in her new responsibilities is a different matter. Friedrich might be young, but he *is* the count of Zweibrücken, etc."

"No, Anchen." Eva slowly shook her head. "It's very kind of you, and I thank both you and your Friedrich, but I want to spend my life doing research on natural science."

"At Quedlinburg? Abbess Dorothea wants you there, and our brother would probably dower you, but you didn't seem in favor of the idea when Eleonore mentioned the possibility."

"No. I want my own laboratory."

"You'd need a wealthy patron for that. Like the alchemists. But they were old male scholars, not young girls. Who would offer to pay your bills?" Anchen sounded distressed, but at least she was listening and taking Eva seriously. "Especially since it would almost certainly make our entire family his enemies."

"Or I need to come up with something that'll earn me a lot of money, and preferably gain me a reputation as a very capable scientist in the American style as well."

Anchen's frown changed into a broad grin. "Absolutely wonderful, little Sister. I totally approve. You figure out what it should be, and I'll help you bring it about. We could probably enlist Litsa and Sister Maximiliane as well. Let us get the dresses out of the way, and go have tea at the House of Hesse. There's a small gathering today, and they should both be there."

# Chapter 36

*Cologne, Hatzfeldt House*
*February 12, 1635*

"Lock up your daughters! The Saint and the Wolf hast come!"

At the laughing shout just when the carriage entered the courtyard, Charlotte looked questioningly at Dame Anna on the seat beside her.

"Ah, that would be young Wilhelm of the Weisweiler Hatzfeldts. Please pardon his levity, my dear Charlotte. It is based on a very sincere affection for his older cousins, and there is no insult intended, just joy at seeing them again."

"Certainly. Melchior has been telling me about the new set of family that I have acquired, and this must be the young son of Adolpha von Cortenbach. He is the one your uncle Georg has taken under his wings." Charlotte gathered her lap rug and prepared to leave the carriage.

"I assume the Saint mentioned must be your husband, dear Charlotte," Madeleine's voice from the faraway corner of the carriage held more than a lacing of acidity, "but I really don't see why anyone should need to lock up their daughters on his behalf."

"Ah, my dear Madeleine," Dame Anna's mild smile was in no way echoed in her suddenly sharp eyes, "I'm afraid there have been several instances where Melchior's very chastity has made

223

him a challenge to women who really should be old enough to know better."

Charlotte hid a grin at the sudden red color in Madeleine's cheeks. The older woman probably wouldn't have gone as far as to actually seduce Melchior in Bonn, but there was no doubt that his failure to appreciate the charms of the temperamental beauty had made him an almost irresistible challenge.

But no harm had been done. Dame Anna and Frau Benedicte had neatly blocked Madeleine after that single scene on the evening of their arrival. Still, that scene had been embarrassing to everybody involved. Everybody, that is except for Wolf, who had apparently considered it the greatest joke he had ever heard, and been no help at all.

"Milady?" Charlotte looked at Allenberg holding out a hand to take the fur-lined rug. When it had first been suggested that Charlotte should employ her husband's female quartermaster as a secretary, she had assumed that it was a joke, but she had decided to give the big woman a chance, and Allenberg—as everybody including Charlotte's husband called her—had proved extremely capable and with a surprisingly big store of knowledge about the most diverse subjects. Mostly concerning trade, but still quite impressive.

In the swirling snow of the courtyard of what must be the newly refurbished Hatzfeldt House, Melchior was gently hugging a younger woman wrapped in a hooded blue cloak and leaning on a cane, while Wolf was laughing and slapping an elderly man on the shoulder. The obvious source of the shout turned out to be a very young man, grinning broadly and almost dancing like an eager horse around Melchior and Wolf, and on the staircase a spindly looking man with narrow shoulders and a big smile stood with his arm around a decidedly overdressed young woman, whose ribbons were blowing around in the gathering wind. All around there also seemed to be an endless number of copper-curled children, cats and people dressed as servants, but—despite variations in build and coloration—the people of interest to Charlotte had a pronounced family likeness.

"The old man is Uncle Georg, the couple is Hermann and Trinket, and the woman in blue is Lucie." Dame Anna's beautiful voice was pitched low enough to reach only Charlotte. "The children are the Peters, the illegitimate children of Lucie's late husband. Their status is about like that of fostered pages."

"Thank you." Charlotte kept her own voice low, and went to greet her husband's family with a smile.

"And then I told Father Johannes that I simply had to have my parlor done over in pale lilac silk instead of that common pink, but he said..."

"Trinket, my dear." Dame Anna's voice cut across Trinket's chatter in a gentle rebuke. "This is a very pretty room, but both Lady Charlotte and I need to freshen up a little before sitting down to lunch, which I'm sure shortly will be ready to serve."

"Oh! Yes. Yes, of course. I'll show you there." The young girl's fair skin blushed to a much deeper red than the walls of her—in Charlotte's opinion—much too garish room.

"Yours is truly a beautiful room. Was the stained glass window with the white rose your own idea?" Charlotte linked her arm with Trinket's and started walking along the corridor. The girl might be both silly and vain, but she was obviously trying to impress Charlotte, and there was no reason not to be kind to the silly chit.

"Yes. I've always loved the way the light from the windows in the cathedral made the floor and walls look like a garden of flowers even in winter. Father Johannes suggested a white rose, and made the drawing for the glass maker. I would have liked a pink rose and in one of the bigger windows, but Father Johannes pointed out that the smallest window was the one getting the most light, and that any other color than white would make it difficult to change the color scheme." Trinket regained some of her liveliness while talking about her pretties. "He had spent years in the American town called Grantville, and had there seen a room supposedly looking like the bottom of the sea, and another with the ceiling like a sky with stars of small glowing glass bulbs. He also had some magazines called *Simplicissimus* with drawings of the rooms. They were very pretty. I did ask Archbishop Ferdinand..." Trinket stopped, and stood looking at the closed door. Charlotte threw a quick glance at Dame Anna, who shook her head at the silent question. No, Trinket didn't know about Charlotte's treatment in the hands of the archbishop. Dame Anna reached out a hand to touch Trinket's shoulder.

"Oh, sorry. I was woolgathering." Trinket shook her head and opened the door. "I did ask Archbishop Ferdinand, and there's nothing seriously wrong with having a stained glass window in a secular room. But he didn't approve. Of course. Any money one could spare should be given to the Church."

"Ah! But then glassmakers have nowhere to practice before working on the big windows in churches—and would either starve or be forced to rely on the Church's charity as well."

At Charlotte's words Trinket's face lit up, and she gave the first completely unguarded smile Charlotte had seen on her face.

"I'd not thought about it that way." She impulsively gave Charlotte a hug. "I'm very glad my brother-in-law married you. The rest of the family just makes fun of me." She gave a sigh. "I know I'm vain and silly, but I really want my pretties so much. But never mind that now. I'd better go be sensible in the kitchen, and see that the table is set for lunch in the big dining room. Lucie runs the household, when Maxie isn't here, but they are both moving to Magdeburg, so I'm supposed to take over."

After she left, Dame Anna poured the warm water from the big jug into the basin and handed Charlotte a washing cloth. "Not a complete dimwit."

"No. I take it she was Archbishop Ferdinand's ward after her parents died."

"Yes. And I don't envy her that. I had a word with Thomas, our old head groom, while you were greeting the rest of the family. The archbishop is still supposed to be somewhere near Aachen and showing no signs of returning. Could be just the weather stopping him, but Franz's former secretary, Otto Tweimal, has been here to talk to the council, and supposedly brought reports back to his new master."

"I see. And I think I'll leave all worries about Archbishop Ferdinand and his doings to Melchior. But let's hurry to that lunch. I'm starving."

"So, come spring I'll move myself and all the Peters to Magdeburg." Lucie smiled at Charlotte and offered her the platter with spicy roast duck and honeyed quiches for a second serving. "Maxie—that is Sister Maximiliane—has bought a fairly large house in that town, and invited me to make my home there. I'll take all the Peters with me, as they'll have better opportunities for an education there. Father Johannes—he's a painter and a very good friend of both me and Melchior, who has recently started a production of porcelain—might try the oldest Peters as apprentices, but in any case there should be plenty of opportunities for them there."

"That sounds like a very good idea." Charlotte smiled back and passed the platter on to her husband. Lucie had seemed a little quiet, until she started talking about the children. It obviously wasn't a problem to her that they were the offspring of her husband and his mistress. "But are they really all named Peter?"

Everyone around the table laughed. "Oh, no. Two of them are even girls," Melchior said, refilling the goblet he shared with Charlotte with wine. "It is Father Johannes' doing. During his stay with the Americans in Grantville, he had read a book about Peter Pan and something called the Wild Boys, and he claimed that the Peters were all wild boys at heart, and therefore started to call them all Peter."

"I suspect that he also couldn't tell them apart, but it really was a most amusing story, and the Peters absolutely loved it." Lucie glanced around the table to see if anybody wanted more of the meat dishes before nodding to the maid by the door to signal the serving of the next course. The Hatzfeldts set a very nice table for a household in a town that had been under siege for the entire autumn, so Charlotte took the opportunity to change the subject.

"I am surprised at the speed at which your larder has been restocked." She smiled first at Lucie then to Hermann on the other side of the table to indicate that she wasn't talking simply about food. "How far around do you normally trade?"

"Oh, it's fairly much all the way up and down the Rhine." Hermann answered. "We do not get quite the same amount of exotic trade as the ocean ports, and of course any wars or rebellions touching the Rhine will disturb things for a while, but as one road closes, so another gains importance. If the present trouble in Bavaria continues, the trade along the southern route east from the Rhine via Basel is almost certain to increase. Are you familiar with Bernhard of Saxe-Weimar?"

"Not really. We met briefly a few times after my marriage to Wolfgang, but we've never spoken more than a few commonplace greetings."

Charlotte appreciated the discretion shown by Hermann by not mentioning Essen, but Bernhard and the upper Rhine was not the direction Charlotte wanted the conversation to take. "I am however more interested in the possibilities along the lower Rhine. According to the letters we have received from Magdeburg, the USE plans to support Essen's claim-by-conquest to the Düsseldorf area, while my brother is expected to receive the rest of Berg, and join the USE. I would of course have preferred to keep Berg—all of it—for my son and myself, but I have no intention of jeopardizing the prosperity of Jülich by refusing to take advantage of the trading possibilities with Essen as well as the USE—much less create a break with my family."

"Ah! Spoken like a true ruler." Uncle Georg at the end of the table raised his goblet and nodded, smiling at Charlotte. "Have you also sought information about the needs of your realm, and the possibilities available?"

"Frau Benedicte Eigenhaus in Bonn mentioned several possibilities, and Allenberg, my new secretary, knew of a few more. But I'm afraid Jülich needs almost everything." Charlotte smiled back at the charming old man. "Wolfgang's campaign against Essen was brief as such goes, but he threw every resource he had into that undertaking."

"A sound enough decision in itself." Herman looked toward Melchior, who nodded in agreement. "A halfhearted attack against someone as strong and resourceful as Essen would be a complete folly. And whatever else your first husband was, he was definitely no fool." Hermann hesitated. "Though some of his latest decisions looked a bit odd from the outside."

"Spoken like a true diplomat, Brother," said Melchior. "But do you know of any particular needs and problems in Jülich, Uncle Georg?"

"We have of course been rather isolated by the siege," Georg replied, "and later fully occupied by repairing as much of the damage as possible. The number of casualties grew extremely high during the later part of the cannonade, when Hesse knew he had to win before he was stopped. But both young Wilhelm's mother, Adolpha von Cortenbach, and your foster-brother, Johan Adrian, have written. Jülich has not been under direct attack from either Essen or Hesse, but there have been minor raids and some looting, mainly from Archbishop Ferdinand's mercenaries. The people left in charge by Duke Wolfgang have proven somewhat wishy-washy, so there hasn't been much in the way of central coordination, but Johan Adrian and Adolpha have made contact with the surviving members of the old administration to form a kind of emergency council. From what they can tell, the main problems are in the short term: a serious lack of food due to most of the harvest being stolen by raiders, a shortage of weapons for local defense of what's left, and no money to buy either. In the long term: the loss of all the local men killed by the Essen army could cripple Jülich despite its fertile land, but if Melchior plans to keep even a minor part of his regiments around him, that should solve that problem quite neatly."

"Oh, I do. And we've got the weapons as well," Melchior said. "Any signs of activity from the Low Countries?"

"Patrols watching the border, certainly." Herman took over. "But Don Fernando has so far stayed mainly on the west bank of the Meuse, De Geer on the east bank of the Rhine, and nobody but Archbishop Ferdinand has shown any interest in the area south of the Aachen-Cologne road."

"Most likely everybody has been waiting to see what decrees came out of Magdeburg." Lucie interrupted her brother. "Jülich's valuable for its farming potential—and from what Father Johannes told about the likely effect of the industries now growing around Magdeburg, it's only likely to become more so in the future—but no sane ruler in this part of the world is likely to want a war with the USE."

"No, but that's not necessarily enough to protect Jülich, unless I follow the rest of the family and join the USE." Charlotte looked at her husband. "We'll need someone to look into buying food in bulk for immediate delivery, but preferably delayed payment until after next harvest. And I'd like us to move to Jülich Town as quickly as possible."

Melchior nodded. "Allenberg with someone local."

"One of my assistants," Herman interrupted.

"Yes, and contacting the Abrabanels," said Lucie.

"Good." Melchior leaned forward to look at Wolf at the other end of the table. "You take the Old Boys into Jülich the day after tomorrow. Simon would have left messages with either Adolpha or Johan Adrian in Jülich Town. Find out where they've gone, leave a garrison, and move on. If no trouble reported, head for the Meuse. Don Fernando is far more likely to start an aggression than De Geer."

"I really think it would be better to send Lorentz or Dannwitz. My reputation isn't suited for calming people down," Wolf said and reached to pour more wine for Madelaine and himself. "On the other hand, I'm not at all sure it's safe to ignore Archbishop Ferdinand, and alarming him would have no drawback that I can see. So why don't I move the Old Boys to Düren, and tell Dannwitz to take his regiment north into Jülich?"

"Nice try, Cos, but you're not going anywhere near Irish Butler if I can prevent it." Melchior hesitated. "You do however have a point about alarming people. I'll take the Old Boys myself, and you'll be personally in charge of Charlotte's safety, both here in Cologne and during the move once I've made sure it's safe."

Wolf's response was a word not previously known to Charlotte.

# Chapter 37

*Between Aachen and Cologne*
*February 15, 1635*

"Shit!" Simon tried to throw himself off the horse as it slipped on a patch of ice beneath the snow, but his stiff snow-covered legs refused to respond, and both he and the horse hit the ground hard. Struggling to keep his wits about him despite the fog that came from having been tired and cold for too long, Simon took stock of his situation. No one was shooting at him or waving around edged objects—which was always good. His horse was heaving for breath but not screaming, so it might be foundered or lame, but probably wouldn't have to be killed—which was really good, since cavalry horses were expensive. His face, toes and hands were all hurting, but they had been doing so for hours, and it wasn't until they stopped hurting that frostbite became a real danger. So if nothing was broken, he could probably walk to some kind of shelter. The bad news was that while his small compass could keep him going in the right direction, he'd lost the road after crossing the Rur river, and had no idea how far he was from Cologne.

Simon twisted himself around to reach the saddle and free the foot still caught in the stirrup. At his touch the horse scrambled to its feet, and Simon slowly stood up. Nope, nothing broken, and while the horse held its head so low it was almost touching

231

the ground, it did seem to be resting evenly on all four legs. Normally he would have found shelter—or rather have stayed where he was three days ago when the snowstorm came racing in from the northwest—but the news Simon was bringing just couldn't wait. A large Habsburg army had crossed the Meuse at Maastricht and was moving eastward. Don Fernando had obviously heard that Jülich was not yet a part of the USE, and decided to try expanding his border all the way to the Rhine. The storm would have hit Rosy before he could have reached Cologne, and Simon had no way of knowing if the general even knew about the attack on Geilenkirchen. The troops at Geilen-kirchen had probably been an advance force aimed at securing the road to Jülich Town, but all movements would be stalled by the storm, so if only he could reach the general, there was still time to beat them back.

Fumbling to get the compass out from its pocket in his coat Simon would have dropped it in the snow if it hadn't been attached with a thin chain. West. That was probably still his best direction. Sooner or later he would hit the Rhine—though hope-fully not literally. Picking up the reins Simon started walking.

## Cologne, Hatzfeldt House
## February 16, 1635

"They've left." Wolf slammed open the door to the muniment room.

"Really! Wolf, you are the rudest, most inconsiderate..." Lucie grabbed her blotter and tried to soak up the ink she had just spilled.

"Mind your manner, Cos, and help Lucie clean up the spill." Melchior reached across the big oak table to remove the most important of the papers he'd been studying with Charlotte, Lucie and Allenberg.

"I'll do that!" The tiny Peter on duty as Lucie's page quickly pulled a lambskin off a chair, threw it on the table, climbed on top of it and started scrubbing by stamping his feet.

Lucie looked at Charlotte and grinned. "At least it wasn't one of the cats."

"Cats work as an ink blotter?" The Peter stopped stamping, and looked questioning at Lucie.

"I don't know. And you'll not try to find out. Nor will any of the other kids. And you must not get Old Thomas to try it for you either." Lucie lifted the child down and removed the lambskin. The table was a mess. "You acted very quickly to stop the ink. That was fine. Now take the skin down to the laundry room and give it to one of the maids."

The child bundled up the skin and ran towards the door, forcing Wolf to step aside.

"The Peters really have too much energy to be locked up in the house by this snowstorm with no real duties, dear Sister." Melchior started blotting the stained papers with a piece of scrap paper before passing them on to Allenberg.

"I know, but they are still just kids, and I don't want to work them too hard." Lucie stretched her body carefully to ease her crippled muscles. "This table will need both sanding and scrubbing with bleach."

"And just how long do you all plan to ignore me?" Wolf, who had remained by the door tapping his foot in irritation, walked to the table and dropped gracelessly into a chair.

"Grow up, Cos." Lucie's smile took the worst edge off her words. "You sound like a sulking child, and that is quite unbecoming for a man your age."

"Apologize for startling the ladies, and you can tell us what's wrong." Melchior leaned back in his chair and raised an eyebrow at his second-in-command. Wolf was always a problem when idle in garrison, and while he was obviously trying to behave himself, he was also chafing under the snowstorm that was keeping them all from moving on with their plans.

"Ladies, my apology." Wolf stood up and made a small bow, his temper under control, if only barely so. "Irish Butler and the rest have left the archbishop and gone east or south. Abrabanel had sent someone from his caravan back to Cologne, and he mentioned seeing the bastards on the road to Trier, when I bought him a drink."

"And the archbishop?"

"Still holed up somewhere south of Düren, as far as anybody knows. Cos, I really, really want to go after them."

"No. Once Simon and his patrol get back and report on the situation in Jülich, I'll consider giving you furlough. But I'm not going to rob myself of my second in command when facing an unknown situation. You're far from useless to me, my Wolf." Melchior smiled as he added the compliment.

"Thanks." Wolf scowled at Melchior. "How useless would I have to become in order for you to let me hunt?"

"Useless enough for me to hang you, Cos. You are not going." The steel in Melchior's voice made it clear that the discussion was over.

Simon staggered into the court of Hatzfeldt House, and was knocked down by somebody rushing out without looking where he was going. It would probably have been smarter just to have remained at the gate tower where he'd left his horse, but Simon was no longer really thinking, and the old habit of reporting only to the general was too strong.

There were a lot of people talking, moving him around, and replacing his cloth with warmed blankets, but it wasn't really until he was sitting in an inglenook that he started recognizing anybody. He was propped up against Wolf and with the general on the other side feeding him honeyed milk from a mug. That was weird.

"Report, Simon." The short order from the general got Simon talking.

"Don Fernando has crossed the Meuse with a large army, taken Gangelt, and is besieging Sittard. Geilenkirchen was under attack. Cavalry and dragoons. Pr'bly one regiment at Geilenkirchen, at least three at Sittard. Schaden gone north, Rosy to warn you and Adolpha. You haven't seen him?" His worry for Rosy finally cut through Simon's foggy mind.

"No, but the road to Jülich Town has been closed since the storm started. Impassible drifts by Elsdorf. Any details?"

"No. I turned back as soon as I knew they had a stronghold at Gangelt. Slow going in the snow. Wouldn't have moved much since then." As the heat seeped into Simon, he could feel himself relaxing, and the world started spinning in circles.

"Wolf, take the siege specialists to Düren and lead Dannwitz west to Aachen, then move north and see if you can gain control of the road to Sittard. I'll take both Lorentz and the Old Boys and get the road cleared to Jülich Town, then aim for Gangelt by way of Aldenhoven and Brunssum. Meet me . . ." Melchior's orders were the last thing Simon heard before passing out.

# Chapter 38

*Brunssum*
*February 20, 1635*

The small village of Brunssum would have looked quite cozy nestled between the snowy hills, but the massed men and horses on the low slopes rather spoiled the picture of rural idyll. Melchior sat quietly on his horse waiting for the villagers to spread the carpet on the cleared hill top and get the small table with the two chairs in place. It was still quite cold, but the sun combined with the absolute lack of wind meant that his meeting with Don Fernando could take place outdoors, and in full sight of their men. Strictly speaking, that wasn't necessary as both he and Don Fernando were in full control as leaders. But quite aside from the fact that they were formally two Habsburg armies facing off, they also both knew the value of making a display of poise and calm for the men they led.

Wolf had sent a message yesterday that he had regained control of the road north from Maastricht after a brief fight, and was moving north toward the now occupied Sittard. Don Fernando had holed up in Gangelt during the snowstorm, and managed to take the neighboring Sittard as soon as the snowstorm had ended, but with only two newly conquered towns as a base he was in a vulnerable situation—and knew it. Had he managed to take Jülich Town as well as all the fortifications along the Meuse

235

before Melchior could bring his regiments into play, the situation would have been entirely different. But despite having far more resources to call in from the Low Countries than Melchior could muster, Don Fernando had now been willing to meet for a negotiation with only minimal conditions.

Melchior slid off his horse and motioned Simon to follow him. Simon had bounced back from his ordeal with a speed that made Melchior feel positively old, and was once again following Melchior around as a combined courier and aide de camp. They had found Rosy laid up at a farm delirious with fever, and with serious frostbite in his feet, and Schaden had simply attached himself to the regiments again yesterday with a brief report of no major military movements to the north.

That actually made good military sense to Melchior. Normally it would have been best for Don Fernando to sweep down on Jülich Town from the north to support his attack from the west, but his treaties with both the USE and Essen were new, and moving major forces towards their borders could—and probably would—be taken as aggression. Jülich, Luxemburg and the area in between on the other hand were all fairly disorganized, and with no major military forces to oppose him.

"Don Fernando, Your Royal Highness." Melchior gave his best court-bow and went to take the chair across from the already seated man. That Don Fernando was of much higher rank made it necessary that Melchior was seen accepting his own lower status without appearing subservient, but Melchior was also a capable and respected military leader, and at least in the field he could meet with any other military leader as a near equal.

"My wife, Countess Palatine Katharina Charlotte, sends her regards and best wishes for you and your esteemed wife. And if you would be so kind as to read these papers from your brother-in-law before we start this meeting?" Don Fernando carefully read the papers and looked thoughtful as he passed them back to Melchior.

"Archduke—now king—Ferdinand placed quite a lot of trust in you for someone trained by Wallenstein. And I can see that our cousin has phrased this to indicate that this trust was not expected to change when he followed his father on the throne." Don Fernando's rigid posture would have indicated displeasure in most men, but Melchior had met enough Spanish noblemen in Vienna to ignore that impression, and instead watch his opponent's eyes.

"Yes," Melchior made sure he replied with a small bow of his head without bending his back. "I have never cared for politics or lent myself to intrigues. And unless you believe my liege lord to be mistaken in his trust, I suggest we get right to the point."

Don Fernando inclined his head slightly, but said nothing.

"My wife's claim on Jülich has been accepted by the most important members of her family as well as by the USE government. And I have the men and money to turn any attempt to take it from her into a most costly undertaking."

This extremely blunt speaking produced a raised eyebrow followed by another small nod.

"My wife wishes Jülich to keep its sovereignty, but realizes that keeping Jülich an independent state among such powerful neighbors is likely to lead to attempts to change that. Such as this." Melchior indicated Don Fernando and his army with a wave of his hand, and continued. "My wife has natural alliances to the USE through her family, and while she has no interest in pursuing a policy of conflict with Essen, a close alliance with those who killed her first husband would offend everybody—including herself. She might still find it necessary to join the USE, but would like to make it clear that such would not be her first choice."

Only because Melchior was watching Don Fernando so closely did he spot the glint of amusement in the man's eyes. Apparently the increasingly erratic behavior of the late Duke Wolfgang had been a source of worry for his western neighbor, but since the duke had been related by blood or marriage to just about every aristocratic family in Europe, appearances had to be maintained—and especially against a merchant upstart like De Geer. *Nil nisi bene.*

"The patchwork of interests and alliances to the south must be dealt with if this region is to take advantage of all the new possibilities," Melchior continued, "but that can wait for a later occasion. This leaves my wife and me with our relations to the Low Countries, and thus the possibility of some kind of alliance with you. We would of course have preferred a more orderly occasion for discussing the possible arrangements, but we believe that there is still time to limit the damage. We also believe that such an arrangement would be vastly preferable to you compared with having my wife join the USE before you can finish your campaign here in Jülich."

Don Fernando gave a small nod. "A liege oath from your

wife to me? I have no wish to poach on my cousin's territory by asking one of you." That Don Fernando was now unbending enough to actually make a suggestion was a most promising sign.

"That could be a possibility, but could also cost my wife dearly in terms of support from her family, who are very strongly in favor of having Jülich join the USE. What we had in mind was something with a slightly more modern twist. Are you familiar with the works of Grotius, and the concept of a buffer state?"

"Certainly." Don Fernando unbent as far as to give a real smile. "And you are quite right in assuming that I would prefer such an arrangement. The actual contract must involve lawyers to get all the pesky little details in place, but your word on good intentions would be enough for me to end hostilities and withdraw my companies from this side of the Meuse." He's smile turned wry. "I would—naturally—like to expand my territory to gain as much of the Rhine as possible, and Archbishop Ferdinand's latest troubles have left the prize of Cologne dangling in the air, as bait for many schemes and dreams. But I myself would engage the USE in open hostility only as a last resort, and I pride myself too much on my good sense to expect you to be any different."

"My freely given word on good intentions, and our sincere wish for peaceful relations and cooperations." Melchior smiled back and nodded.

"Yes, and speaking of cooperations: I would like to make a suggestion concerning the rather problematic southern area." Don Fernando now smiled a little broader. "I've been negotiating with the two largest interests involved in the Eifel area. They have been dragging their feet, and wasting my time with political maneuverings. The governor of Luxemburg and the administrator of the Province of the Upper Rhine are both coming to Aachen in a couple of weeks, and I would like to invite you to join us there."

"Ah! And the two of us coming to that meeting together, and with our combined armies behind us, should ensure the speediest possible conclusion to any negotiations." Melchior kept smiling, but also gave a small shrug. "My wife and I have no territorial aspirations in that direction, but we are most interested in stable government and trading opportunities. I shall be delighted to accompany you to Aachen."

# Chapter 39

*Bamberg, Geyersworth Palace, SoTF administration*
*election office*
*February 25, 1635*

"Hi Sister Sister, I'm so sorry I'm late." Terrie rushed into the office, and embraced the young woman in a brown nun's habit standing at the tall lectern desk.

"We have time," Sister Tabitha answered. "Sister Evangelina had problems with the Bavarian yeast she brought with her, so rather than starting right after Vesper, the meeting will start an hour later."

"Ah! But I have newer news. Mother wants us both go by Frau Anna Eberhart's house and escort her to the meeting."

"Frau Eberhart?"

"Yes, she is one of the finest Rauchbier brewers in Bamberg, but after her sister Maria mysteriously disappeared a few months ago, she has been very nervous, and has refused to go out after dark. Mother talked her into coming to the Women's Institute's Brewer Evening by promising to send her own daughters to escort her."

"I know American women are supposed to be fine fighters, but why would two young girls make her feel any safer?" Sister Tabitha smiled fondly at her new friend, who seemed determined to turn her into a sister as well as a Sister.

239

"I am carrying the new gun my father gave me for Christmas, but her husband is sending an apprentice along for brawn. Your holiness and my American ingenuity are supposed to deal with anything else. Abracadabra." Terrie waved her hands around. "She lives up by the cathedral so we better get going. Have you banked the fire?"

"Yes, I'll just grab my cloak and blow out the candles."

Outside the palace the fog was rolling thick and wooly along the river, and the streets were slippery with wet snow. Only the nearest houses were visible, but the bells of the invisible churches were tolling, and a man selling hot pretzels could be heard somewhere in the nearby streets. As the two young women started walking up the hill from the river the bells stopped to signal the start of the evening service and Sister Tabitha took out her rosary and starting whispering her prayers as she walked. Terrie walked in silence until the rosary was put away.

"How did you decide to become a nun?" Terrie asked.

"I just never considered anything else." Sister Tabitha slipped a little on the frozen cobbles and Terrie grabbed her arm. "I overheard your father mention that you've not yet settled on a profession, or decided what you want to do after graduation."

"That's right. Most people—even in Grantville—do what their parents did. Father wants me doing some kind of administration, but laws bore me silly. Mother thinks I should study medicine or nursing, and I do like both chemistry and biology, but I just don't want to spend my time with sick people. I suppose you think I'm shallow?"

"No, I've never been interested in nursing either."

"It must be easier when you have a vocation. I know you're only twenty, so you must have known what you wanted from when you were very young." Now it was Terrie's turn to slip a little.

"That's not quite how it was. In fact I'm really just doing the normal thing and following my mother's profession." Sister Tabitha smiled at Terrie, who had stopped and looked up at her in amazement. "My mother was raped, when her convent in Hungary was sacked. She fostered me with the owner of a nearby vineyard, so she could visit me. Once I was old enough to become a postulate, I just went to live with her, and moved to Bavaria when she did. She died of the pox shortly after we moved. The whole convent fell ill, and many died. Those of us who survived with only a few scars"—she pointed at the group of small scars on her cheek—"had to gather all our resources to keep the convent going. I had been just about ready to take my first vows, but ended up running the winemaking and selling. I'm still more than a year from taking my final vows."

"I see." Terrie walked on in silence until they stopped outside the Eberhart brewery. "Have you ever wanted to own your own vineyards?"

"No, not really. What I would like the most would be to work directly with the plants. Breed new and better varieties. Frau Kacere has kindly helped me find some books from your homeland. They are very interesting, and I would like to have more time to study them." She smiled. "Perhaps someday. I like it here." She looked back down the cobbled street to the river hazy with mist. "Father Arnoldi was bad, but there are good people here opposing him, and those who support him."

"Yes, and we want you here." Terrie reached for the knocker on the wooden gate. "Wine. I think I'll talk to Mother about arranging an evening about wine like this one about brewing."

Sister Tabitha shook her head. "Winemaking is a man's profession, while brewing is mostly done within the household and thus a woman's task. It would be considered odd."

"Good."

## Mainz, Church of St. Alban

*To Franz von Hatzfeldt, Prince-Bishop of Würzburg*
*From Johann Philipp von Schönborn*

*My dearest Franz,*
*Due to the recent upheaval I hear is taking place around Cologne, I am directing this letter to your brother in Mainz, asking him to forward it to you, wherever the Lord has seen fit to lead you. I hope this finds you in good health and prosperous circumstances, and look forward to the day when we shall meet again. In case you feel the time for our return to your bishopric draws near, I believe that you should grant me my wish, as I am afraid there are some problems in Würzburg, and it might be to*

*your benefit to first come to me here in Bamberg. Recent unfortunate circumstances have made it seem appropriate for me to relocate to Bamberg, but these I believe would be best told to you in person.*

*It pains me to talk about rivals or competitors within Our Holy Mother Church, but as you know Father Arnoldi felt that he should have been Ehrenberg's successor in Würzburg, and he has slowly been building up support for himself during your exile, both in secular circles and within the Church. He cannot depose you, and I do not know of him to be plotting your demise, but in order to save yourself unnecessary struggles my advice to you is to come directly here to join me in Bamberg.*

*The new USE administration is considering making Bamberg its center for the entire province, and I believe things would go far more smoothly if you met the Americans here in person. I do not agree with all their ideas—far from it—but regardless of their secular views concerning church property and taxes, they are also very firmly opposed to any kind of witch-hunt, and that is what Father Arnoldi seems to be trying to stir up again.*

*Herr Salatto, whom I mentioned to you in the letter containing your safe conduct, is based in Würzburg, while the person in charge of the secular administration here in Bamberg is Herr Vincent Marcantonio. Both are well-meaning men of good hearts, whom I believe would appreciate your talent for administration, and especially all your many contacts in the other major towns of the province and beyond. I am sure you can imagine the herculean task it would be to set up an entirely new administrative headquarters, and if you were to approach one or both with an offer to help—rather than making demands on their time and resources—there should at present be the best possible opportunity for establishing a cordial relationship with this new power.*

*It pains me to admit that I have not been able to prevent the new administration from taking over most of the properties belonging directly to the Prince-Bishops of both Bamberg and Würzburg—alas, I lack the skills of negotiation so prominent in you and your esteemed family—but the vineyards and estates that you acquired before ascending to your present prominence should still be yours, and most of the buildings by the Cathedral are still considered part of the properties of the Church. The new administration's headquarters is being established in the Geyerswoerth Palace here in Bamberg, and with the aim of improving relations I have taken upon myself to lend as well some clerks and various records to both Herr Marcantonio and Herr Salatto. I beg of you not to consider these actions an act of betrayal. Contrary to the beliefs expressed by Father Arnoldi and his secular associates, I'm quite certain that the new structure is stable and will be toppled by neither civil unrest nor nefarious schemes.*

*I have done my best for you my friend and mentor, and am shamed that it is not more, but to preserve and further the beautiful and prosperous kingdom that you once dreamed, is in your absence far beyond my abilities.*

*Written by my hand and under my seal on
the 1. of January 1635 at the Cathedral of
Sct. Peter and Sct. Georg in Bamberg*

*Yours as ever,
Johann Philipp von Schönborn*

Franz put down the letter and looked at his friend breathing slowly in the bed beside his chair. Franz Wilhelm's stomach had taken a turn for the worse the day before they had arranged to leave, and despite the careful nursing he had received, the illness showed no signs of abating.

"What's in the letter?" Franz Wilhelm's voice was little more than a whisper.

"It's from Schönborn. He's getting along quite well with the Americans."

"Please read it for me."

Franz hesitated. Without Franz Wilhelm's help with getting free of Archbishop Ferdinand's schemes, he would still be stuck in that god-forsaken camp—or worse.

"Please, my friend." Franz Wilhelm moved his head on the pillow to look at Franz. "It's my body that's deteriorating, not my head."

Franz read the letter out loud.

"As I thought." Franz Wilhelm shifted his body a little. "You have to go as soon as in any way possible. Coming from Schön-born that letter is a shout for help."

"Yes, I know. But I also cannot abandon you after all the help that you have given me."

"You would be wasting that help if you stayed. And besides, my illness has delayed both of us, Franz, and I no longer think I can afford the time a detour to Bamberg would cost me. Hesse's campaign has come to an end, and I want to be in Minden before he turns his attention northward. Minden might not have been included in the province of Hesse-Kassel, but according to the rumors your brother Herman brought from Frankfurt, Hesse had orders via radio from Magdeburg to stop bombarding Cologne, but didn't stop. I need to get there in person, Franz. I'll write my people, and have them come here to escort me north. Carrying me if need be." Franz Wilhelm's voice now sounded stronger.

"And getting bumped around in a carried chair would make your sore stomach feel so much better. Be sensible, my friend." Franz looked around the sparsely furnished little room. It was warm and clean, and the best care possible would be given freely. "I'll go talk to Heinrich."

"About arranging for your travel?"

"About arranging for my travel."


## Magdeburg, House of Wettin

Eva stepped back towards the wall and turned her head from the light. That some of the men in the Danish delegation were unusually attractive didn't make their various reactions any easier to ignore. Eva smiled a little at her own thoughts; if there was one thing she would not waste her time and thoughts on, it was wishing for a husband. That she was expected to become the sister-in-law to the new prime minister had brought a few ambitious men sniffing around, but refusing to even consider that was the one thing regarding Eva that everybody agreed on. Most her relatives felt that Eva had best devote her life to catering to their comforts in various capacities, while Eleonore and Wettin wanted Eva to return to the school at Quedlinburg and become a nun or a teacher. Eva had been happy at Quedlinburg, studying the American books and making new and better medicines to sell for the school. But she wanted her own territory; and besides, Quedlinburg just wouldn't be the same without her sister Anchen, and their friends Litsa and Maria.

All four of them were here tonight, but separated by their new interests: Anchen with her fiancé, the young Count Friedrich von Zweibrücken, both looking besotted, Litsa gathering political news for her journalistic writings at the elbow of her cousin Amalie Elisabeth of Hesse-Kassel, and Maria... Eva sighed and started moving quickly across the brightly lit ballroom. And pretty Maria managing to flirt with the entire Danish delegation, while they were being introduced to Abbess Dorothea and Maria's newly arrived mother, Ehrengard. Eva had never liked the haughty and quarrelsome woman, but someone really should warn her that Anchen's betrothal had made Maria even more determined to marry well and early.

# Chapter 40

*Cologne, Hatzfeldt House*
*March 10, 1635*

"I really think you would be better off joining the USE, Sissy," said Friedrich.

Charlotte looked at her young brother with a mixture of fondness and irritation. He was obviously off on one of his wild enthusiasms, and had not stopped singing the praises for all things American since his arrival with Johanna von Anhalt-Dessau and Maxie.

"You've mentioned that a time or two—or ten—since our arrival." Maxie's usual vivacious entrance sent everybody smiling. Even Friedrich didn't sulk the way he usually did at even the slightest hint of reprimand.

"But Maxie, they are negotiating to join the Habsburgs in the Low Countries."

"An alliance, Brother, just as we plan to have an alliance with the USE. I know your tutor set you reading Grotius, and according to Melchior the Americans are really in favor of balancing powers and buffer states." She hesitated. "The Crown Loyalists might be less in favor of that than the old government, but I'm still trying for something that'll leave Jülich with more independence than joining the USE. The purpose—or one of them—of the negotiations my husband is presently undertaking is to establish something stable and acceptable to all for the entire Rhine-Mosel-Meuse triangle so the French cannot play Peter against Paul to strike north again. No matter how much you prefer adventure to politics, you must be able to see the benefits from that. Can you imagine what kind of trouble it would create if France managed to gain control of this side of the Rhine? Perhaps all the way to Düsseldorf? The Habsburgs would much rather Jülich joined the USE, and the USE—at least the old government—would much rather see us join the Low Countries. At the moment it could go either way, and I'm not ruling out that we'll end up joining the USE. Don Fernando and my husband are getting along really well, and some of the trading agreements that Allenberg suggested would be very favorable to everybody involved."

"Yes, yes," Friedrich waved the argument away and scowled at his sister, "and that's another thing. That husband of yours. You are a Countess Palatine from an old and fine family, and a jumped-up imperial count..."

"Friedrich! Melchior von Hatzfeldt is one of my closest friends." It was the first time Charlotte had seen Maxie that angry; she really did have quite a temper.

"Sorry, sorry. I'm sure you would not befriend someone who isn't of good character. But Charlotte is my sister, and she could marry royalty."

"No thanks, Brother. And that's exactly why I wanted to be married before I met my loving family again." Since Charlotte had expected precisely this kind of reaction from her family, she wasn't particularly upset about her brother's lack of enthusiasm for her marriage. "But did you get the letters sorted, Maxie?"

"Yes." Maxie's mood changed suddenly to worry. "I have opened the letter from Cardinal-Protector Mazzare directed to my cousin's palace in Bonn. No one seems to be contesting Ferdinand's position as archbishop of Cologne, and as far as the USE is concerned he can return, and providing he's willing to follow USE's laws, he can remain. I wonder if I should go talk to him myself. He's too proud to like returning in anything less than triumph, but his health isn't good, and much as he has annoyed me, I am fairly fond of that stubborn old fool."

"I'll go!" Friedrich looked ready to rush out of the house and jump on the first horse he encountered.

"No. That would be too cruel towards Johanna." Maxie's kind words made Friedrich hesitate.

"She could go with me. She's just spending her time here shopping with Trinket anyway."

"No. It would be too dangerous, what with all the small groups of mercenaries still lurking around. And besides: I know she has all kinds of plans for things the two of you could do together once she has made some additions to her wardrobe. We did leave Magdeburg rather abruptly."

"Wolf took off after the Irish mercenaries as soon as he brought his regiment back to Cologne, and young Simon is still with Melchior, so I think your best course of action is to wait for my husband's return," Charlotte said. "His last letter indicated that the negotiations were nearly finished, and he would have more authority in dealing with Archbishop Ferdinand than anybody else."

# Chapter 41

*The Inn of the Good Shepherd outside Frankfurt am Main*
*March 15, 1635*

"This is the last bloody, sodden straw that broke the donkey's back."

Franz looked up from his meal in alarm to see a rugged soldier standing scowling at him on the other side of his table.

"No preaching." The man sat down, grabbed Franz's wooden bowl and started shoveling the food into his mouth.

Franz looked towards the alarmed innkeeper, who had reached for something below the bar but stopped when Franz shook his head and held up two fingers to signal two more servings. Franz pushed his clay mug across the table and leaned back regarding his cousin, Wolf von Wildenburger-Hatzfeldt.

"It must be bad when you reach for food before ale," Franz commented as Wolf mopped up the last of the stew in the bowl and reached for the new serving just set down by the serving maid. That Wolf scowled at the pleasantly rounded maid was in fact even more unusual than that Wolf only now seemed to notice the mug and drain it.

"I said no preaching."

"I'm not. But I am capable of adding two and two. And starving plus a sudden dislike of bar maids plus the state of your boots adds up to you getting rolled and ending up stranded with

249

no horse and no money, trying to walk to Frankfurt and find one of Herman's contacts there. Am I correct?"

Wolf's only answer was a snarl.

Franz's father had taken Wolf into his household and raised him with Franz and his brothers. The careful and bookish Franz had had very little in common with the wild and adventurous bigger boy, and Franz knew that Wolf considered him a complete ninny. Still, their upbringing had turned the cousin into a brother in anything but name. An often annoying, and usually short of money brother, but still a brother, so Franz continued. "I have no funds to spare before I reach my destination, and what I'll find there is unknown. But we can redistribute the few packs on my second horse, and you can come with me."

"You have a second horse?" Wolf stopped eating and looked at Franz like a predator viewing an uninteresting morsel that might be worth eating after all.

"Yes, and you may not take it for your own unless you are on a mission from Melchior, which I doubt, or you wouldn't be here alone. Does he even know where you are?"

Wolf shrugged. "He knows I've gone after Irish Butler and his cronies. They've deserted Archbishop Ferdinand and gone south. Melchior kept me from following immediately after they left, and I had faulty information when I tried to pick up their trail. They must be south of here."

"You think they're heading for Bavaria?"

"Bound to. Who else would hire those traitorous buggers? The question just is how far south they'll go before crossing the Rhine. They wouldn't be welcome anywhere, so they'll probably look for the weakest area."

"Sorry, Cousin, but military weakness is outside my field."

"Yes, you never could fight your way out of a wet paper bag." Wolf frowned. "So how come you're traveling alone?"

"I parted from Franz Wilhelm von Wartenberg in Mainz. He's the prince-bishop of Minden in case you don't know. We escaped Archbishop Ferdinand together, and planned to borrow some money from Archbishop Anselm in Mainz, hire some guards and continue together to Würzburg. Franz Wilhelm had intended to make some contacts within the American administration before he went north to Minden, but instead he fell ill, and our plans changed. I'm simply moving south as quickly as the weather permits. Hence the second horse, though I have few belongings."

"But still going to Würzburg."

"No. To Bamberg. There're some troubles in Würzburg."

"I'll come with you. I leave most worrying about contacts and contract to Melchior, but the Americans are very good at gathering information, and they might know where Irish Butler went."

## *Magdeburg*

"This is so *unfair*!!! I want to stay in Magdeburg!!!"

Eva put her book down on the wide carriage seat. Maria's whining was already grating on her nerves, and they were barely out of Magdeburg yet. Unless she found some way to shut up that stupid little airhead, she'd surely strangle her before they ever got to Rothenburg. Eva had tried to arrange for them to travel by train at least as far as Grantville, and preferably from there to Kronach, but Eva's mother had insisted that her daughters should travel in her own horse-driven carriage as befitting for nobility, rather than to mingle with all sort of low-born riffraff on a public transport. That this would mean several extra weeks of rumbling along badly kept snow-covered roads, of course, meant nothing to the haughty woman.

"The balls to celebrate the election were barely getting started, and I'm being sent off to my mother's obscure, rural friend. I want to stay in Magdeburg!!!"

"Then you shouldn't have let your mother catch you alone with that Danish secretary." Eva took a firm hold on her temper and tried a little reason. "That is not the kind of behavior that'll gain you the kind of husband you want."

"We were only kissing." Maria defended herself. "And with his golden curls and mine, we would have the most beautiful little angel-babies. Ever since she arrived at Magdeburg, mother has been talking about nothing but my sister Katharina's new baby."

"Ria, he was already married."

"Well, I didn't know that."

"Abbess Dorothea was standing right beside you when she told your mother."

"Not that I heard." Maria sniffed and pressed her nose against the new glass panels in the carriage door, trying to look back at the town behind them.

"No you were probably too busy batting your eyelashes over your fan." Eva gave up. Reason didn't really stand a chance of making an impression on Maria von Schwarzenfels anyway. Staying with her cousin Amalie Elisabeth, wife to the landgrave of Hesse-Kassel, might have been the pretty young girl's first contact with the most powerful people in Europe, but Maria was the youngest—and prettiest—of her family, and had been spoiled all her life. Especially by her doting father. Eva was the youngest of her own family, but in the ducal family of Anhalt-Dessau it had been the sons and the oldest sisters who had been the center of attention, and she had mainly been left to the servants and her books.

"Why didn't you talk the abbess into stopping my mother? She's been doting on you ever since we stayed at her stupid school."

Eva didn't answer. Yes, the abbess had tried again to get Eva to return to Quedlinburg, tempting with extra lessons by teachers from Grantville and her own still-room and hinting at a teacher's position with or without becoming a nun, but Eva was getting more and more determined to have her own laboratory. And besides: trying to teach a room full of girls like Maria would drive her crazy.

"I want to stay in Magdeburg!!!"

Eva took a deep breath and picked up her book.

## Bamberg

Terrie stopped with her hand on the latch to open the gate to the brewery, and listened to the loud shouting inside. Normally the Eberhart household was very quiet with no one raising their voices except when the apprentices got a little boisterous. Part of this was Frau Eberhart's recent dislike of loud noises, but judging from the apprentices' behavior, Herr Eberhart had always been a gentle giant, who might not accept shoddy work, but didn't need to shout to make his point. Of course a leaking barrel tended to make its own point, but still, the roaring seemed totally out of character.

"That sounds like Councilor Bitterfeld." Terrie looked over

her shoulder at Sister Tabitha standing behind her.

"You mean the roaring? I thought that was Herr Eberhart finally losing his temper over something."

"No, it's Bitterfeld. When Father Arnoldi had us locked up in Würzburg awaiting the torture and trials, Schönborn needed something to cover the sounds of our escape. He created that by getting into a quarrel with Councilor Bitterfeld. A very brave thing to do. Councilor Bitterfeld is strong, and he likes to hit people."

"Likes to hit people?" Terrie let go of the latch and turned to stare at her friend.

"Yes." Sister Tabitha smiled at her friend's surprise. "Many household masters beat their servants, apprentices and children, and some also their wives. But there was almost constantly someone in Councilor Bitterfeld's household with a broken bone. At least it happened often enough for it to be gossiped about."

"But why didn't anyone stop this?"

"It's not illegal."

"It most certainly is."

"Then I just don't think anyone noticed that." Sister Tabitha considered her outraged friend. "Don't American men ever beat the members of their household?"

Terrie started to answer, then hesitated. "American households don't often have servants, and certainly no one is allowed to beat them. But I must admit that some couples fight."

"Oh yes, the American Amazons." Sister Tabitha smiled. "I can imagine that knowing that your wife is perfectly capable of grabbing a gun and shooting you keeps American men from being too eager to use their fists." She continued. "Here it's more that being unable to hold on to your authority without damaging your dependents is seen as a flaw. When Councilor Bitterfeld's wife died, he wanted to marry the daughter of one of the wealthiest guild masters, but despite his wealth and influence none would accept his suit."

"I most certainly hope so." Terrie reached again for latch. "So he's unmarried?"

"No. His first wife bore him no living children, so he still needs someone to provide him with an heir, even if she cannot give him the money and connections that he wants. His new wife is said to be from a family that he has ruined." Sister Tabitha smiled a little bitterly at her speechless friend. "Quite like one of those horrid novels you lend me. Only without the handsome young nobleman coming to her rescue."

From inside the building came a loud crash, and Terrie wrenched the door open and stormed inside.

# Chapter 42

*Rhine Highlands near Zuelpich*
*March 15, 1635*

Melchior pulled up his collar against the icy wind blowing unhindered across the moorish plateau, and led his small troop of cavalry towards the few tents huddled together. A single plume of smoke quickly dispersing above the flapping tent sides was the only sign of human life.

The long-winding negotiations in Aachen involving seemingly everybody, including the USE's representative and councilors from Cologne and Bonn, were still going on, but at least everybody had pulled back their armies. At the moment both he and Don Fernando had left the treaties to the lawyers and gone home for the rest of the winter, and now there was just this final knot to be tied before he and Charlotte could settle down for some time together.

Inside the biggest of the scruffy tents sat Archbishop Ferdinand of Cologne. In the seven months since Melchior had last seen him, the forceful church politician had become an old and obviously ill man, sitting dull-eyed and hunched over as if his stomach pained him.

"Archbishop Ferdinand." Melchior had expected it to be harder not to give in to his anger at the man causing so much trouble with his personal ambitions. "It's time to go home."

"Home?" the old man's eyes slowly focused on Melchior, "There is no home. It's all gone."

"No, it's not." Melchior squatted down in front of him. "The Archdiocese and City of Cologne will probably end up joining the USE, but the palaces in Cologne and Bonn are still yours as well as some of the land. You might not find it much, but it's there, you can come, and you are still the archbishop of Cologne. I have a letter for you from Cardinal-Protector Mazzare. It was forwarded to me from your palace in Bonn." Melchior reached inside his doublet for the letter, and held it towards the archbishop.

"No! I will not end my life as a powerless parish shepherd, consoling myself with the glories awaiting me in Heaven. I will not! The power is mine! I am the Archbishop of Cologne, I will not fail!" The old man's voice rose to a scream as he pushed himself up from the stool; only to collapse, clutching at his stomach, vomiting blood.

Melchior caught him and waited for the spasms to pass, wiping the contorted face with his handkerchief. Maxie had mentioned her cousin's troubled stomach in the letter asking Melchior to find him, but this was far worse than she had indicated.

"Archbishop Ferdinand, please becalm yourself, you are obviously making yourself ill with your obstinacy. What you dreamed and hoped for is not to be. Or at least you cannot reach it by the path you walked." Melchior lifted the old man's head, looked into the eyes filled with equal pain and fury and tried again. "I'll tell what is left of your Guard to strike the camp and arrange your transportation. And please remember: the Kingdom, the Power and the Glory, those belong to God and God alone. Always and forever. You must now take up the task that you have been given for whatever glory it may bring."

"Never."

"I believe you heard the archbishop's answer, General von Hatzfeldt," Melchior looked up into the attenuated face of Sister Ursula.

"You here, Sister? That is unexpected."

"I am a servant of the Lord, Herr General, and fulfill the tasks He sends my way to the best of my abilities." To Melchior's great surprise the usually weak and brittle woman actually managed to look somewhat dignified.

"Very well." Melchior stood up and gave up being kind. "If

the two of you do not wish to go to Cologne, I must ask you to choose some other destination. Leaving you here is not acceptable."

"Oh." Sister Ursula's voice was suddenly exactly as Melchior remembered it. "And does this letter from Cardinal-Protector Mazzare place a general of the Holy Roman Empire above a high-ranking prelate of the Catholic Church?"

"Not at all, Sister. I am acting on behalf of Sister Maximiliane, who worries about her cousin's health. Would you care to take up this discussion with her?" Melchior didn't wait for an answer but continued, "I am presently in military command of the area between Koblenz and the Dutch border, and once you tell me where you wish to go, I'll issue the necessary papers. The roads are passable, but given the state of affairs in Bavaria, I am afraid I cannot suggest any other destination for you than Bonn or Cologne. I shall be lodging with my men at the Inn of the Gray Squirrel outside Zuelpich, and await you there tomorrow. Good Afternoon."

# Chapter 43

*Bamberg*
*March 25, 1635*

The river was running high with melt water under the bridge as Franz stopped to look beyond the lower town and up the hill toward the cathedral. It was getting late, and the dusk was quickly turning to darkness as the light faded from the sky. Riding into a town with important meetings and negotiations ahead of him was nothing new, but this was personal; this would be his chance to regain his Kingdom, fulfill his plans and dreams. All the years he had worked in the service of one high-ranking prelate or another, using all his diplomatic skills and knowledge to further other people's ambitions, it all came down to this: this battle would be entirely for his own.

"Would you get your bloody arse moving. I want warm beer and hot stew." Wolf's hoarse voice cut through Franz's calm and brought him back to the here and now.

"You're right. We are both cold. It's been a long journey." Franz's pleasure at having finally reached his destination even made him feel charitable towards his grumpy cousin. Not that Wolf had been a bad traveling companion. He was really very useful when it came to getting good service, and making shifty looking individuals back away, but his impatience with all the unavoidable delays that came with traveling in wintertime had been somewhat annoying.

The two men started their horses and slowly made their way along the streets until Wolf stopped outside a large tavern. "I think we better gather information separately, Cousin. What's in your purse?"

Franz sighed and threw the small leather sac to Wolf. "Not enough to buy the brewery, but you should have enough to buy a few rounds for your table. I'll tell the porter at the cathedral's dormitory to expect you and give you a room."

Wolf didn't answer, just got off the horse and threw the reins to Franz before disappearing into the large tavern. Well, Wolf would make his own way up the hill, or just roll himself in his cloak and sleep wherever he could—or he might get over his aversion to barmaids. But fortunately Wolf's morality—or lack of it—wasn't Franz's problem.

Franz continued slowly across the lower town with its still bustling shops and markets. It was a lot cleaner than it used to be. No dung heaps blocking the gutters, no signs of chamber pots being emptied into the streets. There were hardly even any horse-droppings and all of those fresh, as if the streets were cleaned daily. Father Johannes had told that this was how it was done in the American town, Grantville. Rather pleasant. Made the streets seem inviting, and speeded up the movement, which should encourage trade. It should also encourage wealthier people to go to the shops themselves instead of always sending the servants. Not the nobility, of course, they had the traders come to them to show them their wares. Still, clean streets probably increased luxury trade, and the American idea of emporiums, and perhaps some kind of trading arrangement with the Abrabanels similar to what Heinrich had arranged in Mainz...

Franz's musings only stopped when he reached the Geyer-swoerth Palace. It had been the residence of the prince-bishops of Bamberg, and was now supposedly where the Americans had their headquarters. The quite brightly lit rooms showed that they had not stopped working at dusk to save the candles, but he really needed much more information before making contact, so Franz turned the horses up the steep street to the cathedral.

"My dear, dear friend. Oh, if only we could sit and talk the night away, as we used to do. This would give me the very greatest of pleasure. But the best possible opportunity for you is right now. Are you in immediate need of anything?" Schönborn was obviously dressed to go out. And for something quite formal to judge by the quality of his black cassock.

"No, not really. I'm fairly hungry, but if you still keep sweets in that bonbonier I see on your desk, I'll make do with a few of those." Franz smiled at Schönborn clasping his hands and almost dancing with enthusiasm.

"Oh, we can do better than that." Schönborn grabbed Franz's hand and pulled him out of the room and along the corridors to the kitchen, where he grabbed a platter of small pies and was out the door to the courtyard before the cooks had time to do more than shout in alarm. "These were for Domherr Bitterfeld and his cronies. They supposedly gather to play chess, but in reality they just stuff their heads and gossip. Here fill your pockets."

The two men emptied the platter, and Schönborn gave it to a stable boy along with the last pie.

"Bitterfeld is also in the center of your present opportunity." Schönborn continued as the two men walked down the street to the river as quickly as the slick and half-frozen cobbles permitted. "Only it's his cousin, Councilor Bitterfeld, rather our Domherr Bitterfeld. Councilor Bitterfeld is newly elected to the Würzburg City Council, and one of Father Arnoldi's strongest supporters." Schönborn turned to look briefly at Franz. "When the news about Archbishop Ferdinand's flight from the Hessian attack reached us, Councilor Bitterfeld tried to get the council behind making Father Arnoldi some kind of interim bishop until it was revealed whether you had survived."

"The council can have nothing to do with such a decision. That is entirely a Church matter, and something to be even considered only in the most dire emergencies. I think the last time it happened was during the plagues."

"Yes, and who in the Würzburg Council was in support of the proposed petition and who was against it was quite illuminating." Schönborn's smile held nothing of its usual cheer. "But Councilor Bitterfeld's newest scheme involves you in a different way. Do you remember the Dreimark vineyard?"

"Yes, a large south-facing field that has belonged to the Eberhart family practically since the deluge. It is—or at least was five years ago—planted with golden grapes brought north from Bois on the Loire by an Eberhart, who went there as a journeyman, two generations ago. When left to ripen completely the grapes produce a very good golden wine. It's a bit tangy when young, but matures exceptionally well. I think the area suffered some damage when the Protestant army attacked."

"I stand in absolute awe of your memory." Schönborn detoured around a puddle where a cobble was missing and continued. "Councilor Bitterfeld has been trying very hard to get his hands on that vineyard. First he tried to buy it from Maria Eberhart, the widow who owned it, and when she refused to sell, he tried to claim that her husband, Zacharias Eberhart, had given it as collateral for a loan. Recently he has tried to get it from Maria Eberhart's sister, who is also an Eberhart, and also married to an Eberhart, and who inherited it after Maria Eberhart disappeared under mysterious circumstances last autumn. Maria Eberhart, by the way, was declared dead after an indecently short time— although her body wasn't found. Right now Councilor Bitterfeld is trying to get the American administration to support his claim on the basis of two documents. One is supposedly a copy of Herr Zacharias Eberhart's testament donating the field to the Würzburg cathedral, the other a document stating the sale of the field to Councilor Bitterfeld under your seal and written by your old secretary, Otto Tweimal. Right this moment Frau Kacere, who is in charge of such disputes, is holding a formal hearing of the case. She is most learned in matters of laws and contracts, but she is sorely missing the archives you brought with you into exile."

"Yes, she would. I can see that." Franz started walking faster as they reached the foot of the steep street, and headed straight for the Geyerswoerth Palace. "I remember the testament, and that field had been a part of his wife's dower, and would not have been Herr Eberhart's property to donate or sell. Tweimal's role in this is more dubious. I haven't seen him since last autumn, when he disappeared from Archbishop Ferdinand's camp, and I wouldn't trust that little turncoat to shave me. What can you tell me about Councilor Bitterfeld?"

"Pompous, bad-tempered bore, who has only the friends that he can buy. Very, very easily offended, and reacts all out of reason to the slightest insult. He has amassed a suspiciously large fortune since the Protestant attack. And he hates women, especially those who are young or outspoken. He tries to hide that, but having Frau Kacere in charge is a serious problem

for him, and that her assistants are usually women—and often
nuns—only makes it worse."

The room had been a large formal dining room when Franz
had last been in Bamberg. The richly decorated walls were the
same, but this evening benches in rows lined three sides of the
room while a big table filled with documents and a tall lectern
occupied the fourth side. Two groups of people clustered around
the benches at opposite sides, while what were obviously specta-
tors filled most of the benches by the door, but Schönborn took
him directly to the big table where a smiling young girl in a
blue dress was sorting papers under the directions of a pleasant-
looking older woman, while a young nun in a simple brown habit
was setting up a secretary station with paper and writing tools.

"My very best greetings on this glorious evening to you and
your delightful handmaidens, Frau Kacere." Schönborn gave a
deep bow while pretending to swing a hat from his head to his
chest in the French style. "It gives me the greatest pleasure to
introduce to you the esteemed Bishop Franz von Hatzfeldt, who
has just this hour arrived in Bamberg." He turned to Franz.
"My dear friend. This is the learned Frau Kacere, who has most
valiantly taken on the task of putting the land and its owners to
the right. It's my most sincere belief that the two of you would
reap the greatest of benefits from working together."

"I am very pleased to meet you, Frau Kacere." Franz thought
quickly through what Father Johannes had told him about American manners and stuck out his hand. "I have a friend, Father
Johannes the Painter, who spent more than a year in Grantville,
and who has told me about the American preference for getting
directly to the point." He gave a slight bow with the handshake
and continued, when Frau Kacere smiled and nodded. "The
Würzburg bishopric's archives, which you must most sorely need
are presently in Cologne. They have been mixed somewhat with
papers from Fulda, but my sister, Lucie von Hatzfeldt, has almost
completed the process of separating and listing the documents.
I have brought along the lists, and would like to present them
to you in the morning."

Frau Kacere's smile was getting bigger and bigger, so he went
on. "As for your present undertaking: I well remember the Dreimark vineyard, and it was part of Frau Maria Eberhart's dower

when she married her cousin, Herr Zacharias Eberhart. It was set aside as part of her widow's share in the bridal contract, and would only have belonged to Herr Eberhart's side of the family after her death. Not only would I have remembered if this very fine vineyard had come to the Church, but I am willing to swear on the Bible that the Dreimark vineyard was not Herr Eberhart's property to dispose of when I left Würzburg."

"The papers were handled by your secretary, Otto Tweimal." A big blustery man in rich velvet robes broke away from the group on the left side of the room. "It was just before you fled from the attack, and the papers were lost, and have only recently come to light. They are there on the table with your seal on. And besides: how come you claim to remember such details from a minor marriage contract?" He looked up and down Franz's threadbare and dirty appearance and sneered.

"The dispensation for the marriage between the two cousins was my very first act as bishop, and may I see the document of sale and the testament?" Franz was much too used to diplomatic maneuvering to let the other man's insults affect him and simply accepted the papers from the broadly grinning young girl in blue. Judging from her excellent teeth she was almost certainly an American, though a bit tall for her to be Frau Kacere's daughter. The tall lectern had two lamps mounted on a moveable brass rod in a construction that Franz wanted to copy as soon as possible, and was by far the best lit surface in the room, so he placed the papers carefully under the light and started to examine the seal and the details in the writing.

"Here. This is Frau Kacere's personal property. Please be careful." The young girl hurried to bring Franz a wooden box containing a big lens set in a gray material and wrapped in yellow velvet. Franz looked to Frau Kacere for permission before using the lens.

"Beautiful. This is by far the finest lens I've ever seen."

"Old eyes fade." Frau Kacere had taken a seat behind the big table, and was obviously prepared to give Franz as much time as he needed.

"Oh, so is this by any chance borrowed from your father?" The light compliment came automatic from Franz, while almost all his attention was on the papers.

"Frau Kacere, this is an outrage, and I have wasted enough

time on this. I bought the vineyard in good faith from the Würzburg cathedral, though I knew it might be destroyed by the attacking army. That the papers were somehow mislaid has given me no end of trouble and bother. First with that insolent widow Eberhart, and now with her sister, whose husband is definitely derelict in keeping his chattel in line!" Councilor Bitterfeld now sneered towards the group of people by the benches on the other side of the room, where an older man with big hands started walking towards them.

"Is that Frau Eberhart that you describe as chattel?" The young girl in blue came round the table towards the councilor. "You must be in your dotage not to have realized..."

"Terrie!" Frau Kacere's voice brought the young girl to a stop. "Please leave the room." She turned towards Councilor Bitterfeld, and Franz was impressed at how well such a small woman could look down her nose at a big man. "Councilor Bitterfeld, your private opinion about your opponents in the case is of no interest to me, and if Herr Zacharias Eberhart made an illegal bequest in his testament, then that does not make the vineyard the Church's property to dispose of." She turned to Franz. "Bishop Franz, have you any remarks upon the documents?"

"Yes, Frau Kacere. Both documents are written in the hand of Otto Tweimal, both are equally faded and on the same type of paper suggesting that not much time had passed between the writing."

"So, that just means that a farmer made a new will in a turbulent time, and had a church clerk write it for him," Councilor Bitterfeld interrupted. "There's nothing unusual in that. And if the Church didn't own the vineyard then it owes me the money back I paid."

"That sounds reasonable." Frau Kacere looked towards Franz. "Would you agree to that?"

"I would, except for the seal."

"Isn't that your seal?"

"Yes, but my seal suffered a small damage during my exile, and I had the edge re-cut with tiny facets along the bottom. If you compare this seal with the one attached to the documents in the ironbound ledger I recognize over there, you'll see the difference. The seal on the bill of sale is less than two years old. I last saw my seal—and Otto Tweimal—last autumn." Franz considered Councilor Bitterfeld; much as he disliked the man, it was possible that he was guilty of nothing more than an unpleasant personality. "Herr Eberhart was killed when the Protestant armies attacked, so the sale must have taken place just as we were leaving Bamberg. To whom did you pay your money?"

"Otto Tweimal. But he was acting as your secretary."

"And who provided you with the testament and the bill of sale now in this room?"

Franz fully expected to hear the name of his former secretary again, but instead Councilor Bitterfeld looked as if he was biting into something sour, and said, "I am not at liberty to say. A story was told me in confidence."

"In that case," said Frau Kacere looking up from examining the seals, "and if no one has any further information, I must conclude that the Dreimark vineyard belongs to the Eberhart family. The seal on the bill of sale is not identical to the one used on the old documents." She looked at Franz. "And as the two documents by all appearances were made at the same time and by the same hand, I would also reject the testament as proof of the Church ownership of the vineyard."

"Of course. I would myself protest such a claim."

"Whether or not the Würzburg cathedral owes Councilor Bitterfeld a return of payment is a matter beyond my jurisdiction. I now declare this hearing over. You may all leave."

As the people from the benches started to rise and move towards the doors, Councilor Bitterfeld stood scowling at everybody, then stormed out of the room, forcing everybody to jump aside. Schönborn took Franz to the big table where the young nun was finishing her writing and then passed the ledger over to Frau Kacere for signing.

"Sister Tabitha, may I introduce to you Prince-Bishop Franz von Hatzfeldt of Würzburg with the assurance that had he been present when you and your order arrived, your reception in his bishopric would have been entirely different."

"I should most certainly hope so." The young girl in the blue dress had returned, and didn't hesitate to interrupt. "That stinking Father Arnoldi was downright persecuting them, when they came to Würzburg as refugees. And why does Schönborn call you a prince?"

"Terrie! You are rude tonight far beyond what is acceptable," Frau Kacere said. "Apologize to Bishop Franz."

"No need for that. I am not at all offended." Franz considered the young girl and continued. "While Father Johannes the Painter has told me much about the American irreverence and informality, this is the first time I've met your people in more than passing. And I am learning that Father Johannes did not at all exaggerate." He stuck out his hand, and smiled. "Pleased to meet you, Miss Terrie. And prince combined with a clerical title is mainly an indication of independence. I do not intend to go on using it. Except," he continued with a grin, "when I want to 'Dupe the Joneses.' Is that the correct expression?"

"Exactly." Terrie smiled and shook his hand in return. "And normally I am more polite. But Sister there," she nodded towards the nun, "and I were visiting Frau Anna Eberhart when last Councilor Bitterfeld came to bully her. The things he said and the threats he made would have gotten him arrested in Grantville. Frau Anna is quite fragile, and her husband is too slow to be much help with anything but making and moving barrels of beer. I think you should stop giving the Eberharts dispensations to marry so closely within the family." She took a deep breath, and continued before Frau Kacere could comment. "And I know I shouldn't have said that either. Sister, if you are finished we could walk each other home."

"If I may be permitted to escort the ladies?" Franz had noticed Frau Kacere looking slightly worried.

"No need. We both live only a few streets away and in the same direction."

"Please, Miss Terrie, it would be my pleasure. And an escort for the two of you right now would make it easier for Frau Kacere to concentrate on finishing her work."

"Oh, yes. Councilor Bitterfeld." Terrie hesitated. "We could ask one of the guards." Then she grinned at Franz, and took his offered arm. "Or are you trying to curry favor with the judge?"

"That is entirely possible. Though I did believe the curry was a spicy dish."

"You stupid little twerp!" the slap from the big man sent Otto Tweimal crashing to the floor. "The bishop's seal had been altered during his exile!" Otto considered trying to defend himself, but judging from the bulging veins on the big man's head, he'd do better not to call any attention to himself.

"And I had to stand there meekly accepting the insults from that insolent old witch and her sluttish tramps. They should be taught a lesson. Learn their place. To the fires with the lot of them. All women deserves to burn. Spawn of Satan..."

As the rant went on Otto crept slowly towards a corner and waited for a chance to escape.

# Chapter 44

*Cologne*
*April 1, 1635*

"Your tisane."

Archbishop Ferdinand of Cologne nodded briefly, but didn't turn his head as Sister Ursula placed the cloth-wrapped pewter goblet on the table beside him. The sweet smell of honey and herbs reached his nose, but sweets had never been his preference, and everything that now entered his mouth seemed to take on the iron taste of blood.

"Leave it!"

At his words the old woman stopped her reach for the bottles still standing on the table.

"The doctors..."

"The doctors have said that I'm bleeding inside, and if it doesn't stop I'll eventually die. Just like from a knife in the stomach from the outside. It's taking too God-damned long! Leave!"

At the sound of the door closing softly behind him Archbishop Ferdinand used the strength from his anger to get up from the chair, grab the rough clay jug, and totter to the window. For the two weeks since his arrival to Cologne he had slowly been getting weaker, and was now leaving his bed only to receive the few people he had sent for, to see what might be saved. Nothing! His plans with Duke Wolfgang and Marshal Turenne set into

268

motion exactly a year ago had been completely crushed and it looked like nothing could stop that damned USE from spreading its tentacles into the Rhine.

He felt the blood rising from the fire in his gut as he stretched to open the catch holding the leaded glass-panels closed, and fell down on the narrow window-bench, clay jug still in hand. Why sea-captain Morrison would have a preference for that rotgut made from the leftovers of winemaking was incomprehensible, but according to the doctors, anything containing strong spirits was the worst he could possibly put into his stomach. Not poison, but while it might briefly dull the pain, it would eventually kill him. He wrestled open the stopper at the top of the jug. The raw woody smell of the Marc rose to his nose.

The Rhine River glittering in the moonlight seemed to mock him with the possibilities it appeared to offer. False promises. The old man leaned his head against the side of the window, too weak to lift the jug.

"Jumping would be faster. If you are so keen on dying."

Startled, the archbishop squinted his eyes to see into the darkness of the room behind him.

"Sister Ursula. I thought you'd left." Archbishop Ferdinand could hear his own words slurring with fatigue. "I cannot. Better some Hell here on Earth than suicide and not seeing my beloved brother, Philip, in Heaven." He sighed. "Philip has been dead for..." Archbishop Ferdinand stopped, but gave up trying to calculate the number, and sat again staring out the window.

Sister Ursula came out from the shadows to stand beside him. "And is a slow suicide all that you have left to hope for?" The old woman's voice was bitter enough to startle the archbishop out of his musings.

"What else is there? Bavaria is impossible right now. Even if I could reach it. And nothing remains for me here. Surrounded by commoners snickering at my fall from power. And that sanctimonious Hatzfeldt can't even be relied upon to have me assassinated. If I only had Felix Gruyard with me, there might still be something I could do, but all that I have left are incompetent ninnies."

"I see." Sister Ursula looked down on the man she had loved and served all her life. "Then do as the doctors tell you, and retire into rural seclusion until you heal. By then there might be new possibilities. New resources. The Crown Loyalists just won the election. You could work with them!"

"Such as Hesse? The hell I will." He lifted the jug and drank, only to fall forward over the windowsill vomiting blood down the stone wall.

In the room behind him the old woman's face was a pale emotionless mask in the dusk. Then she bent down to grab his ankles, and straightened to give a heave, sending him out the window to his death on the courtyard below.

"One last service," she whispered, and went to take the bottles back to the wine cellar.

# Chapter 45

*Bamberg*
*April 5, 1635*

Terrie rushed into the Eberhart brewery and smack into an object not inclined to move out of her way, but as she bounced back, an arm reached out and grabbed her before she could land on the tiled floor.

"Easy, my pretty sweet, you made me spill my beer." The big soldier's smile was surprisingly charming. "This must have made the floor quite slippery." He put down his mug on a barrel and swept Terrie up in his arms.

"Put me down! Right now!" With Frau Eberhart standing shaking her head with a fond smile, Terrie didn't feel the least frightened, but the broad grins from the apprentices annoyed her.

"Yes, but where? You wouldn't want to break one of those pretty ankles."

"Fräulein Terrie is an American, Colonel von Hatzfeldt, and as such quite independent. She would probably prefer to navigate the floor on her own. Terrie, my dear, Colonel Wolf von Wildenburger-Hatzfeldt is Bishop Franz's cousin and, as you have already seen, a bit of a flirt. He is here inquiring about some troop movement south of here, but it was my husband who talked to the trader, and he has already gone to the vineyard with the new wine barrels. Weren't you and Sister Tabitha supposed to go with him?"

271

The big soldier had put Terrie back on the floor—not too quickly—leaned back against the whitewashed wall, and picked up his mug again.

"Yes, Frau Eberhart, but Frau Kacere needed Sister at the office, and we decided to wait to another day. I just came to tell you." Terrie shook out her skirt and scowled at the soldier. On principle. He really looked quite charming—and had had a bath and a shave quite recently, which automatically gave him a few bonus points.

"What a pity, my dear. I know how much you had looked forward to a spring day in the sun after spending all winter studying."

"Yes, I've probably annoyed everyone by talking of little else all week." Terrie sighed. "I could just have gone with your husband on my own, but by the time I thought of it, he had already left."

"Well, I'm going to talk with Herr Eberhart as soon as I've arranged for the delivery of a barrel of this beer to the cathedral. You could ride behind me on a saddle pillow. It's not that far."

Terrie considered the offer from the smiling soldier, who continued, "And while I don't claim to be harmless—and like pretty young girls as much as the next man—I also badly need the help of your people in tracking down an old enemy. I give you my word of honor that you'll come to no harm that I can prevent."

"I accept. Can you pick me up in front of the Geyersvoerth Palace? I'll tell Frau Kacere and Sister where I've gone."

When Terrie worked her way out the heavy palace doors carrying a fairly large hamper, there were two men on horses waiting in the cobbled courtyard.

"With your permission, Fräulein Terrie, I would like to invite myself along for your outing to the Dreimark vineyard," said Bishop Franz, smiling and taking the hamper from Terrie. "I have longed to see those hills again in the spring time for five long years. And chaperoning my wayward cousin Wolf provides the perfect excuse for playing truant from my duties."

"Certainly come with us. The more the merrier. Frau Kacere suggested I get a picnic hamper from the kitchen, and I asked for enough for Herr Eberhart as well. Judging from its weight, the content could easily stretch for another person." Terrie had seen Bishop Franz quite often since his arrival, but usually deep in somber discussions with Janie Kacere, or buried in ledgers and documents. This morning, however, he seemed a completely different person, obviously enjoying the prospect of a ride in the fresh air, and bent on teasing his cousin.

"Herr Eberhart is a kind and pious man, and I am sure he would like nothing better than to share his bounty with my psalm-mongering cousin." Wolf lifted Terrie up to the pillow tied behind the saddle of one of the horses, then lifted her down again and started adjusting some ties. She was pretty sure he'd felt the gun tied to the small of her back, but he just continued teasing his cousin. "Franz also tried to insist that you should sit behind him, rather than me, but that is out of the question. He must console himself for the loss of lovely young girls with food as becoming for a priest. And besides, my stories are far more entertaining."

"It would be kinder to the horses, Wolf." Bishop Franz grinned at his cousin and winked at Terrie. "Even with all the walking you did after that barmaid stole your money and horse, you are still a good deal heavier than me. Why don't you start with telling us that story? You've never really been clear about what happened?"

## The Dreimark farm

"Well, unless you want to travel the rest of the way to Rothenburg with the servants in their wagon, we'll have to wait until the broken wheel is repaired," Eva said. "Personally I wouldn't mind. I just want to get you delivered, and get back to my own life." Eva pulled up the hood of her brown cloak and started walking up the hill toward the vineyard behind the farm, waving away the guard who started to follow.

"What! Are you not staying with me in Rothenburg?" Maria almost tried to run to keep up with Eva, but had to place her feet carefully to avoid having her wooden heels slipping on the gravel.

"No. Why should I?"

"But who'll keep me company? Mother's friend is old and never goes anywhere because of her gout."

"I neither know nor care. You are a spoiled and thoughtless brat, and I've had to listen to your endless whining for three weeks. I've had enough. Go back to the farm, and wait for the smith they are sending for to repair the wheel."

"I don't want to." Maria sniffled a little. "That dung heap really stinks."

"I noticed."

"Can't I come with you? I'll be silent."

Eva stopped and looked over her shoulder. "I seriously doubt that you can, but as long as you don't mention Magdeburg, you can come along."

"Where are we going?"

"Just among the rows of grapevines. There's a track for driving the wagons along during harvest. The ground should be covered with rubble soaking up the heat from the sun, so any herbs sprout earlier here than in the woods."

"You and your herbs."

"We've had almost a week of full sun, so there might be violets too."

"I like candied violets. And a posy would both brighten up that dull brown of your dress, and look good against my blue one."

Otto Tweimal huddled himself deeper into his cloak, and sneaked a watchful peek at the small group of ruffians in front of him. If he had to be involved in this demeaning business, he should at least have been in charge. After all he was the graduate of a prestigious convent seminar (regardless of how he had managed that), and had spent most of his adult life in the confidence of men of power (and made the most of the bribes and other opportunities that had come with that), so how dare they belittle him by saying: "and take along that useless twerp. At least he can hold the horses." Of course there was no reason for him to care what a group of rough hired bullies thought about him, but while a few threats and slaps from an employer in private might be excused—after all men of power were also men under pressure—insults in front of people from the lower classes undermined his authority, and that was totally unacceptable. If only Bishop Franz had not returned, there might have been a chance for Otto to offer his service to the Americans in the new administration, but the bishop had made no secret of his disgust at Otto's behavior in Archbishop Ferdinand's camp, and would certainly tell everybody if Otto came out of hiding. On the other hand, Bishop Franz had loathed the archbishop's torturer and might be forgiving if Otto made the most of his fear of Felix Gruyard. It would not do to appear sniveling when presenting himself to a new employer, but . . .

The ruffian in charge signed for his men to move forward, and Otto raised his head. The plan had been to watch the farm for the arrival of a wagon filled with barrels plus an older man and two young girls. One of the girls should be wearing a brown nun's habit and have a few pockmarks, while the other would probably be dressed in the bright blue color said to be preferred by the Americans. The ruffians had orders to grab both girls, or—if that wasn't possible—at least the one in blue. If the opportunity was there, they should also beat up the man driving them as badly as they liked; if he died so much the better. The girls would then be taken to a collier's hut in the hills above Untersteinbach, where they should be kept until someone came to pick them up.

Otto had quietly snickered at the ruffians' confusion when the wagon had arrived with no girls sitting beside the driver, and when shortly afterwards a closed carriage had rolled in slowly and two girls fitting the description had descended. The two girls had now started to walk towards the vineyard, and apparently the leader of the ruffians had decided that the opportunity was too good to miss. And it might be so for Otto as well: what better opportunity to gain favor than by Otto foiling the kidnapping of one of the Americans' daughter and a nun under the protection of Bishop Franz's crony, Schönborn. Otto became quite cheerful at the thought, and quickly tied up the horses to creep after the ruffians as they started moving forward.

As Eva and Maria reached the edge of the vineyard a small man burst out of the stand of trees sheltering the vines from the eastern winds.

"Run, run. They are going to kidnap you! I'll save..." he shouted before slipping on the loose gravel and tumbling into the posts supporting the vines.

Eva quickly grabbed the screaming Maria's arm and tried to pull her along, but their shoes were not made for running, and before they reached the wagon track dividing the vineyard a group of men in rough leathers had reached and grabbed them.

"Quickly. Get them to the horses."

"And the twerp?"

"Leave him. They are stirring at the farm. This hellcat has the lungs of a fish-peddler."

✧          ✧          ✧

"There's something wrong." Wolf stopped in the middle of the story he was telling and touched his spurs to his horse. "Hold on tight."

With the horses suddenly running at full speed Terrie had no opportunity to look around for whatever had alarmed the soldier, but once they had reached the farm, Wolf and Franz both slowed down to pass an expensive carriage standing on three wheels.

"Who were the riders above the vineyard?" Wolf shouted the question at an old woman staring up the hill to where a group of people had gathered around something on the ground.

"We don't know, but they took the two noblewomen from the carriage."

"Terrie, off!" Wolf turned around to lift Terrie down.

"No I'm coming along. My gun is more accurate than anything you could have."

"No time to argue." Franz had already started up the hill. "I think I see somebody I recognize."

In the center of a group of people dressed for farm work mixed with what must have been the driver and the guard from the carriage stood a shaking Otto Tweimal.

"I thought you'd be hiding under a rock somewhere." Franz frowned at his former secretary. "And I'll have my seal back, Herr Tweimal, plus a full account of everything you have been using it for."

"No time for that now." Wolf had now arrived. "Who were those men, and where were they taking the girls?"

"They are hired by Councilor Bitterfeld—or perhaps—Father Arnoldi." Otto tried for a somewhat shaky servile smile. "I tried to save them. The girls I mean. A-and there's a collier's site, where..."

"You'll guide us. Franz, leave the hamper, and take Tweimal up behind you."

## The hills between Bamberg and Würzburg

"Who are these girls, and where's Tweimal?" The big, beefy man in velvet standing beside a lean priest in a black cassock outside the derelict wooden cabin scowled at Eva and Maria.

"They're the ones you told us to pick up at the Dreimark

vineyard: a pretty one in blue and a pockmarked in a brown habit. And that little turncoat you saddled us with did his best to warn the girls. I hope he broke his neck when he fell." The leader of the ruffians growled.

"No, they are not. You idiots kidnapped the wrong girls. And now they've seen us. Cut their throats and go get the right ones or you'll not get paid." The man in velvet was interrupted by the priest grabbing his arm.

"Wait. Young girls. No chaperone I presume. One already scarred by God's scourge. One obviously given to Vanity. Perhaps they might be candidates for purification even if they are not those who offended you, Councilor."

Witch-hunter! Eva had been relieved at the priest's interruption until she realized what he was saying. She cast a quick glance around the clearing where the burnt-out remains of several large fires suddenly looked much more ominous. *If I am to get us out of this, I've better come up with the biggest lie ever,* she thought. A glance at Maria, who looked close to fainting, but still obviously wellborn and delicate, gave her an idea.

"I am Princess Eva Katharina von Anhalt-Dessau, and my scars are considered a sign that I should devote my life to a higher purpose," Eva said. "As a part of this I am escorting this young girl to Rothenburg to meet her intended. According to the American books this is a union from which the pope shall come, who will save the Christian world from a Muslim invasion."

"I didn't know that." Maria now looked totally confused, and swayed a little. "I thought Mama was sending me away because she was angry with me."

"It wouldn't be seemly to let you know." Eva cut off Maria before she could mention any details about just why her mother would be angry with her.

"Both the House of Anhalt and the Americans are heretics, and destined for the eternal fires. The Americans, their arrival, and all that they bring are the work of the Devil." The priest sounded quite uncompromising, but Eva thought he did hesitate a little.

"There are many people who agree with you, Father." Eva bowed her head to the priest. "Maria's intended is, however, a devout Catholic, and a powerful general in the service of the Holy Roman Empire. And it was a cardinal who personally brought the information to Maria's parents. I did not speak to him, but was told that the most holy and learned scholars of the Vatican had been convinced that the threat to all of Christianity was real, and that the salvation would come from the son of this young Maria." The priest still didn't look convinced, so she tried a little flattery. "I am a firm believer in the guiding hand of God, and feel certain that there must have been a purpose to our carriage breaking a wheel just where it did. Might it perhaps be that we were to meet with you? Could it be that you are to come with us?" The priest frowned, so Eva hurried to continue. "Or perhaps give us instruction? As you noticed, young Maria is a bit inclined towards worldly finery—though that is mostly at her family's insistence. Her parents are good people, but unfortunately mainly concerned with worldly matters and ambitions."

Her ruse worked. Eva pulled Maria down beside her on a sooty log, and with their hands firmly gripping sat meekly listening to the wilder and wilder ravings of the priest.

# Chapter 46

*The hills between Bamberg and Würzburg*
*April 5, 1635*

"It's beyond the next hill." At Otto Tweimal's words Franz gave a whistle to stop Wolf, and they pulled the horses to the roadside and dismounted.

"What's the layout?" It was the first time in all their lives that Franz had seen Wolf when he was fully focused and alert before heading into battle, and he suddenly understood why Melchior accepted all the problems Wolf's taste for trouble and adventures caused.

"I, I . . ." Under Wolf's intense frown Otto slipped into stammering confusion.

"Concentrate, Tweimal. Or I'll wring your scrawny neck." Wolf grabbed Otto by the collar and gave him a shake.

"It's a small cabin. A collier's hut. One room. In a clearing. It's used for making charcoal. And bur-burning witches. F-Father Arnoldi. They said . . ." Otto stopped and swallowed.

"Never mind that now." Wolf gave another shake. "Do they post guards and where?"

"I don't know. There're hills all around."

"There were four riders at the vineyard. Are there more?"

"No. I don't know. Perhaps Father Arnoldi. And the councilor sometimes brings along a servant. Or sends one as a messenger.

He was there when we left. He brought them all guns and horses, but not so many bullets. They complained. There's a keg of powder in the hut."

"For charcoal they would need tracks—if not roads—to bring the logs to the clearing." Franz looked at the beautiful bright green surrounding forest. He had to win back his kingdom. Not so much from the new administration—despite their differences they really had many of the same goals—but those powerful men ignoring the law and grabbing what they want simply because they wanted it; that had to be stopped. And witch-burning and terrorizing people were just totally unacceptable.

"So, do we sneak or ride in shooting?" Terrie was checking her gun, while walking around working the kinks out of her back.

"Is that one of the new guns?" Wolf asked.

"No, it's old." Terrie looked at Wolf with suspicion, and didn't put it back in its holster. "And you may not borrow it. And I definitely know how to use it."

"I think"—the devilish sparkle was suddenly back in Wolf's eyes—"that we should use subterfuge."

"Oh no. What are you up to now?" Franz looked to where Wolf was taking a piece of rope from his saddle.

"Don't worry, my priestly little cousin. Remember my crazy schemes usually work." Wolf started tying Otto Tweimal's hands in front of him with one end of the rope despite the smaller man's protests.

"Not always. That trick you pulled with Frau Mittelfeld's goats brought me the worst beating in my entire childhood," Franz said with bitterness, "and I wasn't even involved."

"Ah, but that was your own fault. If you had been involved, you would have had an alibi too." Wolf was obviously in a fine mood. "In an unknown situation one needs information. We could gather that by sneaking closer, and then withdraw and plan an attack."

"Or send for reinforcement. That would be remarkably sensible, so I presume that is not what you intend to do." Franz looked sourly at his grinning cousin.

"And leave two lovely young ladies in the hands of villainous villains, while we dither around? Of course not." Wolf started tying the other end of the rope to Franz's saddle.

"You are not going to pull me after the horse!" Otto Tweimal started tearing at the rope in panic. "Bishop Franz, help me! It was only my fear of Felix Gruyard that made me desert you, and of Father Arnoldi here. They are the same. And at school..."

"Shut up!" Wolf reached out to slap the back of Otto Tweimal's head. "And stop pulling the rope. It's tied so you can free yourself, and we'll walk the horses." He looked at Franz and Terrie. "The main problem is to keep the kidnappers from barricading themselves in the cabin with the two ladies as hostages. The main resources we have are three guns with enough bullets to kill all the kidnappers, plus that everybody at the cabin would know Tweimal by sight, and no one would know me. Father Arnoldi and Councilor Bitterfeld would know the two of you, but are unlikely to think either of you dangerous enough to consider your presence an attack. Sweet Terrie, can you shoot to kill? And smile until you do so?"

"Yes." Terrie hesitated and took a deep breath. "I might ordinarily have problems shooting first, or killing in cold blood, but Father Arnoldi is the priest who tried to burn Sister, and Bitterfeld threatened her as well. I promise, I'll make an exception."

"Good girl. I'm quite opposed to people wanting to burn women myself." Wolf smiled with approval. "Franz has always been completely useless, when it comes to fighting, so I'll leave it to him to get the two hostages out of the way. This is how we'll do it..."


"Horses coming!" The shout interrupted the priest in a way the councilor's attempt to question Eva had not been able to do. The councilor grabbed Eva and Maria and started pulling them towards the hut, while the priest went to stand holding his cross in the middle of the clearing facing the wagon-track leading downhill, and the ruffians spread themselves on either side of him with various weapons ready to fire.

Into the clearing came two horses walking quite slowly: the first with a rider dressed in a black suit, and leading a walking man tied to the saddle with a long rope, the second with a big soldier in the saddle and a smiling young girl in blue sitting behind him.

"That's Bishop Franz and Otto Tweimal. And that American bitch!" The councilor let go of Eva and Maria and pulled a gun from his belt when the girl on the horse grinned and waved at him.

"I think this belongs to you now, Councilor Bitterfeld." The man in the black suit got off his horse, untied the rope, and started walking towards the councilor, dragging the bound man after him. Behind him the soldier and the still smiling girl had also dismounted and, ignoring the priest demanding an explanation, had started walking towards the armed ruffians on either side of him.

"Are you the general of the Holy Roman Empire?" Pulling Maria with her towards the soldier, Eva got both of them out of reach of all their kidnappers.

"No, my lady, that's my brother." The soldier gave Eva a smile while continuing to walk towards the ruffians, who slowly lowered their guns, waiting to find out what was happening.

Franz had reached the councilor, whose gun was still pointed towards the center of the clearing, so he dropped the rope, grabbed the gun stuck to his belt and pointed it toward the councilor's stomach. "Don't move, Bitterfeld. I'm not a very good shot, but I really cannot miss at this distance. And I have quite a few questions I want to ask you." He twisted a little so he could keep an eye on the two kidnapped ladies without looking away from the councilor. "Tweimal, come take the gun from the councilor. And while, as I'm sure you realize, Bitterfeld, I'm not very fond of my former secretary, I will kill you if you try to grab or shoot him."

As a series of shots sounded behind Franz, startling him, Councilor Bitterfeld knocked aside the gun pointed at his stomach, and swung his own gun around as a club to knock Franz down. Before Franz could recover, there was a quick movement to the side, and then the heavy councilor landed on top of him, knocking the breath from his lungs.

As Franz tried to push himself free, somebody dropped a fairly large branch beside them and wrested the councilor's gun from his hand, and when Franz finally managed to get away from the groaning councilor, the young lady in brown stood holding the gun as if she knew how to use it.

"Thank you, my lady." Franz remembered the gun in his own hand and pointed it towards the councilor as well, while looking around. In the center of the clearing Wolf and Terrie obviously had everything under control with Father Arnoldi and all the four ruffians lying unmoving on the ground, but Otto Tweimal was nowhere to be seen.

"Where did Tweimal go?" Franz asked. "I really have a score to set with that little rat."

"I think he went scuttling into the bushes." Wolf and Terrie had reloaded their guns and picked up the weapons from the fallen before making their way to where Franz and the two ladies were standing over the councilor. "That was some very nice shooting, Sweet Terror." Wolf smiled at Terrie with obvious approval. "No messy, screaming wounded left to clean up."

"Yes," Terrie looked away. "Father Arnoldi definitely deserved to die for what he tried to do to Sister and the other nuns, but..."

"They were going to burn the women they planned to kidnap, and would have killed Maria and me, when their henchmen caught us instead. I am Eva and this is my friend Maria." Eva held out her hand and smiled at Terrie. "Thanks for saving us."

"Is he handsome?" Maria smiled at Wolf. "Your brother, the general I am to marry. Is he handsome? It was so clever of him to send you to save us."

"Melchior is already married." For once Wolf looked confused when a pretty girl smiled at him.

Eva groaned. "That was a lie I told to stop them from killing us, Maria. I knew the people at the farm or our servants would have sent for help, and I had to keep us alive until they could find us."

"Then what about the prophecy?"

"There is no prophecy and there is no general."

"Well, actually there is a general, but as I said, he's married now." Wolf was now looking intrigued and obviously amused.

"Married to whom?"

"The widow of Jülich-Berg." Wolf started tying up Councilor Bitterfeld, who was slowly coming to life.

"I suppose I cannot compete with that." Maria looked pensive and a little sad.

"Ah! But it is the grandest story. They married to save Bonn from an attack and she fought by his side on the walls. Why don't all you lovely young ladies go sit down while my priestly cousin finds the horses, and I'll tell you the story of The Romance of Charlotte and Melchior?"

# Chapter 47

*Bamberg*
*April 25, 1635*

"I really cannot express the depth of my gratitude for your warning against the American wine pests, Lady Eva."

Franz and Eva stopped for a moment at the top of the cathedral stairs and looked out across the town to the lush green vineyards along the river valley. "The drawback of having an area especially suited to a single produce is that the entire economy comes to depend on it, and most years, wine is one of the major exports from this entire area. Our cash crop, as the Americans have it. If we are to rebuild, and make the most of stability and inventions the Americans have brought, we'll need the wine for trading." He smiled at her and offered his arm as they descended the stairs, walking slowly in the bright spring morning.

"I'm glad I could offer you something in return for coming to our rescue." Eva replied. "My family will naturally send gifts for you and your cousin, and probably to Terrie's family as well." Eva laughed a little. "My brother will find it quite odd to gift a woman—and a fairly wellborn woman, too—for shooting bandits, but after all, Terrie is an American Amazon, so he'll probably do it."

She sighed. "But the information about the spreading pests was what I personally had to give to you, Bishop Franz."

"And to the entire area, Lady Eva. I have no intention of keeping the problem and its cure to myself."

284

"Your kingdom." Eva smiled. "I heard your cousin tease you."

"Yes, my kingdom. And with Father Arnoldi dead, I can clean up Würzburg's administration. They are even offering me Bamberg as well, both the clerics and the city councils. At least those not involved with Father Arnoldi. Councilor Bitterfeld is singing like a canary."

"Congratulations. And have you ever heard a canary?" Eva enquired with a smile.

"No, but I find it such a delightful expression."

In the center of the cathedral square Wolf was looking over the horses with the driver and the guard, while Terrie and Sister Tabitha were helping Maria settle in the repaired carriage. Despite their very different temperaments the three girls had formed a firm friendship, and Terrie had even had her parents write to Maria's parents and persuade them to let Maria return to the safety of her family in Magdeburg after the terrible kidnapping. That Maria seemingly had shrugged off the experience and was mainly concerned with ferreting out if Eva had really, really, really made up all of the story about the prophecy and the general, had not been passed on to Maria's parents.

"The Lady Maria seems to be of a very resilient nature," Franz remarked to Eva as they crossed the square.

"A most diplomatic way of expressing that she's totally self-centered and only concerns herself with anything affecting her here and now. And you are right. But on the bottom she's also quite kind, and would probably be more intelligent if everyone around had not always talked about her beauty as if that was the only thing about her worth paying attention to."

"Please, allow me to compliment you on your ability to pay attention to everything outside yourself, Lady Eva. And may I enquire if you are as resilient on the inside?"

Eva looked away from Franz, letting her eyes follow the swallows flying between the trees and their nests under the eaves of the buildings. "Bamberg has taught me that I can do more than I think. In the future I will spend more time among people, and less in my books and my still-room." She turned her head and looked straight into Franz's face. "I am not at all certain what I want to do with my life, but I will not let my scars define me. I am worth more than that."

"Most certainly, Lady Eva, whole kingdoms more. And did I remember to thank you for saving my life?"

"Likewise, Bishop Franz." Eva smiled. "Please, give us your blessing for our journey, and we must be on our way. There also appears to be a messenger heading for you."

The vaguely familiar looking courier had dismounted and started patiently walking his horse to cool rather than approaching Franz until everybody had finished their goodbyes and the carriage had rolled from the square.

"My, my. If that isn't Peckerbun, joy of the ladies' eyes and other parts. What have you got?"

At Wolf's words Franz stopped and turned to him in outrage. "Ladies present! Your garrison language is not acceptable, Wolf."

"If they understand it, they've heard it before and have no cause for taking offense, and if they don't understand it, they have even less cause." Wolf grinned but stopped and turned to Terrie and Sister Tabitha. "Come say hello to Lieutenant Simon Pettenburg. His sweetheart is Melchior's quartermaster."

"I should perhaps start by assuring you that the person referred to is female, and was forced by circumstances beyond her control to take on a male's disguise and seek employment." The fresh-faced young man bowed and smiled at Terrie and Sister Tabitha before handing a bulky message bag to Franz. "There is no urgent military or political news, and everybody in your family is doing fine, Bishop Franz. General von Hatzfeldt assumed that the American radios would have brought the most important news, such as the recent death of Archbishop Ferdinand, but was uncertain how many details were shared. The information about the negotiations concerning the USE's western border is not confidential and might be of interest to the Americans in the administration here. Also I went by way of Mainz, and there is trading news from your brother Heinrich, who suggests that you read those without delay."

"While Franz does that, and Pettenburg stables his horse, I'll go for a walk with the lovely ladies. We'll meet for lunch in Franz's dining room," Wolf said and turned to offer his arm to Terrie.

"No, please wait." Terrie interrupted. "Let me invite you all instead. Geyersworth Palace at noon. I very much want to hear about Bishop Franz's family and Lieutenant Pettenburg's sweetheart, and Wolf can go help with the horse and ask his military questions at the same time."

"Lively lady. Is she American?" Simon asked, looking after Terrie rushing down the street pulling Sister Tabitha after her.

"Yes, very." Wolf answered dryly. "And one hell of a neat shot with that American gun she's packing. Now tell me if anyone knows the certain whereabouts of Irish Butler and his cohorts?"

# Chapter 48

*Bamberg*
*April 30, 1635*

Franz left the Geyerswoerth Palace just as the bells started to call to evening service and the start of the Walpurgis waking night. Overhead the setting sun was starting to color the slowly drifting clouds and with no wind stirring the surface of the river, it was turning into a slowly flowing ribbon of rose and gold. He was expected at the cathedral, but with Schönborn leading the service and holding the sermon, there was plenty of time to get there before the doors closed and anyone might miss him. Plenty of time to sit down of one of the benches the Americans had placed on the squares and along the river as if public spaces were taverns encouraging people to hang around and spend money.

"Good evening Bishop Franz. May I join you?" Frau Kacere's voice interrupted Franz's thoughts.

"Please do, Frau Kacere." Franz stood up and saw the older woman seated on the bench before sitting down again to watch the sunset.

"They hung Councilor Bitterfeld in Würzburg the day before yesterday. Did you know that, Bishop Franz?"

"Yes. Good riddance to bad rubbish, I believe your saying goes." Franz kept his eyes on hills darkening as the sun descended behind them. "Not a very Christian reaction from a priest, I'm sorry to say, and I'll probably try to find it in my heart to pray for his soul tonight, but..." He hesitated. "I had a visit from his widow today. She came straight from his funeral to thank me for my part in his death. She is now at the cathedral, where she'll be spending the night in prayer. Praying for the strength to forgive." He turned his head to look at Frau Kacere. "If you and your people can stop people like Bitterfeld and Father Arnoldi from polluting the world with every breath they take, then I'll support you with every skill and thought I possess."

Frau Kacere shook her head. "I can only promise you we'll try."

They sat for a while in silence.

"On a lighter note, Frau Kacere. When you arrived, I was just thinking about the benches you had placed around town. Some of the clerics are quite opposed to that, claims it encourage people to loiter and gossip when they should be working to God's honor."

"How Protestant of them. And do you agree, Bishop Franz?"

"Not necessarily. Clean streets, benches, even trees planted as if the town were a garden, those all encourage people to linger. It probably makes a town a healthier place to live, but I was wondering if it might not also be a way of encouraging trade?"

"There's something of both those reasons involved, plus civic pride, public relations, and many others, but my personal reason for wanting to spend money on things like benches is in fact somewhat religious. I don't know if you've noticed, Bishop Franz, but in addition to those placed where people gather, there's also quite a few placed with a view to God's creations such as the hills, the river, and even for watching the sun set."

"I see. It's certainly a beautiful view. I do not believe I've ever heard you mention your religion before, Frau Kacere?" Franz made the last sentence questioning.

"No, I consider that a private matter."

"No offense intended."

"And none taken. Me not talking religion is an old decision based on some incidents in my youth. Someday I might tell you about them." She smiled and continued, "Schönborn mentioned that the two of you were holding a Walpurgis wake tonight in the cathedral. I would have thought you'd start at sunset. Aren't you going to be late?"

"I know a back door, and Schönborn is perfectly capable of

starting without me." Franz smiled back. "I just need to compose my mind before heading uphill to join the others. A wake is all about contemplation and prayer and it's been a very long day. And also a very long year." Franz nodded towards the north-west and Cologne. "It was only about a year ago that I learned about Archbishop Ferdinand's plans to regain control of Bishop's Alley and the middle Rhine. Until then my life had been," he hesitated, "understandable. Not smooth, what with the Protestant armies driving me and so many of my peers into exile, but still something I could understand and deal with. Make plans about what to do. Then the landgrave of Hesse-Kassel attacked and the archbishop seemed to fall completely apart, and I decided to stop putting my faith in princes and to trust God for a change." Franz smiled wryly. "I tend to plan, negotiate and occasionally scheme to make my way rather than to pray and trust God."

"Nothing wrong with that. God helps those who help themselves."

"Yes, but sometimes God might have other priorities, and I have absolutely no taste for gambling." Franz hesitated. "I'd hired Father Johannes the Painter to restore our family home in Cologne. He'd spent a lot of time in Grantville, but I don't know if you ever met him there?"

"Certainly, I attended most of his lessons about the political structures and alliances. The books in our libraries didn't have anything near the details we needed."

"From what Father Johannes told me, the ideals and goals, if not necessarily the means, on which your nation was based are very close to what I hoped to achieve for my 'Kingdom,' but if there's one thing all my years as a diplomat has taught me, it is to always keep an eye on what the people around me are after. Not necessarily to oppose them, but I have some serious problems with accepting idealism as the primary motivation. Please don't take offense, Frau Kacere, but just what are you and your fellow Americans after? It doesn't appear to be entirely power, and certainly not mainly riches."

The old woman beside him sat silent for so long that Franz started wondering if he might have destroyed their highly valued working relationship with his direct question.

"What we want?" She finally answered. "I suppose we want what everybody wants. A life for ourselves and our children, as pleasant as possible, and with a good balance between security and freedom. The culture we came from placed more importance on freedom than the one that shaped you, but getting thrown nilly-willy across time—and whatever—shook most of us badly, so we might be more interested in security than when we felt safe at home in the world we knew." She smiled at Franz. "We are really very much like you in that we plan and negotiate, rather than just sit down and pray that God will take care of everything. We might be more inclined to fight than scheme, but whatever the means: freedom and security are pretty much the goals."

"And according to the news Pettenburg brought, you now have the Rhine and thus access to the Sea."

"Yes, now we have the Rhine."

# Afterword

When Eric Flint announced that the anthology he was putting together for the 1632 universe would be open for stories from Baen's Barflies as well as from the invited professional writers, I wrote my first serious attempt at fiction in the form of the short story "Family Faith" featuring the Jesuit priest and painter Father Johannes Grünwald. The story was accepted and published in *Ring of Fire I*.

Later the second Father Johannes story, "A Question of Faith," was published in *Grantville Gazette V*, but when I had the third story, "Faith in Princes," ready for submission, I was asked to join what was then called the Torturer of Fulda project. The project was a collaboration intended to deal with the western border of the USE, and with my story taking place in Cologne, it would fit right in. In the following years I added other storylines to cover what was going on around Cologne in 1634/1635, while the other authors involved did things to their stories.

Eventually my Cologne Cabal became the novel *1635: The Wars for the Rhine*.

It contains:

- the original story of Father Johannes going to Cologne to work for Prince-Bishop Franz von Hatzfeldt, and to search for his missing friend.

- the story of Archbishop Ferdinand of Cologne's attempts to regain the power he lost when the Protestant armies moved west, and what that did to Charlotte von Zweibrücken and Franz's older brother, General Melchior von Hatzfeldt.

- the story of the Hessian attack on Cologne mentioned in the story "Prince and Abbot" by Virginia Demarce.

- the story of four young girls in the middle of the political scene.

- the story of Wolf von Wildenburger-Hatzfeldt's ride across Bavaria.

- the story of Bishop Franz's return to Würzburg and Bamberg.

All those story lines have now been incorporated into one continuous story about the various attempts to gain control of the Rhine and especially the city of Cologne, and thus the gate between central Europe and the Atlantic Ocean.

I hope you enjoyed my story.
Anette Pedersen

# Cast of Characters

*The Hatzfeldt family and associates:*

In the late fifteenth century three brothers started the families which around 1632 had grown to the seven lines of the extended and intermarrying Hatzfeldt family. They were mainly lower nobility in the Middle Rhine area serving rulers and high-ranking prelates on both sides of the Rhine as Amtmen and administrators, but also becoming wealthy landowners in their own right.

The Hatzfeldts playing the major roles in this novel are the members of the Crottorf line, which are the four sons and one daughter of Imperial Knight Sebastian von Hatzfeldt of Crottorf, and those of the Wildenburger line, who are the son and two grandchildren of Bernhard von Hatzfeldt of Wildenburg.

**Hatzfeldt, Melchior von:** imperial count and general, once studying to become a Knight of Saint John on Malta, later a mercenary general working for Wallenstein and the Holy Roman Empire.

**Hatzfeldt, Franz von:** prince-bishop of Würzburg, fled into exile when the Protestant armies conquered Würzburg, formerly a diplomat in the service of the prince-bishop of Bamberg, owner of the family Castle Crottorf, Melchior's younger brother.

**Hatzfeldt, Heinrich von:** domherr at St. Alban in Mainz, remained in Mainz during and after the Swedish conquest of the town, Melchior's older brother.

**Hatzfeldt, Hermann von:** former mercenary colonel, now about to get married and devoting himself to the family's business interests, Melchior's youngest brother.

**Hatzfeldt, Lucie von:** widow, crippled after a carriage accident, Melchior's only surviving sister.

**Wildenburger-Hatzfeldt, Wolf von:** Melchior's second-in-command and cousin.

**Wildenburger-Hatzfeldt, Anna von:** Stifts-dame in Bonn, Wolf's sister.

**Wildenburger-Hatzfeldt, Georg von:** former dean in Fulda, Wolf's father's brother.

**Allenberg:** quartermaster in Melchior von Hatzfeldt's regiments.

**Backenfoerde, Margaretha von:** wealthy widow after Franz Wilhelm von Hatzfeldt-Merten, Melchior von Hatzfeldt's stepmother.

**Backenfoerde, Sophia "Sobby" von:** Margaretha's niece.

**Cortenbach, Adolpha von:** widow of Johann Wilhelm von Weisweiler-Hatzfeldt, wealthy landowner and Amtman in Jülich.

**Dannwitz, Dehn, Lorentz, Mettecoven, and Schierstedt:** officers in Melchior von Hatzfeldt's regiments.

**Eltz, Captain:** distant cousin of the Hatzfeldts, formerly serving in Melchior von Hatzfeldt's regiments, killed in Würzburg during the Swedish attack.

**Grünwald, Johannes, Father:** Jesuit priest and painter ("Family Faith" in *Ring of Fire I*, and "A Question of Faith" in *Grantville Gazette V*), hired by Bishop Franz von Hatzfeldt to refurbish the Hatzfeldt family's house in Cologne.

**Hatzfeldt, Sebastian von:** imperial knight and minor nobleman in the service of the archbishops of Mainz, owner of Castle Crottorf, killed when the Protestant army attacked the estate. Married three times.

**Hatzfeldt-Fleckenbuehl:** branch of the Hatzfeldt family with estates in Hessen.

**Hatzfeldt-Merten, Anna von:** Stifts-dame in Cologne, Margaretha von Backenfoerde's daughter from her first marriage.

**Hatzfeldt-Schönstein:** branch of the Hatzfeldt family with estates in Jülich.

**Hatzfeldt-Werther, Johann Adrian von:** wealthy landowner in Jülich-Berg, Sebastian's ward and Melchior's foster-brother.

**Hatzfelt-Weisweiler, Wilhelm von:** major landowner in Jülich, a distant cousin of Melchior von Hatzfeldt.

**Hatzfeldt-Wildenburg, Maria von:** Sebastian von Hatzfeldt's cousin and second wife, Wolf von Wildenburger-Hatzfeldt's grandfather's sister. Dead.

**Lenz, Marsch and Niederthal:** couriers in Melchior von Hatzfeldt's regiments.

**Madeleine:** Bavarian noblewoman, Wolf von Wildenburger-Hatzfeldt's mistress.

**Mansfeld, Maria von:** Melchior von Hatzfeldt's dead sweetheart and the mother of his illegitimate child.

**Mittelfeld:** sergeant in Melchior's regiment, cousin to Karl Mittelfeld in Bonn.

**Moreau, Paul:** a Protestant painter and friend of Father Johannes Grünwald.

**Peters, the:** illegitimate children of Lucie von Hatzfeldt's husband.

**Pettenburg, Simon:** lieutenant and courier in Melchior von Hatzfeldt's regiments.

**Schaden:** soldier in Melchior von Hatzfeldt's regiments.

**Scot, Ross "Rosy":** assisting quartermaster in Melchior von Hatzfeldt's regiments.

**Sickingen, Lucie von:** Sebastian von Hatzfeldt's first wife and mother of five surviving sons and one daughter. Died shortly after the birth of daughter Lucie.

**Tweimal, Otto:** Bishop Franz von Hatzfeldt's secretary.

**Worms-Dalberg, Maria Katharina "Trinket" Kaemmerer von:** orphan heiress and ward of Archbishop Ferdinand of Cologne, she's engaged to Hermann von Hatzfeldt.

## *The Zweibrücken family and associates:*

The Zweibrücken family was German high nobility with large estates on the German-French border, and a long tradition of intermarrying with the Swedish royal Vasa family.

**Katharina Charlotte "Charlotte," Countess Palatine von Zweibrücken:** married at age sixteen to Duke Wolfgang of Jülich-Berg, age fifty-three.

**Elisabeth, Countess Palatine von Zweibrücken:** Charlotte's sister.

**Friedrich, Count Palatine von Zweibrücken:** Charlotte's brother.

**Harbel:** Charlotte's lackey.

**Merode:** general in Jülich-Berg.

**van der Berg, Frau:** Charlotte's chatelaine.

## *The Bavarian ducal family and associates:*

The Bavarian ducal family was among the most powerful German nobility, and the younger sons were usually given the most important clerical domains in Germany.

**Ferdinand, Archbishop of Cologne:** highest ranking prelate in the Rhine area after the Protestant conquests, younger brother to Duke Maximilian of Bavaria.

**Maria Maximiliane "Maxie":** former Countess von Wartenberg, now a nun, illegitimate daughter of Archbishop Ferdinand's uncle Ferdinand.

**Albrecht of Bavaria:** Duke Maximilian's youngest brother, wife Mechthilde recently killed.

**Butler, MacDonald, Deveroux and Geraldin:** mercenary colonels once serving Wallenstein, now hired by Archbishop Ferdinand of Cologne.

**Franz Wilhelm:** bishop of Minden, Maxie's younger brother.

**Gruyard, Felix:** Archbishop Ferdinand's torturer and minion.

**Maximilian, Duke of Bavaria:** ruler of Bavaria.

**Maximilienne:** illegitimate daughter of Archbishop Ferdinand's uncle Ernst, the former archbishop of Cologne.

**Philip, Bishop of Regensburg and Cardinal:** Archbishop Ferdinand of Cologne's older brother, dead.

**Ursula:** a nun, Archbishop Ferdinand's former mistress.


*The Hesse-Kassel family and relatives:*

**Amalie Elisabeth, Countess von Hanau-Münzenberg, Landgravine of Hesse-Kassel:** Hesse's wife.

**Wilhelm V "Hesse," Landgrave of Hesse-Kassel:** ruler of Hesse-Kassel.

**Elisabeth "Litsa" von Schwarzenfels:** Amalie's cousin.

**Maria Juliana "Ria" von Schwarzenfels:** Litsa's younger sister.

**Albrecht von Schwarzenfels:** Litsa and Ria's father, Amalie's father's brother.

**Ehrengard, Countess von Isenburg-Büdingen:** Litsa and Ria's mother.

**Hermann, Count von Hesse-Rotenburg:** USE secretary of state, Hesse's brother.

**Katharina von Schwarzenfels:** Litsa and Ria's older sister.

**Philipp Moritz, Count von Hanau:** Amalie's brother.

**Rutgert, von:** lieutenant and Hesse's secretary.

**Uslar, von:** mercenary general in Hesse's army.

## *The Anhalt-Dessau family:*

**Eleonore, Princess of Anhalt-Dessau:** wife to Wilhelm Wettin, former duke of Saxe-Weimar, who's running for prime minister in the first general democratic election in the USE.

**Johanna Dorothea "Anchen" von Anhalt-Dessau:** Eleonore's younger sister.

**Eva Katharina von Anhalt-Dessau:** Eleonore's youngest sister.

## *The Neuburg family and the other heirs to Johann the Insane:*

**Johann (the Insane), Duke of Jülich-Berg-Kleve:** major landowner, died without offspring, and his lands were divided between his four sisters and thus passed on to the Neuburg, Brandenburg, Zweibrücken and Habsburg families.

**Wolfgang Wilhelm von Neuburg, Duke of Jülich and Berg:** first marriage to Duchess Magdalene of Bavaria, Duke Maximilian's younger sister; second marriage to Countess Palatine Charlotte von Zweibrücken.

**Philipp von Neuburg:** Wolfgang's son and heir from his first marriage.

**August von Sulzback:** Wolfgang's younger brother.

**Hedwig, Duchess von Holstein-Gottorp:** August's widow.

**Johann von Hilpoltstein:** Wolfgang's youngest brother.

**Sofie Agnes von Hesse-Dramstadt:** Johann von Hilpoltstein's wife.

**Anna Maria von Neuburg:** Wolfgang's sister and dowager duchess of Saxe-Altenburg.

## *The Eigenhaus family, servants and associates:*

**Eigenhaus, Benedicte:** matriarch of a Bonn-based family trading up and down the Rhine, married to a councilor and wine trader in Bonn.

**Eigenhaus, Irmgard:** midwife and owner of an apothecary, Benedicte's illegitimate half-sister.

**Eigenhaus, Jakob:** Benedicte's youngest son.

**Hilda:** Benedicte's cook.

**Steinfeld:** old handyman in Benedicte's household.

**Stina:** Benedicte's maid.

**Ilse:** Benedicte's young kitchen girl.

**Heidi:** the cook borrowed from Benedicte's sister Clara.

**Madelaine:** the French cook borrowed from Benedicte's sister Elisabeth.

**Mittelfeld, Karl:** former soldier, now fisher and smuggler on the Rhine, a friend of the Eigenhaus family; he and his family live in Bonn.

**Wickradt:** Commander of Bonn's defenses, and a distant relative of the Hatzfeldt family.

## *Americans in Bamberg plus friends and enemies:*

**Kacere, Jane Aurelia Mora:** Department of Internal Affairs, SoTF administration in Bamberg, assigned to work with down-time lawyers to try to make sense of Franconian jurisdictions and land tenures.

**Marcantonio, Theresa "Terrie":** Barbara and Vincent Marcantonio's daughter.

**Norris, Bennett:** inspector of elections, based in Bamberg.

**Arnoldi, Father:** priest at the Würzburg cathedral.

**Bitterfeld, Councilor:** member of the Würzburg city council, supporter of Father Arnoldi.

**Bitterfeld, Domherr:** domherr at the Bamberg cathedral, cousin to Councilor Bitterfeld.

**Eberhart, Anna:** rauchbier brewer in Bamberg, Maria Eberhart's sister and heir.

**Eberhart, Maria:** the widow who owned the Dreimark vineyard, disappeared and is presumed dead.

**Eberhart the cooper:** Anna's husband and distant cousin.

**Eberhart, Zacharias:** Maria's husband and first cousin, killed when the Protestant armies conquered Würzburg.

**Ehrenberg:** former prince-bishop of Würzburg, dead.

**Evangelina:** a Bavarian nun and refugee.

**Haun, John "Johnnie F.":** head of the "Hearts and Minds" program in Würzburg.

**Marcantonio, Vincent "Vince":** chief of SoTF administration in Bamberg, Terrie's father.

**Marcantonio, Barbara Corbin:** nurse, Terrie's mother.

**Salatto, Steven "Steve":** head of SoTF administration in Würzburg.

**Schönborn, Johann Philipp von:** canon at the Würzburg cathedral, close friend of Bishop Franz von Hatzfeldt.

**Tabitha:** a Bavarian nun and refugee, Terrie's close friend.


*Other Characters:*

**Andrew the Scot:** the innkeeper at the Black Goat outside Bonn.

**Anselm von Wambold:** archbishop of Mainz.

**Banér:** general in the Protestant armies.

**Beauville, Claude:** shop owner in Cologne.

**Beekx, Alain van:** a painter from Holland.

**Bernard:** ruler of Swabia.

**Cohen, David:** rabbi in Mainz.

**De Geer:** ruler of Essen.

**Dorothea:** abbess of Quedlinburg.

**Ferdinand:** archduke of Austria, heir to HRE.

**Fernando, Don:** coruler of the Netherlands.

**Gustav II Adolf (Gustavus Adolphus):** king of Sweden, emperor of USE.

**Hardenrat, Peter von:** an important man in Cologne.

**Horn:** general in the Protestant armies.

**Johan Georg:** former prince-bishop of Bamberg, dead.

**Katharina:** princess of Sweden, Gustav II Adolf's sister, married to Charlotte von Zweibrücken's uncle.

**Maria Anna:** archduchess of Austria, once betrothed to Maximilian of Bavaria, now married to Don Fernando of the Netherlands.

**Nasi, Francisco, Don:** head of the Abrabanel family's financial network in Germany, and unofficial head of the Americans' information network.

**Nicholaus:** former innkeeper at the Black Goat outside Bonn.

**Old Pegleg:** Nicholaus' friend from Beuel across the Rhine from Bonn.

**Oberstadt:** the mayor of Bonn.

**Oxenstierna, Axel:** chancellor of Sweden.

**Schweinsberg:** prince-abbot of Fulda, dead.

**Turenne:** marshal in the French army.

**Wallenstein:** former mercenary general, now ruler of Bohemia.